Red Eyes

by

Gary H. Hensley

DLD Books

ISBN: 151746188X
ISBN–13: 978-1517461881

To Sherry, my wife

AUTHOR'S NOTE

The characters in this book are purely fictional. However, some of them are inspired by a combination of people I knew while growing up in the Kingsport, Tennessee area. I owe a debt of gratitude to the many people of the East Tennessee and Southwest Virginia region who piqued my interest with their colorful lives and stories.

I gratefully acknowledge the assistance and support of the following people: my wife, Sherry, for her loving patience, support, and typing skills; my editor, Leonore H. Dvorkin, for her professional editorial assistance and encouragement; her husband, David Dvorkin, for his additional editing assistance and his expert work on the book layout and cover; Emily Medley, a recent graduate of Maryville College, for her critical review of the first three chapters; Oliver "Buzz" Thomas, an author, attorney, educator, and community leader, for his review of the courtroom scenes; and Dr. Jim Stovall, author and Professor of Journalism at the University of Tennessee, for reading the book and giving me excellent feedback.

I am especially indebted to my parents, Howard and Iva Nell Hensley, who taught me to appreciate "the telling" almost as much as the story itself.

And finally, I am grateful for the encouragement given by my family and extended family, as well as many friends and associates.

Gary H. Hensley
Maryville, Tennessee
October 2015

INTRODUCTION

They came out of the hills of Southwest Virginia to enforce the law in and around Dawson, Tennessee. "The Big Three"—that's how the newspaper referred to them. Actually, the headline read "Last of the Big Three Dies." It was the 1976 story of the death of James Taylor, a long-tenured lawman in upper East Tennessee. He left behind a wife, four children, and a legacy. The first of the three to die was Jimmy Ray Johnson; the next, Cam Barker.

This trio of crime fighters grew up on small farms, where their parents eked out a meager living. They also had in common a determination to break out and find work off the farm. The three young men were poorly educated but street smart, and they worked in Tennessee, just across the state line from where they had grown up in Virginia.

Johnson was born in a house on the river and many years later died there, although by then it was a second home—a party house of sorts. He succumbed to complications from diabetes, which had claimed a leg two years earlier. Jimmy Ray was a jovial man, the life of the party. He loved to sing and make music. He was also fearless—a trait he had in common with the other two. Johnson once stood in the middle of Main Street in Dawson and traded gunfire with two bank robbers. Without seeking cover, he reloaded twice. One bank robber was shot dead and the other wounded. Jimmy Ray never received so much as a scratch.

Cam Barker may have been the bravest of the three. He shot and killed two men in his career. The first was a domestic situation in which a distraught husband turned his anger from his wife to the deputy. Barker was stabbed twice before he could draw his gun and fire.

The second incident happened when an escaped prisoner barricaded himself in a house and traded gunfire with sheriff's deputies. Cam went inside to get him. He worked his way through the house to a back bedroom. The cornered escapee jumped out of a closet and shot Barker in the abdomen. Cam fired back and hit the fugitive in the right eye, killing him instantly. The deputy then made his way to the front porch, holding his stomach with one hand and trying to light a cigarette with the other. Deputies rushed to help him, but he refused to go to the hospital until he could finish his Pall Mall.

After that, he lived another 28 years, making moonshine and enforcing the law. He never hesitated to arrest moonshiners, rationalizing that he only made 'shine for his friends and family—and it was good, safe stuff.

Jim Taylor was cut from the same cloth. He had been through similar scrapes. Like the other two, he was a simple man, but his life was much more complex.

CHAPTER ONE

April 1968

Jim Taylor awoke with a start, jolted by a dream that had transported him to the top of a towering bluff. His old friend, guilt, washed over him like an unwelcome bath. The familiar white ceiling and pale green walls of the hospital greeted him for the fifth consecutive day. He flexed his hand, sore from the IV needle, and noticed a hint of early morning light outside the fourth-floor window of the cardiac unit.

I'm glad that Lilly finally decided to sleep at home last night, he thought. She's probably getting up about now. It was good to see the kids, but it was awkward if not downright embarrassing. My latest heart attack and the circumstances surrounding it have once again interrupted their busy lives. The last few days seem like a dream, or more precisely, a recurring nightmare with which I have finally come to grips.

The day before, he had confessed to his astonished wife, Lilly, the entire story of his hidden life—the good, the bad, and most of all, the unforgivable. Speaking for several hours, he had told her the sordid details of his transgressions as well as the guilt-ridden reasons for his occasional nagging bouts with depression over the years. He had recounted the depths of his intense, lifelong love for her and the inexplicable betrayals of that love.

Finally, he had explained the cause of his latest heart attack and what he intended to do. Lilly had cried intermittently, but she had never interrupted, as if sensing that it was critical to allow him to get it all out. Then she had begun to fill in the gaps and lapses of his memory to complete the story.

It had begun when they met as kids.

*****

Southwest Virginia, 1924

Jim Taylor walked slowly, feeling his way up the moonlit path leading to the swimming hole at Cove Creek. The cloudless sky amplified the light of the crescent moon and the millions of stars that peppered the sky. The warm night was perfect for lovers. He wondered if she would hear his heavy boots crunching the earth as he approached, or if the loud cries of the cicadas would drown it out. He questioned if she would even be there at all. Although Lilly Mae had agreed to meet him, she didn't impress him as the kind of girl who would sneak out for a late night swim.

At just 15 years of age, he was 5' 10" and already barrel-chested and powerfully built. His slightly oval-shaped face was punctuated by a straight Grecian nose and a soft mouth set in a persistent, impish grin.

He finally came close enough to see the silhouettes of the massive river boulders that he and his best friend, Robby Boatwright, had leapt from earlier that day. Shaking the wavy black hair from his piercing blue eyes, Jim strained to see her. Sure enough, there she was.

She sat on a quilt at the edge of the water with her legs stretched out in front of her and her hands supporting her from behind. Lilly Mae gazed upward at the night sky, framed by the twin peaks in the distance.

Jim edged forward quietly, taking in her lovely features. The luminescence of the stars and moon gave her skin an angelic glow. Her toes dangled in the water, sending ripples into the slow–moving stream. Dark hair waved past her shoulders, and it was the first time Jim had ever seen it not woven into a tight braid.

Only a few feet from her now, he slowly lowered himself to his knees and began to crawl. Her shoulders tensed from the sensed presence, but before she could turn around and see him, he had his arms wrapped around her waist and his face buried in her neck. He gently nuzzled his rough cheek against her smooth skin, breathing in the crisp smell of lye soap. He was captivated by the dark, silky hair against her fair complexion and the large brown eyes set perfectly in a soft, round face.

"Jim Taylor, you need to shave!" she said. She squirmed away from him and playfully hit him on the shoulder.

He took her soft cheek in his callused hand and moved her face to within inches of his. Her coffee–colored eyes lowered and seemed to focus on his mouth.

"It's good to see ya, Lilly Mae," he whispered.

Her lips parted, and he accepted the invitation. Bringing his lips to hers, he wove his fingers into her warm hair and drew her soft body against him. His other hand glided to the small of her back, and he tensed when he felt her tongue dart into his mouth.

This can't be real, he thought.

He felt the blood rush to his groin as Lilly Mae's tongue slid around the inside of his lips. Something between a moan and a whimper vibrated in his throat, and the young woman pulled away from him. For several moments, they said nothing. Jim worried that he might have taken it too far. She stared at him with a blank face.

Finally, Lilly Mae rose, turned her back to Jim, and slowly pulled the thin cotton dress over her head. He held his breath as she bent over to spread the dress on the quilt. Her undergarments revealed a curvy figure, and Jim felt a pang of excitement and fear.

"What are you doing, Lilly Mae?" he finally croaked. He felt his groin bulge against his overalls.

"I thought we came here to swim," she said as she stepped into the water. She glided toward the middle of the swimming hole until her shoulders were submerged, and then she turned to gaze at him expectantly.

Jim removed his boots and stood to unbuckle the straps of his overalls. Would it bother her that he wore nothing underneath? He figured it didn't matter, except that she would see her effect on him. He decided to at least turn away from her until he could hide his waist in the water. He slid off his overalls and moved backwards off the bank in Lilly Mae's direction.

"What're ya doin', Jim?" Lilly Mae's voice rang out from behind him. "Walk forwards, or you're gonna slip and fall!"

Jim hesitated. "I can't, Lilly Mae."

"Oh, don't be shy, silly!"

Jim turned around. This can't be real, he thought again.

The water was freezing cold, fed by mountain springs which ran freely throughout the year. Despite the chill, he could feel his crotch straining beneath the water.

Lilly Mae took a few steps forward, revealing her breasts just above the rippling water. Her nipples were taut and erect beneath the thin, soaked material of her undershirt.

He pushed through the water in mad desperation. From the short distance between them, he could see her cheeks dimple with a smirk, and she had a mischievous spark in her dark eyes. The water felt like thick mud, and no matter how hard he worked, he didn't seem to get any closer to his prize.

"Hurry up, Jim!" she begged. "I want you."

"I'm tryin', Lilly Mae!" Jim gasped. "Can't you head more over this way?"

Every step Jim moved forward, it was as though she was moving several paces back. Soon, she was standing near the other bank, and Jim still hadn't gotten any farther than the middle. Lilly Mae eased out of her undergarments and sensuously motioned for him to come to her. He could see that she was naked, but his vision was fuzzy in the diffused moonlight. He was frantic to reach her.

"Jim!" she yelled. "*Jim!*"

There was something strange about her voice. Was it because she was so far away from him?

Suddenly, he felt himself sinking. He struggled to stay above the surface, but it was as though something had caught him around the ankle and was pulling him to the bottom. He flailed as fast as he could toward the moon's reflection on the surface above him, but the force was too strong.

"Jim!" Lilly Mae's voice was muffled by the water, and it still didn't sound quite right.

"James Taylor!"

*****

Jim bolted upright and shouted, "Help!"

"You better get out of bed before your daddy comes up here and whoops you!" his mother warned. "This is the third time I've hollered at you."

Of course, Jim thought. It was just a dream.

Mama Taylor stood over him with the now-empty water bucket.

Wet and shocked, Jim quickly pulled up his knees to hide his nakedness. He wondered how long Mama had been standing there and whether or not she had noticed anything. It wasn't like she had never raised a boy before. Surely she had accidentally walked in on his brothers, John or Ray, at least once when they were his age.

Esther Taylor's height, 5' 10", was her most striking feature. She was of slender build except for the slight bulge of her lower belly. Her "baby pouch," as she called it, was the result of birthing nine babies—four boys, including Benjamin, who died as a baby, and five girls. Her salt-and-pepper hair, drawn back into a tightly wound bun secured by the ever-present, rust-colored combs, gave her a somewhat severe look. Her dark eyes, rather long face, and thin lips added to that first impression. However, Esther's natural disposition was kind and empathetic. When she smiled, her face was transformed by crinkly black eyes that signaled love and compassion.

"Get up and get yer milkin' done," Mama said. "Breakfast is nearly ready. And hang that pallet and them sheets up to dry on your way to the barn."

"Well, that cow ain't goin' nowhere."

"Don't you talk back to me, boy! Get on up and get busy, or you won't get to see Robby till the sun goes down."

With that, Mama left his room.

As he pulled on his overalls and fastened the buckles, he thought about his dream and how amazing Lilly Mae had felt in his arms. It wasn't the first time he had dreamed about her. Ever since they had cake-walked together at the school party last year, all he could think about was when he could see her again. It used to be every weekday at school and then at church, but since his dad had pulled him out of school after eighth grade, now he only saw her every other Sunday at church. He would have liked to stay in school, mainly just to see her, but his dad had made the decision, and it was final.

"Eighth grade is enough school," his daddy, George Taylor, told him whenever he protested. "You can read and write, and that's enough for any man to run a farm."

His daddy assumed that all of his boys would be running a farm and that all of his girls would be raising babies. John, Ray, Opal, Ida, Mamie, and May—one by one, they all grew up and moved away from the Taylor household, which meant there was a lot more work to do on the farm and around the house for Jim and his younger sister, Annie.

George Washington Taylor was tall and slender, with a dark complexion that hinted of his Melungeon ancestry on his grandmother's side. His permanently slightly bent back implied that he personally carried the weight of the world on his shoulders. He was born in 1866—no doubt conceived shortly after his father returned from the Civil War. His prominent mustache hung to just below the corners of his mouth, giving balance to his angular face and partially hiding his sunken jaw.

When Jim walked to the clothesline cradling his wadded, wet bed clothes in his arms, Annie followed him.

"Well, don't you look like a mess!" she said as she took the sheets from Jim. "What happened to you?"

"Mama decided to give me a bath this mornin'," Jim said as he slicked back his dark, wet hair.

"You don't smell like you had no bath," Annie said with a giggle. "You smell like you was in the outhouse and Old Nell kicked it over!"

"Aw, hush."

Annie threw back her head and laughed. Her sandy brown hair hung in two plaits behind her ears. Her freckled nose wrinkled and her sleepy blue eyes danced when she laughed. In four or five years, she would be a beautiful young woman, and not long after that, she'd be married off, like her sisters. Jim hoped to be moved out before then, because it'd be awful quiet and lonely without her around.

"You sure do look pretty today, Annie Bird," Jim said. "Have any young fellers been flirtin' with ya?"

"Oh, no, they're all afraid of Daddy, especially when he sits on the front porch cleanin' his shotgun!" she laughed.

"Good," Jim said. "Don't let none of them fool with you, ya hear? Boys are pigs, every single one of 'em. And they don't care about nothin' but one thing."

"Well, that can't be true about all boys. You're a boy."

"Ain't a single one of us perfect, Annie. Some of us are better'n others, but you still gotta watch out. If anybody tries to mess with you, you let me know, all right?"

Annie giggled. "You gonna borrow Daddy's shotgun?"

"Don't be silly. I'll make sure the punishment fits the crime."

"Well, you can't hit the broadside of a barn, noways!"

"Yes, I can!"

"I seen you the other day out back shootin' that pellet gun Daddy gave you. You'd have to ask the feller if he'd stand still for ya!"

Jim shook his head while Annie shrilled with laughter. Suddenly the front door swung open and Mama came out on the porch. She crossed her arms over her chest and glared at her children.

"That's not the sound of working, you two," she scolded.

"Sorry, Mama!" Annie said. "It was my fault. Jim stopped to help me stack the kindlin', and I started teasin' him."

"It's all right, but get busy and get goin'. You can play later."

Annie winked at Jim and walked back to the house with an armful of firewood. Jim grabbed some wooden pegs out of a pail, hung up his bed clothes, then headed to the barn. As he milked Sally, the cow, he wondered where he fell between being a decent young man and a pig. He wanted to think he was the kind of boy that treated girls right, just as he was raised to do. However, the rhythmic sound of milk squirting into the pail pulled him back to Cove Creek and Lilly Mae's soft, naked body. Dang, if his mother hadn't woken him up...

* * *

"I brought something for us, Scooter," Robby Boatwright said with a mischievous grin. Robby was spending the night to celebrate the beginning of the school's spring planting break.

Jim, whom Robby had called "Scooter" since second grade,

could hardly see two feet in front of him in his loft bedroom. There were only two small windows—one on each end—that allowed the pale light of nighttime to stream in. The boys sat in the shadows, untouched by the light of the stars and the moon. The air that flowed through the loft was unusually hot and humid for a spring night. With their shirts off, they sat across from each other on a blanket they had spread on the dusty floor. Jim held a scrap of fabric and would occasionally wipe it across his forehead.

Robby fumbled in his bag for the big surprise. He finally pulled it out and held it triumphantly above his head. Jim couldn't really make out what it was, but judging by its silhouette, it seemed to be a jar of something.

"Maybe we should light a lamp," Jim suggested.

"Oh, you don't want to do that, buddy."

"What is it?"

Robby unscrewed the lid, passed it to Jim, and giggled at the sound Jim made as his lips touched the rim of the jar of moonshine.

"Shhh!" Jim admonished him, and then added, "If I get caught, I'm dead."

"Okay," Robby whispered, "let's slip out to the barn."

Jim screwed on the lid of the foul-smelling 'shine, then stealthily followed Robby down the ladder to the living room floor below. They paused for a few seconds at the bottom, listening to Mr. Taylor's rhythmic snoring, then eased out the door and headed for the barn.

Jim took a sip and handed the jar to Robby. His throat and stomach were instantly on fire as he half coughed, half whispered, "That's good stuff!"

They quickly hatched a plan and headed up the "hollar" behind the house. As the boys quietly tipped over and lowered Mr. Keller's outhouse to the ground, a dog barked and others joined in. The two friends panicked and ran through the pasture fields to the adjoining farm. The Widow Staley lived there alone with her cats.

Jim and Robby sat on a log trading sips while the barking dwindled in the distance.

"Let's get her outhouse while we're at it," Robby suggested.

"No, she's all alone. Let's get back."

"C'mon, let's get it," Robby insisted as he stood up and started toward outhouse.

Jim grabbed his arm and said emphatically, "We're not turning it over! Now let's go."

Robby jerked his arm loose and faced his friend. They stood staring nose to nose in the moonlight. Finally, Robby said, "The hell with it. Have a drink, Scooter."

As they slowly drank their way back, Robby and Jim talked about everything from the girls at church to the kinds of guns they hoped to own someday. As the jar passed from hand to hand, their speech became slurred and their eyelids grew heavy.

They talked as loudly as they dared and occasionally snickered at something the other said. They stumbled and bumped into each other as they walked back to the Taylors' farm.

Jim wondered how a preacher's son had managed to get his hands on moonshine. Jim had never been drunk before in his life, and he felt dizzy and queasy as they walked.

The wave of nausea hit him as they reached the barn, and he doubled over and retched into the weeds. Robby laughed at him, then suddenly vomited, too. The boys turned around to head back to the house, and Jim's heart stopped when he looked up. Someone was standing in front of them, a few feet away.

"Annie...?" Jim finally croaked.

"Jim Taylor, what in Sam Hill are you doing?" she demanded.

Jim stammered. Annie stood before them with her arms crossed over the white nightgown that billowed around her ankles. Her hair hung in waves far past her shoulders, and the warm evening breeze blew some strands across her scowling face.

Jim looked at Robby, who was staring down at his feet, seemingly embarrassed by seeing Annie in her nightclothes.

"We were just going for a walk—" Jim said.

"What is that rotten smell?" Annie broke in. "Have you two been rollin' around in cow manure?"

Jim didn't know what to say. Any explanation he could think of besides the truth was still bad enough to get a whipping from their father.

"Look, Annie," Jim began. "Please don't tell Daddy we snuck out, all right?"

"And why shouldn't I? It's dangerous out here after dark, and you know it. Somethin' could've happened to you!"

"Well, nothin' did, but you know somethin' will happen to me if you tell Daddy."

Annie stared coldly at Jim for a long moment. Jim hated being at her mercy, but he knew that she was just worried about him. He felt guilty, because he knew she was right.

"You would deserve it," she finally said. "But I won't say nothin' to him on one condition."

"What's that?" Jim asked with relief.

"Don't you dare ever do it again. Next time, I'll tell on ya. Do you promise?"

Jim hesitated. He was still feeling dizzy from the alcohol, and he wanted nothing more than to get this over with and pass out on his bed.

He knew that once he said those two words to her, he'd be bound to them. He had never broken a promise to Annie.

"I promise," he said.

Annie hugged him. When she was closer, Jim could see the tears in her eyes.

"Come on. Follow me," she said as she stepped away.

As they stealthily slipped onto the porch, Annie whispered, "Stay here. I'll make sure they're asleep."

Annie reappeared and motioned for her brother and his friend to come in. They eased into the house and made their way silently—she to her bed, and they to their pallets in the loft.

* * *

Annie had been sound asleep for several hours when she heard the sound of her bedroom door slowly creaking open. She struggled to rub the sleep from her eyes.

"Jim..." she said through a yawn.

"Shhhh..."

"What's wrong?"

"Nothin'."

Annie closed her eyes again as she felt the bed sag as he sat down. When she was younger, Jim used to sneak into her room and make sure she was all right, especially if she had gotten in trouble with Daddy or if someone had made her cry earlier in the day. The last time was two years before, when a girl at school made fun of her favorite dress.

He stroked her hair softly and pushed the stray locks behind her ear.

"Thanks for saving me tonight. I love you."

CHAPTER TWO

Two Weeks Later

On Saturday morning, it was daylight long before Jim saw the morning sun. The "potato" hill on the east side of the Taylors' little house blocked the sun until most morning chores were completed. This was a blessing in the summer and a curse in the cold of winter. Today, though, it didn't make too much difference. The spring air was already perfect.

He whistled as he plodded through the drudgery of his daily chores, including his least favorite tasks of slopping the hogs and hoeing two acres of corn and beans. Normally he dreaded waking up every morning and repeating this routine. But today was Saturday—the day of the church ice cream supper—and his chance to see Lilly Mae.

Jim finished his chores earlier than usual and decided to beat everyone else to the washtub. He fetched three buckets of water from the spring out back and poured them into the tub. Normally he would heat one of the buckets, but today he was in a hurry. He stripped off his sweaty clothes and eased into the cold water.

As he scrubbed the grime off his skin, his thoughts turned again to the ice cream supper that he would be attending in the early evening at his church. He wondered if Lilly Mae would even be there. Jim sure wanted to see her, but part of him was scared at the thought of approaching her. What if he said something dumb? What if she ignored him? What if one of the other boys got her attention? Would her parents even let a boy go near her?

He thought about how his dad was very protective of Annie—and of all his other sisters, for that matter. "Oh, they always go runnin' off when they see Daddy on the porch, cleanin' his shotgun," Annie had said the other day. Surely Lilly Mae's father wasn't anything like his father, George Taylor. Even so, Jim knew he would eventually have to win over her parents if he wanted to be with her. And that thought made him feel even more nervous than before.

He remembered seeing her naked in his dream, and he realized how ridiculous it all was. He hadn't even held her hand during the cake-walk. But all he had done since then was fantasize about kissing and touching her. And now his stomach was in knots just at the thought of speaking to her. He knew he was going to have to make some move if he ever wanted her to notice him, and there was no sense in being nervous about it. He would definitely look like a fool to her if he let his nerves get to him. He had to at least try.

Regardless, the thought of approaching her gave him chills. Or maybe he had just been sitting in the cold water too long.

Jim's stomach was still churning when Mama, Daddy, and Annie finally piled into the buggy to head to the church. The young man would ride Old Nell and follow his family to Piney Level Primitive Baptist Church. As they made their way, the buggy rattled as it creaked over the rutted dirt road. The persistent bounce of the horse's trot did little to ease the nervous quivers in Jim's stomach. It wouldn't be too long before he would see her.

Finally, they made their way slowly up Johnny Mack Hill, and once they neared the top, Jim could see the one-room structure built of logs with a shake roof. The family that owned the adjacent farm had donated the land, and men of the church had raised the building. Inside, cracks in the chinking between the logs were beginning to show the effects of the freezing and thawing of many seasons past. Both the plank floor and the oak benches were worn slick from use by the Baptists and Methodists who shared the building on alternating Sundays.

After parking their buggy and tying up Old Nell, the Taylors approached the church. Jim scanned the many familiar faces for the one that had stolen his heart. Adults and children congregated in small groups throughout the yard, but there was no Lilly Mae.

Am I too late? Jim wondered. Did some other boy already get her a cup of ice cream?

Jim continued to look around, but she was nowhere to be seen. Maybe she hadn't even arrived yet. Finally, his heart skipped a beat. He noticed Lilly Mae's parents standing by the corner of the church, talking to Jim Godsey and his wife. But where was Lilly Mae?

Just then he spotted his best friend, Robby, cranking the wheel of the ice cream machine. Every boy was required to take a turn or two at the crank while the adults caught up on the latest news from the county seat in Batesville. There were girls nearby handing out cups for the ice cream, which they would later serve.

As Jim approached, Robby asked, "Where've you been, Scooter?"

"We got a late start."

"You might be late, but you ain't late enough to miss your turn. Pour some more salt in there!"

Jim lifted the bag of salt and poured. Robbie continued to turn the wheel, and Jim knew he was ready to give it up. But he couldn't let himself get stuck there, cranking the machine. At least not yet. He *had* to find her.

"Have you seen Lilly Mae Larkey?" Jim asked.

"Nope. Why do you wanna know where *she*'s at?"

"My sister's looking for her for some reason or other. Guess she's not here. I gotta go pee. I'll be right back to relieve ya."

"*Sure* you will. Just go relieve yourself before you relieve me!" Robby joked. "I see how it is."

Jim ignored him and walked off toward the outhouse behind the church. As he rounded the back corner of the church, he came to an abrupt stop. Lilly Mae was sitting on the back stoop with her face turned down to the yellowed pages of a book. Her dark hair was woven tightly into two braids that fell past her ears and onto her shoulders. She wore a green cotton dress that complemented her glowing, tanned complexion. Whatever she was reading must have been really good, because she didn't even notice Jim standing there, staring at her as though she was some sort of exotic creature. Lordy, he could hardly catch his breath.

"Hey, Lilly Mae," he finally got out.

Lilly Mae's head turned in his direction and her dark, doe-like eyes washed over him like a warm rain. It seemed as if he had pulled her out of a pleasant dream.

"Oh. Hello, Jim," she replied.

What now? He hadn't lied to Robby when he'd said he had to pee. He had to go badly, but now he had Lilly Mae's attention, and he couldn't let her see him go to the outhouse. He tried to forget about his painful urge as he made his way up to near the stoop.

"What're ye readin'?' he asked.

"Oh, just a story about a girl that grew up in the Kentucky coal mining country."

Jim shifted from one foot to the other. "Sounds interestin'. Is it fer school?'

"No."

Jim tried to smile, but it came out as more of a grimace from his discomfort.

"Why don't you go do your business," she said, "and I'll tell you about it when you get back."

Jim blushed. Just like that, she had said it—like it was nothing at all for a girl to tell a boy to go use an outhouse in plain view. Jim wanted to tell her he'd be all right, but clearly he wouldn't, and he didn't want to seem too prideful. He walked down the path to the small building, and before he went in, he looked back toward the small porch. To his relief, she wasn't watching him; her face was turned back down to the book.

He went inside and was immediately hit by the overwhelming smell. He grappled nervously with his overalls, praying he would pee fast lest she think he was doing the other one. When he was done, he strapped his bib and was out the door in a flash.

Jim made his way back up the path, feeling relief in more ways than one. At least her book would give them something to talk about. He couldn't think of much else she'd be interested in hearing about, especially not his and Robby's sleepovers or his daily farm routine.

"So, does this girl work in the coal mines?" he asked, taking a seat next to her.

Lilly Mae laughed as she slid the scrap of newspaper, used to mark her page, into the book.

"No, silly. Her father and brother do. Girls don't go into mines. You know that!"

Jim felt embarrassed. Of *course* the girl wouldn't work in the mines. Mines were dirty and dangerous places.

"Well, then, what does she do?"

"She stays at home and helps her mama with the cooking and cleaning—like most girls do," Lilly Mae said.

"Well, what's so interesting about that?"

"Oh, but that's not what the story's about. It's about how she falls in love with a man that comes in from out of town, but her daddy doesn't like him because he thinks he's an outlaw. So she sneaks out while her daddy and brother are down in the mines and meets him in town when she runs errands for her mama. And he really is a charming man," Lilly Mae sighed.

"Is he, now? Well, what does he do?"

"He just treats her like a lady, you know? He buys her nice things and talks sweet to her. He had come down to find work because things weren't going so well for him where he was from. But one day she goes missing and her daddy hunts the man down and threatens to kill him if he doesn't give her back. But he doesn't have her. He didn't even know she went missing. And he's just as desperate to bring her home."

"Do they ever find her?"

Lilly Mae shrugged. "I ain't got that far yet."

"Well, I wanna know what happens to her. Could you tell me when you finish readin' it?"

"Why don't you read it yourself, Jim?"

"I would, but I ain't got time to read. I help out around our farm, y'know?"

"Oh, that's right," she said. "Well, you could make time to read. And I believe I've got the perfect book for you."

"Sounds great. I'll give it a shot."

She seemed pleased. Jim could tell it was going to take quite a bit of work to impress her, but he was ready for the challenge, even if it meant spending a few nights with a dusty old book by the coal oil lamp.

"Say, Lilly Mae, do you think I could walk you home tonight? I mean, I'd really like to hear more about those people in that book."

She smiled. "That's fine by me. I'll ask my mother and let you know later."

Suddenly, Annie joined them on the back stoop, carrying a full cup of ice cream in her hand.

"Robby is lookin' for ye, Jim," she said after swallowing a spoonful of ice cream. "He said you went to the outhouse, and he was worried you'd fell in."

Jim turned red.

"Right," he said, and then turned to Lilly Mae. "I'll see you after a while. I better get back before he comes huntin' for me."

"All right. Have a good time, Jim."

Robby gave him a knowing look when he approached the ice cream machine. Jim ignored his friend's look and just grabbed the wheel and started turning.

"What took ye so long?" Robby asked. "My arm was already sore before ye walked off."

"I got caught up talkin' to people. You'll be all right. Go rest yore skinny little arm."

Robby rolled his eyes, took a helping of ice cream, and walked off.

As Jim turned the wheel, his mind churned with thoughts of walking Lilly Mae home.

Will her mother say yes? he wondered. Is she even gonna ask her at all? How stupid did I sound to her? I guess I'll find out.

*****

As Lilly Mae prattled on about the coal miner's girl, Jim's mind was on Lilly Mae's parents walking 10 yards behind them. They weren't close enough to hear their daughter's breathless description of the girl's romance with the young man, but they were certainly close enough to see them. Jim wanted to make some move to show he was interested, but he didn't want to do anything her parents wouldn't want to see. It was his first chance to make any kind of impression, and he didn't want to be like the poor, misunderstood man in Lilly Mae's book.

"Don't you think it's amazing, Jim?"

His name pulled him back into their conversation.

"What?"

It was dark now, and the only source of light came from the moon and stars. It was hard to make out her facial expression, but he could hear the hurt in her voice.

"Weren't you listening, Jim?"

"Yes! I was listening. It's amazing. I'm sorry, Lilly Mae. I just get nervous with people walking behind me. That's all."

"Why? It's just my parents."

"I know..."

Jim brushed his hand against hers. Each time the soft glow of evening light was cut off by the shadows of the trees, Jim thought about weaving his fingers between hers, and then letting go when her parents could see them again. But how would she react? Today was the first time he had actually worked up the nerve to have a conversation with her, and it was the first time they had spent any time alone. Well, pretty much alone. It was too soon, and Jim was worried she would snatch her hand away. If nothing else, he could at least make occasional contact with her and pretend it was an accident.

"Y'know, Jim, I'm jealous of the girl in this book," she said after an awkward silence.

"Why's that?"

"She makes lovin' seem so easy," Lilly Mae sighed. Jim looked at her, and she seemed to be staring at something far off that he couldn't see. "The man just comes into her life and says all the right things to her. And she says all the right things back. Even if she does have trouble with her family over it, she's just...*lucky.*"

He seized the opportunity to place a comforting hand on her shoulder.

"Well, maybe you'll be lucky too, Lilly Mae," he said. "Don't ya think that it would ever happen to you?"

"I don't know," she said. She didn't move his hand away.

"Then I don't see why you should be jealous of her. It's just a story, and real life is much better than books."

"How would you know, Jim? You don't read books!"

"I ain't gotta read to know that. I'd rather somethin' good happen to me in real life than read about somethin' good happenin' to someone that don't exist."

Lilly Mae was quiet for a minute after that, and then she grabbed his hand and gave it a little squeeze.

"You're right, Jim," she said as she let go of his hand.

Jim didn't know what to say after that. Was it a friendly gesture, or was she implying that she wanted more? He didn't want to find out right then. He just wanted to enjoy the feeling. His hand tingled the rest of the way to her house.

*****

Jim saw Lilly Mae very little in the month after their evening stroll. The Sunday after the ice cream supper, she came down with a cold and didn't come to church. After that, he only saw her briefly a couple of times, and even then, he had to share her attention with the other churchgoers.

He soon realized that he wasn't the only young man vying for her attention. He had noticed James Kilgore talking to her in church just before the service started. He was a year older than Jim, and bigger, too.

Jim had tried to talk to Lilly Mae a few times, and he always tried to think of something smart to say that would keep her attention on him. He had asked her about the coal–mining story, but she said she had already finished it and had moved on to another book. He was just about to ask her how it had ended and what the new book was about when Kilgore butted in.

"Hey, Lilly Mae," Kilgore said as he eased into the pew near her. "You shore look awful pretty today. Is that a new dress?"

Jim could have punched him. How was it that Kilgore could flatter her so easily? Jim wouldn't dare make a comment on her beauty, at least not yet. But here came this other boy, jumping the gun like it was nothing.

"No, I've just not wore it to church before," she said flatly.

She picked up a hymnal, flipped to a random page, and hid

her face behind it. Jim felt relieved that she was at least trying to ignore the other boy.

Kilgore wasn't fazed. "Well, it looks real good on you."

Mrs. Larkey frowned at the young man, and Lilly Mae turned scarlet behind the hymnal.

Jim wanted to say something to Kilgore to make him go away, but he knew that anything he could say would just make it worse.

"Git over here, James," Mrs. Kilgore hissed from the other side of the aisle.

Kilgore groaned and sauntered back over toward his mother. Lilly Mae laid the hymnal in her lap and sighed with relief.

*****

The pace of work on the farm picked up as fall and harvest time approached. Jim was also doing additional farm work on Saturdays for Mr. Ramey. His father had volunteered him, saying that the family could use the extra cash come winter. Jim didn't mind the extra work. The heavy lifting helped keep his mind off Lilly Mae, and his muscles were growing bigger and stronger. As the days went by, Kilgore felt less of a threat.

On Sunday morning, Jim got up early for church. While lying in bed the night before, he had come up with a plan. He would get to the church early, follow the Larkeys in, and hope that there would be an empty seat next to Lilly Mae, or at least near her.

As he washed his face and hands in the pan of cold spring water on the back porch, he wondered if she would find it strange that he had come early, without his folks. What if she figured out that he had come early just to see her? Would she think *he* was strange?

Jim pushed these thoughts aside. As far as he knew, Lilly

Mae liked talking with him. He joined his family at the breakfast table, where Momma had the usual array of eggs, bacon, sausage, and biscuits and gravy, along with plenty of cold milk to wash it down.

After tending to the animals and milking Sally, the cow, Jim announced, "I need to ride Old Nell to the church early and catch Mr. Ramey before the service."

"Why?" his father said with the look of suspicion that he wore whenever Jim did anything out of the ordinary.

"I gotta ask him if he needs me next Saturday."

"Why didn't you ask him yesterday?"

"I forgot."

"Well, why don't you just ask him *after* the service?" Daddy said slowly. He wasn't buying it.

"'Cause he might get gone before I can ask him. Then I'll have to go all the way over to his place and ask him."

His father just stared at him for a minute, his face not changing. This really wasn't as good a plan as Jim had thought.

"I guess we'll *all* go early, then," Mr. Taylor finally said.

Jim shrugged. As long as he got there before the Larkeys, he didn't care who was with him when he showed up.

"I can't go early," Mrs. Taylor objected. "Let him go. I still gotta finish this potato salad."

Mr. Taylor narrowed his eyes at his son. "You had better be on your best behavior, son."

Jim couldn't stand his father's suspicion any longer. He wasn't very good at lying to his father—or his father was just really good at seeing through lies.

He hurried into the yard and out to the barn to saddle up Old Nell. As he tightened the cinch, he said a silent prayer for forgiveness for the lie he had just told his father. He swung into the saddle and placed his feet in the stirrups. As he rode down the lane toward the main road, he felt uneasy—guilty for telling a lie to his father, and excited at the prospect of seeing Lilly Mae.

He pulled up the reins as he neared the main road and looked back at his homestead, hoping to pull himself together a bit before continuing on.

The house sat in the mouth of a hollow with hills on either side. A quarter mile off the main road, it was only partially visible due to a bend in the lane leading up to it. A small branch flowed out of the hollow past the house and barn following the lane until it emptied into Kegley Creek at the main road.

George Taylor had built the board house in 1892 to replace an old two-story log cabin. The new house had three rooms, a loft, and small porches at the front and back. The large living room contained a fireplace and served as a kitchen and living area. Until their daughter May moved out, it had also been sleeping quarters for Mr. and Mrs. Taylor; their bed had occupied one corner of the living area. Now the other two small rooms were used as bedrooms for Annie and her parents. The spring house and barn had been built a year later, and the shake roof had been replaced with tin a few years after Jim was born. The exterior had never been painted, but his dad had kept the place in good shape.

Jim was born in the back bedroom of that house in July 1909. His parents named him James Taft Taylor in honor of President Taft, who had been elected the year before. The Taylors were dyed-in-the-wool Republicans. George Taylor often said that the Taylors had never voted for a Democrat—that is, if you didn't count Andrew Jackson.

After several moments of reminiscing, Jim nudged Old Nell with his knees and turned onto the main road.

It wasn't too long before he arrived at the church, to find that the Larkeys hadn't made it there yet. He killed some time by tying up Old Nell by the water trough and watching her as she drank.

When Jim was a little boy, she was just Nell. Once she started slowing down and her age began to show, she gained her current title. Soon enough, it would be too hard for her to make the trip to church. Lord knew what his daddy would do with her then.

Finally, the Larkeys pulled up.

As they entered the church, Jim hurried in behind them and exchanged glances with Lilly Mae. He felt his stomach flutter when they did. What was she thinking? Mr. Larkey led his family to a pew four rows from the back. Lilly Mae was the first one in, and she didn't go all the way to the end of the pew. Instead, she left some space to the left. Had she left that space for Jim? Or did she just not like sitting too close to the edge? Either way, Jim was ready to take advantage of it. He quickly crossed over the row behind them and moved forward to sit next to her.

"Is it all right if I sit here?" he asked slowly, trying to keep from stammering.

"Of course, Jim," she said.

His heart was pounding. He could hear it beating furiously in his ears, and he could hear almost nothing else.

Mrs. Larkey smiled at him, while Lilly Mae's brother and three sisters gawked at him as though he were a stranger, someone who had just walked right into their home and had sat down at their dinner table. Mr. Larkey stared straight ahead.

Lilly Mae said something to him, but he couldn't quite hear her.

"What?" he said.

"I asked if you were all right, Jim. You don't look too good. Have you caught that summer cold that's been going around?"

"No, I'm fine," Jim answered. If he had caught a cold, he certainly wouldn't want to be anywhere near her.

"You don't look fine. Just relax, all right?"

Jim nodded. How embarrassing! He had finally managed to sit next to her in church, and he had succeeded at nothing but making her worry about him. At least she cared, but he didn't want her thinking he was weak, either.

He finally started to relax halfway through Deacon Greer's 15-minute opening prayer. The congregation went through the a cappella, four-part harmony songs, and Brother John Boatwright was well into his sermon of hellfire and brimstone when the pain shot through Jim's foot. As usual in warm weather, he was barefooted. What had happened? The heel of his left foot was throbbing. He turned around to see James Kilgore staring straight ahead at Brother Boatwright with a very out-of-place smirk on his face. Jim turned and stretched backwards over the pew and saw that Kilgore was wearing brogans. He kicked me, thought Jim, as his face reddened.

"Don't do that again," Jim said to him in a trembling whisper.

Kilgore acted as though he hadn't heard him.

"What happened?" Lilly Mae whispered.

"Nothin'."

Mrs. Larkey gave them a disapproving glance, and Jim refocused his attention on Robby's father. Five minutes later, it happened again. This time, Kilgore kicked him much harder. Jim's vision blurred from a mixture of pain and rage.

He would later say that he couldn't remember leaping over the back of the pew and flailing away at Kilgore. He couldn't remember tumbling with the bigger boy between the pews. All he remembered from that 30-second brawl was Lilly Mae screaming.

"Jim! Stop it!"

The adrenaline didn't subside until Jim realized he couldn't breathe. Kilgore had a death grip on his throat. Jim grabbed Kilgore's wrists and tried to pry the massive hands off his neck. Kilgore's father took hold of the boy's shoulders and tried to pull him off, but Kilgore wouldn't let go. The congregation buzzed around them with excited chatter as people shuffled to intervene.

Jim was near panic when he finally managed to hit Kilgore

directly on his Adam's apple. Kilgore choked for air, and Jim seized the opportunity to pin him to the floor. He began pounding Kilgore's face, and blood splattered onto the back of the pew. They grappled at each other, and Jim was grateful for the extra work he had done that summer. Kilgore was bigger than Jim, but he wasn't as strong. With Jim having the advantage now, Kilgore's only effective punch was an elbow to Jim's face.

The next thing Jim knew, his dad had caught him underneath the arms and broken his grip on the older boy.

Jim choked and sputtered as his father dragged him out of church and threw him off the porch. Jim's mouth was dry and his throat hurt. Mr. Taylor pitched him into the buggy, tied Old Nell to the back, and drove straight to the barn at home.

During the long ride home, George Taylor said nothing. His face said it all.

Jim's rage had subsided and was replaced with something else—fear.

"Fighting in church," Mr. Taylor finally said when they had reached the barn. "Do you *want* to burn in Hell, boy?"

"But he kicked me! Twice!"

"Shut up. You think that really makes things any different?"

Jim knew what was coming. His dad yanked the leather strap from a peg on the barn wall and swung it. The impact left Jim's back stinging. His dad swung the strap over and over at him until he just gave out. Jim was on the ground writhing in pain when he finally heard the strap hit the ground and then his father's heavy boots crunching the straw as he walked out.

For several minutes, Jim lay there in the straw and dirt. He hurt all over—his heel, his back, his throat, his face. He pulled himself off the ground, hobbled out of the barn, and noticed that the buggy was still sitting in the yard. Was Daddy not going to go back for Mama and Annie?

Jim walked over to the branch and washed off. He didn't hear any sounds or movement from the house, and he figured that his father was done for the day.

Still wet from head to toe, Jim untied Old Nell, climbed into the buggy, and headed back to the church. All the way there, he thought about what had happened at church.

What was Mama going to say? Would Annie ever let him live it down? How would they even go on with the service after something like that? What would Reverend Boatwright do?

Jim was certain that he had disgraced his family in the eyes of the entire community. He had never heard of a fight breaking out in a Baptist church—or any other church, for that matter. Was his father right? Would he go to Hell for this?

But the worst thought of all: Would Lilly Mae ever speak to him again?

As he rounded the last curve before starting up the hill to the church, he saw the McMurrays' wagon approaching with his mother and Annie aboard.

They pulled up alongside one another and stopped. Mrs. Taylor and Annie moved into the buggy with Jim after Mrs. Taylor thanked the McMurrays.

"The church prayed for you and the Kilgore boy," Mr. McMurray said. "I told your mama that I seed it all, and it weren't your fault."

"Thank you, Mr. McMurray," Jim said. "I appreciate that."

The ride home was silent. Jim focused on the road, but he could feel his mother and sister staring at him.

Finally, Annie spoke. "Did Daddy give you a whippin'?"

"Annie, hush!" Mrs. Taylor said.

Jim said nothing. He knew Annie was just trying to cut the tension, but her words couldn't slice through it.

Finally, when Jim pulled into the lane beside the branch leading to the house, his mother spoke softly. "Your face is swellin'. We'll need to put a poultice on it when we get in."

The people in the community would talk about the fight for years to come, but George Taylor never spoke of it again. Jim dreaded facing the congregation two Sundays later, and all he could hope for was that the rest of them saw it like Mr. McMurray. He tried to get out of going, but his father wouldn't hear of it.

Jim had no choice but to go back. But how would he face Lilly Mae? Even if his chances with her were ruined, at least Kilgore's would be, too. Still, he didn't think it was fair at all. What could he have done different? he wondered.

CHAPTER THREE

Two weeks later, when the Taylors arrived at the church, the Kilgores sat on one side of the aisle and the Taylors sat on the other. Lilly Mae was two rows in front of the Taylors. Jim hoped that she would speak to him again, but he knew better. Surely Mr. Larkey would never allow it after what had happened.

The service droned on and on: first the songs, then Greer's long prayer, then the sermon by Reverend Boatwright. Next, the visiting preacher, Thurston Spurcheon—an evangelist who would preach at the week-long revival next week—delivered a "short" message that ended 40 minutes later.

After the closing prayer, it was more than an hour past lunchtime. Jim took nothing at all away from the morning's sermons. The whole time, he had been staring at the back of Lilly Mae's head, wondering how she felt about him after what had happened the last time he had sat with her. He also thought about his dreams of her, which would certainly send him to Hell if the church fight didn't. When they bowed their heads for the final prayer, Jim asked for forgiveness on both counts.

After the service, Jim and Robby Boatwright filed out of the church with the rest of the congregation. As Jim passed familiar faces, he noticed a lot of them looking at him with pity.

"Did ya get a whippin' over that fight?" Robby asked as they finally made it outside.

"What do you think?"

"I think I wouldn't be able to walk ever again if I had done somethin' like that. I'd be lucky if my daddy didn't send me off to a boys' home."

"Your daddy wouldn't do that," Jim said.

"How did it get started, anyway?" Robby asked. "Did he whisper somethin' naughty in your ear?"

"Would you just drop it? I don't want to talk about it."

Jim was about to walk away from Robby when he heard a familiar voice call his name. He turned around and saw Lilly Mae walking toward him. He froze up.

"Hi, Jim. Hi, Rob," she said.

"Hello," they replied. Jim stared at his feet.

"Are y'all coming to the revival next week?" she asked.

"What do you think?" Robby said. "It's my daddy's church."

"Oh, well of course *you* are," Lilly Mae replied. "But what about you, Jim?"

Jim couldn't get over that she was even talking to him. He looked over at where her parents were waiting for her in the buggy. Her brother and sisters were giving him that same, strange look as last time, but Jim was surprised to see that Mrs. Larkey was smiling at him. Mr. Larkey was more difficult to read, but at least he wasn't glaring.

"I don't 'spect I'll have much choice in the matter," Jim finally answered.

"Well, good. I thought I might sit with you to keep you out of trouble."

Jim felt himself turn red. He didn't know if she meant to have a good time with him at the revival, or if all she cared about was keeping him under control. Either way, he was excited at the prospect of being with her.

"He needs all the help he can get," Rob said.

Lilly Mae laughed.

"Well, I'll see you, then," she said, and then she hurried to her family's buggy.

"See you there, Lilly Mae," Jim called after her. She turned around and waved.

That night, Jim lay nude on his pallet. All he could do was think about Lilly Mae's smooth skin and soft curves and how great she would feel pressed up against him. He didn't know what to expect at the revival, but surely it wouldn't be anything like the thoughts coursing through his mind right then. He wondered how Lilly Mae could possibly keep him out of trouble when she was the reason he was in trouble to begin with.

*****

Less than a week later, the revival was in full swing. Preacher Spurcheon's altar calls had been very successful, with six conversions and two recommitments to Christ. Lilly Mae had kept to her word and had sat with Jim four of the last six nights to keep an eye on him. Aside from exchanging a few threatening looks with Kilgore, Jim had behaved himself pretty well.

Tonight, a cool fall breeze with the crisp smell of dried leaves drifted through the church.

"Tonight's weather is perfect for a revival—not too hot, not too cold," Lilly Mae sighed. "His presence really is with us here, don't you think?"

"Seems so," Jim said, looking straight ahead toward the altar. The service was long, as usual, and Jim's mind was elsewhere while the preacher breathlessly called the congregation to salvation. After the plans he and Lilly Mae had made earlier in the evening, all he could do was anxiously wait for the preacher to say the words that would put those plans into action.

"I want to talk to you alone," she had said earlier while everyone drifted in and filled the pews.

Finally, the moment came. Everyone rose for the song that would transition to the altar call, and Jim slipped out the door and onto the porch. He peeked anxiously into the church and saw Lilly Mae coming toward him.

"Do you think they saw us leave?" he whispered.

"I don't think so. We need to hurry."

He followed her through the buggies and wagons to a big chestnut tree across the dirt lane from the church. Lilly Mae glanced nervously in every direction. Her shoulders relaxed when she was certain no one was around. Jim was still confused about what she could possibly have to say to him that was so private that they had to sneak around like a couple of bandits. It wasn't like her at all.

She pressed her back against the tree and gazed off at the horizon. The vast Virginia sky was clear, and thousands of stars glittered above them. Jim focused on Lilly Mae, who seemed to be gathering her thoughts. For what seemed like forever, they just stood there, with Lilly Mae watching the sky and Jim watching Lilly Mae.

"How come you always look at me like that?" she finally said.

"Like what?"

She bit her lip and kept her gaze on the sky. Jim could tell that she was really struggling to find the words for whatever it was that she wanted to say. Deep down, he was getting kind of impatient. Why can't women just say things simple? he thought.

"Like I'm the most interesting thing you've ever seen," she said after several painful moments of silence. "I'm quiet, boring, and I keep to myself. Yet you act all nervous around me, like it's some act of God if I say two words to you."

Jim felt trapped. Is this really all she wanted to talk to him about? Had he scared her off?

"Well, I don't know," he said. "I don't think you're boring."

She stared at him, and Jim couldn't tell if she was frowning or just thinking again.

"What's wrong?" he asked.

"Nothing. It's just I'm not used to the attention, that's all."

"Well, Kilgore was payin' plenty of attention to you a couple of weeks back."

Lilly Mae scoffed and rolled her eyes. "Do you really think *that's* the kind of attention I want? Kilgore might tell me I'm pretty, but he ain't gonna sit and listen to me talk about books."

"I don't think I'm quite understandin' ye, Lilly Mae. Did you bring me out here just to ask me why I like to talk to ye?"

Lilly Mae sighed and looked back toward the sky. Sounds of the night rang in their ears—a symphony of katydids and frogs from the woods mingled with strains of "What a Friend We Have in Jesus" from the open windows of the church.

"I guess that's what I'm asking you."

Jim shrugged and leaned against the tree so he was standing right next to her. How could something so simple be so complicated?

"I don't know," Jim said. "I just do."

Lilly Mae seemed a bit disappointed by his answer. She looked down at her feet. "I guess I really don't think there's much special about me. But you act like something is. I just want to know what you think about me."

Jim couldn't believe what he was hearing. He had been a mess from thinking about her all the time, and she seriously thought there was nothing special about her?

"Well, for one, you're smart," Jim began. "You talk about things that I ain't never heard or thought about before. For two, you're nice. You don't act all full of yourself like some girls around here. And three—"

Jim stopped himself. How would she react if he told her how beautiful he thought she was? Would she laugh at him? Would she shoot him down?

"Three?" she asked when he didn't continue.

He figured it was too late, now. What did he have to lose, anyway? Worst thing that could happen was she'd laugh at him.

"You're beautiful," he said without looking at her.

For a moment, all he could hear was Preacher Spurcheon's booming voice beckoning people to come forth. They were running out of time. He could feel her staring at him, and he waited anxiously for her to at least say *something.*

"I'm sorry," he said after a few moments of silence. "I shouldn't have—"

"No, it's okay," she said. She moved in front of him and stared hard at him with her dark eyes. It was hard to tell by just the light of the moon, but she seemed to have a hint of a smile on her face.

The next thing Jim knew, her face was so close to his that he could feel her breath on his neck. She wrapped her arms around him and slowly pressed her mouth to his, then quickly broke away and made a beeline to the church.

It was one of the best moments of his life.

Jim stood there a minute more to calm himself, then headed back. He eased inside the door during the closing song, and for the first time in his life, he sang out loud in church.

He felt at home here. His father, grandfather, and great-grandfather before him had been members of this church. Piney Level Primitive Baptist Church had been on this hill for many generations. No musical instruments were allowed; Sunday school was not permitted; no pictures or "graven images" could be placed in the church. They believed in "shouting" when moved by the Spirit and foot washing to experience and demonstrate humility. No minister of the church had ever been to seminary. Collection plates were not passed, and the pastor received no pay. If something needed fixing, those that could afford it would pitch a dollar or two into a hat.

The roots of this church and all other Primitive Baptist Churches in America could be traced back to dissension that had raged a hundred years earlier, during the 1820s and 1830s. The practice of using Sunday schools in church, seminaries for teaching ministers, and the funding of missionaries gradually spread from England to America in the period of 1800 to 1820. A small group of Baptist churches began to resist the introduction of these practices, believing they were of man, not God.

These churches believed that their faith and practices were those of the "original" English and Welsh Baptists and should be preserved. Thus they became known as the Primitive—original—Baptists. The churches that adopted the new practices eventually became known as Missionary Baptists. This virulent, permanent rift spread through Maryland, Pennsylvania, and Virginia, down through the Carolinas, Tennessee, and Georgia, and then to the West.

Curiously, many of these early Primitive Baptists also came to oppose temperance societies and Freemasonry. They believed that consuming alcohol was sanctioned by the Scriptures and that the secretive nature of the Masonic Institution was contrary to the principles of liberty in general and to Primitive Baptist doctrine in particular.

In later years, these beliefs gradually changed as ministers preached against the effects of "strong drink" on men and their families. In addition, some of the men of this very church would later join the Masonic Order.

CHAPTER FOUR

May 1926

Over the next two years, Jim and Lilly Mae saw each other as often as possible at church functions, and occasionally they would sneak meetings when going for supplies from his uncle's country store down near the river.

In early 1925, George Washington Taylor was appointed a part–time deputy sheriff for Shelby County. Then, in January of 1926, Jim's father was also appointed a part–time revenue agent, to help "bust up" moonshine stills in the backcountry. The revenuers were based in Richmond and needed help in finding stills and arresting the moonshiners.

Occasionally, Jim would tag along to help his father, and this was the beginning of his interest in law enforcement. He was drawn to the excitement of the hunt and the adrenaline rush of the capture.

The agents from the state capital quickly discovered the value of George Taylor's knowledge of the backcountry.

George had heard rumors of a large still operation on Walker Mountain. On May 17, 1926, he decided that the next morning, he would try to find it.

Jim finished the morning chores and came back to the house to wash up for dinner. His father asked him to come along in the morning to help.

"Jim, I want you to go with me. If I find the still, I'll need some help in bustin' it up and carrying the copper off the mountain."

Jim was beside himself. His boring afternoon of farm work was instantly transformed to one of excitement and anticipation.

"I want to go, too," Annie demanded.

"This is no work for a girl," her father sternly replied as he cleaned his shotgun.

Jim walked around to the back porch where Annie had retreated to be alone. Approaching her haltingly, he offered her a dipper of cool water from the pail on the porch rail. She shook her head and turned her back to hide the tears.

Jim slipped his arm around her shoulder and gave her a little squeeze. "Annie, he's just afraid you'll get hurt. You're 12 years old now. It won't be long before you'll be able to ride to the store for Mama, spend the night at Aunt Addie's, and such."

She nodded her head and turned away again.

He had grown especially close to Annie over the last couple of years. She was smart as a whip, and her sweet disposition could melt his heart. Since she and Jim were the only children left at home, she often turned to him with her problems, questions, and secrets. She trusted him, and he had never broken that trust. She shared her innermost feelings with him, and she could count on him to understand. He also confided in her and asked for her advice on things he didn't quite understand. It was Annie who had encouraged him to ask Lilly Mae if he could walk her home from church the first time.

For lunch, Jim had cold biscuits left over from breakfast, along with ham and blackberry jam. He washed it down with a cool glass of buttermilk and headed to the fields. Time passed swiftly as he thought about tomorrow's adventure. He wondered if they would find the still, and if so, whether anyone would be there tending it.

Over the years, he had heard stories about how dangerous it was to "happen upon" a still. Men would kill to protect their livelihood.

Many mountain families had been making moonshine for generations. Making moonshine was not illegal until Prohibition took effect in 1920, but avoiding taxes on it was. Distilling strong spirits was a part of the American heritage dating back to the earliest years of the colonies, and it was an integral part of the colonial economy.

George Washington had a distillery at Mount Vernon, and he kept detailed records of the overhead and profits of the business. During his presidency, angry farmers in western Pennsylvania refused to pay the excise taxes levied on whiskey by a Congressional act of 1791. The tax radically reduced profits from the farmers' chief cash crop. Scattered attacks on federal tax agents grew until it was termed an insurrection in July of 1794.

President Washington called out 13,000 militia men and personally led them into Pennsylvania to put down the insurrection. The show of force succeeded, and only 13 men were arrested, all of whom were later pardoned by Washington.

Some of the moonshiners in these mountains of southwestern Virginia were no doubt descended from those rebels in western Pennsylvania. Tomorrow, George Washington Taylor would pursue them as his namesake had 132 years earlier.

After supper, Jim's father told him to get to bed early. "We need to be in the mountains before daylight," he said.

Jim was in bed by 8:00, but it took over an hour for him to drop into a fitful sleep.

His mother awakened him just after 4:00 a.m. "Get up, Jim. Breakfast is ready."

He joined his parents at the table. His father said a quick prayer. "Lord, watch over the family this day." Jim took it to mean that they would be doing dangerous work and that they needed the Lord's help.

He wanted to ask questions about the trip into the mountains, but he dared not ask at the table. Even though he was almost 17, now, his father's rule of not allowing children to speak at the table still applied to him. He asked his mother once why his daddy had such a rule. She replied, "I don't know, son. I reckon it was jus' the way he was raised."

Jim said, "You were a Taylor, too, before you married Daddy. Was it a rule at your house when you were a little girl?"

"No, son, it wasn't."

"Since you was both Taylors, were you and Daddy kin before you married?'

"I don't know, son. They say that our great-grandfathers were brothers. If that makes us kin, it wouldn't be close kin."

"Well, I guess that makes me a double Taylor, and that's gotta be a good thing."

His mother smiled, but she said nothing further. Jim was jolted from his thoughts by his father's, "Come on, boy. Saddle your horse. We've got to get going."

Once his eyes had adjusted to the dark, the half moon gave enough light to see the road. They would follow the road to north of Holston Landing, then hit the mountain trails. They had packed some biscuits, beef jerky, his father's shotgun, extra ammo, and an axe.

They rode in silence for about three miles before Jim began to ask questions.

"How long will it take to get up in the mountains to where we begin searchin'?" he asked.

"A little over an hour. 'Bout 5:30."

"What do you want me to do when we get there?"

"First of all, you've gotta be real quiet, and you need to keep an eye out for anythin' that ain't natural, like where the ground's been disturbed or where there's a path when there shouldn't be no path. And you need to listen and smell."

"Listen and smell for what?"

"Listen for voices, horses snortin', dogs barkin', metal janglin', and such. If they're cookin' off a batch, there'll be smoke to smell, but I 'spect it'll be too early for them to have a fire. Most likely they won't be there, but we can't depend on that."

"If they are there, what'll we do?" asked Jim.

"Well, first you need to stay behind me if we spot 'em. Then you need to stay where I tell you while I go in and arrest 'em. Don't come in till I tell you. If there's gunfire, stay down and stay put."

"What if they shoot you?"

"Boy, you've got more questions than Carter's got liver pills. It ain't likely to happen, but if I get shot, you ride to Holston Landing for help."

There was silence for the next 15 minutes as Jim digested all that he'd been told.

For the first time in his life, Jim felt like a man. On the ride this morning, his father had talked to him more than he had in the last three months combined. And he had talked to him like a man instead of a kid—well, at least part of the time.

Jim suddenly asked, "Dad, can I have a gun in case you need help?"

"No, you don't need a gun!"

After a minute or two his father said, "Well, I'll give you my pistol, and I'll go in with the shotgun. But you stay back like I told you and only use the pistol if you get cornered, and only if your life depends on it. Do you understand?"

"Yes, sir."

Halfway up the mountain, the forest canopy blocked the light of the moon, so they tied off the horses and proceeded on foot. Mr. Taylor carried the shotgun, Jim the axe. George Taylor would stop every few minutes and listen. Jim heard it first and tapped his father on the shoulder.

Mr. Taylor cocked his head to one side and strained to hear. He heard nothing. Then it dawned on him why Jim had signaled him. It was the "nothing" that he had noticed. The staccato song of the katydids had stopped. It was completely silent on the mountain except for the distant and barely audible rumble of a train in the valley toward Holston Landing.

Finally, they heard a muffled voice, or maybe a laugh. Then the katydids started up again. Mr. Taylor estimated that the voice they had heard was about half a mile away. He whispered to Jim, "With these katydids, they won't be able to hear us coming. Let's go."

They eased through the woods, listening and watching for a lookout or a guard dog. Then they heard voices again—louder this time. Next, they noticed a faint glow among the trees. "Must have a fire goin'," whispered Deputy Taylor. "We'll get close enough to see the operation, then hunker down until daybreak."

They moved close enough to make out the forms of three men. The moonshiners had apparently gotten overconfident and had placed no lookouts. Jim and his father could see them more clearly, now, by the faint light in the eastern sky.

Mr. Taylor slowly and quietly broke down his 12-gauge, double-barreled shotgun. He pulled out the two shells one at a time, looked them over, and then placed them back in the chamber. Then he eased the gun shut, wincing when it made a dull clank.

The men around the still never looked up. They had apparently heard nothing.

"Stay here and stay down," his father whispered. Jim nodded as his father headed for the still. His heart pounded as he watched his father approach the still—slowly at first, then faster. Deputy Taylor was within 20 yards of the still when the boy stoking the fire saw him.

"Shit! Run!" the boy screamed as he reached for a rifle.

Taylor yelled, "Don't move!"

But before the words were completely out of his mouth, gunfire erupted. His father returned fire. Jim was frozen by fear to his spot on the ground. His father was hit—knocked completely down and onto his back!

Jim was halfway to his father before he realized that he was running. He had emptied the six-shot revolver in the direction of where the men were running into the trees. He was hyperventilating as he reached his father. Mr. Taylor sat up.

"Where are you hit?" screamed Jim as he looked for signs of blood.

"I uh, I don't know," replied his father as he checked himself. Then Mr. Taylor checked the shotgun lying next to him, and he began to laugh—just a chuckle at first, then a hearty laugh. His laughter had a calming effect on Jim. He had never heard his father laugh like that. Jim was bent at the waist with his hands on his knees, trying to catch his breath.

After a deep breath, Jim asked, "What's so funny?"

His father pointed to the shells in the chamber. "Look. Both shells fired."

"I don't understand."

"I only pulled one trigger, but both barrels went off. It knocked me down."

Jim slowly began to comprehend what his father had said, but he didn't see the humor in it. "Are we going after them?" he asked, excitedly.

"No, they're long gone by now. Go get the axe, and let's get to work on this still. Another thing, boy: You tell anybody about what happened here, and I'll have your hide."

Jim looked at his father, still sitting there with the gun broken down across his lap. Jim burst into laughter, and his father just shook his head. After retrieving the axe, Jim watched his father chop holes in the boiler.

Mash flowed onto the fire, and steam rose to the treetops.

"Did you recognize any of the men?" Jim asked.

"One of them was a boy by the name of Benson, 'bout your age. I didn't get a good look at the other two. One of 'em was his father, I 'spect. I've seen 'em around Holston Landing a time or two. They was on the far side of the still. They run into the woods with their backs to me, firing wild-like over their shoulders. They'd probably stayed and killed me if you hadn't come runnin' in. You didn't stay put the way I told you to, boy. You can't come along again unless I can depend on you to follow orders."

After a brief pause, his father added, "But I gotta admit, the way you come in a-blastin' probably saved me. They probably thought there was four or five of us 'cause of the way you shot so many rounds so fast."

At the time, Jim hadn't had a clue what he was doing. He had been so scared that now he could barely remember firing. His father didn't seem angry at him, so Jim just nodded.

Taylor had heard rumors that Benson beat his wife and kids when he got drunk. He also knew, from what sheriff's deputies had told him in the past, that Roy Benson was a dangerous man. Since Taylor could identify the Benson boy, he thought he might work a deal to get Roy Benson to confess. It was worth a try.

"That hose there will lead to a spring. Follow it and get ye a drink of water. Then roll up the hose while I get this copper coil off," his father directed.

"Don't you want a drink?"

"I'll get one outta this hose while you find the spring."

The hose was concealed by leaves and twigs the entire distance to the spring. Jim drank the cold water, then grabbed the hose and started back, looping it as he went. By the time he got back to the still, he was struggling under the weight of the hose.

"Do we have to carry this all the way back to where the horses are?"

"No. We'll carry it a ways, then hide it. This is the biggest still I've ever seen. We'll ride to the Post Office in Holston Landing and have them notify the sheriff's office in Batesville that I need help. You can go on home, and I'll come back with the deputies to finish up here."

The ride off the mountain was pleasant, with a cool morning breeze rustling leaves under a cloudless, pale blue sky. On the road to Holston Landing, they were passed by two cars in less than 45 minutes.

"When will we get a car?" Jim asked.

"I don't know. Why would we need a car?"

"Well, it'd be a lot faster to get around."

"You in a big hurry, boy?"

"I reckon not," Jim replied.

As they rode into the Post Office lot, Mr. Taylor told Jim to head for home. "Tell your mother it'll probably be after dark before I'm home. I gotta go in here and get 'em to call the sheriff's office in Batesville."

"Can I go in with you?"

"What for?" his dad asked impatiently as he dismounted.

"I ain't never seen a telephone."

His dad started to say something, and then thought the better of it. After a pause, he said, "Come on in, then git straight home."

"Yes, sir."

On the ride off the mountain, he remembered that his father had told him that he was not to tell anyone about busting up the still. He said it was police business, and nothing could be said until it got to court. Nevertheless, Jim couldn't wait to tell Rob Boatwright. He would swear Rob to secrecy. They had shared secrets before. He'd like to tell Annie, but her having missed the excitement would just make her feel worse. He wondered if he should tell Lilly Mae how he had saved the day on the raid. No, that would be bragging, so he wouldn't mention it. Besides, it would all come out at the trial, and everyone would hear about it.

Suddenly the horse stopped. Jim realized that they were at

the turnoff for the lane that led to their house. Fortunately, Old Nell was not as prone to daydreaming as her rider.

*****

Two days later, George Taylor rode over to Bright's Hollow to talk with Roy Benson. Two coon hounds met him 50 yards from the house. Their snarling and growling threatened to spook his horse.

Benson came out on the porch with a rifle in hand.

"Call off the dogs, Benson. I need to talk to you," Deputy Taylor shouted.

"What do you want?"

"You goin' to come out and talk, or do I need to come back with deputies?"

Benson called off the dogs and approached cautiously.

Taylor explained that he could identify his son and that he would probably go to the pen for it.

Benson pointed the rifle at Taylor. "Nobody's goin' to put my boy in jail."

"That's what I want to talk to you about. He don't have to go to jail if you agree to my proposition."

"What proposition?"

"You meet me at the Post Office in Holston Landing tomorrow morning at 9:00, and I'll lay it out fer ye."

"Lay it out right now."

"Nope. Nine o'clock tomorrow."

Deputy Taylor reined his horse around as he said, "See you there." As he rode off, he wondered if Benson would shoot.

The next morning, Benson showed up along with his son, Tom.

George led them to the Postmaster's office, then laid out the deal. "You confess, and your son doesn't get charged."

"You got nothing on me or my boy."

"I can personally identify your boy. He shot at me. Shootin' at an officer is a serious crime. I know you was there and ran into the woods, but I didn't see your face."

Benson bit his lip as he sat in silence. Deputy Taylor got up to leave.

"I'll take it," said Benson.

"Be at the courthouse in Batesville at two o'clock tomorrow to turn yourself in."

Benson got up and walked out. His son Tom followed George out and whispered, "I'll get you for this, old man."

Taylor turned and said, "Boy, you better get on back to the house before I change my mind."

Roy Benson was sentenced to two years in prison, with 10 years of probation to follow.

CHAPTER 5

May 1927

George Taylor's first automobile was actually a truck. He bought it to augment the wagon they used to haul lumber from the sawmill. George and Bob Johnson were equal partners in the business, and orders for lumber had steadily grown since the first of the year.

George was now a part–time deputy sheriff, a part–time revenuer, and a part–time sawmill owner. Jim drove the truck, helped at the mill, and also worked on the farm.

It was a typical day in late May, hot and dry. The sawmill was down due to a broken belt, and the new one wouldn't be in at Batesville until Monday. Jim had been assigned the task of picking it up, and he looked forward to driving the truck all the way to town and back. In the meantime, he had lots of work to do.

At church on Sunday, he asked Lilly Mae if she could go to Batesville with him the next day.

"I'd love to!" she said. "I'll pack a picnic lunch to have on the way back."

"Good. I'll pick you up at 9:00."

Jim was up early on Monday morning. After a quick breakfast, he rushed through his chores, washed up, and headed to Lilly Mae's. At 9:00 sharp, Lilly Mae came into view, standing by the road with a picnic basket at her side. She wore a simple blue calico dress and a white ribbon in her hair.

She is beautiful, Jim thought as he rolled to a stop.

"What's in the basket?" he asked as she climbed into the truck.

"Ham sandwiches and fried apple pies. I thought we might buy a root beer in town to go with it."

"Sounds good. Maybe we can buy an extra one to take to Annie. She loves root beer."

They drove with the windows down, enjoying the breeze off the river. Jim asked her if she had thought about what she was going to do now that she had finished school.

"I'm not sure. Where are we going to picnic on the way back?" she asked, changing the subject.

"I know a place near the Gap on the river. Can you cross a swinging bridge without falling off?" he joked.

"I'm not walking on a swinging bridge unless you promise not to bounce."

"Okay, I can live with that."

Jim pulled up in front of Gillenwater's Feed and Hardware store. "Do you want to get the root beer next door while I pick up the belt?" he asked.

"Sure. I'll meet you back here."

He handed her a silver dollar. "You brought lunch. I'll pay for the drinks. I'm getting paid four dollars a week now at the sawmill."

"What're you doing with all that money?"

"I'm saving most of it—all except what you'll let me spend on you."

She laughed as she turned toward the store.

When he returned, she was waiting in the truck. He heaved the belt into the back, saying, "This thing weighs a ton!" He started the truck and headed back home.

They rode in silence for a few minutes, enjoying the scenery. Then Jim asked, "Have you ever thought about moving away from here?"

"Not really, but I have thought about traveling—about seeing other places I've read about."

"Like where?"

"Like New England or California."

"My brother Ray says Ohio is as flat as a pancake. You can see for miles," Jim said as he slowed the truck and turned right.

"Where are we going?"

"To that swinging bridge I told you about."

"Okay, but remember, no bouncing!"

Jim maneuvered the truck onto the grass by the river near the bridge. He grabbed the basket and a blanket and walked around the truck to help Lilly Mae out, but she was already out of the truck, ready to go.

They approached the bridge and climbed the steps to 40 feet above the water. As he had promised, Jim did not bounce up and down, but the bridge swayed with every step they took.

Lilly Mae walked slowly, with a hand on the cable rails on either side. Jim matched his steps with the rhythm of the sway.

"This is scary!" Lilly Mae said between little screams of both fright and delight.

"This thing fell last year. It took 'em three months to git it back up."

"Jim, hush!"

They made it to the other side, and none too soon for Lilly Mae. As they descended the steps, Jim told her to turn left.

"But the path turns right."

"There's two houses down that way. This is the only way they can get across the river. Go left and we'll find a picnic place."

Jim had been here before with a couple of friends, fishing and nipping at a quart jar of moonshine.

"Do you know where we're going?" she asked.

"No, but there's got to be a spot on the river somewhere," he lied.

They picked their way through the trees and undergrowth until they came to a grassy opening on the bank.

"This looks good," said Lilly Mae.

"Okay," he said.

The river was low; it hadn't rained in two weeks. The sun reflected light off the green water and cast shadows from the trees by the shore. A few gray rocks rose out of the water and created a white foamy wake, as if they were motorboats headed upstream.

Jim spread the blanket beside a weeping willow tree and sat down. Lilly Mae bent down and opened the basket to make sure the root beer bottles were not broken. Jim saw the swell of her breasts and their eyes met. He quickly kissed her and she kissed him back. He reached for her as she sat down. She quickly pulled two bottles out of the basket.

"You open these and I'll get the sandwiches," she said.

"Are you ready to eat? It's early."

"Well, I thought you needed to get that belt back to get the sawmill running."

"No, they've shut the mill down. Won't start back up till in the morning."

"Oh, okay. You want to go wading, then?"

"Sure. You wanna go skinny dipping instead?"

"Jim, you know we can't do that! But I've got a secret. It's a little embarrassing."

"What?"

"I wet my pants a little on the swinging bridge, and I'd like to wash off in the river."

"Go ahead. I'll hold your clothes."

"No, you turn your back and swear that you won't peek."

"Okay."

"You promise?"

"I promise."

Jim turned his back, and she waded into the river. She

pulled her step-ins from beneath her dress and rinsed them in the water. Then she stepped out of the water and hung them on a birch branch out of sight behind the willow tree.

"Want to go wading now?" she asked.

He rolled up his trouser legs to his knees. She took his hand and waded in.

"Try not to step on the rocks," he said. "They're really slick."

The words were scarcely out of his mouth when he slipped and fell onto his back. She stood over him, laughing uncontrollably. He lay there looking up at her. Then, on impulse, he grabbed her hand and pulled her in. They lay in each other's arms, kissing and laughing and kissing again.

"We've got to dry off. I'm freezing," she said through trembling lips.

"I'm not. I'm hot as a firecracker."

"Come on," she said as she ran out of the water and rolled up in the blanket.

He lay there in the water for a moment, watching her and thinking of the Cove Creek dream. He turned over onto all fours, got up, and walked to the blanket.

"Our clothes will never dry under that blanket," he said. "We're gonna have to hang 'em up."

"Jim, we can't do that."

"Well, we can't go back with wet clothes. Try to explain *that* to your daddy!"

She hesitated. He stood there dripping from head to toe. Finally, she spoke. "You go hang yours up, and I'll turn my back. Then I'll do the same while you look away. Jim Taylor, if you look, I'll never speak to you again. Do you promise?"

"I promise. I never looked the first time, did I?"

"Okay, I'm going to turn over. You go on."

Jim walked around the willow and found the birch tree limb where Lilly Mae had hung her step-ins. He eased out of his clothes and placed them on the same limb. He stood there a minute or two, completely nude, enjoying the freedom of the breeze on his unclad body. He was excited and nervous as he walked back around the tree.

She was covered with her back to him. He eased into the blanket and said, "Okay. Your turn."

"Cover your eyes."

"They're covered."

Lilly Mae hung her dress and petticoat on the limb and peeked around the tree. Jim was under the blanket with his hands over his eyes. She hurried back and slipped into her side of the blanket wearing nothing but the ribbon in her hair.

He reached over and touched the ribbon.

"Can I take it out?" he asked.

"Why?"

"I just want to see your hair better."

She didn't answer, but she didn't object when he removed it. He stroked her hair and her cheek with the back of his hand. She closed her eyes, but for an instant she could still see the outlines of the trees and leaves backlit by the sun.

"Wonder why when you see something bright, you can still see it for a little while after you close your eyes?"

"Well, damn, Lilly Mae, I don't know. What's that got to do with anything, anyhow?"

She turned to look at him and laughed. "I don't know. I just thought of it."

Impulsively, he reached under the blanket, pulled her tightly against him, and kissed her hard on the lips. He could feel her soft breasts and hard nipples against his chest. She could feel his erection against her belly. His hands caressed her back, her bottom, and her hips. She opened her mouth slightly and he could feel the soft wetness of the inside of her lips on his.

He squeezed her breast softly and she moved her body tightly against him. He rolled on top of her and wiggled in between her legs—searching—probing.

"No, no, no!" She jerked, wiggled, and pushed him violently away from her.

"What? What happened?"

"I can't do this, Jim. It's not right."

"Why? What did I do wrong?"

"Nothing. I just can't do this. This is a sin. We're not married."

She realized suddenly that she was sitting up bare breasted. She pulled the blanket up around herself as tears streamed down her face. She sat in silence, staring at the river.

"Lilly Mae, I'm sorry. Please don't cry. I love you. Let's get married."

She answered, "Go get your clothes on. Then we can talk."

He stared at her; she stared at the river. After checking his clothes, he walked back to her, unashamed of his nudity. She watched him approach. Barely above a whisper, he said, "They're still wet."

"Come on, get under the blanket," she said.

He sat down and covered himself.

"Jim, I can't get married. I'm going to college."

"To college? What for?"

"I want to get more education. I want to teach."

It slowly sank in. Women teachers in Virginia were not allowed to be married. He was devastated. "That means you won't ever get married," he said in a voice trembling with both sadness and anger.

"No, Jim, I want to get married someday. I just want to teach a few years first. It's always been my dream to teach. You're the first person I've told. My family doesn't even know."

"When are you going, and how long will you be gone?"

"I don't know when. I'll talk to my parents to see if we can afford it. My father says he wants all his children to go to college. He wanted to go but couldn't afford it. As to how long, it'll take two years to get a certificate to teach."

"Where would you go?

"I want to go to Radford State Teachers College."

"Where's that?"

"Its north, on up in Virginia. I don't know how far it is, but you can get there by train from here."

Jim sat in silence, trying to make sense of what he had just heard. He felt as though he'd been kicked in the stomach by Old Nell.

Lilly Mae spoke first. "Jim, I'm sorry. I know I've hurt you, and I'm really sorry. We can still date when I come home for holidays, and we can write each other."

He didn't answer. He turned to look upriver, to hide the tears welling in his eyes.

Finally, Lilly Mae said, "I'm going to get our clothes. Don't peek."

"I'm not going to look. I don't even want to look," he said testily as he stared straight ahead.

She got up, and once her back was to him, he watched her intently until she disappeared around the tree. She came back fully dressed, carrying his damp clothes. She handed them down to him, and he put them on partially under the blanket, but not trying to hide anything, either.

Lilly Mae handed him a sandwich and a root beer. "Let's eat. It'll make us feel better."

They ate in silence. Afterwards, she placed the half–eaten sandwiches and the bottles in the basket with the untouched pies. Jim folded the blanket, and they headed back across the bridge to the truck.

Other than a couple of feeble attempts at small talk, they rode in silence. When Jim pulled up beside the path leading up to her house, Lilly Mae grabbed the basket, kissed him on the cheek, and said, "We'll talk again."

A flood of thoughts and feelings assailed Jim on the drive home. Would he ever be able to marry Lilly Mae? Would she break up with him once she left for college? Would she meet someone at college? After turning into the lane leading to his home, he stopped to hide the blanket under the seat. When he lifted it, two fried pies toppled onto the seat, along with Annie's root beer.

CHAPTER 6

July 2, 1927

For the previous five years on July 2nd, Jim and Annie had gone blackberry picking together, as their older siblings had done before them. Nobody could remember exactly when the tradition had started, but it was always on July 2nd. But Jim couldn't go this time. Orders were backed up at the sawmill, and he would be delivering lumber most of the day.

"Annie, let's wait until Monday. We can go on the fourth," said Jim.

"Nope. Can't break the family tradition," she answered. "I'm going today. Besides, the way you've been moping around here over Lilly Mae, I doubt that you could make it up that mountain."

He ignored her comment. "Where ya goin' this year?"

"Up by the bluff, where the fattest berries grow," she said as she pulled the bucket out of the cupboard.

"Well, watch out for bees and snakes. Be careful, and make sure you put some coal oil on your legs for chiggers."

"I already did," she said as she stepped off the porch and headed around the corner.

On the hilltop behind the house, a shadowy figure, alerted by the voices below, quickly rose to his feet. Positioned just inside the woodline, some 100 yards behind and to the left of the house, he quickly picked up his canvas pack, securing the canteen and dried beef inside. He had been there since before daylight, watching.

Don't see old man Taylor, he said to himself. Must've already left for work. Bet she's goin' berry pickin'.

Annie made her way up the hollow, bucket in hand. Her route would lead past Aunt Addie's, where she could get a drink of spring water, then over the hill past her granddaddy's abandoned cabin, where the wagon road ended and the foot trail began. From there, she would press on for nearly a mile up the steep, winding trail, but she didn't mind. In fact, she enjoyed it. Sometimes she felt as though God had created this beautiful forest just for her.

He moved to his left and positioned himself to observe her progress up the hollow below. Once she was well past his position, he moved parallel with her, staying above and to her left. He watched as she approached the house. An old woman was hanging clothes on a line.

"Hey, Aunt Addie," Annie yelled as she approached the house.

"Hey, girly gal," answered Aunt Addie. "You goin' berry pickin'?"

"Yes, ma'am."

"Where's Jim?"

"He's workin' at the mill."

"You goin' up on the bluff?"

"Yes, ma'am."

"I'd love to go with you, but I ain't able. Git ye a drank of water 'fore you go."

Annie dipped the gourd into the pail and drank the entire dipperful.

"Gotta go, Aunt Addie. I'll bring you some berries on the way back."

"No, young 'un, you keep them berries. I already have some," Addie said as she wiped the brown snuff juice from her chin.

"Okay. 'Bye, Aunt Addie."

"'Bye, girl. Watch out for snakes."

The stealthy character couldn't make out what they were saying. He thought she might have come to the house to borrow something, but now she was moving again. I guess she's going berry pickin' after all, he thought.

As she proceeded up the next hill, he realized he would have to work his way around the hill to the left and pick her up again on the other side. "Gotta be careful. Someone could be on the other side of the hill," he mumbled to himself.

After Annie crossed the next knoll, her granddaddy's old vacant cabin came into view. He had died when she was barely a year old. He was a Civil War veteran, and they said he loved the Fourth of July—always put out a flag. Annie wished she could have known him.

The stalker saw the old log cabin but no girl. Shit! Had she turned right at the foot of the hill? Had he lost her?

His heart beat faster. The tracker had a decision to make. If he went to the right, he would be in the open. If he continued up the hill to the left of the cabin, he would have cover, but if she had gone the other way, he would never catch up.

Then he heard a noise behind the old structure. Moving quickly and stealthily up the hill past the cabin, he finally spotted Annie in front of a broken-down outhouse. Her step-ins were around her ankles.

Annie had felt the dull ache in her bladder since shortly after leaving Aunt Addie's. She had hoped the outhouse at Granddaddy's was still serviceable. She was wrong. The seat had partially rotted and fallen in. One hinge of the door was missing, and the little building was leaning backwards at a precarious angle. She let the door go and jumped back as it slammed shut.

Shortly after leaving home, she had stuffed a handkerchief into her budding cleavage to catch the sweat. Now it would come in handy. She looked around, then lowered her step-ins and raised her dress to her waist. She squatted, peed, and wiped herself. What a relief, she thought, as she picked up the bucket.

He couldn't believe what he was seeing. Her legs were beautiful, with tanned ankles and snowy white thighs. She was a mature 13-year-old, with long, light brown hair and a pretty face. Her adventurous spirit, coupled with a caring and cheerful personality, captivated the hearts and minds of boys and girls alike.

His tongue flicked over his dry lips. His rate of breathing picked up as blood rushed to his groin.

This was Annie's favorite part of the hike, the man-trail up the mountain. She had encountered bears on two occasions while walking this trail, but she wasn't afraid of them. As soon as they saw or smelled a human, they moved off quickly into the mountain laurel. There were still some blooms on the laurel—some pink, some white. June was the best month to see the blooms, but there were some still on in early July.

There was a good spring about a third of the way up the mountain. She would stop for a drink before the final push to the top.

The stalker was relieved that they were finally on a trail. He could move freely, now, without fear of the noise made with each footstep through the underbrush. The path was steep as it wound back and forth up the mountain. He had to be especially careful. His quarry now had the high ground, and he could be seen at each switchback if he proceeded too fast.

She was out of sight. He could move now. As he rounded a turn, he saw Annie, sitting next to the trail in plain view. Hitting the ground fast but silently, he low-crawled backwards very slowly until he was hidden from view. She must be taking a break, he thought. The pursuer removed his hat and peeked around a bush, staying low to the ground. The girl was drinking from a spring that was dripping from tree roots protruding out of the rocks on the bank above the trail. He often wondered how trees that seemingly grew right out of limestone boulders could survive.

Annie rested while the water dripped into the bucket. She missed her time with Jim. I wish he could've come, she thought. This would've been a good time to get him talking about Lilly Mae. It would be good for him to talk about it, rather than holding it inside. Her wanting to leave for school sure threw him for a loop. He hasn't been himself for over a month. I saw them talking after church last week, and it was obvious that he wasn't happy. When I asked him what the matter was, he finally said that Lilly Mae was leaving in the fall for college. He shouldn't be upset over that. I understand how she feels. I'm going to college when I graduate from Holston Landing High. I like school. I'm not going to get married young and quit school, like my sisters did.

She was now on the steepest part of the path and would be on top in a few minutes. She continued her thoughts.

I'm going to pick a man that understands that a woman can do things in life besides have children. I want children, but I want to work, too. I'm thinking I might want to be a nurse or even a doctor. That article in the magazine at Aunt Lois's was about a woman doctor in St. Louis. I bet I could be a doctor!

He was breathing hard, now, both from the steep climb and from the mental pictures flashing through his mind. He was almost to the summit. Where would she go now? Be careful, patient, he warned himself. She could be sitting at the top of the trail. He left the trail and worked his way through the mountain laurel and doghobble. There she was!

She was walking away from him along the ridge, with the bluff to her left. The trees here on the ridge were larger and farther apart. There were openings as much as 50 yards across where unobstructed sunlight fed the blackberries, wild azaleas, and an occasional cedar tree. She walked straight to a large patch and began picking.

He stayed in the woods and inched around to her right and

rear. He had stalked animals many times the same way. He liked to pretend that he was a large cat: paw up, hesitate; paw down, ever so slowly; never a sound, never taking eyes off the prey. Stop! Hunker down, eyes on the target. Wait. Patience. Pounce!

Annie ate almost as many berries as she put in the bucket. Her thoughts turned again to her melancholy brother. I may get to have that talk with him up here after all. I got a feelin' he'll take off early and come on up. He'll probably ride up on Old Nell, and I can ride double back with—*"UHHH! Ohh!"*

He had approached her from behind, wrapped his arms around her, and pinned her arms. Her entire body shuddered with paralyzing fear. She tried to scream, but her vocal cords did not respond.

"Calm down! You're goin' to like this. We can be secret friends."

She blacked out for an instant, then awoke fighting. She clawed, kicked, and even tried to bite him. "Stop, stop!" she tried to scream, but there was still no sound. She broke free and reached for a stick. It wasn't much of a weapon, but it was all she had. Annie swung for his head. The attacker ducked to one side, and it bounced harmlessly off his shoulder.

"Why? Why?" she cried. "Why are you doing this?"

He panicked and delivered a vicious punch to her face, knocking her to the ground.

He carefully removed her step-ins and cast them aside. She came to as he was shoving his pants to his knees. She screamed, "*Why?*" This time her voice was loud and shrill.

On startled impulse, he hit her hard in the face, causing flashes of brilliant white light, then pain, then numbness. On the ground now, she kicked wildly with one leg, then the other, her screams reverberating in his head.

She kicked free, but before she could rise to run, he leaped on top of her, with a hand gripping each wrist. His hands moved to her throat in a frenzied effort to stop the screams. "Shut up!

Shut up! Someone will hear! Trust me. You're going to like it."

Now her screams were hoarse, croupy. She slowly realized that he was choking her. As light turned to dark, the calmness spread in her mind like an unfurling blanket, and her thoughts were crystal clear.

Yea, though I walk through the Valley...

She was gone.

He spread her legs. "Wake up, girl. You're gonna miss the fun."

He shook her shoulder with one hand and rubbed her crotch with the other. Finally, he inserted two fingers to open her up. He was ready. "I'm starting without you, girl."

He tried to enter her, but she was too small. He grabbed her buttocks and lunged hard. He was in her now, rocking back and forth.

"Wake up!"

For the first time today, he looked at her eyes. They were wide open and blood red.

"Damn! Damn! *Damn, damn, damn*!"

He tumbled backwards, pushing with his feet to scoot away from her. He got up and wiped himself off with her handkerchief, careful not to look at her eyes again. He ran across the meadow, retrieved his pack, and returned to sit down near her to think and have a drink from the canteen.

Somebody will come looking for her, he thought. I need to bury her and get away. But wait! What if it was an accident?

He saw her bucket and ate some berries while he formulated a plan. It finally came to him—she fell off the bluff. She got too close trying to reach some berries. That's it!

He got up and walked around the large briar patch to the bluff side. There were blackberry bushes within five feet of the edge. He looked at the river some 700 feet below.

I reckon if her body could fall all the way to the water, that would be just fine, just fine, he said to himself.

Working her feet through the step–ins and inching them up her legs to her waist, he was careful not to look at her face, her eyes. He picked up her limp body and carried it to the edge. Looking away from her, the killer said, "I'm sorry," as he threw Annie off the bluff. Next, he reached for her bucket and placed it on its side near the rim. Spotting a rock on the edge about 18 inches across, he pulled it up and turned it over. Then, making his way back around the blackberry patch, he picked up the handkerchief, placed it in his pack, checked the area, and headed off in the opposite direction, from which he had originally come.

*****

Jim delivered his last load for the day and headed home. He drove the truck across the spring–fed branch and parked close to the barn. His mother was sitting in her cane–bottomed chair on the porch, snapping beans.

"Where's Annie?" he asked. "I want to see how many berries she picked."

"She's not home yet. I 'speck she's at Addie's. Ride up there and tell her to get on home. They're probably makin' a blackberry cobbler for the Fourth of July. I hope there's some berries left for us!"

Jim walked back to the barn, saddled Old Nell, and rode up the hollow to Aunt Addie's house. She was sitting on the porch, whipping a funeral home fan back and forth.

"Aunt Addie, that snuff's goin' to stunt your growth."

"Good. Maybe it'll take some of this fat off'n me."

"Tell Annie to come on out here. I'll give her a ride home."

"Annie ain't here. I figured she took the wagon road home."

"She's ain't at home," Jim said. There was a hint of worry in his voice.

"She's probably sittin' up there on the bluff, daydreamin'. You know how she is."

"I'll go give her a ride home," Jim said, as he squeezed Old Nell's sides with his legs.

He rode past Granddaddy's old cabin and up the mountain trail. He thought, *She's sitting up there eating berries and reading one of Aunt Lois's magazines, no doubt.*

After reaching the top, he rode through the first clearing. No Annie. Then he guided Old Nell through the woods to the next clearing, but she wasn't there either. He dismounted and walked around a half dozen blackberry patches, but she was nowhere to be seen. He called her name several times. Could he have missed her at the last clearing? Back at the first clearing, he dismounted and let Old Nell graze while he walked around the bushes calling for her.

Finally, he worked his way around to the bluff side. "Oh, Lord!" he exclaimed.

Her bucket was lying on its side, with berries scattered on the ground. He ran to the bucket, saw the overturned rock, and cried loudly, "Oh God! Please! Oh, God. Please, no!"

Jim was on all fours, working his way down between rocks, holding onto crevices, roots, and saplings. Carefully descending, he recited over and over, "Please, Jesus, let her be okay!"

He reached a small ledge—"Please, Jesus, please!"—and looked over. A strange, animal-like sound caught in his throat.

She was 200 or so feet farther down the bluff, face up, wedged between a boulder and a tree.

His heart was racing; he couldn't breathe. Jim gulped for air. The harder he gasped, the less air he could pull in. He felt faint. He willed himself to stop, to breathe slowly, and finally he was breathing in rhythm. He lay there for a minute, talking to himself. "I've got to go for help. No. She might be alive! Maybe I can help her!" Even as the words formed on his lips, he knew it was not true, but he had to try.

He quickly studied the terrain below, straining to see through tear-drenched eyes. He would have to work his way down in a zigzag fashion. He eased off to the right and began the descent. Within five or ten minutes, he realized that he not only had to find the best way down, but he needed to concentrate on the best way back up. He paused occasionally to study the terrain. Thinking clearly, now, he focused on his task.

He approached her slowly. The body didn't bear a resemblance to Annie, but that was definitely her dress. When he saw her face, his body recoiled—literally jumped back—and that almost sent him over the small ledge. Her eyes were open wide, and they were red. Not like bloodshot, but totally red. He gathered himself and gently closed her eyes.

His sister's face was swollen beyond recognition, and her head was wedged between the blood-splattered rock and a tree. He tried to gently raise her head, but it wouldn't budge. Then, working his hand up her back, he was finally able to free her. After gently propping her body against the tree, he wiped his shaking, bloody hands on his britches and studied the bluff above.

Next, he cradled her in his arms and started up, but quickly discovered that he couldn't keep his balance. "I'm sorry, Annie, but I have to carry you over my shoulder," he apologized.

It took over an hour for him to wind his way up—carrying, pushing, and pulling. Reaching the top, Jim lay down, exhausted, with his back to her. He couldn't bear to look. After catching his breath, he carried her body to the horse and draped her over Old Nell's neck. After mounting the horse, he turned her over and cradled her in his lap. Once on the trail, he could hold her in both arms. Old Nell knew the way home.

At his granddaddy's abandoned cabin, he took a left onto the wagon trail. He didn't want Aunt Addie to see Annie this way.

Despite trying to block the tragedy from his mind, he cried most of the way off the mountain. Visions of Annie kept flooding his mind. She was so sweet, had such a good heart, and would never realize her dreams. He needed to compose himself and be strong for his parents. Their baby was gone.

*****

Annie's father went inside himself. He sat alone for hours on end, alternating between the back porch and the barn. Esther wailed uncontrollably as family and friends tried without success to console her.

The sheriff came with Doc Smith, the county coroner. Sheriff McConnell talked in hushed tones with George out at the barn. Preacher Boatwright gathered everyone around the front porch of the tiny house and had prayer. Jim stayed out back with his friend Rob.

Everyone brought food, until there was no space left in the kitchen or spring house. Lilly Mae came with her family. Cars, buggies, and horses filled the yard and overflowed down the lane almost to the road.

Jim steered Lilly Mae around back and up the path behind the house. She walked with him arm–in–arm until they were out of sight. She stopped and hugged him tightly.

His body shook with silent sobs. He took a deep breath and said, "I'm glad you came."

"Of course I came. I came as soon as we heard. I want you to know that we can see each other every day. I want you to talk to me, to talk it out. Don't keep it inside."

He nodded, unable to speak.

Lilly Mae said, "Let's walk. It will do you good."

They walked all the way to Aunt Addie's and then sat alone on her porch, talking for over an hour.

Finally, Jim said, "We better get back."

As they neared the house, they noticed that everyone including his mother was outside.

"What's going on?" he asked Rob.

"They ran everybody out of the house. Dad's got them all corralled out here, giving a little talk and a prayer, I guess."

"What do you mean, they ran everybody out? Why?" Jim asked.

"Said it was the law—that Doc Smith had to examine the body."

Jim spotted his mama and daddy on the front porch and approached them.

"What's goin' on?" Jim asked.

"Doc Smith's checking the body," his father replied.

"What for?"

"To make sure there was no foul play."

"What's that?"

"To make sure it was an accident, son. But he's sure taking his time," he added.

"He don't need to be poking around on my baby. It ain't right," his mother said.

Jim rejoined Lilly Mae and Rob, who were listening to preacher Boatwright.

Sheriff McConnell and Doc Smith came out on the front porch and apologized to George and Esther for taking so long. The sheriff asked George to walk with him out to the barn. Doc Smith tipped his hat and headed for his car. Esther went back inside.

By late afternoon, friends and neighbors had begun to start out for home, leaving only those who would stay for the wake. Lilly Mae squeezed Jim's hand and said, "I'll be back tomorrow. I wanted to stay for the vigil tonight, but mama said no, I could come back tomorrow."

"Okay. I'll see you tomorrow," he replied.

Jim went inside to check on his mother.

She said, "Jim, go check on your daddy out at the barn."

Jim walked through the barn, but his dad wasn't there. Then he walked outside and around to the back of the barn. His dad sat on the ground with his back to the wall, staring straight ahead.

"Dad?" He didn't answer. "*Dad!*"

His father finally looked at him.

"Come here, Jim, and sit with me."

Jim eased down beside his father, not knowing what to say.

"Jim, there's something you need to know." He paused, and then added, "What happened to Annie was no accident. She was murdered."

Jim was stunned and confused. He had trouble processing the words, the meaning. He had struggled so hard to find Annie and to get her up the bluff. Even on the long ride back, it had never entered his mind that what had happened was anything but an accident. He sat in silence, then finally asked, "How do you know it was murder?"

"The doctor said so—said she had been strangled so hard that it busted the veins in her eyes."

"Why would anyone kill Annie?'

"She was, uh, raped." His voice broke, and he started sobbing.

Jim's eyes filled with tears as he imagined what she must have gone through.

Mr. Taylor got to his feet. "Jim, I don't know how to tell your mother, but I've got to tell her. It'll be in the reports and even the newspaper. Everyone will know, so she's sure to find out about it. I asked the sheriff to keep it quiet till after the funeral. We'll tell her then."

"Okay," Jim said as he got to his feet.

Mr. Taylor—Deputy Sheriff Taylor—said, "I'm goin' to find the son of a bitch that did this and make him pay." Then he walked back to the house.

Jim had never heard his father curse before. He got to his feet, then eased back down. His legs were unwilling to cooperate. He thought, If Dad catches that man, he'll kill him.

Then it dawned on him that his father would go to prison, and that, in turn, would kill his mother.

I can't let that happen! he thought.

It was after dark when his Uncle Mel found him sitting there alone. "Come to the house and get something to eat, Jim," he said.

"I'm not hungry."

"I know, son, but if you'll eat something, maybe we can get your mother to eat, too. Come on, now."

Jim followed his uncle to the house.

They had Annie laid out in the front room. Someone had placed a scarf over her face. The extended family was there, interspersed throughout three rooms and the two porches. The men were mostly outside, the women inside. They would spell each other throughout the night so that there would always be a small group awake with Annie.

Jim nibbled some, but mostly pushed the food that Aunt Grace had prepared for him around on the plate. Then he retired to the heat of the loft to think and hopefully get some rest. He was totally exhausted, both mind and body. Flashbacks from the day's events kept sleep at bay.

After finally drifting off, he awoke with a scream. "Red eyes! Red eyes!"

He was sitting up, drenched with sweat. His mother was holding his head to her breast.

"It's okay. Mama's here, mama's here, honey."

He tried to mouth words, but finally decided to keep quiet and catch his breath.

"I'm all right," he finally said. "I'm okay, Mama. Get some rest."

"You're my baby now," she sobbed.

"I'm okay, Mama. Promise me you'll get some sleep."

"Okay, son. I'll be downstairs if you need me."

She carefully descended the ladder, but there would be no

sleep for her that night or for many nights to come.

*****

Jim awoke with a start. A wolf with red eyes had been chasing him through the woods.

It was still hot in the loft. He lay there until he heard the chime of the clock on the mantel below. He counted the chimes; five o'clock. He was hungry. He could smell bacon frying. He pulled on his shirt and reached for his britches. They were stiff and crusty with Annie's dried blood. He rolled them up and grabbed his overalls instead.

I've got to wash these clothes, he thought. I don't want Mama to do it.

He eased downstairs and asked his aunt for a bacon biscuit. "Where's Mama?" he asked.

"She's in the bedroom with your dad," she replied.

"Are they asleep?"

"I don't know, honey."

"When they get up, tell 'em I'm going to ride down to the river and take a bath."

"You can bathe out back. We'll run everyone around to the front, darlin'."

"No, I'd druther go to the river."

He walked outside into the pitch darkness and immediately felt the chill of fear. Afraid in the dark, he mingled with the men outside, half-heartedly answering questions that he didn't want asked. Someone mentioned the Fourth of July picnic at the church tomorrow afternoon. He was astonished that they would celebrate the holiday two days after someone had murdered his sister.

There was a faint light now in the eastern sky. He gathered up his soiled clothes and rolled a bar of lye soap up in a linen towel, then walked to the barn to saddle his horse. After tying the two rolls to the saddle, he mounted Ole Nell and headed for the river. As he rode, he tried to make sense of how life goes on like normal after such a tragedy. Less than 24 hours before, a precious soul like Annie had been lost. Yet there would be a party tomorrow afternoon, the mail would run on Tuesday, and people would go back to work. It didn't seem right.

After bathing and washing his clothes, he lingered for almost two hours at the river. When he returned home, he saw Lilly Mae sitting on the porch, talking to Aunt Addie. He joined them. Later, the couple walked to Aunt Addie's house, where they sat in rockers on her porch.

"Jim," Lilly Mae said, "I've been thinking about college. I've been accepted, but I'm not going for fall quarter. I'm going to stay home and be with you to help you through this. If everything is okay, I might start winter quarter."

"Funny, I've been thinkin' about the same thing. Down at the river this mornin', I made a decision. Annie had dreams, too, but now... Well, what I'm sayin' is, you have to live for today. You never know what's around the next corner. If you don't go to college, you'll always wonder what it would've been like. I ain't goin' to be the one responsible for killin' your dreams. I can't do that to you. I want you to start in September. Don't wait, don't wait for nothin'. I love you, Lilly Mae." He reached over and kissed tears from her eyes.

The funeral the next day was a typical Primitive Baptist affair. Reverend Boatwright said all the appropriate things about Annie's short life: how in some respects she was lucky that her trials here on earth were over; how the Lord had a purpose in her death; how it would be a witness to others to get right with God before their life was suddenly snatched away; how only God knew the reasons for such a tragedy; how Annie was with the angels now, looking down and saying, Don't weep for me. I'm in a better place, one of eternal bliss.

At least some of the hymns they sang were Annie's

favorites.

Reverend Boatwright explained that the greatest tribute to Annie would be to bring the message of Christ to the assembled flock and to present the opportunity for someone today, here and now, to save their soul and live for Christ.

No doubt the message would somehow be a comfort to his parents, but it did nothing to assuage the hatred in Jim's heart. He looked for his best friend, Rob, to walk to the cemetery with, but he couldn't locate him. I guess Rob is already up there, he thought.

Annie was laid to rest in the Taylor family cemetery a quarter of a mile up the wagon road from the church. The land for the graveyard had been provided by her great–uncle 47 years before. The site was less than a mile, as the crow flies, from where her life had ended.

CHAPTER 7

The day after Annie's funeral, Jim rode up to the bluff with his dad to a meeting requested by the sheriff's department. When they arrived, two deputies were there, walking back and forth through the clearing. They asked Jim to tell them exactly how he found Annie. He recited how he had searched for her, what he had found, and how he had gotten her up the bluff. Mr. Taylor asked them if they had found anything.

"No, not really," answered Deputy Johnson. "We did find where she was, uh, where we think the crime occurred."

"Where?" Taylor asked.

The deputies walked them over close to the blackberry bushes and pointed to where the grass was matted down. There, Deputy Goins pointed to a small patch of dried blood, along with strands of Annie's hair on the grass.

"We think he carried her to the bluff from here," the deputy said.

They discussed the case for a few more minutes, and then the deputies moved on. Jim's father asked to be taken down to where she landed.

"It ain't safe, Dad," Jim replied.

"I want to see it."

"What if we just go to the first ledge and look at it from there?"

"Let's go."

As they proceeded slowly down to the ledge, his father began to realize just how hard it must have been for Jim. They finally reached the ledge and lay on their stomachs to look over. Jim pointed to the place below. The rusty color on the rock where her head had lain was plainly visible. Jim closed his eyes.

Mr. Taylor studied the scene. At last he said, "I don't see how you done it—how you got her up outta there."

"You ready to go, Dad?"

"Yeah."

They walked back around to the crime scene and sat there a while, talking and looking.

Mr. Taylor said, "I think that somebody was up here picking berries—somebody Annie knowed and maybe trusted. I believe that's how it happened. That means they live around here."

Jim was shocked to hear this. "How can we find them?"

"I don't know. Keep our eyes and ears open, I guess. The sheriff says I can't take part in the investigation. Too personal. But if I can find him first, they won't need no trial."

*****

Over the next week, Jim visited Annie every day, alternating between the cemetery and the bluff. Lilly Mae went with him once, but he preferred to be alone. It felt good to sit and talk to her.

Meanwhile, his father racked his brains trying to think of anyone in the neighborhood that might be the killer. He finally settled on three possibilities. Jim was surprised when his father shared his theories with him. I guess he thinks I've grown up, Jim thought.

"It could've been Ira Shelton's boy, the one that's not right in the head. They live on Fowler's Branch, which is not more than a mile from the bluff. Or it could've been John Baker, that lives down on the river. He's been in jail for all manner of things."

"Well, let's go pay them a visit," Jim said.

"No, son. I've thought better of that. We need to let the law handle this."

Jim nodded, but he didn't agree.

"One other thing. I've been concentratin' on folks here in the neighborhood, but I had another idea. Do you remember that moonshiner, Benson, I sent to prison?"

"Yeah."

"Well, the day I convinced him to confess, his son told me he would get me back fer it. He coulda done it fer payback."

Jim asked, "What do we do next?"

"I'm going to see the sheriff the day after tomorrow. I'll ask him to check them out. By the way, son, you need to come back to work. You've been off for a week. The best thing for you is to stay busy."

"Okay," Jim replied. "How 'bout if I start back Monday?"

"Good enough."

The next day, Jim rode up to the bluff, convincing himself along the way that his father was right. He needed to get back to work to help get his mind off this. He would sit on the bluff and explain it to Annie; she would understand.

As Jim rode out of the woods into the clearing, he was greeted by bright sunlight and a stiff breeze.

He dismounted and walked to the spot where Annie had spent the last few terrifying moments of her life. He normally sat on the edge of the bluff looking at the river and valley below. But today he wanted to sit here and tell her about Lilly Mae going to college this fall. How she would catch the train at Batesville, and—

What was that?

Something in the blackberry bushes caught his eye, like a tiny flash. He focused on the spot but didn't see anything out of the ordinary. Then, as the breeze picked up, there it was again; fleeting, like the silvery side of a sunlit fish in shallow water.

He crawled on all fours to the bush and carefully surveyed

each individual branch.

Coulda been a drop of water on a blackberry reflecting the sun, he thought.

The wind picked up again, and he saw the flash. He began to carefully pull the branches apart, taking care to avoid the thorns. There! It was a chain, some sort of chain.

He retrieved it and examined it carefully. It was about seven inches long, with a tiny clasp on one end. The last link on the other end was broken, as if it had been pulled or jerked apart. The slow realization of what he had began to press down on him.

This belonged to the man who raped and murdered my sister! She jerked it off him during the struggle!

Jim ran to his horse, stopped suddenly, and returned.

"Annie," he said, "this is the clue we need. I promise you I'll make him pay. I promise."

After mounting Old Nell, he silently said goodbye to Annie, then headed home.

"I can't wait to show Daddy. On the other hand, maybe I should keep it to myself," he whispered to himself. Dad has changed his mind about how to handle everything. He'll hand it over to the sheriff as evidence.

Jim vacillated all the way home. As he approached the barn, he made the decision. He would give it to his father.

When his father came home from the sawmill late in the afternoon, Jim met him at the barn. He showed him the chain and explained exactly where he had found it.

His father examined it carefully, squinting through sawdust-encrusted eyes, turning it this way and that. "You see any writing on it anywhere?" he asked.

"Nope. I looked at every inch of it. No writing."

"It's off a pocket watch," his father mused. "It means Annie fought back."

Jim let this sink in, then asked, "What'll we do with it?"

His father hesitated, started to say something, but didn't. Finally, after taking a deep breath, he exhaled the answer. "We'll turn it over to the sheriff. Have to. It's evidence."

Jim nodded.

The sheriff was very interested in the chain. "George, this chain belongs to the killer. It's been jerked in two—like in a tussle. I've been askin' around, and they ain't hardly anybody goes up on that bluff. It used to be fer summer grazin'. Couple of families would drive cattle up there and leave 'em all summer, then drive 'em back down in the fall. If it weren't fer that, they wouldn't even be a path to git up there."

George just nodded. He wanted to say that he already knew that, but decided to stay quiet.

"By the way, one of my deputies is on his way over to Shelton's on Fowler's Branch. I'll let ye know what we find."

"What about John Baker?"

"Oh, yeah, well, he couldn't've done it. Found out he's in jail across the line in Tennessee, serving 11/29—violation of probation. Been there since April. As for the Benson boy, I'm goin' to check on him myself. Benson's wife, Elvira, goes to my church in Holston Landing. I'm goin' up there this afternoon."

"Okay, Sheriff. I'd appreciate anything you can find out."

On Sunday, after church, Jim went home with Lilly Mae to have dinner with her family.

The Larkeys always had a large dinner on Sunday. In addition to the family, there were almost always some guests: a relative or two, and frequently Reverand Boatwright and some of his family. Mrs. Larkey had cooked enough to feed a small army. There was fried chicken, mashed potatoes and gravy, green beans, beets, tomatoes and onions, Virginia ham, fried okra, squash, corn on the cob, biscuits left over from breakfast, fresh baked cornbread, milk, lemonade and buttermilk, two pies, and a cake.

After dinner, the men found chairs on the porch, where

they discussed the weather and other important things. Sounds from the kitchen filtered through the screen door—eight women and girls, four conversations, then a second of silence broken by shrill laughter from all. The light breeze off the river made the hot and humid July day almost bearable. Jim eased off the end of the porch and headed around the house so the men could swap theories on who could have raped and killed his sister.

Lilly Mae joined him on the swing in the backyard. They hadn't planned the meeting, but each instinctively knew the other would be there.

"How's your mama doing?" she asked.

"As well as can be expected, I guess. She stays in bed a lot. Aunt Addie makes her get up and tries to do things to keep her busy."

"I've decided to take your advice. I'm leaving for college in September, September 17th," she said proudly.

"Good. I'm glad for you. You'll make a fine teacher."

"I'll write to you every day!" she promised.

"I'll write you, too."

"Let's walk down to the river," Jim said. They walked hand in hand to the river path, then turned upstream.

Jim spoke first. "I've made a decision, too. I'm going to Ohio as soon as Mama is on her feet."

"Ohio? What's in Ohio?"

"I'm going to stay with my brother Ray until I can find a job. I've got some money saved. I could pay some rent, but he probably wouldn't take it. I wrote him a letter last Friday. I should hear back in a couple of weeks."

"When did you decide all this?"

"Just in the last week or so. I promised Annie I would find her killer, but I've got to get away from here. I knew you would be leavin', and with Annie gone and all..." His voice trailed off.

He looked downstream, willing himself not to cry. Lilly Mae

placed her hand on his cheek and pulled his head around to face her. She stood on her toes to reach his lips. They stood there several minutes, in silence, in a tight embrace.

Still holding her close, Jim said, "We'll write every day."

"Every day," she answered with a squeeze. "Let's go before they come looking for us," she said as she broke the embrace.

"Wait." He pulled her back to him and kissed her passionately. His hands could feel the softness of her back and the firmness of her buttocks through the thin summer dress.

She broke away and pulled him by his hand down the path toward the house.

*****

On Monday, Sheriff McConnell came to see George at the sawmill.

"George, I went to the Bensons' up at Bright Hollow last Friday. As you know, the old man is in prison. It's just the two of 'em there. The boy answered all my questions. Didn't seem nervous or nothin'. Elvira confirmed that he was at home the whole Fourth of July weekend. I asked her if the boy owned a pocket watch or if her husband owned one. She laughed at me—said they couldn't afford a clock, much less a pocket watch.

"That watch fob appears to be gold. I think we're looking for someone that's not dirt poor, and I think it's someone right here in the neighborhood," the sheriff added.

"I think so, too," George agreed. "I appreciate you checkin' it out."

"We'll keep workin' on it, George. We ain't goin' to rest till we get to the bottom of it."

"Thank ye, Sheriff."

George was disappointed but not surprised. I'll keep on it, on it till the day I die, he thought.

Jim went back to work. It was good therapy. His mother

was slowly returning to some normalcy, taking one day at a time. George Taylor had that far–away look in his eyes from time to time, but as days eased into weeks, they all learned to live with it.

Ray had answered Jim's letter and assured him that they could make room for him. Jim bought a train ticket and wrote his brother that he would be there on Saturday, September 24th. Jim had mixed emotions—guilt over leaving, excitement over leaving.

He bought a new pair of work boots, two sets of clothes, and a suitcase. After he explained his plans to Aunt Addie, she assured him that she would look after his mother. Mr. Taylor was not pleased, but finally gave his approval in a strange way. He gave Jim a snub-nosed .38 pistol.

"Jim, take this with you for protection. Don't play with it. It ain't a toy. Use it only in self–defense and only if you absolutely have to."

"Thanks, Dad. I'll be careful. I need to tell Mama. I've been dreading it."

"I already told 'er this morning."

"I'll talk to her," Jim said.

"She's not here. Addie took her up to her house to talk. They're cannin' beans."

That night, Jim talked to his mother and explained how he felt. He assured her over and over that he would write often and be home for Christmas. She nodded more than she talked, but finally said, "Jim, you're growed up, and you've got to make your own way. Be careful, son, and don't forgit yore raisin'."

CHAPTER 8
Fall 1927

They stood waiting under the wide eave of the train station—Jim, Lilly Mae, and her parents. It was time to board. Mr. Larkey, a suitcase in each hand, stepped into the gentle rain and handed the bags to the porter. Jim kissed Lilly Mae, and her parents chatted nervously as if they didn't see it. Lilly Mae gave hugs all around and boarded the train.

Exactly one week later, Jim repeated the process with his parents. He boarded the train that would, for the first time in his life, carry him out of the county of his birth. Before leaving for the train station in Batesville, Jim rode up to the cemetery to say goodbye to Annie. He placed flowers on her grave and told her he was leaving, that he would be back for Christmas, and that he was not giving up on finding her killer.

"'Bye, Annie. I love you."

The fog from his breath on the passenger car window hampered his view. Jim was practically glued to the window after the train passed through the tunnel at Riverport. As he wiped the glass once again, he observed that it was all new territory now, but it looked much the same as home. There were mountains, hills, and the river. He passed farmers in their fields too busy to look up, but the children waved without fail.

The gentleman next to him asked him where he was headed.

"To my brother's place in Ohio," Jim replied. "Where're you

goin'?"

"I'm going to Chicago to visit my daughter."

"You ever rode a train before?" Jim asked.

"Yes, many times. I have to change trains in Cincinnati. How about you?"

"I, uh, I don't know. This is my first train ride. Why would you get off? Is there somethin' wrong with this train?"

The man smiled. "No, no. This train doesn't go to Chicago. I have to catch another train in Cincinnati that does go to Chicago."

"Well, where all does this train go?" Jim asked in a worried tone.

"It goes to Cincinnati. Then I'm not sure, from there. Where are you going?"

"I'm goin' to Oxford, Ohio. My brother's meeting me at the station. He lives near there."

"Would you like for me to ask the conductor if you need to change trains?"

"Sure would, mister."

"My name is John Hartsook, but call me John. What's your name?" he asked, extending his hand.

"Mine is Jim," he said as they shook hands. They chit-chatted a while longer before Jim asked, "When you goin' to ask him?"

"Oh, I'll ask right now." He paused, then said, "Why don't you come with me? We'll ask him, and I'll show you where the latrine and the dining car are."

"Thanks, mister. I mean John."

They toured the train and Jim was careful to memorize the layout.

The conductor told Jim that there was a layover of an hour and 30 minutes in Cincinnati, and that he didn't have to change trains. "You can get off there and stretch your legs or you can stay on the train," the conductor informed him.

They stopped in Middlesboro and nine other communities in Kentucky. Jim watched the hustle and bustle at each station until well after dark. He thought of many questions to ask, but John had fallen asleep.

When John awoke from his nap, he said, "We'd better get something to eat."

They made their way to the dining car and took a seat. Mr. Hartsook handed Jim the menu. After reading it twice, Jim said, "I'll have the potato soup. Reckon they got cornbread?"

"No, I don't think so. The soup comes with crackers. What do you want to drink?"

"Milk," Jim replied.

Their meal arrived, and Mr. Hartsook marveled at how Jim devoured his food. He told Jim that his daughter in Chicago had a new baby—his grandson—and he was anxious to see the child. Jim told him about his family, but he didn't mention Annie.

"Jim, what are you going to do in Ohio?"

"I'm goin' to stay with my brother and help on the farm till I find other work."

"Have you considered going to college?"

"Not really, but my girlfriend is going."

"Really? Where?"

"Radford. Radford, Virginia."

"Well, what a coincidence! My daughter went there. It's a very fine school. She loved it. There was always some sort of party going on, fancy dances, and lots of clubs to join."

"Dances? There must be some mistake," said Jim. "It's an all–girl school."

"You're right, it is, but the boys from nearby colleges come for the balls and various social gatherings."

Jim looked out the window, then down at the table. Mr. Hartsook quickly realized his mistake and changed the subject. "Jim, let's have dessert."

"No, thanks. I'm not hungry."

"Well, I'm going to order for both of us. We can take it back to our seats and have it later. I'm buying."

"No, sir. I've got money."

"I'm sure you do, but I insist. The next time we meet, it'll be your time to buy."

Jim nodded.

Back at their seats, Mr. Hartsook read the paper. Jim stared into the darkness on the other side of the window until the motion of the train put him to sleep.

They arrived in Cincinnati just before daylight. Mr. Hartsook was already awake and gathering his belongings.

"Jim, you should get off the train and walk around. Do you drink coffee?"

"No, sir."

"Well, maybe you can get hot chocolate and some breakfast. Just remember the platform number. This is car seven, and the seat number is on your ticket. Don't lose your ticket, by the way."

"Thanks for everything Mr. uh, John."

"Thanks, and good luck to you."

They shook hands, and Mr. Hartsook made his way down the aisle.

Jim sat for several minutes, trying to decide whether to stay in his seat or get off. Finally, he worked up the courage to get off. He checked the platform number. He walked around the station repeating in his mind: Platform 3, car 7. Platform 3, car 7.

The station was magnificent. Jim had never seen anything like it—the high arched ceiling and mural-etched walls, the hustle and bustle of the crowd, and the sounds of locomotives clanging and rail cars banging.

Back on board, the train lurched and pulled slowly out of the station, one of five depots serving seven different railroads in Cincinnati. Less than six years later, they would all be replaced with the Cincinnati Union Terminal, a $41,000,000 project consisting of 22 buildings.

With no one seated next to him, Jim rode in silence, thinking of Lilly Mae, Annie, and his other family members.

It was daylight now, Sunday morning. He wondered if Lilly Mae had met a nice person, like Mr. Hartsook, to show her the ins and outs of train travel. He also thought about the boys she would meet at college; his stomach felt queasy.

The hills of Cincinnati slowly gave way to the flat land of the Midwest. He had never seen anything like it. The crop fields stretched all the way to the horizon. He was excited, now, anxious to see Ray and his family, to see how they worked such large farms, and to begin a new chapter in his life.

Ray was there to meet him. He grabbed Jim's hand and shook it vigorously, then backed up and looked him over.

"You've growed up, Jim."

"Mama's good cookin', I guess," answered Jim.

"How's Mama and Daddy gettin' along?" asked Ray.

"They're takin' it one day at a time—doin' pretty fair," Jim answered as they loaded his things into Ray's 1923 Ford.

"You've got your own car!" Jim observed.

"Pretty much gotta have a car up here. Tractor, too. Everything's far apart here, not like at home. Farms are so big, you'd never get 'em plowed with a team of mules. What about Old Nell—she still alive?"

"Yeah, still kickin'. Gittin' old, though."

"We're sure sorry we couldn't make it to Annie's funeral. It was pretty much over by the time we got the notification. The car was broke down, anyways." He added, "You know, Josie and me were talkin'—we never saw Annie but three or four times after she was three years old. Tell me about her and what happened."

Jim told him the story, leaving out the more gruesome details. After a long pause, Jim said, "I'm goin' to find her killer and make him pay."

Ray nodded, but he wondered how Jim expected to do that from 400 miles away.

They turned off the road into a long driveway guarded by a lone postal sentinel, with *Taylor Rt. 6* free–handed on the side.

The house and lot resembled a small island surrounded by oceans of yellow and green fields. Chickens pecked at the flat ground around a large barn that was located to the right of the house. The pigpen behind the barn contained more pigs than Jim had ever seen in one place. A large door in the second–story loft of the barn was accessed by a cable and pulley. Jim also noticed an above–ground tank mounted on stilts, which he would later learn contained fuel for the farm equipment.

The two–story house was weather–beaten by years of Ohio rain, wind, and snow. Over time, half the paint had surrendered and fallen off. The other half clung in curls here and there.

The first floor contained a large kitchen, a living room, a dining room, and a small room used as a pantry. Upstairs accommodated four bedrooms: one for Ray and his wife, Josie; one for their two sons; one for Jimmy Roberts, who helped work the farm; and the fourth, which would be Jim's.

Josie ran out to greet them. The two little boys stayed on the porch.

"Jim, we're so glad you came!" she said as she hugged him. "Come here, boys, and say hello to your Uncle Jim."

"Hello, boys," Jim said.

"Hi," they said in tandem.

*****

Over the next two weeks, Jim gradually settled into life on a big farm—up early before daylight, a big breakfast, hard work, a big dinner, hard work, and a small supper of mostly leftovers.

As promised, Jim wrote Lilly Mae almost every night. He told her about the train ride and the farm. She described the campus and explained her daily routine, the subjects she was studying, and all about her two roommates.

The first three weeks were the toughest. Jim felt uneasy after the second day. He missed home and its familiar surroundings. Ray didn't seem to notice, but Josie realized he was homesick. She made a point to have a chat with him each night after supper.

He hurried to the mailbox every day before dinner and read the letter on the walk back to the house. This routine allowed him to think about the news from his parents or Lilly Mae while working in the afternoon.

By Thanksgiving, he and Lilly Mae were exchanging letters twice a week. Jim finally asked her if she was seeing other boys. She answered no and asked him if he was seeing other girls. He replied that he wouldn't do that to her, and besides, there weren't any girls around here to see.

The Saturday after Thanksgiving brought exciting news. The pastor at Ray's church, Reverend Bivens, told Ray that his brother in Oxford needed a driver. He was in the wholesale grocery business and made deliveries all over that area. Jim was to go see Mr. Bivens on Monday.

"How will I get there?" Jim asked.

"You can take our car. I'll draw you out a map. It's just 20 miles from here," answered his brother. "Do you want me to go with you?'

"No, I can do it. Thanks, Ray. I really appreciate it."

On the way to church the next day, Josie reminded Jim to thank Reverend Bivens for the referral.

Monday morning, Jim was up earlier than usual, anxious to get started. Josie convinced him that it was much too early to leave for Oxford. She prepared breakfast while instructing him on how he should respond to Mr. Bivens's interview questions.

The wholesale house was on the far side of town, and Jim proceeded with caution up the main street. Mr. Bivens was elderly but not frail. He was considerably older than his brother.

"Do you know how to drive a truck?" he asked.

"Yes. I hauled lumber at my father's sawmill in Virginia," Jim replied.

"Can you read and write and do figuring?"

"Yes, sir. I helped make out the cartage bills for my father."

"How old are you, Jim?"

"I was 18 last July."

The boy reminded Mr. Bivens of himself at 18. He had left Harlan, Kentucky when he was 17 to work as a laborer on the railroad. He wondered if the boy was as homesick as he had been his first time away from home.

"Son, are you a Christian?"

"Yes, sir. I was raised in the Baptist Church."

"You'll be handling money from the storekeepers. I need an honest man. My brother says you've been to church every Sunday since you got here."

"Yes, sir. You can trust me."

"Okay. When can you start?"

"Right now," Jim replied eagerly.

"Well, you'll have to get settled first. You got a car, a place to live?"

"I drove my brother's car here, and I live on his farm."

"Okay. Can you start next Monday at 6:00 a.m.? The job pays $6.25 a week."

"Yes, sir. I'll be here!"

They shook hands, and Jim headed back to the farm. He was excited and couldn't wait to write Lilly Mae and his family about his new job.

Ray had more free time since cold weather had set in. He and Josie were by the fire in the front room, waiting to hear about the interview.

"How'd it go?" asked Ray.

"I got the job."

"Good for you!" exclaimed Josie.

Jim filled them in on the details. Also, he told them that on the way home, it had occurred to him that he couldn't tie up their car every day.

"I've got $270 under the mattress upstairs. How much does a car cost?" he asked.

"Lordy, Jim, you shouldn't have traveled on the train with that much money. It's a wonder you didn't get robbed! Where in the world did you get that kind of money?" his brother asked.

"I've been saving my pay for over two years."

They discussed various cars, the best place to buy one, convertible or hardtop, and so on.

"I think you ought to pay cash," his brother advised. "Maybe a '21 or '22 Model T."

"I'd like to buy a new one, one that'll make it to Virginia and back. I'm going home for Christmas."

"Jim, you can't go home for Christmas," Ray said incredulously. "You can't get time off that soon after starting a new job."

"Well, I'm goin' to ask Mr. Bivens if he'll let me go."

"Jim, that's not a good idea."

They sat in silence.

Finally, Jim asked, "Can you make me a loan? I figure I can pay $150 down and make time payments on a loan for the rest. That would leave me $120 to put back for savings."

"I'd like to, but with winter coming on, I just don't have it."

After further discussion, Ray suggested, "We'll go look at cars and pick out two or three tomorrow, then I'll take you to our bank. We'll tell them about your job and tell them they can check with Mr. Bivens for proof. Then you tell them how much you can put down and have them to figure the payments on what's left. Whatever payments you can afford will be the car you buy. You can deposit what's left over in a savings account there."

"Sounds good. I sure appreciate your help, Ray."

The plan worked. The banker's trust in Ray, coupled with the impressive savings amassed by his young brother, sealed the deal.

Jim picked a maroon 1928 Standard Model A Ford sedan with black fenders. The brand-new car had been delivered to the dealer only a few days earlier, on December 2nd. The salesman explained that the Model T had been discontinued, and that he could give him a great deal on one of those. Jim wouldn't hear of it. He wanted the new Model A.

After Ray helped him with the registration at the courthouse, Jim attached the license plates and drove back home alone. He was proud, thankful, and maybe a little smug. Deep in his heart, he realized that part of the reason for holding out for a new car was to show off to all the folks back home. He drove through the countryside thinking of Annie and how she would have been the first one back home to have ridden in his new car.

Unlike southwest Virginia, the road ahead was straight as an arrow, stretched out before him like an endless board from his daddy's sawmill. When he had arrived there in September, the farmhouses that anchored the 640-acre plots had been hidden by green trees, like oases in a desert of wheat and corn. Viewed now through the leafless trees, the houses stood stark against a gray winter sky, vulnerable, lonely.

I haven't forgotten, Annie, he thought. I'll get him. I haven't forgotten.

CHAPTER 9

Winter 1927–1928

Jim reached the wholesale house at just after 5:45 a.m. Mr. Bivens saw him and called him into the office.

"Good morning, Jim."

"Good morning, Mr. Bivens."

"Sit down, and I'll explain the job to you."

Jim sat down and listened as Mr. Bivens explained that he would get any route change assignments every morning in the warehouse from Mr. Calhoun. Also, he would ride the route with Johnny Bartow the first week. He was told to pay close attention, and Johnny would train him well.

"By the way, do you know how to use this?" Mr. Bivens asked, pulling a pistol from a desk drawer.

"Yes, sir, but I already have a pistol that my father gave me before I left home."

"Do you know how to shoot?"

"Yes, sir."

"You need to carry it on your route. You'll have a lot of money on you. Don't use it to protect the money. It's for protecting yourself. Absolutely only in self–defense, do you understand?" he said emphatically.

"Yes, sir," Jim answered as he thought, That sure sounds familiar.

"Any questions?" asked Mr. Bivens.

"No, sir. Uh, well, I would like to ask your advice on

something. I'm thinking I need to rent a room closer to work. Do you know how much that would cost?"

"Your best bet would be a boarding house. I'll call Mrs. Lowery up the street and see if she has a vacancy. I'll let you know this afternoon when you get in off your route. Come on, I'll introduce you around."

Jim met Johnny last; he was waiting by the truck smoking a cigarette. They exchanged greetings, then Johnny said, "It's your lucky day. I've already loaded the truck."

Jim observed Johnny throughout the day. He liked him instantly. He was funny and full of life. It occurred to Jim that this job was a snap compared to sawmilling and hoeing corn.

Mr. Bivens caught Jim at the end of the day and informed him that Mrs. Lowery would have a vacancy as of a week from Saturday. He gave Jim the address and wished him good luck.

Jim quickly found the boarding house, as it was only three blocks from the warehouse. Mrs. Lowery informed him that the rent was two dollars a week and included breakfast and supper. They agreed that he would move in the Saturday that it became vacant.

Jim quickly adjusted to the job. Handling the truck was easy compared to the logging truck back home, and that allowed him to better concentrate on the route, the customers, and the paperwork. He enjoyed getting to know the customers, and he especially liked the folks at the smaller country stores. He had met a person or two from Virginia and a few from Tennessee and Kentucky. They were always willing to talk to him about home for a few minutes.

Christmas was approaching. He was not looking forward to asking Mr. Bivens for time off. When he did ask him about it, Mr. Bivens didn't seem too pleased.

"Is your mama or daddy sick?" he asked.

Jim paused, wondering if lying would help. "No, sir, but I sure would like to see 'em."

Bivens thought about himself at Jim's age and finally said, "All right, you can go. But I want an honest answer. Are you coming back?"

"Yes, sir," Jim assured him.

Ray and Josie indicated that they might want to go, too.

Ray said, "This is the first Christmas for Mama and Daddy without Annie. I guess we all should go. Reckon we can all fit in your new car?"

"Sure we can," said Jim.

*****

Immediately after work on Friday, December 23rd, they headed home, with Jim and his brother up front taking turns driving and Josie and the two kids in back. They had a flat tire about halfway down into Kentucky, but Ray and Jim had come prepared, and they were quickly back on the road.

They had driven just under 13 hours when they turned into the lane and approached the house, a little before 8:00 a.m. Mama Taylor was waiting on the porch as they drove past the barn and parked in front of the house. The smile on her face was well worth the drive.

"Got any breakfast around here?" Jim asked his mother after hugs all around.

She grabbed his shoulders, shook him and said, "What do you think, young man?"

"Bet there is."

"Git in that house right now!" she said.

Jim was apparently a man, now, in his father's eyes. He included Jim in the breakfast conversations. As Esther cleared the table, Mr. Taylor said, "Ray, that's a good-looking car you've got out there."

"Not mine. It's Jim's."

The shock on George's face was evident as he turned to look

at Jim. Ray explained the details of the purchase while Jim suppressed a smile. Jim described his job and how the boarding house seemed a lot like the dorm life that Lilly Mae had written about.

Esther said, "Speaking of Lilly Mae, she's home from school and was asking about you. Said she'd like for you to come over today."

"What time?"

"Didn't say."

After his mama and daddy had looked over the car, Jim took a bath, put on fresh clothes, and headed for Lilly Mae's.

She glanced out the front window for what must have been the twentieth time that morning. Finally, she saw him walking up the path from the road below and ran to meet him, anxious to feel his arms around her.

"Hey, college girl," he said as she ran into his arms.

"Hey, working man," she countered. They went inside and sat with her family in front of the fire. After an appropriate period of catching up, Lilly Mae announced, "I want to see the new car."

"Okay, let's go."

To Jim's surprise, she also informed her family that she and Jim were going to Dawson to see the Christmas decorations.

She was impressed with the car. "Jim, it's the prettiest car I've ever seen!"

"Thanks. You wanna drive it?"

"You know I can't drive. Maybe you can teach me sometime."

"I can teach you right now."

"No, not now. I want to hear all about Ohio."

As they drove, she told him all about Radford, and he relayed stories about the men at the boarding house. They toured downtown Dawson. It was anchored by Church Circle on one end of town and the railway depot on the other. Lilly Mae marveled at the huge, decorated tree in the center of Church Circle. Later, they walked through the railway station and Jim bought an orange at the market next door. They had lunch in the dining room of the station, the Clinchfield Café.

Jim finally broached the subject that had been gnawing at him for the past three months. "A man on the train told me they have dances and parties at Radford and that boys come in from other schools. Is that right?"

"Yes, we've had a couple of dances and the annual charity auction." She rattled on nervously about dresses for the occasion, the number of chaperones, a critique of the foods served, and so on. She hardly paused for a breath, as if her monologue could prevent the inevitable question from being asked.

"Did you dance with boys?" Jim asked bluntly.

"Yes, a few times. The social director believes it's part of a college education, part of learning the social graces. We even had a session on dining—you know, learning which spoon or fork to use, things like that."

"Did they hold you close and kiss you?"

"Absolutely not, Jim! It's not like that."

"Have you been on dates?"

"No! Yes! Jim, I'm not going to lie to you. I've been on two dates, if you can even call them that. They were double dates with my roommates, one to go out for hot chocolate and another to go out for dinner."

"Did they kiss you goodnight?"

"Jim, please!"

"Did they?"

"One pecked me on the cheek. Jim, they meant nothing to me. I don't even remember their names," she lied.

The ride home was tense. Lilly Mae tried to make conversation, but Jim's replies were one-word, sullen quips. He let her out at the road by the path to her house.

"I'll see ya," he said without looking at her.

She kissed him on the cheek and got out, then leaned back in the door and said, "Jim, no one but you has held me close and kissed me. I know you're upset, but I've done nothing wrong. When are you going back to Ohio?"

"Early Tuesday morning."

"Are you coming to see me before you go?"

He paused, then said, "I reckon so."

"I'll be looking for you tomorrow," she said with a smile.

He shifted into first gear, said goodbye, and drove off. On the way home, he turned up the hill at the church and drove out to the cemetery. The graves were on a knoll in a clearing in the woods. The ground was frozen and the trees were bare. Someone had wired to the fence an old two–man, cross–cut saw blade with the name *Taylor* painted on it.

He eased open the gate and approached Annie's sunken grave. "Hi, Annie," he whispered. He told her about Ohio, his job, and the new car. He retrieved the orange from his overcoat pocket and placed it on her grave.

"No surprise," he said. "It's the same thing I gotcha last Christmas."

He stood staring at the orange, thinking how it was like a little ball of sunshine to keep her warm. He recalled how excited she would get at Christmas time, how she enjoyed being "the baby" of the family. He tried to think of happy times to drive the images of her terrible death struggle from his mind's eye.

He wiped his eyes, said goodbye, and walked to the gate. As he turned to push down the U–shaped latch, he repeated his promise to her. "I'll find him, Annie, and make him pay."

*****

Sunday, Christmas Day, was sunny and cold as the whole family crowded into the packed church. After church, Jim stood by his new car, answering questions and enjoying the attention.

"Hey, Rob, I haven't seen you in a month of Sundays," said Jim as they shook hands.

"Yeah, it's been a while," replied Rob.

"What've you been up to?"

"Well, Dad's teaching me to preach. I've been called, you know."

"Yeah, I heard. You'll make a good 'un!"

"I'm starting business college in the spring over at Brighton. That'll take a year. Then I'll be looking for a job."

As they walked around the car, Rob said, "Wow! What a car!"

They got in and sat down.

Rob said, "Jim, I've been meaning to tell you. I'm sorry I wasn't at Annie's funeral. I can't take funerals. I'd rather remember people as they were."

"Don't worry about it."

"When you comin' in again?"

"Probably next summer," answered Jim.

They got out of the car as Jim's family approached. They shook hands, promised to write, and said goodbye.

Back home, the family sat by the fire and greeted family members as they trickled in and out.

The conversation turned to politics, and Mr. Taylor said, "We'll elect a Republican next year. Herbert Hoover'll win by a landslide. Al Smith's a Catholic, and this country won't never elect a Catholic."

Uncle Mel mentioned that Hoover had a good business head and that there'd be a lot of jobs created.

Finally, Annie was mentioned. The room grew silent except for the crackle of the fire. George spoke first. "I thought it was hard when we lost Benjamin, but this is harder."

Silence. Esther left the room.

Jim broke the silence. "Heard anything from the sheriff?"

"No, nothing," his father replied as he stood up and headed for the back porch.

Later, Jim went to check on him and saw that he was headed for the outhouse. As George came out, he spotted Jim on the back porch. Jim turned to go back inside, but his dad called for him to wait up.

"Stay right here. I've got somethin' for you," he said as he went past him into the house. He came back out and opened his hand, revealing the broken watch fob. He handed it to his shocked son and said, "I want you to have this to remember Annie by."

"Don't they need it for evidence?"

"The attorney general told the sheriff they was no need to keep it. Said even if they found the owner, he could say he must'a lost it there when he was huntin' or somethin'."

"I think it means they've give up on finding the killer," said Jim.

"Don't think so, son, but I 'spect they're not spending much time on it, either."

"Well, I ain't given up."

"Me neither, son, me neither. Fact of the matter, I've looked at every watch and chain on every man I've seen in the past six months."

*****

Monday morning was sunny and unusually mild. Jim picked up Lilly Mae and suggested they drive to Batesville.

"That'll be fun," she said. "But first, I'd like to visit Annie's grave, if that's okay with you."

"Sure. We can do that."

As soon as they were out of sight of her home, she scooted over next to him. He taught her to shift gears as he worked the clutch. She fingered his hair and studied his face.

"You know, you're kinda cute when you get jealous."

"Who's jealous?"

"You are, and I love you for it. I thought about it a lot last night. It shows how much you care for me, and I want you to know that you don't have to worry about it."

He didn't reply, but he felt relieved. They turned right up the road to the church, then left onto the old wagon road that led to the cemetery.

"Better let me have the gears now," he said as they bounced along the rutted lane. After pulling up on the grassy knoll beside the cemetery, they got out and approached Annie's grave.

Lilly Mae saw the orange and turned to Jim with tears in her eyes. She hugged and kissed him. "You're so sweet," she whispered.

He didn't know what to say and just enjoyed the moment.

Later, in the car, he kissed her tenderly, slowly. She switched positions to face him, her back to the steering wheel, her head on his chest. They sat there awhile, not talking, arms around each other. He peered out the windshield, taking in the fresh smell of her hair. She listened to his heart beat, her eyes closed.

Finally, he lifted her chin and kissed her. She responded immediately, passionately, and with both hands in his hair, she pulled his tongue inside her mouth. His free hand rubbed her hip, and then back and forth on her soft leg until her dress was almost to her waist. He was hard now, throbbing. She felt a warmness, a wetness, she had never known.

She was suddenly aware of his erection against her hip. She rose up, and he scooted to the right and extended his legs to pull down his trousers. She grabbed his hands and stopped him, and then on impulse she squeezed his hardness with her right hand. He tried again to lower his pants. She said, "No," as she calmly straddled him. They kissed as their clothed bodies ground into each other with clumsy jerking movements until they found a mutual rhythm. Her climax came in short, shuddering bursts, his in one huge eruption.

They sat there in each other's arms until he felt her body shaking in sobs.

"What's wrong, Lilly Mae? What's wrong? I'm sorry. Please don't cry!"

She quickly moved over to her side of the car, wiping tears and staring intently at the dashboard. Finally, she said, "I'm sorry, Jim. I should never have let this happen. It's not right. We shouldn't be doing this."

He said, "I'm sorry, too. I didn't mean to upset you. I want you to be happy. It hurts to see you cry."

She looked over at him, studying his face, then touched his cheek and said, "I know, I know."

As they pulled away from the cemetery, she fixed her eyes on the passing countryside, and Jim concentrated on the bumpy trail. Once on the main road to Batesville, Jim relayed some of the funny stories told by the men at his boarding house. Lilly Mae just smiled at first, but eventually laughed and asked for more.

After lunch, they took the long route back to enjoy the scenery of the mountains and river. Jim wanted to show her the watch fob and tell the story behind it, but decided against it. He remembered his father's admonition and kept it to himself.

Once back home, they kissed and promised to write often. Early the next morning, the promises were repeated to his parents. Then, along with Ray and his family, he began the long drive back to Ohio.

*****

Shortly after arriving home, he washed the car and cleaned the inside. Something fell as he lifted his canvas bag.

What in the world? he wondered.

It was a blackjack with a piece of paper secured by a rubber band. He removed the paper and read the message: *Carrying Money on Route is dangerous. Keep this in your truck. Your father—G.W. Taylor.*

Jim smiled and put the blackjack under his car seat.

Back at work Wednesday morning, Jim thanked Mr. Bivens for the time off. Mr. Bivens asked him if his parents were well, and Jim assured him they were. He also mentioned that they sent their thanks as well.

Jim fell back easily into his delivery routine and life at the boarding house.

Mr. Calhoun, the warehouse boss, caught Jim as he completed his route on Thursday.

"Jim, could you come in Saturday and help me with the year–end inventory? My assistant will be off for the New Year holiday. Since you don't have family here, I thought you wouldn't mind."

"Yes, sir. Be glad to."

"We should be done by 6:00 or 7:00, and it pays double time."

"What do you mean, double time?" Jim asked.

"Means you work one day but get paid for two."

"Oh, yes, sir! I'll do that anytime you need me."

"Okay. Be here at 8:00 a.m."

On Saturday and Sunday, breakfast was served late at the boarding house—8:00 a.m. on Saturdays and 8:30 on Sundays. On New Year's Eve morning, Jim grabbed a sausage biscuit from Mrs. Lowery in the kitchen and walked to work.

He and Mr. Calhoun worked well together. Calhoun was impressed with how quickly Jim caught on to the inventory routine.

While they were working on the next–to–last shelf of inventory, three men with masks and guns suddenly appeared from the rear of the warehouse. Mr. Calhoun bolted for the front office, and one of the men opened fire. During the diversion, Jim drew his father's pistol from his back pocket and opened fire. The men ducked behind shelving, fired several rounds at Jim, and ran for the back door. Jim crouched behind boxes, shaking so badly he dropped the gun. Quickly recovering, he scooped up the gun and ran for the office. It was locked.

"Open up, open up!" he shouted. There was no reply. "It's me, Jim!" he yelled again. Finally, the lock clicked. Mr. Calhoun peeked out, then let him in and quickly locked the door behind them.

"Call the police!" Jim stammered.

"They're on their way. I've already called. Are they gone?"

"I don't know. They ran toward the back of the warehouse."

He heard the sirens in the distance as Mr. Calhoun proclaimed, "Jim, you're shot!"

"What?"

Mr. Calhoun pointed to Jim's arm. There was a patch of blood on the upper left sleeve of his shirt.

The police arrived, and a hearse from the local funeral home transported Jim to the clinic. A policeman came in to question him while the nurse treated the wound. It wasn't much more than a deep scratch. Her swabbing hurt him a lot more than the bullet had.

"How many were they?" the officer asked.

"Three," answered Jim.

"Did you recognize any of them?"

"No. *Ouch!* Their faces were covered," Jim answered as he stared at the offending nurse.

"How did they get in?

"Don't know. They were already in when I saw 'em."

"What were they wearing?"

"I don't know. One of 'em started shooting. It happened real fast. Their clothes were dark, but I don't remember exactly what color."

"What about height?"

"The one that shot at Mr. Calhoun was about my size. The other two, I couldn't say."

"How many rounds did you fire?"

"I don't know."

"Was the gun fully loaded?"

"Yes, sir."

"Then you shot six times. All the cartridges in the cylinder were spent. You hit one of 'em. There were blood drops at the back of the building. Did you ever loan keys to the building to anyone?"

"No, sir. I don't have keys to the building."

"If you think of anything else, let us know, okay?"

"Okay," Jim replied.

"Mr. Bivens has your gun. By the way, son, you did a good job."

"Thanks," said Jim.

Mr. Bivens came in as the officer was leaving. He was genuinely concerned for Jim and asked two or three times if he was all right.

"I want you to take some time off, Jim."

"No, I'm fine, Mr. Bivens," Jim replied.

"I insist. I'll see you Tuesday morning. I'll pay the folks here at the clinic, then take you home. Oh, I almost forgot. Here's your gun."

While Mr. Bivens paid out front, Jim examined the gun. Six spent cartridges.

This is the second time I've emptied a gun in the general direction of somebody, he thought. If this ever happens again, I'm going to stay calm and take careful aim.

Jim enjoyed New Year's Eve that night at the boarding house, entertaining the men with details of the day's events. However, every time a firecracker exploded outside, he jumped, and the men laughed.

He used the time off on Monday to shop and catch up on letters to Lilly Mae and his parents. Then he drove out to visit Ray and his family.

They showed him the front-page article on the robbing foiled by a 20-year-old employee. Mr. Bivens was quoted as proclaiming him "a real hero," and he indicated that Jim would get a bonus as a reward. Other than his age, the facts in the story were essentially correct.

Jim asked Ray not to send the clipping to his mom and dad. "It'll worry Mama to death," he said. After leaving Ray's, he picked up a day-old Sunday paper in Oxford. He wanted to keep the clipping but had decided not to send one to Lilly Mae, either. She would worry, too.

When he reported for work on Tuesday morning, Mr. Bivens handed him an envelope and thanked him. Jim took the envelope and looked it over.

"Well, aren't you going to open it?" Mr. Bivens asked.

Jim opened it and was shocked at the contents—$50.

"Uh, Mr. Bivens, this is too much. I don't deserve this."

"You deserve every penny of it. You probably saved Mr. Calhoun's life as well as your own—not to mention the money in the safe. Jim, there was a lot of money here, 'cause we didn't make a deposit due to the holidays. I appreciate what you did. You better get on your route; you're going to get a late start."

"Yes, sir. Thank you."

It took longer than usual to load the truck. Other employees came by to congratulate him and ask questions. In the conversations, he learned that there was no sign of forced entry at the warehouse, and that it was apparently an inside job. The most shocking thing he learned, however, was that Johnny had not shown up for work the day before. No one had seen or heard from him, and the police were looking for him.

Jim deliberated about it all day while making deliveries. It was hard to believe that Johnny had anything to do with the attempted robbery.

Did I shoot Johnny? he wondered. I guess you never know what's in someone's mind or who to trust.

CHAPTER 10

Spring 1928

Jim was happy and content with his job, and he was less homesick with each passing day. He quickly mastered the routine of the route, and for the most part, the people he met on the stops were interesting and friendly. His favorite stop was Toby's, and he usually spent extra time there. The owner, Connie Evans, was originally from West Virginia. She entertained him with stories about the coal mines there, and he countered with descriptions of farming life in southwest Virginia. Over the course of several weeks, he learned that Connie was divorced and had come to Ohio to help her ill father with the store. Her mother had died several years before, and her father was alone. Then he passed away, and she inherited the store, along with several of his debts.

The store building consisted of three rooms. The large main room out front served as the store, and there were two small rooms in the rear. One was for storage, and Connie lived in the other. The store's walls were lined with shelves, and an L-shaped counter separated the more expensive items from the groceries and other goods. A potbellied stove and six chairs dominated the center area. The two windows on either side of the front door were the only windows in the building. Out the back door from Connie's quarters were a storage shed, an outhouse, and the hand pump for the well.

Connie's easy manner and bright personality naturally

appealed to Jim. She was just two inches shorter than he was, and she usually kept her black hair pulled back tightly in a ponytail. Her face brightened when she laughed, revealing tiny creases streaming away from her mossy green eyes. A hint of rouge on her pearl-tinted cheeks gave a soft, rosy glow to her smooth skin. She was a pretty woman with full lips that were usually colored with just a dab of lipstick. Jim often wondered why she didn't have a husband or boyfriend.

"Hi, Toby! What do you need today?"

"You mean besides a rich husband?" she joked, and then added, "Just stock up anything I'm low on, honey."

He did a quick survey and headed back to his truck. He came back with a load and began restocking her shelves. They talked as he worked.

When he finished, he asked, "How about a baloney sandwich and a glass of milk?"

She prepared the sandwich as he figured up her bill. "Why do you call me Toby?" she quizzed. "You know my name is Connie."

"I don't know. It's the name on the store, and it just fits you better."

"Then I'm gonna call you Rascal," she quipped.

"Why Rascal?"

"Same response. It just fits you. You've always got that little smile and a twinkle in your eyes, like you're lookin' for mischief to get into. By the way, I read about you in the papers, but I didn't make the connection till one of the customers told me."

"Yeah, it was me. You ever been robbed, Toby?" he asked, changing the subject.

"Lord, no, honey. There's nothing here what anybody would want."

"That's not true. You're a pretty woman here by yourself. You need to be careful. The same thing that happened to me could happen to you."

"Oh, I'll be all right. Don't worry," she replied.

"Do you have a gun?"

"Yeah, I've got Daddy's gun in my room."

"Do you know how to shoot it?"

"Not really. I've just never took the time to learn."

"Well, I'll be glad to teach you. You really need to learn in case you ever need to use it."

"I'll think about it," she replied.

They settled up and Jim left for his next stop.

*****

Winter grudgingly gives up to spring in Ohio. Warmer weather comes in fits and starts as it battles the constant cool breezes from the northwest. The tractors kick up dust in the fields, signaling that a new cycle has begun.

Between stops on his route, Jim enjoyed observing the activity. He also missed the hills of home. Talking with Connie and hearing her experiences of growing up in West Virginia helped ease his frequent bouts of homesickness.

He pulled into Toby's and went inside. Toby was all alone. "Business slow today?" asked Jim.

"Yeah, it's been awful slow," she answered.

"You know, it's hard to get my truck completely off the road. Why did your dad build the store so close to the road?" he asked.

"He didn't. The road came to him."

"I don't understand."

"Well, he told me that when he built the store, it was about 50 feet off the road. Then the county moved the road to where it is now."

"Why'd they move it?"

"Don't know. He never said. By the time I moved here, he was sick and probably didn't really care about it."

Jim ate his lunch in silence.

"You're mighty quiet today, Rascal," she noted. "What's the matter? Come on, you can tell me, hon."

"I don't know. Just thinking about home, I guess."

"Thinking about that girl back in Virginia?"

"I guess that's part of it. Sometimes I worry about Lilly Mae. She's learning things at college—things that I don't know anything about. Sooner or later, she's goin' to figure out that she'd be better off pickin' one of those college boys."

"Things like what?"

"I don't know, the things she learns in class and—dancin'!"

"Dancing?"

"Yeah, they have dances in a big ballroom."

"I tell you what, Rascal. You teach me how to shoot, and I'll teach you how to dance. Deal?"

He hesitated, and then said, "Deal."

Over the next several weeks, they exchanged lessons—target practice out back, then dance lessons in the store. Connie had a hand-cranked Victrola machine and a few records. Her goal was to teach him the Charleston. His goal was to teach her to hit a target without hesitation.

He first taught her the basics: how to make sure there were no rounds in the cylinder or the chamber, how the cylinder and hammer worked together, to never point the weapon at anyone, loaded or unloaded, and how to fire by trigger pressure or by cocking the hammer. Then he showed her how to hold the pistol and how to aim. He cautioned her to expect the kickback and to ignore the ensuing noise.

Finally, they were ready to fire the first shot. She assumed the shooter's stance. Jim stood behind her and placed his arms beside her outstretched arms. Then he leaned into her in order for his hands to reach and cup hers. He was immediately aware of his groin pressed against her taut fanny. Lord, please don't let it get any bigger, he thought.

"Fire!" he commanded.

Connie fired and hit the upper right edge of the target. She jumped up and down, squealing with delight.

"I did it, I did it!" she cried.

"Very good!" Jim said. "Very good."

She gave him a quick hug as she said, "Thank you. Let's do it again." She fired 18 rounds in all, getting a little more comfortable each time.

As they finished for the day, she said, "I hit the target four times. Is that good?"

"Yes, it is, but we'll keep workin' on it till you hit it every time."

They went inside to eat and start working on the Charleston.

They practiced twice a week, until she could hit the target with every shot and his jerky dance movements turned into a fluid Charleston.

After two months of trading lessons, she announced, "Tonight we start the waltz." She told him that it would be difficult in her small quarters, but they rearranged the store to create a small ballroom, with the stove in the center.

"Where'd you learn to dance, Toby?" he asked.

Her answer surprised him. "I learned in college."

"I didn't know you went to college!"

"I went for over a year, before I dropped out to come out here. Several years after the divorce, I decided that I wanted to go to college. I got a part–time job at the school, and they let me work around my class schedule."

"How come you never had children?" he inquired.

"You're full of questions tonight! I can't have kids. We tried for a long time. I finally went to the doctor, and he said I probably wouldn't be able to get pregnant."

"Does that bother you?" he asked.

"Jim Taylor, you're just stalling 'cause you don't want to

learn the waltz! Now, assume the position."

He placed his right hand behind her back, and she took his left hand. She walked him through the steps, counting and pausing at the appropriate times.

"We don't have music," he said.

"We don't need music yet. Just concentrate."

They did it over and over before taking a break.

"How about a glass of wine?" she asked.

"Sounds good."

She came back with two glasses of wine, and they fell into easy conversation beside the potbellied stove.

"You're easy to talk to, Toby. I don't get nervous with you, like I do with most girls," Jim volunteered.

"It's probably because you don't feel like you have to prove anything with me, Rascal."

"What do you mean?"

"Oh, I don't know. Maybe you feel like you can mess up and I won't laugh at you—like when we're learning a dance step."

"Maybe that's it," he agreed.

"Okay, enough talk. Let's get back to work," she said as she cranked the Victrola.

They eased around the makeshift dance floor to the shrill, tinny voice from the record player. He counted the steps in his head.

"Ouch!" she exclaimed.

"Sorry, sorry!" he said as he stopped dancing.

"It's okay, baby, it happens. That's part of learning."

He held onto her and stared into her green eyes.

"What?" she asked.

"You've got beautiful eyes."

She looked at him, but didn't reply.

He continued to stare at her face.

"Rascal, no," she finally got out as she looked away.

He kissed her, now with both arms around her.

She kissed him back. They swayed with the music, never taking their lips from each other.

Finally, she pulled her head back from him and asked, "Where did that come from?"

"I don't know," he said as he placed his cheek on hers. "Toby, teach me lovemaking." It was a statement rather than a question.

She leaned back from the waist, staring at him, reading his face. "Have you ever made love to a woman?" she finally asked.

"No," he whispered innocently, honestly.

Clutched in an embrace, they stood there nervously looking at each other until Jim's eyes dropped and his face began to redden.

Finally, she broke away, walked to the Victrola, and removed the needle. She paused with her back to him, staring at but not seeing the wall in front of her. Finally, she came back, took his hand, and led him to her room.

On the left wall of her room, a sink was anchored by a stove and icebox on the near side and a small counter with cabinets and shelves on the other. Just past the counter was the back door. Along the wall on the right, her small bed was neatly made. A table and two chairs occupied the center. The far wall was balanced by a closet hidden by a curtain on the right and recessed shelves full of pictures, knick–knacks, and books on the left.

Jim reached up to unfasten his shirt, but she took over and kissed his chest as each button was freed. On her knees, now, she removed his pants, then slipped his underwear to his ankles. As she began to orally massage his erection, he released onto her face and cried out.

"Oh, oh, *oh!* I'm sorry, Toby, I'm sorry, I'm sorry!"

"Don't worry, honey, don't worry," she said in a low, husky voice. As she wiped them both with his shirt, she explained that it was normal for the first time.

"Lie down on the bed," she said as she gathered up his shirt. "I'll wash this out and hang it up to dry."

In a few minutes, she returned with a pan of water and a cloth. After washing him, she lit the candles on the shelf opposite the bed and turned off the light. She slowly removed her blouse, then her skirt. She unlaced her bra to reveal her ample breasts and rigid nipples. Then she slipped off her panties and stood naked before him, watching him grow large again.

He looked at her face and her half-closed eyes, then her breasts with the dark rings. He was mesmerized by the curve of her hips and the flat tummy with the black triangle below. As he marveled at her long, slender legs, she turned around and took the clasp from her hair, letting her black locks cascade onto her back. He was captivated by the contrast of the dark hair against the creamy skin of her back and the shapely roundness of her bottom below.

Connie turned and crawled across him to the side of the bed against the wall. He shifted to his left side, and she lay on her back. He kissed her and began to awkwardly caress her. Connie placed her hand on the back of his and began to move it gently over her neck and face. She guided him to her chest and lightly rubbed her breast and nipples. Next, she moved his hand to her tummy and hips, then back to her breasts. Together, they caressed her face and hair and stroked the softness of the side of her breast, then down to her belly.

Connie opened her legs and moved his hand to the softness of the inside of her thighs, feeling first one then the other. Finally, she pressed his hand into her crotch, then back to the thigh. He brushed each thigh in turn while she guided his mouth to her breast. Now his fingers were exploring all of her secret places, learning where to feel and what pressure to use.

She opened her legs wider and drew him to her. He began to move, but she said, "No, let me."

Just as he felt the explosion coming, she stopped, and he

willed himself to stop, too. He forced himself to concentrate on the pattern of flowers in the wallpaper beside him. When the feeling of urgency passed, he took over and began to move against her. She matched his rhythm until he finally made sense of the screeching noise. Was it the bed? No, it was Toby. Little squeals of delight turned to "Rascal, Rascal!" and, *"Now! Now!"*

They lay entwined, spent.

"Thank you, Toby," he whispered, once their breathing slowed enough to talk.

"No. Thank you, Rascal. It's been soooo long."

"It's been a long time for *you*? Try never!" He chuckled.

She laughed out loud, then kissed him.

They lay in bed talking, staring at the ceiling. The ceiling appeared to be plaster of some sort. The flickering light of the candles danced across it like ripples of water in the river back home. A single bare lightbulb, suspended from the end of a cord, hung in the center of the small room. A short string with a small bell at the end dangled from the base of the bulb. He wondered when his parents would be able to trade their lanterns for electricity.

Finally, Jim gave up the fight and let the thoughts of Lilly Mae and the guilt seep in.

"I'd better go," he said.

As if she could read his mind, she asked, "Feelin' guilty?"

He paused before answering. "A little, I guess."

"Me, too," she replied.

"You? Why?"

"Because I'm older. I shouldn't have given in to the lust. Honey, I'm 33 years old. I should know better."

"Didn't you like it?'

"Oh, yeah. I liked it a whole lot, but that's no excuse for going to bed with a 20-year-old boy."

"Toby, I'm not a boy. I've got a lot to learn, but I'm not a boy," he said, failing to correct his age.

"Well, you're right. You're a young man, certainly not a boy."

He sat up on the edge of the bed. "You've got a lot of books on that shelf. What're they about?"

Unashamed of her nudity, she got up and stood by the bookshelf, pointing out the various novels. "Mystery, crime, and love stories. Take one with you to read," she suggested.

He joined her and began to examine the titles. Connie blew out the candles, pulled the light string, and admired his naked body as she slipped into a robe. He knew she was looking at him; it felt good.

Jim selected a book called *Crime and Detective*. Then he spotted the pocket watch. It hung inside a glass dome with a wooden base.

"Whose watch?" he asked.

"It was my father's. There's quite a story as to how it came to me. I'll tell you sometime," she said.

"Tell me now," he said excitedly as he sat down.

Connie lifted the glass and unhooked the watch and fob. She sat down beside him and began the story.

"When my father died, the watch was passed to my brother in West Virginia. He managed to lose it a few months later. A Methodist minister found it and took it to a jeweler to see if there was some way to trace it to its owner. The jeweler traced it to the watch company that made it, and they traced it to my father. The minister tried to find my dad and was told he had passed away. Well, bless his heart, the minister didn't give up. He found my brother and gave it to him. My brother decided that it should be here at Dad's store. So he gave it to me, and I bought this display jar to keep it in. Isn't that a great story?"

He ignored her question and asked, "How did the jeweler trace it?" His mind was racing, fully alert.

"I don't really know. By some number or something on it, I suppose."

He stood up and hurriedly picked up his socks.

Connie said, "Wait a minute, buster!" Then she slowly opened the robe and extended each side like great wings. "Don't you want to take a bath with me before you go?" she invited.

He pulled her against him and kissed her. "I've got to go. I'm meeting a man at Mrs. Lowery's, and I'm running late," he lied. "Can we do the bath next time?"

"I don't know. I'll have to think about it," she pouted.

"Promise me," he said as he kissed her again.

"Okay, I promise. Now go on to your important meeting."

He dressed and hastily made his way to the car. He was excited and anxious as he drove home. He parked the car, raced inside, and bounded up the steps to his room. Nervously, he pulled the watch chain from its hiding place and looked for what seemed like the hundredth time for a number on the broken fob. Nothing. Dejected, he put the chain back in its secret, safe place.

He lay down on the bed as the heavy weight of guilt spread over his chest and stomach.

"What have you done?" he asked himself aloud. You've betrayed Lilly Mae, that's what you've done, he thought.

He asked the Lord for forgiveness and promised himself that he would break off the relationship with Toby.

He got up to write Lilly Mae, then thought the better of it and lay back down. Sleep was a long time coming, and when it did, it was filled with dreams—some good, some bad.

*****

It was difficult to concentrate on work the next day. On Thursday, two days from now, he would see Toby and tell her they would have to break it off. He practiced different scenarios of how he would tell her, what he would say. How would she react, he wondered?

He was nervous and tentative all morning on his Thursday

route. I'll tell her when I make my deliveries, he thought. He practiced more scenarios as he drove between stops. Finally, he pulled up in front of Toby's and went in to check her stock.

There were five or six customers in the store and two men playing checkers. A woman that Jim had never seen before was talking to Toby in hushed tones. Jim made a list of needed items and went back to the truck to retrieve them. He finished restocking the shelves, tallied the bill, and waited for the woman to finish.

"Excuse me," Toby interrupted her. "I need to pay Jim."

As Toby counted out the cash, she asked, "What're you having for lunch, Jim?"

"Can't stay today. Gotta run," he replied.

"Oh, okay. I'll see you next time." She winked.

I'll just have to talk to her tonight, he thought as he walked to the truck.

Later that night, he arrived at the store just after closing time. She let him in, then greeted him with a long kiss. The floor was already arranged and the music was playing. The pistol was lying on an oilcloth on the store counter. She had obviously cleaned it with the kit he had bought for her a few weeks earlier.

"Let's have supper to music," she said. "It'll get us in the mood for dance lessons."

She is beautiful, he thought.

She wore a thin, summery dress he had never seen before. Her hair was in a ponytail that exposed her pretty, slender neck with each toss of her head.

She had prepared his favorite meal: soup beans, fried potatoes, and cornbread. As they talked over supper, Connie noticed a difference in his demeanor. She had noticed that he had not been particularly responsive to her greeting kiss.

After supper, she busied herself cleaning and stacking dishes while he looked over her books. It occurred to him that the one she had lent him was still on the front seat of his car. He had forgotten to take it to his room.

He asked her casually if he could look at her father's watch.

He examined it carefully. On the back were a company name and serial number. He studied the fob chain, looking for any letters or numbers. Nothing. She finished cleaning up, then joined him as he carefully returned the watch to the display jar.

Connie took him by the hand and headed for the dance floor.

"No, no," Jim admonished her. "You've got target practice first."

"Let's skip it tonight, Rascal."

"Nope. The only way to get really good is to keep at it. Besides, I need the practice, too."

After the usual safety reminders, Jim set up the targets and loaded the gun.

They shot until dark. Connie hit the target consistently, and she had a tighter shot group than Jim.

"Who's teaching who?" he asked her as they headed back inside.

"Just luck," said Connie.

"No, you're a very good shot, a very steady hand," he said emphatically.

Jim placed the pistol on the oilcloth and reached for the cleaning kit. Toby stopped him with a kiss.

"I'll clean it later. I need to practice that, too."

She took him by the hand and led the way to the dance floor.

"Tonight, we're going to count steps for a few minutes, and then we'll stop counting and just flow with the music," she instructed.

He counted the steps out loud, then in his head.

"Okay," she said. "Stop counting in your head and just move with the music."

They danced around the room. The numbers came back to

him: one, and two, pause.

"Stop counting," she admonished.

"How do you know I'm counting?"

"I can see your lips moving."

He did as instructed and just moved with her around the room. The count numbers would creep back into his mind, especially if he misstepped. Eventually he was moving more naturally.

After a while, she exclaimed, "Very good! You've got it."

He was proud, delighted. He gave her a hug, lifting her a few inches off the floor. He swung her round and round. They laughed, then kissed hungrily. She curled one leg around behind him. He took her rounded bottom in his hands and lifted her higher. Both legs were around him now. They slowly danced and moved against each other. He tried to flip up the back of her dress, using one hand at a time. She tightened her arms around his neck to signal him that she could support her weight. He slid his hands under the dress and back up to her bottom. Bare skin! No panties!

With her hands in his hair, she sucked his tongue into her mouth. Flashback! Lilly Mae was on top of him in the car at the cemetery. He fought the battle of emotions in his mind. Still embracing, and with her legs tight around him, they kissed as he walked her slowly to the bedroom.

As he bent to lower her to the bed, she said, "Wait! Don't move. I'll be right back."

He stood there feeling guilty and anxious. She returned with a pan of water, soap, and a cloth. She undressed him, then knelt and washed him.

Toby massaged him with both hands, then slowly began a lesson on oral sex. He felt the unbearable sensation building, but she stopped it with the tight ring of her fingers.

As the feeling subsided, she released him and began again. Careful not to nick him, she transported him to where he had never been before. He thought his legs would buckle. She washed and dried him, then emptied the pan out back.

He sat on the edge of the bed, thinking, listening to the screech of the well pump handle. Toby returned and placed the empty pan on the table. She sat down beside him and gently kissed his lips.

"What did you think of lesson two?" she asked.

"Unbelievable," he answered. "I feel like all the energy was sucked right out of me."

He quickly realized the double meaning of what he had just said, and they began to laugh. She bent over, her body shaking with laughter. After the laughter subsided, they sat in silence until she became aware that the music had stopped. She walked to the machine in the store, lifted the gyrating needle, and placed it on its stand. He followed and hugged her as she turned off the machine.

He looked into her green eyes and asked, "What's lesson three?"

"It's part two of today's lesson. You do for me what I did for you."

She noticed the quizzical expression on his face and added, "Don't worry. You'll do just fine."

"Are you sure men *do* that?"

"Men do that as surely as women do that," she replied. "But don't worry. If you don't like it, we won't do it." She kissed him. "Okay?"

"Okay."

On the drive home, he tried to understand the mixed emotions he felt. He thought about how much he loved Lilly Mae and how he was betraying her. He knew he was not in love with Toby, but he also knew he loved the sex even though he had to deal with these feelings of guilt each time. He tried to convince himself that he was doing it for Lilly Mae, so he could please her in bed after they were married. But he knew that was a lie. He was doing it for himself.

He remembered what Toby had said the week before: "It's lust, hon, not love."

He knew he would go back to her bed on Monday.

CHAPTER 11

Friday's weather was warm and sunny enough to allow Jim to work his route in shirtsleeves. He owed Lilly Mae a letter, and he thought over the various things he would write that evening.

He had shared his worry with Connie that Lilly Mae's education and his lack of it could be a problem in the future. Connie had suggested that he take advantage of the program at the local high school. She explained that it was designed for working people to complete their high school education. Classes were held two nights a week, and there was no time limit. "You just take classes until you can pass the test for the diploma," she said.

Jim decided to check out the program. Lilly Mae would be proud of him. He tried to remember all the things he loved about her. He loved her good heart, her courage to go to school so far away, and her determination to become a teacher. He loved the way she tossed her hair and how she talked out of the side of her mouth when making a point in conversation. He loved her beauty and her body. He respected her for insisting that they postpone sex until they were married, and the memory of how they had climaxed with their clothes on was never far from his mind.

Whoa! He had missed his stop. He turned the truck around and pulled into the parking lot of the market.

Back on the road, his thoughts turned to Annie.

What had Connie said? "The minister took the watch to a jeweler."

I don't see how a jeweler could help me, he thought. I don't have the watch. But he owed it to Annie to give it a try. It couldn't hurt, he mused.

After breakfast on Saturday morning, Jim wrote Lilly Mae a letter that was much longer than usual. He took half the morning to relay how much he cared for her, but then he tore it up and started over. The words had to be just so, in case her parents or someone at school read it. He finally finished and sealed it.

Next, he turned to the two letters he had received over the last few days: one from his father, the other from his oldest brother, John. He read them again. They essentially said the same thing. John and his family had moved to Detroit, Michigan, and John had gotten on at the Ford Motor Company plant. The plant was hiring and paid well, and Jim should go up there, they both said.

Jim had considered it over the last couple of days and decided he would stay in Ohio. He wrote his father a short letter, then began the letter to John. He couldn't concentrate, so he left it for later. His mind was on the jewelry store and the watch fob.

He walked up town to Whaley's Café. Over lunch, he fingered the chain in his pocket and practiced the story he would tell the jeweler. He would say that he had found the chain and had a gut feeling that it was important or sentimental to the owner. He wanted to know if there was any way to trace it so he could return it.

Jim walked into the jewelry store two doors down from the café and was greeted by the shopkeeper.

"Yes, sir, can I help you?" the jeweler asked.

"I hope so." Jim pulled the chain from his pocket. He laid the fob on the glass counter and told the jeweler the story he had prepared. He offered to pay the man for his trouble.

"That won't be necessary," the jeweler said. "I'll help you if I can."

He studied the fob while telling Jim that if he had the watch, it would be fairly easy to trace. He explained that Jim might be right about the fob being important to the owner. "This fob is 18-carat gold," he said.

He pulled an eyepiece out of his pocket and slowly examined the entire length of the chain. Finally, he spoke. "I don't know how the owner could have lost this without knowing it."

"Whatta ye mean?" asked Jim.

"Well, by the looks of how the metal was yanked apart, it was obviously jerked with some force. I can see something inside the broken link. I can't make out what it is, but I can open it and then fix it if you like."

"Yeah, go ahead," Jim said anxiously, without asking what it would cost.

The jeweler clipped the link and bent it open. He looked at it through the loupe and said, "It's a number four, a one, and a nine. I'm afraid that doesn't help us," he added. "We need to know what company made it."

"Any way to find out?" asked Jim nervously.

"Probably not. There's an outside chance that a company stamp could be inside this false clasp."

"What do you mean, false clasp?"

"Well, this is not a clasp. It's for decorative purposes. The fob actually attaches to the watch by another link. I've seen it before, but it's a bit unusual. See, this clasp doesn't have a hinge and won't open. I could force it open by cutting around the top, then soldering it back. Not sure I can make it look brand new, but it wouldn't be very noticeable."

"Let's give it a try," urged Jim.

The jeweler took the fob in a back room to work while Jim waited.

Jim repeated the mantra over and over in his mind: It's a long shot. Don't get your hopes up.

The jeweler was smiling as he returned with the fob. "I'm really surprised, but I found it."

"What's it say?"

"Look for yourself," the jeweler said, handing the chain and the loupe to Jim.

Jim looked through the eyepiece. Everything was a blur. He finally found the range and read the letters: *SgtCo*.

"That ain't a word," Jim said.

"It stands for the Sergent Jewelry Company."

Jim's hands were trembling as he laid the fob on the counter. "What's next?" he asked.

"Well, I've done a little business with them over the years. Got one of their catalogues here. I could call them and see if it could be traced. They're located about 80 miles from here, in Indiana."

Jim's mind was racing back to the bluff in Virginia. "What? I'm sorry. I didn't catch all that."

The jeweler repeated it and asked Jim if he wanted him to call them. "I'm gonna have to charge you a little bit for the soldering and the long distance call," he added.

"That's fine. I'll be glad to pay for it."

"Tell you what, young man. On second thought, I'll not charge for the repair, just the phone call. That'll be my contribution to solving this little mystery."

"That's sure nice of you, but I'm happy to pay."

"No, no, I insist." He offered his hand and said, "I'm Sam Ely."

"I'm Jim Taylor. Glad to meet you."

The jeweler told him to come back on Tuesday to pick up the repair. Jim asked if he could call the Sergent Company today. The jeweler said they were probably closed today and that he would try them Monday.

Jim thanked him and left the store, his feet barely touching the ground as he walked to Mrs. Lowery's.

"Jim. *Jim!*"

It was Mrs. Lowery. He had apparently walked right by her.

"Here's your laundry, Jim."

He retraced his steps down the stairs. She handed him the clothes, and he paid her.

"I've seen that far–away look before. Who's the lucky young lady?"

"Oh, no, Mrs. Lowery. I guess I was just daydreaming."

"Like I said, I've seen that daydream before," she joked.

He smiled and said, "I've got to get upstairs and write my mama."

She cocked her head to one side and thought, What a nice young man.

Once in his room, Jim could feel an unsettling fear creeping into his belly. Up to now, he had felt mostly anger over Annie's death, but at this moment, he felt the lonely burden of responsibility.

What if I *am* able to trace the fob? he thought. Could I really kill him? Should I turn it over to the law?

Then he remembered what the attorney general had said: "The killer could just say he lost it while hunting." There wouldn't even be a trial. He would never pay for his crime. He must be killed!

But, he thought, the sheriff would suspect Dad or me or one of my brothers. Regardless, if I find him, I'll kill him. How could I let some monster like that go free? How many other little girls will he rape and kill?

Jim tried to push the images from his mind: Annie struggling, begging, and having to endure him pushing inside her—being torn apart, then choking, not able to breathe—and the red eyes.

"Oh, yeah, I'll kill him. I'll kill him," he said aloud.

Jim felt sick. He made his way to the bathroom and threw up, then washed his face at one of the two sinks.

The boarding house had been converted from an old inn. The common bathroom that served the eight occupants consisted of two bathtubs, two sinks with mirrors, and one commode. All the bedrooms were upstairs except for Mrs. Lowery's. A large dining room and a parlor were downstairs. The remaining space had been converted to an apartment, now occupied by Mrs. Lowery.

Jim went back to his room and finally fell into a disturbed sleep.

On Sunday morning, he awoke hungry. He took a bath and wrote Lilly another letter to occupy his mind. In Lilly's last letter, she had announced that her name had changed. Her friends at Radford had begun calling her Lilly. She informed Jim that she liked it better than Lilly Mae and was asking everyone to call her by her shortened name. He turned it over in his mind. Lilly Mae, Lilly; Lilly Mae, Lilly. He wasn't sure he liked it and wondered what else would change in the days ahead.

He began the letter to her with "Dear Lilly." This time, he relayed how the weather in Ohio was warming up, told her about Mrs. Lowery's comment that there must be a young lady in his life, and so on. He wanted to tell her about the night classes and how he hoped to get his diploma, but he thought the better of it. He would check out the program first. If it didn't work out, he didn't want her to know he had failed. He told her he missed her and looked forward to seeing her in the summer. He wanted to say more regarding his love for her, but he had covered that in his letter the day before.

It was almost 10:30 when he finished the letter. On impulse, he decided to go to church. He changed clothes and walked the three blocks to the Methodist church. During the opening prayers, he asked for forgiveness of his sins and promised he would do better.

After the service, he crossed the street to check the hours of operation of Ely's Jewelry Store. His work day ended at the same time as the store closed. Maybe I can finish a little early and get here in time, he thought. Mr. Ely had told him to come back on Tuesday, but he didn't care about the repair. He wanted to find out about the phone call.

He spent the afternoon on the porch of the boarding house with the older men. Not counting Jim, the youngest man there was 31. Jim mostly listened, absorbed what he heard, and occasionally asked questions. The men treated him as an equal and patiently explained anything he didn't understand. Mr. Raley, a World War I veteran, taught him how the war had started, who fought in it, and how it was won. Mr. Johnson was a railroad man. He explained how the train system operated, how to read the schedules, and how to make transfers. A couple of the boarders were local. The others were from all over the South and Midwest.

Jim arrived at work early on Monday morning, hoping to start early and finish early. He raced through his morning schedule and ate a quick lunch at Toby's. There were two customers there, one of them having lunch like Jim. Toby was busy, but he finally got a word with her.

"I can't make it tonight, Connie. I've got an errand in town, and I have to go by the night class at the high school to see if I can get into the program." He could read the disappointment in her face.

"That's okay, Jim. Maybe next time."

He thought for a minute, then said, "What if I come late?"

"Yeah, that'll work," she said and gave him a smile.

Jim hurried through his afternoon, but he was delayed at the warehouse. His money and receipts had a discrepancy of $30. He and Mr. Calhoun finally found the mathematical error and balanced with his day's receipts. He rushed to Ely's and turned the handle of the front door. Locked. Too late! His shoulders drooped as he slowly exhaled. I can wait, he thought. It's only one more day.

Back at Toby's, Connie locked the door and turned the sign to *Closed*. She decided not to rearrange the store. Instead, she would reread the chapter on oral sex, Part Two. She took the book from the drawer and opened it. As she read the "Pleasing Your Lady" section, her mind turned to Rascal. What would he think if he knew that much of her "experience" had come from the pages of this book? Her ex-husband had never performed oral sex on her; he had thought it unmanly and dirty. He was not a lover; he quickly had his pleasure, then fell asleep.

She tried to convince herself that she was merely teaching Rascal what he needed to know. That was certainly part of it, but the larger part was that she yearned to have a lover who could fulfill her fantasies. Ever since she was a teenager, those fantasies had been fulfilled primarily through self manipulation. Rascal could be the perfect lover, she thought. He's handsome, smart, and very willing to learn. His body is beautiful—those muscles, flat stomach, and dark, wavy hair!

Jim received the brochure and application forms from Mrs. Gladden and thanked her. He looked them over as he walked to his car. When he arrived at Toby's, she greeted him with a hug and locked the door.

He began to move the chairs to one side.

"Rascal, let's skip the dancing tonight. I've got soup and crackers ready to eat."

He looked at her as he eased the chair back to the floor. She wore a gown that was thin and very revealing. Her silhouette suggested that she was wearing nothing beneath the gown.

"Okay, but first I want to show you a new dance I've learned."

He took her in his arms and kissed her as he slowly turned in place, his hips never leaving hers.

When they stopped, she asked him, "What's this new dance called?"

"It's called the 'Any Excuse to Kiss a Beautiful Woman'

dance."

"Well, I like it. Now let's eat."

"Wait. I've got a question. Are you familiar with a place called The Barn?"

"Yes, I went there once with a girlfriend. Why do you ask?"

"Well, I heard some of the men at work talking about it, and I was wondering if you would like to go sometime with me. We could practice our dancing."

"Oh, Jim, we couldn't do that."

"Why not?"

"Well, you're too youn— I mean, I'm too old to go out with you in public. Darling, everyone would be talking and starting rumors and such. Lordy, they would run me out of town! You understand, don't you?"

"Yeah, I guess," he said hesitantly.

"Come on, let's eat!"

After supper, he helped her stack the bowls. Then he reached for the pan of water warming on the stove. She took the pan from his hands and said, "Leave the dishes. We'll wash them later."

She set the pan on the small table next to the bed and placed a linen towel next to it. She lit the candles and removed her gown. Just as he had thought, she had nothing on under the garment. He reached to turn off the light.

"Leave it on," she directed. "We'll need it tonight."

She sat on the bed as he stood over her, watching. She swung her feet onto the bed and stretched out on her back. Finally, she patted the bed beside her. He removed his clothes and lay down beside her. They kissed as their hands explored, caressed, and fondled.

"Wash me," she whispered.

"Huh?"

"Wash between my legs."

He reached for the cloth.

"Leave one end dry, Rascal."

He sat up and wet one end of the towel, then wrung it out.

"Wash gently, very gently," she instructed.

"Like that?" he asked.

"Yes," was her husky reply. "That's enough."

He placed the cloth on the table, then turned and kissed her long and deeply. She took his tongue as she wove her fingers in his hair. Then Toby guided his head as she instructed him on how to please her. He learned the exact movements and pressure needed.

Gradually, her little groans turned into, "Yes! Yes! *Yes!*" Then, "Rascal! Oh, Rascal!" As her back arched, she was racked with intense, rippling waves of pleasure. Toby moved his head to let it lie on her belly as her fingers toyed with his hair. He lay there several minutes, feeling the occasional little tremors of her body.

Eventually Jim sat up and asked, "What's next?"

She sat up and placed a hand on each of his shoulders. "This lesson is on pleasing your lady. Sorry, buddy."

"What am I supposed to with this?" he asked as he looked down.

"I know it doesn't seem fair, Rascal, but the whole point is to show your woman that you're willing to sacrifice your own pleasure for hers."

He thought it over, then slowly said, "You mean that your woman will love you because you want to please her as much as you want to please yourself?"

"That's pretty much it," she answered with a grin.

"What's the next lesson?"

"It's masturbation. We pleasure each other and then finish up by watching each other masturbate."

"You mean you're goin' to watch me masturbate?"

"Yeah, and you're going to watch me, too."

He was quiet, lost in thought.

Connie studied his reaction and then said, "Look, Rascal, if you don't want to do it, that's fine. You don't ever have to do something sexually that you're not comfortable with."

"Yeah, well, okay. I'll think about it," he said as he stood up.

They dressed and he offered to help with the dishes.

"No, you go home and get some sleep," she said. "I'll clean up here."

"Nope. You wash and I'll dry."

They finished the dishes, kissed, and said good night.

Back in his room, he masturbated himself to sleep.

CHAPTER 12

He awoke Tuesday morning to the sound of rain hammering the tin roof. The sound transported him back to his home in Virginia—the musty odor of the loft, the smell of bacon frying, and the muted voices of his parents below.

Suddenly, Jim realized that today he would visit the jewelry store. He rushed down the hall for a quick bath and then nibbled his way through breakfast downstairs. The workday dragged by with small talk at each stop. But in the back of his mind, the thought was repeated over and over: Don't get your hopes up. It's a long shot.

At the end of the day, he quickly settled with Mr. Calhoun and hurried to the jewelry store. Thank God, it was open.

"Well, I've got good news. We found who bought the watch," Mr. Ely said.

"Who?" Jim blurted.

"If it had been bought at a store, it could never have been traced. But it was bought through the catalogue, and they keep good records on those."

Jim thought his heart would burst. Get to the point, man, he screamed inside his mind. He willed his heart and breathing to slow down.

"So here it is," Mr. Ely said. "Mr. Taylor? Mr. *Taylor*?"

"Huh?" Jim recovered.

"I *said*, here it is—the paper with the name and address."

Jim looked at the paper, trying to focus his eyes: Mrs. Elvira Benson, Rt. 6, Bright Hollow, Holston Landing, Virginia.

It slowly sank in.

Her son, he thought. I forget his name. It's the one that shot at Dad at the still. His father was sent to prison over it. Maybe the *father* killed her before he went to prison. No, he went to prison before Annie's murder.

"Mr. Taylor. Mr. Taylor?" Mr. Ely said, without getting the young man's attention. Then the jeweler glanced at the first name on the repair invoice. *"Jim!"* he tried.

"What?" Jim finally answered as he tried to snap back to reality.

"I was saying that they also had a copy of what was written on the gift card. They don't ordinarily give that out, but I convinced them that it was necessary to find the owner. I wrote it there at the bottom of the page," he said as he pointed to it.

"Oh, yeah," answered Jim as he read. *To my son, Tom, on his 18th birthday. Your Mama.*

The sick feeling of anger and fear was coming back. He needed to get to his room.

"Twenty-five cents ought to cover it," said Mr. Ely.

"Yes, sir. Thank you," Jim said as he handed him a quarter.

"Are you okay, son?" inquired the jeweler as he handed Jim the watch fob.

"Oh, yeah. I've been sick," he lied. "Gettin' better, though."

Jim put the paper and fob in his pocket and headed for Mrs. Lowery's.

Shaking and wobbly, he made his way home and sat on his bed—head in hands, trying to recover, trying to concentrate. Sweat trickled down his chest as he got up to wipe his hands with a towel. After opening both windows of his room, he stretched out on his bed and stared at the ceiling. Thoughts flashed through his mind, but one was overriding, pressing down on his chest. Annie, I promised, and I won't forget.

I need a plan, he said to himself. But I need to take my time.

Jim had a terrible night, tossing and turning, dozing more

than sleeping. He awoke well before daylight with a gnawing desire to share the story with someone and enlist their support, to share this heavy burden.

It was difficult for Jim to concentrate on his work, and he was making mistakes on his route. He decided he had to put the situation out of his mind during the day and concentrate on it only at night and on weekends.

A rough plan was beginning to form in his mind. He would have to travel to Virginia and find out more about Benson. He would have to figure out a way to catch him alone.

Also, he would have to break it off with Toby in order to concentrate on the task at hand. Tonight was "dance night," as they had come to call it. After the lesson tonight, he would explain to Toby that he was going to concentrate on his night classes and needed to take a break for several weeks.

*****

The music was playing and the dance floor was prepared when Toby met him at the door. "We're skipping target practice today, and I don't want to hear any argument about it," she insisted with hands on her hips.

With his mind on Benson, Jim forced a smile and saluted as he replied, "Yes, ma'am."

She hugged him and immediately started the waltz. One, two, pause, he counted in his mind. It was coming back to him, now, and he stopped counting. They waltzed around the room, he in his work clothes, she in a pretty gingham dress bought from a Montgomery Ward catalogue.

They had a light supper, then washed and dried the dishes. She lit the candles and switched off the light.

"What now, Miss Teacher?" he asked.

She began to undress him without answering. When he stood before her completely nude, she said, "Undress me."

When all her clothes were on the chair, she took him into her arms. They kissed and caressed hungrily. She took a small bottle of baby oil from the shelf and led him to the bed.

Connie lay on her side next to him and poured a few drops of oil in her palm, then began to massage him. When she handed the bottle to him, he dribbled a few well-placed drops and began to gently rub and caress.

When she sensed that he was near release, she stopped and became engrossed in his manipulation of her. As she arched her back, she grabbed his hand and held it tightly against her, then removed it and placed it on him.

She stood up and said, "You better be careful. I might walk in and see you."

He lay still with his hand gripping his erection. Finally, he spoke. "Toby, I'm not sure I want to do this. It's a little embarrassing."

She stretched out beside him and said, "Jim, I understand. Remember, you should never do anything sexually that you're not comfortable with."

He pulled her close and kissed her. Then he oiled his fingers and began to knead where she needed him—gently at first, then gradually to a firmer frenzy of motion. Unfamiliar sounds started in her throat and moved breathlessly out of her mouth between clenched teeth.

Later, she did the same for him. Then they collapsed and embraced in euphoric joy.

He eased out of bed to get a wet cloth. After cleaning each other, they dozed off in each other's arms.

After the nap, they lay cuddling and talking. Finally, he asked, "What's the next lesson?"

"Positions," she answered.

"What's that?"

"You'll have to wait and see," she answered.

Jim broke the news to her regarding the night classes and

apologized for having to be out of pocket for a few weeks.

"Oh, that's not a problem. I'm glad that you're going to get your diploma. If you need any help with studying, just let me know," she offered.

"Thanks, I appreciate it."

"Rascal, it's getting late. Do you want to spend the night? It would be nice to sleep just like this, together. You could get up early and be gone before daylight."

"I'd love to, but I have to get back to my room and fill out the application for class."

He saw the disappointment as she lowered her eyes. "Oh, yeah, I understand," she said.

He kissed her tenderly, then stood and pulled the sheet up around her. "You stay right there and get some sleep. I'll lock up on my way out."

"No, no," she said as she got out of bed. "I've got a few things to do in the store before I open tomorrow."

She blew out the candles and helped him convert the dance floor back to the store configuration. They kissed and said good night.

He drove home, and she went back to bed and cried herself to sleep.

*****

Jim slept in Saturday morning. He had been up late reading Toby's book the night before. He would try to finish it today after breakfast. The conversation at breakfast was lively, but Jim had little to say. His mind was 400 miles away, in Virginia. He had to make a scouting trip home—but when?

Back in his room, he finished the book and started to put it away when he noticed the epilogue. What on earth is that? he wondered.

He turned the page and read with renewed interest. It was

an explanation of the essentials for committing a murder. To his amazement, it ended with the essentials of avoiding detection:

I. *Leave no evidence at the scene, your home, etc.*
II. *Insure that there are no witnesses.*
III. *Do not be seen near the crime scene.*
IV. *Establish an alibi.*
V. *The body must never be found.*
VI. *The weapon must never be found.*
VII. *Do not be the last person to have seen the victim alive.*
VIII. *Under no circumstances ever confess.*
IX. *Have no apparent motive.*

Observations of this detective after working well over one hundred homicides.
John Tickerling
Chicago Police Detective, Retired

His plan began to fall into place.

He would have to make quick trips to Virginia. First, locate Benson without anyone knowing he was ever there. Second, learn his routine and plan a way to catch him alone. Third, prepare everything needed for doing away with him. Then, do the deed and dispose of the body—all without ever being seen.

He was excited now. He had a rough plan for payback to the man who had killed his sister and shot at his dad. The scouting trip to Holston Landing would take how long? It had taken just under 13 hours with Ray's family at Christmas. He could trim a couple of hours off that because he could eliminate the stops required by Josie and the kids. So maybe figure 11 hours each way. If he left at 6:00 on a Friday after work, he could be there by around 5:00 a.m.

That's before daylight, he thought. That would work. I could leave Saturday night and be back here on Sunday morning. I could sleep Sunday and be ready for work Monday morning.

What then? he asked himself.

I could hide my car and hike to a place where I could observe his house. I would have to take food and water. What else? I'll need field glasses. What else? Think!

He imagined himself hidden on high ground, watching Benson's house, observing his routine.

How many trips home would it take just to figure out his routine and be able to catch him alone? What if I drive all the way back down there only to find that his routine has changed?

"Lordy, this is not going to work," he said aloud.

"Okay, stop!" he commanded himself as he began to gather his thoughts.

I have to take this one step at a time. I need to slow down. I get a week's vacation this summer, and I can use part of the time I'm there in Virginia to figure out the next step. I can borrow Dad's shotgun and tell him I'm going hunting. That will give me a chance to take a look at Benson's house. I remember it's up Bright Hollow, but I'm not sure exactly where.

He was getting a headache.

I need to take a break, he thought. Maybe I'll take a walk, then write to Lilly Mae. To Lilly, I mean.

It occurred to him that this was the Saturday of the Dogwood Ball at Radford. In Lilly's last letter, she had told him that everyone was going and not to worry. How did she say it? "The boys there are of no consequence to me."

*****

Lilly was nervous and suffered from incessant, nagging guilt. She had written Jim and told him about the ball and not to worry, because the boys at the ball meant nothing to her. The Dogwood Ball tonight was the premier event of the year. She would be home about a month from now. Jim would question her. What would she tell him?

This was her sixth or seventh date with Robert Leatherwood. He was attentive, handsome, and from a wealthy Virginia family. She was fond of him, but she was in love with Jim. Or was she? I'm not even sure what love is, she thought.

"Hey! Are you listening?" asked Margaret.

"What?" asked Lilly as she snapped back to reality.

"You've got to get your chin off your chest so I can see what I'm doing," demanded Margaret.

"Oh. Sorry."

They helped each other slip into their gowns and then went downstairs to greet their dates. The young men, corsages in hand, were waiting under the watchful gaze of the chaperones. The boys nervously pinned the flowers, carefully trying to avoid touching a breast. Margaret's date finally gave up and looked to a chaperone for assistance.

The scene at the Dogwood Ball was reminiscent of the Old South, with couples gliding around the ballroom as if on a floor of ice. Between dances, they sipped punch, some of which was spiked with good Kentucky bourbon from flasks brought by zealous young men.

"Lilly, you're absolutely beautiful tonight. You take my breath away," Robert said as they waltzed around the room.

"Thank you, Robert. And you look very handsome."

As the night progressed, Robert held Lilly so close she began to worry about a reprimand from a chaperone.

"Let's slip out for a few minutes, Lilly."

"No, we can't do that. We'll be seen," she replied.

"Not if we're careful."

"No. I'm afraid."

He steered her over near a hallway door. "I'm going into the hall. You wait a minute, and then come, too." He took a quick look around and slipped through the door before she could say anything.

The music stopped. She was apprehensive. As everyone

turned toward the orchestra to applaud, she impulsively opened the door and closed it behind her.

The hallway was dark except for the dim porch light that filtered through the window at the end of the corridor. Robert stood in the shadows against the wall in front of her. He pulled her into his arms with a tight embrace and kissed her. His lips opened as he searched for her tongue. He had kissed her before, but not as passionately as this. She hesitated, thought about pulling away, and then parted her lips. His hands caressed her hips, then up under her arms. His hand moved to her breast and squeezed as their tongues met.

She broke away breathlessly. "No," she said as she turned and reentered the ballroom.

Robert followed a couple of minutes later. He carefully surveyed the ballroom. No Lilly.

Lilly turned the water on and looked in the mirror. She wondered if anyone had seen her smeared lipstick as she had hurriedly made her way to the washroom. She dabbed at her eyes and wiped her lips. She was reapplying her lipstick when her roommate Edith appeared in the mirror.

"You okay?" Edith asked.

"Sure. What do you mean?" she asked Edith's reflection.

"I saw you making a beeline for the washroom, and I didn't see Robert in the ballroom."

Lilly remained silent.

"Lilly!" Edith scolded.

"Oh, *all right!* Robert got a little fresh, and I thought it was time to retreat."

"How fresh?" Edith asked as she patted her hair in the mirror.

"*Edith!*"

"Oh, okay. But you've got to tell us all about it later tonight."

"That's not going to happen," Lilly said emphatically.

"Oh, we'll get it out of you," Edith said as she turned and left the room.

CHAPTER 13

By Sunday evening, Jim had made several decisions. Next month, on summer vacation, he would travel to Virginia. In addition to spending time with his family and Lilly, he would find out as much as possible about Benson and his routine.

In the meantime, he would enroll in the night class program. It would help occupy his free time, keep his mind off Benson, and possibly serve as an alibi later. And he would not see Toby other than when he was working his route.

The next day, he took a sandwich with him to work. Instead of breaking for lunch, Jim dropped by the high school and turned in his application.

"Hello, ma'am," he greeted the lady in the school office. "I need to turn in this application for night classes."

"Oh, yes," she said as she took the envelope. "Wait and let me make sure everything is in order." She carefully reviewed the two pages. "Looks good," she said. "You'll be notified by mail."

"Thanks."

Jim returned to his route, wondering how he would fare in the classes. After all, he thought, it's been almost six years since I was in school.

Later, Jim slowly restocked the shelves at Toby's and stalled for time, waiting for an opportunity to talk to her. Several customers had paid and gone, but the lady talking to Toby droned on and on. Finally, she was free.

"Hi, Toby."

"Hey, Rascal," she replied.

"I turned in my application for classes today," he said.

"Great! How do you feel about it?"

"Nervous," was his one-word reply.

"You'll do just fine, Rascal."

"Hope so. Gotta get to work."

"Rascal," she whispered as a customer walked in the door.

"Uh huh?"

"When do classes start?"

He hesitated, trying to quickly decide what to say. He decided on the truth. "They're goin' to let me know by mail."

"So you're free for 'dance night' Thursday?" she asked in hushed tones.

"Yeah, I guess so," he answered unenthusiastically.

She sensed his hesitation and chalked it up to his apprehension about the classes.

"We'll just play it by ear. If you're not here, I'll understand. You've got a lot on your mind."

"Thanks, Tob—" He quickly changed it to "Connie" as the customer walked up to the counter.

Back on his route, he tried to push Annie and Benson from his mind, but they were always there, *always there*. His thoughts returned to Toby and "dance night."

Positions, he mused. Must mean doing it different ways.

The images of himself and Toby were still vivid as he pulled into his next stop. He checked his paperwork long enough to allow the bulge in his pants to recede before exiting the truck.

*****

Lilly had not dated Robert since the Dogwood Ball. He had a history class with her and had been pressing her to see him. As English class ended, she gathered up her books and, as promised, she headed for the café to meet him for lunch.

"Hey, good lookin'," he greeted her.

"Hi, Robert."

"Roast beef sandwich is today's special," he said as they picked up their menus.

She put the menu down. "Sounds good to me."

They ordered, and as the waiter walked away, he said, "I wanted to ask you if I could visit you this summer."

"No, Robert. I have a boyfriend, as I've told you before."

"I know, Lilly. I'm not trying to steal you away from him. I just thought it might be nice to do some fun things together. I'll be on my best behavior."

"No, I couldn't. Jim is coming in this summer."

"Coming in from where?"

"Ohio," she answered. "I thought I told you he was working in Ohio."

"Well, yes, I guess you did. Surely he won't be there the entire summer, though!"

She hesitated, trying to formulate her reply. "He's coming in on vacation," she finally said.

He reached for her hand. "Lilly, you're not engaged, right?'

"Right."

"Then there's nothing wrong with a harmless date. There's an inn in Batesville. I can stay there, and we can bum around for a couple of days."

"How do you know about the Arcadia Manor Inn?" she asked.

"Researched it," he replied proudly as the waiter delivered their sandwiches.

As they ate, he regaled her with descriptions of all the day trips he had discovered within a couple of hours of her home. Just as she mouthed the word "No," he quickly added that these were all daytime activities. "We don't have to see each other at night!" he promised.

"I don't know, Robert. I'll think about it."

He quickly produced a pencil, wrote his address, and placed the paper in front of her. He tore off another piece of paper and offered it, along with the pencil, to her.

She sat looking at it. He nudged it a little closer. She took it, wrote her address, and handed it back. She wasn't altogether pleased with herself, but she was impressed with his determination and persistence.

They walked across campus to her small dorm. He touched her arm. "Lilly, I look forward to seeing you again."

"Yeah, I'll see you in history class."

"That's not what I meant," he smiled.

"'Bye, Robert."

*****

On Thursday, Jim was already on his second stop when the sun broke over the eastern horizon. By 9:00 a.m., he was driving under a pale blue sky dotted with fluffy white clouds. This is going to be a beautiful day, he thought. He was anxious to get back to Virginia, and it was only a couple of weeks until his vacation.

He had wrestled over the last two days with the decision regarding dance night tonight. Reasoning that he really didn't have an excuse to give to Toby until the classes started, he would go tonight, and then break it off once classes began. He didn't want to hurt her feelings. That's what his mind said, anyway. His body said something very different.

By 11:00 a.m., he was restocking the shelves at Toby's. He tallied her bill and waited patiently for the man next to him to conclude his conversation with Connie. Finally, Jim slid the bill across to Toby and tapped his finger on the top of the invoice.

Toby glanced at the note: *See you tonight.* She paid him and nodded that she understood.

"See ya next time, Connie," he said, as he picked up a bread rack.

"Okay, Jim," she replied. She watched him walk through the store and pause to look at the new telephone. He approached it and looked it over carefully.

He arrived 45 minutes after closing time and walked with her to the telephone.

"How does it work?" he asked.

"You put a nickel in this slot," she said. "Then the operator will ask for a number. You tell her the number, and she connects you. Unless it's a long–distance call, that's all you do."

"What if it's a long–distance call?"

"You put a nickel in and tell the operator you want to call long distance. She'll ask you what number you want, and she'll tell you how much to put in. Then you'll be connected." Then she added, "Oh! You might have to put more money in if you talk too long."

"What do you mean?"

"The money you first put in buys a certain number of minutes. If you go over that amount, the operator will tell you how much to put in if you want to continue talking."

"There's a phone at our office. Mr. Bivens talks on it, but I've never used one," Jim explained. "How much did it cost you?"

"Nothing. The Ohio Telephone and Telegraph Company put it in for free. Supposedly, it will bring me more customers. But now the telephone lesson is over! Ready to dance?"

"Ready to waltz," Jim answered.

She put on the record. It was Charleston music. He looked at her questioningly.

"Just don't want you to forget it," she said.

They danced breathlessly through the long song.

"Let's eat," Jim said quickly before Connie could pick another tune.

After supper, she began washing the dishes and asked him to light the candles. He lit them, then stood behind her with his hands on her hips. As Jim nibbled and kissed Toby's neck, he pulled her shapely bottom into his groin. Moving his hands to her breasts, he started to unbutton her blouse.

Connie left the dishes to air dry and turned to embrace him. She whispered, "Tonight is positions. I'll move to different positions, and you do whatever comes naturally. One rule—no talking."

"No talking?" he asked with raised eyebrows.

"No talking," Toby replied as she undressed in front of him. He undressed and joined her in bed.

She lay on her back and wordlessly invited him to caress her body with his lips and hands. Later, she pulled him on top, and they moved as one until she withdrew and turned over onto her tummy. She raised her bottom and lowered her head as she spread her legs wider. He approached her from the rear, grasped her hips, and made love to her in this new and wonderful way.

To his disappointment, a few moments later, she pulled away and pushed him down onto his back. She straddled him to demonstrate the pleasure of another position. He caressed her breasts as she moved on him, rocking back and forth. She laid her breasts on his chest and kissed him, moving faster now. She felt his release, and in an instant, she too was transported there.

*****

He read the letter a second time to make sure he understood the instructions. He could report for class at any time. The classes met every Tuesday and Thursday night at 7:00, and each student progressed at his own pace. In addition to class work, there would be assignments to work on outside the class. Homework, he thought.

It went on to say that each student would be scheduled a time to attend the "Learning to Use Your Library" class held at the public library in Oxford. At the bottom of the page, a note "For Those Who Cannot Read and Write" indicated that they would be attending a separate class on the same days and times as noted above.

If they can't read and write, he wondered, how will they read this note?

I'll start on Thursday to learn more about the program, he thought. Then I'll tell Connie at lunch today that my first class is on dance night. I'll miss the classes during my upcoming vacation, but that shouldn't be a problem, since I'll be working at my own pace.

As he told Toby, he searched her face for a reaction. To his surprise, she seemed to be genuinely happy for him.

"That's great, Jim! I'm proud of you, and I know you'll do well. Study hard and make sure you keep me up to date on your progress." She looked around to make sure no one was watching, then quickly squeezed his hand.

He listened carefully in class Thursday evening. After completing a short test to measure his grade level, he was given two books and a workbook. At the end of class, he informed Mrs. Gladden that he would be on vacation back home in Virginia the first week of June. She assured him that it would not be a problem.

Over the next two weeks, he adjusted to his new routine: going to classes, studying in his room, and working every day. His class work was progressing well and was not as difficult as he had expected. Mrs. Gladden told him he had tested at the 10th–grade level.

He made a list of what he needed for the trip home. He would buy a rucksack, a canteen, and a pair of field glasses. Also needed were food and water for the drive on Friday night. He would stop only for gasoline. He would also need everything required for repairing a flat tire.

Jim had written Lilly three weeks before to tell her he

would drive home on Friday night, take a nap Saturday morning, and be at her house by 11:30. He suggested that they go to Dawson for lunch and asked her to write him to let him know if it was okay with her.

Lilly received two letters on the same day. One was from Jim suggesting that they see each other on Saturday, the first week of June. The other was from Robert, asking to call on her and her family the same Saturday. He suggested a short excursion by train on Sunday and a day trip by car on Monday. She panicked. Oh, Lord, what have I gotten myself into? she thought.

She nervously penned Robert a letter informing him that she would be out of town that week visiting relatives. She thanked him and basically said, "Maybe some other time." She wrote Jim and informed him that Saturday would be fine and that she was very anxious to see him.

On Thursday's stop at Toby's, Jim told Connie that Mr. Bivens's nephew Bobby would be filling in for him on next week's route. She asked about school, and he informed her that he had completed almost half of the workbook. They sneaked a squeeze of hands and said goodbye.

*****

Jim was packed and ready to go. He checked the time as he pulled out: 6:15 p.m. Thoughts bounced around in his head throughout the night: Lilly, Annie, Benson, and his parents.

He was anxious to hear about Lilly's first year of college and what she expected the final year to be like. He would visit Annie and place some flowers on her grave. And he would go hunting—not for game, but for Benson.

What if Dad wants to go with me? he asked himself. He would have to figure out a way to go alone without causing suspicion.

He wondered how his parents were doing, now that Annie had been gone almost a year. He still felt the guilt of not going with Annie on that July 2nd.

He pushed the images from his mind by singing out loud. He thought of the music at Toby's, and he relived the dance nights in his mind. Then he felt guilty about that and pushed those thoughts from his mind as well.

He made himself two promises: I will not ask Lilly about boys, dances, dates, or parties. It's the least I can do, given what I've been doing with Toby. Also, I will not push her for sex. She feels strongly about waiting for marriage, and I will respect that.

By 3:00 a.m., he was nodding at the wheel. He tried singing and talking to himself. When he crossed into Virginia, the pull of home brought him fully awake and alert. It was 5:05 a.m. when he pulled into the lane at the home place. Just under 11 hours, he noted. He drove past the barn and parked in front of the house.

His mother saw the car lights and shouted at George. They met him on the porch steps. His mother gave him a hearty hug and exclaimed, "You're a sight for sore eyes!" His father shook his hand and said, "Breakfast is about ready. Come on and tell us how ye been doin'. Did ye have any trouble on the drive down?" he asked as he took Jim's bag.

"Nope. Made it in under 11 hours," Jim replied as they made their way to the table.

"The biscuits are almost ready," his mother said as she alternately stirred the gravy and the scrambled eggs. The country ham was already on the table, floating in red–eye gravy. Jim ate as though it was his last meal on earth. They caught up on the last six months, then Jim made his way up the familiar steps to get some sleep.

He was up before 10:00, taking a bath and thinking of Lilly. He shaved and put on fresh clothes and informed his mother that he was having lunch with Lilly.

"Don't 'spect we'll see you before dark," she said, smiling.

Jim blushed, then asked, "Mama, what do you think of Lilly?"

"Lilly Mae's a fine girl, son. You think y'all be gettin' married?"

"Maybe. Maybe someday, if she'll have me. She's got to finish school first, and then she wants to teach awhile, I guess. She can't get married as long as she's teaching."

"No, they changed that, son."

"Changed what?" he asked.

"Teachers can marry now. Your father read it in the newspaper several months back."

Jim was both shocked and pleased. He tried to show neither emotion as he looked away. He quickly recovered, and as his mother walked him to the porch, he asked if his father was working that day.

"Yeah, they can't keep up with orders at the sawmill. He's working six days a week, now that it's turned warm."

He gave her a hug and said, "See ya later today."

Jim pulled off the road by the path leading to Lilly's house. She was standing there waiting for him. He reached for the door handle, but she jumped into the car and into his arms before he could exit the car. They held each other close and kissed passionately. Finally, they broke away and made eye contact.

"Hello, college girl."

"Hello, working man."

They kissed again and talked a few minutes, then got out of the car and walked up the path to the house. Her parents greeted Jim warmly and asked him questions about Ohio, his work, the trip down, and so forth.

Lilly Mae—her parents were having nothing to do with this business of changing names—told them they would be back from Dawson before dark. As they drove down the valley, Jim suggested that they stop at a store and buy sandwiches.

"We can go back to our special place on the river," he said.

She looked at him, trying to formulate an answer that wouldn't hurt his feelings.

He quickly added, "No wading, no wet clothes, and no hanky-panky."

"You promise, Jim?'

"I swear," he answered.

They came out of the store with two paper bags full of picnic essentials. As they drove to the river, she wondered when Jim would ask about the boys at college. He had asked her about her classes and showed a special interest in the subject matter. He asked about the exams, what questions were on them, how she studied for them, and so on.

She asked him about his work and how he spent his time off. He decided to share with her the story about the robbery attempt and the shootout. He had weighed in his mind the temptation to make her proud of him against the possibility of worrying her. He also wondered if he should mention that the bonus he received was in a savings account for an engagement ring. No, he thought, I should probably keep that to myself for now.

"Jim, you could have been killed!"

"Aw, it wasn't that big a deal." He changed the subject quickly. "You're not gonna pee in your pants this time, are you?" he jokingly asked.

"What?"

"You know, on the swinging bridge."

"*Jim Taylor!* Have you ever told that to anyone?"

"No, ma'am. I swear," he said as he held up his hand as if taking an oath.

They made their way slowly across the bridge and quickly found their spot. He handed her the bags and spread the canvas. They sat and talked as Jim pitched stones into the water.

"It's a beautiful day," she said as she looked at the sky with a hand shading her eyes.

"For a beautiful girl," he said, as he kissed her cheek. She explored his addictive blue eyes and smiled. Embarrassed, he lay back and pulled her with him. Holding hands and looking at the clouds moving through the trees above them, Jim broke the silence, "Lilly?"

"Uh–huh?"

"Have you ever noticed how when you see something bright, then close your eyes, you can still see it for a second?"

She thought for a moment. "Jim Taylor, you're awful," she exclaimed as she sat up and slapped his chest.

He laughed uncontrollably as she tickled and poked him.

"You ready to eat, smart aleck?" she finally asked.

"Yep," he said as he sat up.

They talked over lunch, mostly about what Lilly would do at home during the summer. He considered telling her about the classes he was taking, but instead, he described the towns of Eaton and Oxford, Ohio—the stores, the farms, the Methodist church, and the cafés.

She turned onto her tummy and closed her eyes, trying to picture the town in her mind's eye as he talked. He lightly rubbed her back and pulled strands of her hair gently through his fingers.

Goodness, she's beautiful, he thought. He admired the curve of her bottom and recalled his promise to himself not to push.

"Lilly?"

She didn't answer. She was asleep. Propped on his elbow, he lay looking intently at her and thinking about how much he loved her.

She opened her eyes and blinked a few times to focus on his smiling face. She bolted upright.

"I'm sorry. How long was I asleep?"

"Just 20 minutes or so."

"Jim, I'm so sorry. I guess it was the lunch and the warm

sun. You're the one who was up all night."

"Nothing to be sorry for." He kissed her lips, then each eye. "I hope someday we can wake up together in our own home."

She smiled and touched his cheek, looking into his eyes and thinking how mature he was for his age.

"You ready to head to Dawson?" he asked in a low voice.

"Yes," she said, somewhat surprised. "Anytime you are."

In Dawson, Tennessee, they walked hand in hand, window shopping. At Lilly's request, they went inside a few stores. She admired a silver bracelet and tried it on. Over her protest, he paid the clerk and put it on her wrist.

"It'll be to remember me by until the next time I can get back to Virginia," he said.

Later, they sat on a bench near the public library, eating the ice cream cones they had bought at Farley's Drug Store.

"Oh, I almost forgot. Mama has invited you to dinner tomorrow after church. She's invited Preacher Boatwright and his family and thought you would like to see Rob."

"Yeah, I sure would. What's Rob into these days?"

"I really don't know. Last Sunday was the first time I've seen him since Christmas," Lilly replied.

"Has he started preachin' yet?"

"According to Mama, he's led prayer a few times."

On the drive home, Jim mentioned to Lilly that he wanted to help his mother in the garden one day and also wanted to go hunting one day.

"Sure," she said. "I want you to enjoy being home."

"Do you think your parents would mind if I came over one night?"

"No, that'll be fine. We can sit on the porch and listen to the katydids," she said.

He pulled up in front of the house. They kissed in the car, then he walked her to the house.

*****

The next day at church, Jim sat with Lilly. Rob spoke a few minutes to open the service before turning it over to his father.

"He did pretty good," whispered Jim.

She nodded her agreement.

After church, Jim spoke at length with friends and relatives. Then he invited Rob to ride with him and Lilly.

As always, Rob entertained them with funny stories about people in the community, and they laughed all the way to Lilly's. At the Larkeys', the men gathered on the porch and the women busied themselves in the kitchen. Jim and Rob walked to the river and back, talking over old times.

Jim and Lilly took the same route later in the afternoon to steal a few minutes alone. They paused at the oak tree swing and embraced as their lips came together. He moved his hands to her hips and pressed her tightly against his hardness. Curious as to how it would feel in her hand, Lilly opened her lips to receive his tongue and struggled to push the salacious thoughts from her mind.

He released her, interrupting her thoughts. "We'd better get back, Lilly." He gave her one last hug and walked her back to the house. "I'm going to try to go hunting tomorrow. I'll see you on Tuesday, if that's okay with you," he said.

"That sounds great," she replied. "I hope you enjoy it."

CHAPTER 14

Instead of heading home, he drove through Holston Landing and turned up Bright Hollow Road. Actually, it was a wagon trail, rutted by over a hundred years of use. He passed two houses about one half mile apart, and then a mile or so farther, the road terminated at a log cabin with a turnaround. A young boy was playing with a dog near the road. Jim drove the car around the turn and stopped. The boy came out of the yard and looked the car over.

"How ya doin'?" asked Jim.

"Fair to middlin'," the boy answered as he walked around the car.

Two mailboxes stood near the entrance of a trail up the hollow. One box must belong to the Bensons, thought Jim.

"Is there a house up that trail?"

"Yep," the boy answered.

"Is it the McMurrays?"

"Nope, Bensons," answered the boy. "You lost, mister?"

"I guess so. Anybody besides the Benson family live up that trail?" asked Jim.

"Nope."

"So the trail ends at their house?"

"Yep. My daddy says it used to go all the way to Caney Creek 'fore the loggin' folks bought it."

"Well, you take it easy," Jim said, as he depressed the clutch.

He drove back down to the road and turned right onto the Holston Landing Highway. About four miles up the road, he turned right onto Caney Creek Road and began looking for signs of the old wagon trail on his right. There were many candidates, and he was about to give up when he spotted an old man hoeing creek–bottom corn. Jim pulled up, and the man stopped hoeing and looked at him and the car. Finally, he walked over to the fence.

"How ye doin' today?" Jim asked.

"Right pert, I reckon."

"Good lookin' corn crop," Jim said as he nodded toward the corn field.

"Yeah, we got a right smart bunch of rain this sprang."

"Can I ask ye a question?"

"I reckon so," the old man said as he looked at the car.

"I'm lookin' to go squirrel huntin' tomorrow. Somebody said to go up the old wagon trail that used to go from Caney Creek across over to the Holston Landing Highway," Jim said. "Ain't sure where the old trail takes off from this road."

"That trail ain't been open for over 40 years. All growed up now. Takes off there at Estill Springs."

"Yeah, I know where that's at. Sure appreciate it, mister," Jim said as he pulled away.

*****

Jim borrowed his father's shotgun and hunting vest and asked his mother to get him up at 5:30. She awakened him, then wrapped up two biscuits and placed them with his hunting vest.

He turned off the road near the two large springs and parked the car behind a grove of locust trees. After placing the field glasses and canteen in the hunting vest, he sat on the running board and ate a sausage biscuit while waiting for dawn. Light approached slowly as he labored to see the trail. Finally, he spotted the depressed contours of the old trail. He loaded the shotgun and began his trek. His plan was to bag a couple of squirrels as he worked his way up the mountain, then find a vantage point to observe the Benson house.

Squirrels were barking and cutting on hickory nuts, and he shot number three as the sun peeked over the hills behind him. At the top of the mountain, he sat on a log, catching his breath and studying the terrain in front of him. He heard a rooster crow in the distance and wondered if it was at the Benson house. The trail was covered with 40-year-old trees, but it was easier to traverse than the underbrush on either side.

It was almost 8:00 a.m. when he spotted the log house below. He moved to his right until he could see both the front and rear of the cabin. He pulled out his canteen and settled in to watch and wait.

Within 30 minutes, he saw movement and adjusted the focus on the field glasses. It was a woman. Chickens came running as she sprinkled what must be corn around the bare yard. Later, he observed her hanging clothes to dry in the back yard. At lunch time, he ate the ham biscuit without taking his eyes off the house. He spotted the woman several times over the next three hours. He finally decided that Benson was not at home. He must have left early.

Must have a job, Jim reasoned.

He gathered up his things and headed back across the mountain.

Back home, he cleaned the squirrels and gave them to his mother. When his mother commented on how long he'd been gone, he told her that after the flat land of Ohio, he had just been enjoying the hills. In late afternoon, he helped his mother in the garden. After his father returned from the sawmill, they talked over supper about Ray and his family and John's new job in Detroit.

That night, they sat on the front porch catching up on the last six months. His father explained how things were going at the sawmill, and he also informed Jim that he had broken up two stills over the last three months.

"Speaking of stills," said Jim, "is that Benson fella still in prison?"

"Yeah, he's got a year to go."

"I was thinking a while back about what his son said to you—you know, about how he would get you," said Jim.

"Well, to tell you the truth, I did keep an eye over my shoulder for a while. Don't guess I have much to worry 'bout now, though. He's gone."

"Gone? Gone where?" Jim asked.

"The sheriff says he's working in Kentucky. I believe he said Richmond, Kentucky."

Jim's head was spinning. Dad jimmit! he thought, I wasted a whole day of vacation. "What was his name again?" he asked as casually as he could.

"Uh, let me see. The sheriff mentioned his name. What was it? Bob? No, Tom. That's it, Tom. Tom Benson."

On Tuesday morning, Jim asked his mother if she would like to go with him to visit Annie's grave.

"Sure would," she said.

They picked some flowers from the yard and headed out in Jim's car.

"Do you think they'll ever catch the man that done it?" his mother asked.

Jim hesitated and then said, "I don't know, Mama. I sure hope so."

As they got out of the car, Jim picked up the flowers, all except for a purple iris. He left it on the back seat. Annie won't mind if I take one for Lilly, he thought. They pulled a few weeds, placed the flowers, and then talked quietly as they stared at her marker.

Back home, Jim took a bath and then headed for Lilly's. He sat in the kitchen and talked to Lilly and Mrs. Larkey as they prepared dinner. Jim walked to the car and retrieved the iris.

Then he climbed the steps to the front porch and sat on the swing. The house was larger and much nicer than the house he had grown up in.

Bottom land, he thought. That's the difference. Mr. Larkey's great–grandfather was an early settler here and wisely picked the fertile soil adjacent to the river.

"Jim. *Jim!*"

"What?" he answered as he was jolted from his thoughts.

"Dinner's ready," Lilly answered. "What have you got there?" she asked.

"For you," he said as he handed her the iris.

"Thanks! How sweet." She gave him a quick kiss.

In mid–afternoon, they sat on the bench by the river, talking and holding hands. He looked over his shoulder to make sure they couldn't be seen from the house. Good, he thought. He studied her brown eyes and inched closer until their lips met. He held the kiss as their tongue tips danced back and forth. She squeezed his hand hard and gave him her tongue. He turned onto his back, with his legs over the arm of the bench. She scooted over to take his head in her lap. Her fingers played in his hair as he talked.

Jim stopped talking and looked at her. Then he raised his head and softly kissed her breast through her blouse. She cradled his head with her arm, drew him against her, and kissed his hair. He pressed his lips firmly against her, then held her breast with both hands.

"You're going to get my blouse wet," she whispered as she released him to unbutton her blouse.

Lilly opened her blouse and drew his mouth to her bra. He tried to slip her breast from her bra, but she held his hand tightly against her. He could feel her nipple in his mouth through the bra and she could see the bulge in his pants.

He took her free hand and placed it on his erection and squeezed her hand hard around it. He moved his hips up and down against her hand.

"Lilly Mae!"

"Yes, Mama!" Lilly yelled as they both bolted upright.

"Time to come in, honey!"

They stood up breathlessly and smoothed the wrinkles from their clothes. Once Lilly had her blouse buttoned, they slowly headed back to the house.

*****

Back at the Taylor home, Jim helped his mother again in the garden. She was full of questions about his job, Lilly Mae, Ray and his family, John's offer to help him get a job in Detroit, and so on.

The days passed quickly, too quickly. He saw Lilly every day and spent time with his family, his relatives, and Rob. He and Lilly hiked to Begley Falls, visited Batesville, and drove all over Northeast Tennessee.

Every night, alone in the loft, he thought of Benson and Richmond, Kentucky.

He weighed the advantages and disadvantages of Benson's move to Kentucky. The main advantage, of course, was that it was closer to his home in Ohio. Also, he thought, no one knows me there. The main disadvantage was that he didn't know where Benson lived or worked. How could he find out without raising suspicions?

He visited Annie on Saturday morning.

"Annie," he said out loud, "I've got to go back early tomorrow. I've located the man, and I promise you I'll make him pay. Don't worry about me; I'll be careful. I hope to be home for Christmas. I'll come to see you."

He took a last look at the grave marker and the wilted flowers, then said goodbye.

*****

Jim knocked on the door. "Well, good morning, Jim," Mrs. Larkey exclaimed.

"Good morning, Mrs. Larkey. is Lilly here?"

"Why, yes, she's upstairs primping. Come on in. Where are you kids going today?"

"I don't know, Mrs. Larkey. Wherever Lilly wants to go, I guess."

"Did I hear my name?" asked Lilly as she came down the stairs.

"Yes, you did," said her mother. "I was asking where you two were headed off to. Why don't y'all go sit in the parlor and talk it over. I'll get back to my cleaning."

They sat in the parlor discussing their options. Finally, Jim suggested, "How about a drive up to Brighton, on the state line?"

"Sounds good. I'll tell Mama."

They had lunch at the State Line Restaurant, then ambled up the street, peering in store windows as they talked. They stopped at a jewelry store and looked over the merchandise. Jim couldn't help but notice that Lilly was wearing the bracelet he had bought for her.

"Pretty bracelet. Where'd you get that?" he joked.

"My man bought it for me," she said as she squeezed his hand.

Suddenly, Jim blurted out, "Lilly, I'm saving up for a ring!"

"Jim, we've got plenty of time. I'm still in college. We'll talk about it after I graduate." She squeezed his hand, hoping his feelings weren't hurt, then quickly added, "Maybe we can discuss it when you come in for Christmas." As they continued along the street, she sensed that his mood had changed.

"Oh! I forgot to tell you," she said. "I asked Mama if I could stay out late, maybe have dinner with you on your last night."

His face brightened into a smile. "That's great. Where do

you wanna have dinner?"

"Uh, let's see. How about back at the railway station in Dawson? Is that too far?"

"No, that's fine," he answered.

She put her arm in his, and they meandered through downtown Brighton, taking in the sights. Later, he stopped at a newsstand and bought a cigar and a piece of stick candy. He handed the candy to Lilly and placed the cigar in his shirt pocket.

Lilly said, "I didn't know you smoked cigars."

"I don't. It's for my dad. He'll save it till the election in November."

The Clinchfield Café in Dawson was packed, so they decided on Lenny's, across the street.

Lenny lowered the shades to block the early evening sun, then lit a candle at their table.

Lilly pulled earrings from her purse and slipped them on. Jim looked intently at her face and inched his hand toward hers, past the flickering light of the candle. She offered her hand in return as she met his gaze.

"Have you decided?" asked the waiter.

"Oh, uh, no, we need more time," answered Jim.

Lilly smiled at Jim and picked up the menu.

Jim whispered, "Lilly, I've got two forks!"

"I had a class on this at school," she said and then explained the use for each piece of silverware.

"Have you decided, ma'am?" The waiter was back.

"No, give us just another minute, please," she replied.

Once the waiter was out of earshot, they giggled and tried to concentrate on their menus.

They chatted through dinner and ordered ice cream for dessert. As they finished the ice cream, Lilly reached for her purse.

"Jim, I'm going to split the check with you."

He held up his hand and said, "That ain't gonna happen."

Lilly finally relented and said, "I'm going to use the washroom while you pay."

Meeting at the front door, he took her hand and they walked up Main Street for several blocks. Crossing the street, they doubled back to a bench at the railway station and sat holding hands as they watched people going in and out of the depot.

"I'm gonna miss you," he said as he gave her a quick kiss.

"Jim! We can't kiss here," she said, half joking and half serious. Then she added, "I'm going to miss you, too."

The sun had set and dusk was yielding to darkness. Jim stood up and offered his hand.

"I'd better get you back before your father forms a posse."

She took his hand, and they walked silently toward the car in the station parking lot.

I kept my promise, he thought. I haven't pushed her to have sex, and I haven't asked about other boys. He felt proud.

This has been a lovely day, she thought. I think this is what it feels like to be in love. When he mentioned the ring, I should have hugged him and told him that I loved him. I'm really surprised that he hasn't tried anything sexual.

He opened the car door for her. Lilly turned and kissed him passionately, then got in. He pushed in beside her, closed the door, and pulled her to him. They kissed hard, lips grinding, tongues clashing. He squeezed her breast, then moved his hand to her knee. Jim softly stroked her legs under the cotton skirt until he finally reached the softness of her tightly closed thighs. Lilly gradually opened her legs to his gentle rubbing.

Aroused now, she grabbed the bulge in his pants and held it tightly in her hand. He pushed her onto her back and opened her legs. Now he pushed against her as they kissed. She shifted to get him where she wanted him, needed him. As they moved, he clumsily tried to pull her panties down with one hand. She grabbed his hand and moved it away. He fumbled with his pants, still moving his hips. Finally, jerking the buttons free, he pushed them down. He was hard against her panties. As he moved faster, she locked her legs around him. He tried to move her panties to one side, but she jerked his hand away and wriggled out from under him.

"I'm sorry, Lilly, so sorry! I promised myself I wouldn't do this," he said as he sat up.

She didn't answer. Instead, she kissed him and grasped his hardness and began to move her hand up and down. He groaned and guided her hand to go faster.

She looked at it. It seemed huge in her small hand. He was ready to explode.

"Don't stop, don't stop!" He grappled with his pants, trying to find his pocket—his handkerchief. "Now, now, now," he begged as he let go all over himself, Lilly, and the car.

Lilly was amazed, shocked. She still held him in her hand as she looked around the car. He handed her the handkerchief. She wiped her hand, then her blouse.

"I'm sorry, I'm sorry!" Jim said with a trembling voice.

"It's okay, Jim," she said breathlessly as she wiped him off and observed how much smaller he was now.

He sat there, spent, trying to hold her as she wiped off the dashboard.

"Raise up," she whispered as she pulled up his underwear and pants.

"Lilly, you didn't get to finish. Let me do the same for you."

"No, honey, I'm fine," she said as she gently kissed him.

He cradled her in his arms, and they sat in silence for a few minutes.

"Jim, what does it feel like?'

"Feel like? Whatta ya mean?"

"When it spews out like that."

"Oh, it feels like, like the greatest feeling on earth. It's hard to describe. Didn't you feel it that time in the car at the cemetery?"

"I don't know. It felt good. Like a great release of tension," she said.

"That's it! That's a good description," he exclaimed.

"Wanna hear something funny?" she asked.

"Yeah, what?"

"My first thought was, how on earth could something that big get inside me?"

He laughed and hugged her tighter.

"Then I thought, if a baby can come out, I guess that could go in."

"This discussion is making me hard again," he joked.

"Then we better get home, buster," she replied as she straightened her skirt.

They pulled up in front of her house and kissed. He walked her to the porch and squeezed her hand.

"Write often," he said.

"I will. Good night," she said, then added, "I love you."

"I love you, too," he whispered.

CHAPTER 15

On Sunday morning, Jim left at 5:30 for Ohio. Leaving was especially difficult this time, but at least now he could concentrate on locating Benson. He planned to go to Richmond on his way back to scope it out.

Jim stopped for gas in Corbin, Kentucky and studied the map. Route 25 would take him directly to Richmond. He tried to envision how he could find Benson without being noticed. Detective Tinkerling's warning, "Do not be seen near the crime scene," came to mind.

If I start asking questions around town, someone might remember me or the Ohio license plates on my car, he thought.

He decided to drive through town and memorize the main streets and key buildings, then move on.

After driving through town, he headed back to Route 25 using secondary streets.

I've got to concentrate, he said to himself as he pulled into a parking space to think things through. Benson lives in this town, but how can I find where without talking to people? How can I ask without being seen?

Jim saw a drugstore across the street and contemplated just walking in and casually asking the clerk if he knew where Benson lived. He quickly dismissed the idea thinking, How stupid! What are the chances they would know him, not to mention that they might remember me.

He leaned over and tapped the steering wheel with his forehead. Think! Think! Then he saw it in his mind's eye. The sign! he exclaimed to himself.

He looked back at the drug store. The sign said *TELEPHONE INSIDE*. He had been staring directly at it without seeing it.

That's it, he thought. I could call and ask the operator! Do I have to have his phone number to call, or can I just give the operator his name? he wondered. When she connects me, what do I say if he answers? Focus. Focus!

I could tell him I'm calling from the Post Office about a package for him. No, I could be from Western Union, and I need his address to deliver the telegram. What if someone else answers? I could just ask for the address in order to deliver the telegram.

He dried his wet and trembling hands with his handkerchief. Checking his pockets for change, he discovered a quarter and two dimes. I need a nickel for the call, he reminded himself.

Jim walked into the drugstore and spotted the phone. After getting change from the clerk, he took a deep breath and put the nickel in the slot.

"Yes, what number, please?" the operator asked.

"Uh, I don't have a number. I'm trying to reach Tom Benson," Jim said nervously.

"One minute, please. I'll check." Then, "I'm sorry, sir. I don't have a Tom Benson."

"Well, uh, is there any other way I can find him? I have an important message from his mother."

"I'm sorry. Apparently he doesn't have a telephone," she said, then added, "He may live in a boarding house or an apartment building. Some of them supply lists of tenants that use a common phone. Would you like for me to check them?"

"Yes, ma'am. I'd appreciate it."

"It may take a few minutes. Would you like to hold or call back?"

"I'll hold on, ma'am."

Jim stood there, glancing around. No one seemed to notice him.

"Sir, are you there?"

"Yes, ma'am!"

"I found him. He's at a boarding house with a roster of 16 people. The number is CT 116."

Jim panicked; he didn't have a pencil or paper. "Ma'am, can you wait till I can get a pencil and paper?" he pleaded.

"Yes, I'll hold, sir."

Jim put the earpiece down and rushed to ask the clerk. She was helping a customer. Jim shifted from one foot to the other. The clerk glanced at him and Jim mimicked writing on his hand. She slid a pencil and pad on the counter toward him without speaking. He hurried back to the phone. "Yes, ma'm. I'm ready."

"It's CT 116, and the address is 132 Willow Street."

Jim repeated it as he wrote it down. "Thank you, ma'am," he blurted.

"You're welcome, sir."

Jim hung up and headed for the door. An elderly man was reading the label on a bottle of cough syrup.

"Sir, could you tell me how to get to Willow Street?" Jim asked.

After receiving the directions, Jim walked directly to the car. He sat there a moment, amazed at what he held in his hand.

What should I do next? he asked himself. I need to know his routine: where he goes, when he goes, where he works, what time he goes to work, what time he comes home. That means I would have to watch him for days at a time. That's impossible.

Better move on before someone notices me, he thought.

He drove several blocks toward Willow Street and parked. There, he continued his thought process.

I need to time the drive from here to home in Ohio, he thought. Also, I need to get rid of these Ohio license plates on the next trip back here. Where can I get a set of Kentucky plates? I could steal a set. No. I'm not a thief. I've never stolen anything, and I'm not gonna start now.

Jim's growling stomach signaled that it was time to eat. "I need to find a place where my car will blend in—not stand out," he said aloud. Finally, he spotted a restaurant with a lot almost full of parked cars.

Over lunch, he weighed the merits of calling the boarding house. He could say he was an old friend from back home and wanted to surprise Tom.

I could ask about his routine, he thought. Where he works and so on. What if Benson answers? I could just hang up. Once I have the information, I could wait a month or so, and no one would remember the call.

Jim decided he would make the call, but first he would drive by the boarding house.

It was the largest building on the block. He parked across the street, quickly looked it over, and then moved on, looking for a telephone where he wouldn't be noticed.

He came to a T intersection directly in front of a train station. He parked the car and went in. The phone was in the lobby near the ticket window. Jim nervously removed a nickel from his pocket and promptly dropped it on the floor. He retrieved it, took a deep breath, and deposited the coin in the slot. Jim gave the operator the number, and she connected him.

"Hello."

"Yes, ma'am, I'm trying to locate Tom Benson."

"He's asleep. Wanna leave a message?"

"Uh, well, I'm a friend from Tennessee and want to surprise him."

"Honey, he works nights and sleeps till 'bout 3:00 or 4:00 in the afternoon."

"That won't work. Let me see. Uh, where's he work?"

"He's a night watchman at the Coalfield Construction Company, but you don't wanna approach him there—might get shot!"

"Oh, yes, ma'am, that wouldn't do. I tell you what. I'll be back through here in a week or two, and I'll see him then. Please don't tell him I called. I want it to be a surprise."

"Okay, honey, I won't tell. Goodbye."

"Goodbye."

Jim walked to the ticket counter and asked the agent for directions to the Coalfield Construction Company. Directions in hand, he walked to the car, taking deep breaths until he felt some of his tension subside.

He drove slowly by the construction company and closely observed the layout. A tall fence surrounded the compound with a large double-gate main entrance and a man gate adjacent to it.

No wonder they need a night watchmen, he thought. It looks like they've got every piece of equipment known to man in there!

To the left of the compound were a parking lot and a building. That's probably the main office, he thought.

The building was somewhat isolated, with a wooded hillside to the rear, a vacant field on the left, and a gully filled with trees and underbrush on the right. Centered inside the fenced compound was a high bay garage. Jim guessed that the tiny building next to the gate was probably the guard's quarters. He drove a half mile up the road and pulled into a lane to turn around. The lane appeared to bend to the right about 500 yards ahead. I wonder if it goes behind the hill at the construction company? he asked himself.

It's time to go home, Jim thought as he backed up and turned around. He checked his watch—2:41 p.m.—and jotted down the time. He would memorize the phone number, address, and directions, then destroy the paper when he got to Ohio.

Time passed quickly. Jim was deep in thought, planning. It was 8:23 p.m. when he parked the car near Mrs. Lowery's.

Roughly five and a half hours, he noted. That was with one

very brief stop. To be safe, he would allow six hours.

He greeted everyone and told them it was good to be back. Once in his room, he read the letter from John updating him on Detroit, the job at the plant, and his family. He took a quick bath and wrote Lilly a letter.

The next morning, Jim stuck his head in Mr. Bivens's office to thank him for the time off. He greeted folks in the warehouse and began loading his truck. There had been one change in his route, but other than that, he was back to his familiar routine.

He found it difficult to concentrate on his work. His mind was in Richmond, Kentucky, and he now had a basic plan. He would go back there next weekend and observe Benson at the construction company. He would figure out a way through the fence and decide on the best time to attack. He would also scout out a place to bury him.

Six or seven customers were in Toby's, shopping. The new telephone must be working well, Jim thought, as he walked toward the counter.

"Hi, Connie," he said.

"Well, look what the cat drug in!" she exclaimed. "How was Virginia?" she asked, and then in a hushed tone, "Did you see that special girl?"

"Oh, it was good to see everybody," he answered. "Anything other than the usual today?"

"No, just stock anything I'm low on."

After stocking the shelves, he worked on the invoice at the counter.

When she was free, Connie leaned on the counter and chatted with him while he filled out the invoice. "So, are we still doing lessons?" she asked.

"Well, not for a while, Toby. I've got classes Tuesdays and Thursdays, and I have to do my homework the other nights. I'm trying to get my diploma as soon as possible. On weekends, I'm staying at my brother's farm to help. He's short-handed right now."

"I understand, Rascal. Just let me know when you want to see me again."

"Sure will, Connie. See ya later."

*****

In his room Friday night, Jim mulled over the Richmond plan until after midnight. The next morning, he slept in and had a late breakfast, killing time before leaving for Kentucky. He didn't want to arrive early and just sit around in his car. He had decided that would be too suspicious.

Earlier in the week, he had solved the dilemma of the license plates. An entire outside wall of a country store on his route was covered with tags the owner had collected over the years. Jim found a set of Kentucky tags and pried them off the wall, saving the two nails for when he would return the plates. The tags were out of date, of course, but at least the color and design hadn't changed. He placed them in the empty box and secured it in his back seat.

Now that the plates, field glasses, flashlight, and blanket were packed in his rucksack, he was ready to go.

He was within 10 miles of Richmond by 7:30 p.m. He found a road house and took his time eating supper, waiting until the sun was low on the horizon.

After switching tags, Jim headed for Benson's workplace. On the previous trip, he had picked a spot about a quarter of a mile past the compound to hide his car.

He walked toward the building, staying inside the woodline, then up the hill. There was barely enough light to guide him. Weaving his way back and forth on the hillside, he picked a burial site in the underbrush, far enough from trees to allow digging without interference from a root system.

Jim carefully studied the immediate area. When he was

satisfied that he could find the site again, he moved downhill to find an observation point. When he was satisfied with the spot, he removed the field glasses and focused in on the guard shack. No activity. Finally, he spotted movement. It was Benson walking the perimeter fence! Jim watched him slowly walk the fence line, occasionally shining his light through the fence. When he reached the gate, he unlocked it and walked to the office next door. He shone his light, walked around the building, then walked back to the main compound.

Jim watched this routine for over six hours. It varied only once, when Benson took a break for supper, or maybe it was a snack.

It was a difficult night for Jim. His rage was building by the minute, fired by those awful images in his mind. The urge to do it now, to make the man pay, was difficult to suppress. Jim became so agitated at one point that he stood and moved in the darkness toward Benson. He stopped abruptly and repeated the mantra in his mind: Stick to the plan. Stick to the plan. Stick to the plan.

Benson made another round. This time he did something different. He came to the guard shack and switched on a light over a writing ledge. He had a pencil in his hand.

My God! Jim screamed in his mind. It's not Benson!

Jim's breathing was erratic, and his shaking hands made focusing difficult. It was an older man, maybe 50. It raced through his mind over and over: I almost killed an innocent man! Lord, what would I do? I couldn't live with that. Oh, God, forgive me for what I almost did.

Jim made his way to the car and drove to the train station parking lot. He backed into a space between two cars. It took almost an hour for him to settle down, but sleep finally came.

He didn't want to be seen at the railway station again, so after daylight, he walked up the street until he found an open café. Over breakfast, he devised several versions of what he would say, depending on who answered at the boarding house.

He dropped a nickel in the telephone located in a back corner of the café. His hand was shaking as he lifted the ear piece.

"Yes? Number, please."

"CT 116, please."

"One moment. I'll connect you."

"Hello." It was the same woman.

"Tom Benson, please."

"He's not here. Can I take a message?"

"I have a package for him. It's important."

"Well, let's see. Uh, he probably don't want this gettin' out, but he's in jail."

Jim hesitated, then said in his friendliest voice, "Oh, no, not again. What are we gonna do with him?"

"Lordy, honey, I don't know. They got him for drunk and disorderly conduct over at Lucy's tavern last night. He missed work, and the company ain't goin' to like that."

"When'll he be out, you reckon?" asked Jim.

"I'd say this evening or early tomorrow morning. They normally let 'em out to go back to work."

"When's his next off day, if you don't mind me askin'?"

"Hon, he works six days a week, off on Sunday."

"Wonder if he needs bonding out?"

"Naw, the company generally bonds them out and takes it outta their pay."

"Well, I appreciate it, and don't mention the surprise, now."

"Oh, no, it'll be our secret," she replied.

"Thanks again. Goodbye."

"'Bye, honey."

Jim couldn't believe his good fortune. He now knew pretty much everything he needed to know. He walked to his car and headed home.

On the outskirts of town, he pulled over, checked for cars in each direction, and quickly switched plates. On the drive home, he talked himself through his plan for the following week.

It's important that the body is never found. That means I will need to bury him deep. If he were in a shallow grave, animals might dig him up. I need to dig the grave next week, then kill him and bury the body the week after that. But what if somebody discovers the hole next week? I need something to cover it. It's gotta be lightweight so I can carry it in my rucksack.

He finally decided that a net would work. He could cover it with leaves and light brush to hide it.

Then there's that big pile of dirt, he thought. I'll just stack brush over it and hope nobody discovers it. I'll take a flashlight to check it before I kill Benson, to make sure it hasn't been disturbed. There's that word again—kill. Well, I might as well say it. That's what I'm gonna do to the son of a bitch!

I'll need a shovel and maybe a mattock, he thought.

Then his attention turned to what would happen when Benson didn't show up for work. More important, what would his landlady think? No one would skip town and leave all their belongings behind!

What if he left a note? Jim thought. No, the landlady might realize it's not his handwriting. I don't know how far he went in school. He might not be able to write, or maybe he just prints his letters.

He dismissed it as too dangerous to approach the boarding house with a note.

It finally came to him.

I'll print a note that simply says, *I QUIT, TB*, and tape it to the fence or guard shack. Then I'll bury him. The people at work won't think much about it—they'll just hire somebody to take his place. His landlady will think maybe he's in jail in another county. After a few months, she'll give away or sell his things. His mother probably won't miss him for a month or two. I can't imagine that he writes her very often, if at all. The police won't investigate it. There's no body, no crime. They'll figure he stole something and left town on the run.

There were several hours of daylight left when he neared Eaton. He decided to visit Ray and Josie before going to Mrs. Lowery's. Josie convinced him to stay for supper. Jim explained the night school program to them over supper. Josie seemed to be especially interested, but Ray didn't have much to say.

On the way home, Jim considered stopping to see Toby, but he decided to go home and write Lilly instead. He took a bath, then wrote Lilly a long letter once again, telling her how much he had enjoyed their time together. He added, *Especially Dawson.*

CHAPTER 16

Lilly and Robert stepped off the train and headed toward the Arcadia Manor Inn for supper. It had been a gorgeous day. Robert had been the perfect gentleman, and the scenery on the excursion was spectacular.

He took her hand and placed it through his arm as they walked. "It's been a lovely day, Lilly. The vistas were surpassed only by your beauty," he said sincerely.

"You do know how to flatter a lady," she replied. She had enjoyed the day, except for the nagging guilt that she was betraying Jim. On the other hand, she thought, we're not engaged, and we're free to date other people. Then she wondered how she would feel if she knew that Jim was on a date right now in Ohio.

During supper, they heard music strike up in the adjoining room. Robert paid the check and led her into the small ballroom.

"Robert, we need to get on home," she protested.

"Oh, Lilly, it's early. It's at least two hours before dark," he said as he put his arm around her and began to waltz.

He held her close as they danced around the room. They were very good together, and people began to watch them. Gradually everyone stopped dancing to admire the handsome couple. Lilly spotted her Aunt Alma watching them with her hands clasped beneath her chin, a smile on her face.

When the music stopped, Lilly led Robert over to her aunt and introduced them.

"Well, I see that great beauty runs in the family," said

Robert.

"You're too kind, Mr. Leatherwood, but I thank you just the same," Alma gushed.

They walked to the car hand in hand. Once in the car, Lilly said, "Robert, it's been a lovely day. Thank you."

"The pleasure was all mine," he replied and squeezed her hand as he engaged the clutch.

About halfway to Holston Landing, Robert eased the car into a pull–off on the bluff overlooking the river.

"What are we doing?" asked Lilly.

"I thought this would be a great place to watch the setting sun," he replied as he killed the engine. "The end to a perfect day."

He took her hand in his as they admired the various colors of dusk's fading light. As the glowing ball slipped from sight, shafts of red and orange–hued light beamed skyward between the clouds in the center of the horizon.

He put his arm around her and kissed her slowly and tenderly. "It was a beautiful day, thank you," he whispered.

Before she could gather herself to answer, he started the car and pulled onto the road. They recounted favorite sights on the excursion until they reached her house. He walked her to the door and kissed her cheek.

"I'll pick you up at 9:00 in the morning. Thanks again." He turned and walked away.

"Good night. Thank you!" she called.

"Good night," he said over his shoulder.

*****

The following Tuesday in Ohio, Jim bought a large seining net and borrowed a shovel and mattock from Ray. The flashlight, field glasses, and other gear were stowed in his rucksack. He put them all on the back floorboard of his car and covered them with a tarp.

On Friday afternoon, he secured the company truck, picked up his check from Mr. Calhoun, and walked home with Richmond on his mind. He was deep in concentration as he mounted the steps and entered the boarding house. To his surprise, and somewhat to his irritation, Mrs. Lowery and his fellow boarders were throwing him a 21st birthday party. He had not corrected the age given in the newspaper article the year before, and he certainly didn't want Connie to know he was just 19 today.

Being with Toby only sparingly over the last two months had left him feeling guilty and shameful. He went there occasionally when he wanted to talk—and when he needed her.

I've had so much on my mind lately, he thought, as they sang Happy Birthday to him. But that's no excuse. I must apologize and make it up to her.

Mr. Johnson quipped, "We won't have to slip you a drink anymore. You can buy your own, now!"

As the laughter subsided, Mrs. Lowery shook a disapproving finger at Johnson and said, "Just for that, you can help me clear this table."

Later, Jim slipped away to his room as the men on the porch passed a bottle while debating the merits of the two presidential candidates, Alfred E. Smith and Herbert H. Hoover. Once in his room, he pored over the Richmond checklist until satisfied that everything was in order and ready for the next day's trip.

He pulled away from the boarding house just after 7:00 the next morning. The plan was to arrive in Richmond by lunchtime and then determine if he could drive behind the hill in the rear of the construction company. He would hike over the hill to the burial site and dig the grave during the afternoon. If he determined that it was too risky, he would wait until dark and dig through the night.

Jim made it to Richmond a few minutes before 1:00 p.m.

The sandwiches in the seat beside him had been purchased 20 miles up the road. Jim drove a half mile past the company and turned right down the narrow lane. He was in luck. The lane curved right and led him behind the hill in back of the construction company. Apparently the lane had not been used in quite some time. There were muted tire tracks with weeds growing in the center.

The lane halted abruptly at a large rusty gate with a weathered *NO TRESPASSING* sign attached. Jim approached the gate and looked through it at an abandoned rock quarry. Faded evidence strewn here and there confirmed that lovers had parked here at some time in the last few months. He would need to find a place to hide the car.

Finally, he settled on a spot and headed up the back side of the hill. Once he located the burial site he had selected the previous week, he sat down with his canteen and waited and watched. After almost an hour, Jim was satisfied that the place was remote enough to dig during daylight.

He retraced his steps to the car, gathered his gear and lunch, and headed back. Off and on, he could hear the machines running at the company's compound, but he was convinced that no one would be able hear his digging. After a sandwich, he began to dig.

Only two feet deep and I'm already tired, he thought.

He put down the mattock, and as he reached for the canteen, movement slightly below him and to the right caught his eye. He recoiled, frozen by fear, then hit the ground in the shallow hole. Two men were headed straight for him.

Oh, Lord, he thought, what will I tell them I'm doing? Will they report me to the police? Oh, Jesus, please.

Jim decided he should stand up, and if seen, tell them he was digging a grave for his dog. I can't let them see me here lying in a grave, he thought.

He peeked out toward them. Wait, he thought, they're not

men. It's two boys, and they've turned uphill.

He watched them until they disappeared over the rise.

They'll see my car, he worried.

Jim maneuvered up to the top and sneaked a quick look. The boys had veered left and down toward the lane. They wouldn't see his car. Jim watched them go out of sight, then returned to his work.

He looked at his watch. Almost 5:00 p.m., and a little over four feet down. I haven't worked so hard since I was back on the farm, he lamented to himself. He placed his watch beside the canteen and resumed digging. About three and a half hours of daylight left, he figured. I can do it, I can do it, he said over and over as he worked.

Light was fading fast when he finished. The sun had been behind the hill for well over an hour. He struggled out of the hole and took a swig from the canteen. After a brief rest, he placed the net over the hole and anchored it on each side. Then he gathered leaves and other debris and carefully spread it over the net. Stepping back to inspect it, he judged it not good enough. After rearranging it to his satisfaction, Jim gathered the brush that would hide the pile of dirt.

*****

"Lilly Mae!" her mother called.

Lilly jumped. She hadn't heard her mother on the stairs, and now she was standing in the doorway to her room.

"Honey, are you looking at that package again? You need to decide. If you want to keep it, keep it. If not, send it back. Don't keep torturing yourself."

"I will, Mama," she said as she turned her head to hide the tears in her eyes. Lilly put the necklace down and reread the letter for the fourth time. It was a sweet letter urging her to keep the necklace. He recounted their time together—the train excursion and the trip to Cumberland Gap the day after. He described it as a beautiful experience with a beautiful person. Only the two of them knew what he really meant.

He had given the diamond necklace to her as they sat near the falls at Cumberland Gap. She had refused it as too much, too expensive. It must have cost $200 or more, she thought. He had insisted that she try it on.

She remembered the details vividly. As he closed the clasp, he kissed her neck, but she quickly moved away. He asked her to at least wear it for the afternoon and then decide. Back at the car, he steered her to the side mirror and commented how beautiful the necklace looked on her. They kissed, and then inside, they kissed again. The setting was very romantic. The entire two days had been romantic, and things had gotten out of hand.

It wasn't any more his fault than mine, she thought as she looked out the bedroom window. I was upset and immediately insisted that he take back the necklace, but now here it is again. What should I do? she pondered.

*****

Jim sat in the dark, catching his breath and contemplating his next move. I'll put this gear in the car, he thought, then come back with the field glasses and watch Benson.

He returned with a flashlight along with the binoculars. After working his way to the observation point, he focused on the man walking the fence. It was pitch dark except for the night lights at the office and the garage.

He watched the routine for a couple of hours to insure that nothing had changed. When the night watchman left the compound to check the other building, Jim got a good look at him under the office light. It must be Benson; it was a young man of about 20. Jim decided that the tree between the compound and the office building was his best vantage point for jumping Benson. He would like to do it right now, but knew he was too tired. He would hit Benson with the blackjack as he passed the tree, then drag him up the hill. Getting him up the hill would take time and energy.

Jim felt his way up the hillside through the brush and trees. It was much more difficult than he had imagined. Once safely across the crest, he was able to see with an occasional short burst from the flashlight.

He drove through town, then switched the tags. The first three hours of driving sped by as he visualized the plan for next weekend in Kentucky, but exhaustion began to overtake him. When Jim awoke with a start, only the two wheels on the left side of the car were in contact with the roadway surface. He overcompensated and almost ran off the other side of the road before braking to a stop.

I've got to find someplace to park and get a few hours of sleep, he decided.

He flicked the flashlight on to check the time.

What? I don't...

His thought trailed off as he struggled to get his eyes and mind working together. His wrist was bare.

"Where's my watch?" he said aloud as the adrenaline began to kick in.

Dread and fear spread quickly throughout his body and then slowly settled in his gut as he realized that the watch was on the dark hillside in Richmond. He had taken it off to dig. I placed it by my canteen, he remembered.

Over the next 20 minutes, he agonized over what to do.

Do I take my chances and leave it there until next weekend, or do I go back and get it tonight? he asked himself.

After weighing the pros and cons, he decided that he must go back. After turning the car around, he quickly calculated that it would require three hours to get there, approximately 30 minutes to retrieve the watch, and three hours just to get back to this point—still three hours from home.

It was almost noon when he stretched out on the bed in his room. In his mind, he relived that last night with Lilly. "I miss her," he whispered. It would be a long time before he saw her again. His thoughts eventually turned to Toby, and he yearned for dance night as he drifted off to sleep.

After the nap, he cleaned up and walked up the street for dinner. Later, after nodding off while working on his school workbook, he finally gave up and went to bed. Twelve and a half hours had passed by the time he got up to get dressed for work.

Thursday night at class, he completed a progress test and asked Mrs. Gladden if she could grade it right then.

She was about to say no when she looked up at him. She read the anticipation in his face and said, "All right, Jim, have a seat." She quickly graded it as the other students filed out.

"Ten point five, Jim. I'm very proud of you."

"What exactly does that mean, Mrs. Gladden?" he asked.

"It means that you're halfway through your sophomore year in high school," she replied.

"That's good, ain't it?"

"Isn't it," she corrected him. "Yes, Jim, that's very good progress in such a short time. If you keep working hard, you'll have a diploma in a year or so."

"Thanks, Mrs. Gladden. I'll see you Tuesday night."

He sat in the car, his mind racing. I could have a diploma soon. Maybe go to college one day. But what if something goes wrong this weekend? I could go to prison. I would lose Lilly. I would lose everything. But what about Annie? What about my promise to her? *Benson could rape and kill another little girl!*

The rage was back; the images were back. The thoughts raced through his mind yet again. He could hear his little sister begging for someone to help her. No one came.

I wasn't there to help. If only I had gone with her that day!

His eyes filled with tears, and sobs overwhelmed him.

He finally recovered and quickly looked around. No one was there; he was alone. He wished he had someone to talk to, someone to help him Saturday night. But he knew that was impossible. He would do it alone.

Saturday morning after breakfast, Jim sat in his room, thinking through the details. He would need his pistol, blackjack, flashlight, field glasses, shovel, rucksack, and canteen. He went over the list until he was confident that he had everything.

Later, sitting in the car in front of Mrs. Lowery's, he visualized the steps in his plan. When he came to the part where he would drag the body up the hill, it hit him like a ton of bricks. He had forgotten the note! He was nervous again, feeling the panic in his churning stomach.

He returned to his room, printed the note, and took the tape from his nightstand drawer. Back in the car, he went over the scenario again. Certain that he had covered everything, he headed to Kentucky.

After supper on the outskirts of Richmond, he switched the plates and drove through town, past the company, then parked in the pull–off a quarter mile past the compound. He rejected the lovers' lane on the back side of the hill as too risky. A car parked there without an occupant would be out of place, unusual.

When dusk passed into darkness, he put the keys under the seat and headed out, once again staying inside the woodline. He tripped several times over limbs and logs. It wasn't this dark the last time I did this, he thought.

It started sprinkling. He stopped to rest and look around. It dawned on him that it was darker this time because of the clouds and rain. He could see the halo of lights ahead and to his right. Is the rain a problem or an advantage? he asked himself. As he caught his breath, it occurred to him that shoveling mud could be a major problem. Should he call it off and go home? He opted to press on and decide later.

Once he reached the observation point, he quietly lowered the rucksack and shovel to the ground. He pulled out the field glasses and tried to focus. He was shaking uncontrollably. The field glasses were of no use to him.

After talking himself down, he focused the binoculars and saw the man walking the fence. He wasn't sure if it was Benson. The light rain was a problem. I'll edge down the hill to get a closer look, he decided. Finally, he determined it was the younger man.

It's him, the monster, he thought, grinding his teeth.

Jim picked up the shovel and carried it up the hill to the hole. After placing it on the brush pile, he returned to his position. A strange calmness spread over him, and he relaxed. Once Benson's patrol led him to the opposite side of the garage building, Jim moved out with the pistol, the flashlight, and the blackjack.

Jim made it to the tree undetected and readied the blackjack. The pistol was secured in one back pocket, the flashlight in the other. The note and tape were in his right front pocket. He was ready.

Benson came to the gate, unlocked it, and headed to the office building. As he passed the tree, Jim hit him. Benson's body jerked once and then fell to the ground.

Jim picked up Benson's flashlight and searched him for a weapon. Then he removed his billfold to search for an ID.

Jim's hands were shaking again. He fumbled through the wallet, and two pieces of paper fell to the ground. Jim looked around, then flicked on the light: *Employee Number 22, Tom Benson*. Bingo, Jim thought. He returned the two cards to the wallet and put it back into Benson's pocket.

Jim secured his blackjack, rolled the body over, and began to drag it toward the woods. Eventually, every muscle in his body was screaming. This was harder than he had thought it would be.

He dropped the body just inside the woodline to catch his breath and look around. He was calm now, filled with a sense of relief.

"What?" Jim heard himself say as fear charged through his body. Benson was getting up, groaning, now on all fours. Jim reached for the blackjack and dropped it as he jerked it from his pocket. He went to his knees, searching for the weapon.

Jim hit Benson with his fist, but it was a glancing blow. Benson lunged and knocked Jim over. They grappled, and Benson ended up on top with his hands around Jim's throat. Jim swung wildly at him, but Benson tucked his chin to avoid the blows.

Jim was losing strength—couldn't breathe. No, no, he thought, I'm going to die, just like Annie!

He tried to loosen Benson's grip with one hand while the other hand was frantically slapping at the leaves, trying to locate the blackjack.

As his vision dimmed, Jim felt the hard leather. He gripped it and swung for the side of Benson's head. He missed the moving head! He swung again and this time caught the monster's jaw with a sickening thud. Benson's grip relaxed and Jim pushed him aside. Gasping for breath, Jim could hardly move.

Benson was moving again.

Jim hit him with a fist to the face. "That's for my sister," Jim hissed.

Benson mumbled, "Sister."

"That's right, my sister," Jim shrieked, and hit him again. "You raped her, you son of a bitch!" He hit him again.

Jim straddled him, retrieved his flashlight, and switched on the light. He wanted to see his bloody face—the face of the bastard that had killed his sister.

Benson said something through swollen, bloody lips. Jim

switched off the light and reached for his blackjack.

Benson mumbled, "Who?"

"Why?" Jim asked as he grabbed him by the throat. "Why?" he demanded as he shook him.

"Good," Benson said.

"Good what?" Jim demanded as he shook him.

"Stuff...," Benson mumbled through a broken jaw.

Jim began to cry and groan uncontrollably. Now he was choking Benson with both hands, rocking back and forth, sobbing, mumbling Annie's name as he gripped harder and harder, tighter and tighter.

Jim's mind raced with thoughts of Annie's suffering. As he slowly recovered his senses, he was frightened by a strange whining sound. He realized it was coming from deep within his own body. He slowly released his grip and rolled onto his back. He began to cry again. He lay there a good while, slowing his breathing and thinking of Annie.

He tried to swallow, but his mouth was too dry. After walking up the hill to get a drink from his canteen, he sat down to think. Leave no evidence. Leave no evidence.

He walked down to the body and checked to make sure he had everything. He switched on the light briefly and picked up the blackjack. His pistol was still wedged into his back pocket. He checked Benson's pocket for his flashlight. Not there. He turned on the light, spotted it, flicked off the flashlight, and then placed it back in Benson's pocket.

I need to get the note up first in case someone comes by the compound, he said to himself.

He took the note and tape and walked to the tree. Once he had checked to see that no one was around, he hurried to the main gate and attached the note.

Next, he carefully surveyed the area around the body again. Then he walked back up to his rucksack and secured everything inside except the flashlight. Jim took another drink of water and headed for the body.

He grabbed Benson under the armpits and started backwards up the hill. After several breaks to rest, he made it to the gravesite.

Jim sat down and waited for his breathing to return to normal.

Next, he rolled the body over face up, stood up, and switched the light on to make sure Benson was dead.

Jim flinched, jumped back, and dropped the flashlight.

Red eyes!

He was jolted to the core.

"Red eyes," he mumbled as he picked up the flashlight and frantically fumbled with the light switch. He bent over from the waist with his hands on his knees. Benson's red eyes were burned into his mind's eye.

He straightened up, and then, wiping away tears, he jerked the net free. He tried to move the body with his foot. Too heavy. On hands and knees, now, he rolled the body into the grave.

Jim picked up the shovel and began the two-hour task of filling the hole with dirt. The first two or three inches of dirt were wet, but after that, it was easier going. After finishing, he sat down to rest.

Next, he gathered leaves and small bits of debris to cover the mound. Jim knew that over time the grave mound would sink back to ground level and eventually to a few inches below. He briefly turned on the light and looked at his work. He gathered more debris and scattered it on the grave. He flicked on the light again and was satisfied this time.

After putting some of the brush that had previously covered the dirt pile over the grave, he used the remaining brush to cover the dirt pile residue. With a quick burst from the flashlight, he checked the area one last time.

Jim gathered his gear, along with the shovel and canteen, then moved to the observation site and quickly rechecked that area. Finally, he drew the rucksack onto his back and headed toward the car with the shovel. He moved very slowly to avoid falling. As before, he stayed in the woodline.

Once he reached the point in the woods opposite to where he had parked the car, he stopped and hunkered down. He had to cross about 20 yards of open ground, then cross the road to the car. He watched and listened. Satisfied that no one was around, he crossed the open ground, hurried through the barbed wire fence, and ran across the road to the car.

The car! *The car!* Where was it? He dropped the rucksack and shovel, and while frantically looking around, he stumbled over the shovel and fell. Bouncing up quickly, he looked among the trees. Maybe the car had rolled off. No, it was gone. His legs almost buckled. His heart was racing, and intense fear gripped his body. He sat down.

Think! Think!

It slowly dawned on him that the car had out-of-date license plates.

Maybe the police took it! What should I do? he wondered.

Jim carefully formulated a plan, hid the gear in the weeds, and began to walk toward town.

He kept to the back streets as he headed to the railway station. About 40 minutes later, he sat down on a bench beside the station.

Please let this work, he said to himself.

He pretended to be asleep, but kept an eye out.

Finally, he spotted a police cruiser slowly approaching the station.

Should I? Do I dare? he asked himself.

Jim jumped up and hurried to stop the police car. "Officer, I need some help," he said nervously.

"What ya need, son?'

"My car broke down and I was wonderin' if there's a garage open on Sunday."

"Broke down where?"

"On the edge of town, down that way," Jim said as he pointed east.

"What kinda car?"

"It's a Model A Ford."

"We pulled that car in earlier this evening," the officer replied. "Son, it's got old tags. Thought it was stolen. Can ya prove it's yours?" the officer asked as he got out of the car.

"Yes, sir," Jim replied. "The papers are in it."

"You got any ID, son? How'd you get so dirty?"

"Yes, right here," Jim said as he reached for his billfold. "I messed up my clothes trying to fix the car."

"Stop!" commanded the officer. "Put your hands up. I'll get it out."

Jim raised his hands as the officer patted him down. The officer secured Jim's billfold and looked for an ID.

"Jim Taylor, Eaton, Ohio," the policeman read out loud. The officer opened the back door and told Jim to get in.

"What's wrong?" asked Jim.

"We'll go down to the station and figure this out. I said, get in."

Jim thought his heart would jump out of his chest. On the ride to the station, he breathed slowly, trying to calm himself.

The policeman led him inside and presented him to the desk sergeant. After the sergeant was briefed, he said, "Let's start from the beginning. What were you doing here in the middle of the night?"

"Well, I was out on Route 25 headed home to Ohio. I was hungry, and I saw the sign pointing to Richmond. Then I drove through town looking for a place to eat. I started to turn around in a pull–off, and the engine died. I tried working on the car but couldn't get it started. I finally decided to walk to town and wait for something to open so I could eat and find help with getting the car started. Then I found the train station and slept on a bench until I spotted this officer," he said, pointing to the officer who had brought him in.

"If you're from Ohio, why do you have out-of-date Kentucky plates?" the officer asked.

"Well, I guess it was a joke. My friends in Virginia have done it before. You know, hoping I'd get stopped by the law."

"So these so-called friends would keep your plates?" the officer asked incredulously.

"I don't know. The last time they did it I found them on the back floorboard," Jim replied.

The police officer stood up. "The car locked?" he asked.

"No, I don't think so. I don't understand."

"Hold him here," the officer said to the desk sergeant. He returned with the Ohio license plates.

"You mean my car is right here?" blurted Jim.

"It's out back behind the fence," the desk sergeant replied.

"So, can I go try to get it started?" asked Jim.

"There's a tow fee. Four dollars."

Jim paid the fee and pocketed the receipt. As he was leaving, the desk sergeant called out, "We've always got a mechanic in jail back here. Want me to get one up?"

"Well, now that it's getting daylight, I can see. Let me try it first. If I can't get it started, I'll come back," Jim replied.

The police officer headed outside, saying, "Come on, I'll let you through the gate."

Jim's heart was racing again. The officer unlocked the gate and followed him to the car.

"I can take it from here. Thanks, Officer," said Jim.

"I'll wait to make sure it starts."

Jim got in and searched for the key under the seat while pretending to fiddle with wires under the dashboard. The keys were not there! He plunged his hand farther back and felt them. He eased them to the ignition, then got out and raised the hood.

He tinkered under the hood until the officer looked toward

the station. Jim removed a spark plug wire, then got in the car and tried to start it. The engine rumbled but would not fire. Jim got out and bent over the fender, replaced the wire, and got in to try again. The engine fired to life.

Jim thanked the officer and commented that he was going back out to where he broke down and look for his flashlight. He pulled out of the lot and waved to the officer.

Driving past the construction company, he saw the note taped to the gate. After recovering the rucksack and shovel, he headed back to Ohio, his hands unsteady on the wheel.

CHAPTER 17

1928–1929

Over the next few weeks, Jim tried to keep busy in order to push the overwhelming thoughts of Kentucky from his mind. He resumed his schoolwork and helped Ray on the farm on weekends, but he couldn't shake the persistent dark mood that had enveloped him.

Eventually, Connie pulled him aside and emphatically asked what was wrong.

"Nothing," Jim replied.

"Something's bothering you, Rascal. Is it something I can help you with?"

"No, nothing's wrong."

"Well, if you decide you need someone to talk to, I'll be here."

Jim looked away. After a brief silence, he asked, "Can I come by tonight?"

"Sure. What time?"

"How about 6:30?"

"See you then," she replied as a customer approached.

Jim finished his route just after 5:00. After freshening up at the boarding house, he secured the bottle of wine from under his bed and headed for Toby's.

She greeted him at the door, wiping her hands on an apron that partially covered her light blue, knee-length dress. The radiance of Connie's face and her inviting smile were like a beacon of light to Jim.

"Something smells good," he said.

"Well, you should be able to guess. It's one of your favorites."

"Pork chops!" he said. "I can't wait."

Toby did most of the talking as they ate. Finally, she asked, "Rascal, did you break up with your girl in Virginia?"

"No. I told you, nothing is wrong. Everything is fine."

Toby studied his face as she turned on her new radio. "I'm going to find some music and see if you still remember our dance steps."

Jim cleared the table as she searched for a Cincinnati station.

They waltzed around the store as Jim counted steps in his mind. He was stiff and somewhat mechanical in his movements. Eventually he moved without counting, and their bodies became one as they glided around the room.

"I'd forgotten how good this feels, Toby."

"The dancing or my body?"

"Both."

The music morphed into a Redman tobacco commercial. Jim held her close as they stood in silence, waiting for the music to resume. Connie wanted to ask again, but she instinctively knew to wait until he was ready to talk.

The radio host played mostly waltzes, but an occasional dance tune left them breathless.

When the music finally gave way to the news report, Jim led her to the bed, where they quickly shed their garments. As the newscaster reported on the Summer Olympic Games in Amsterdam, they made love—slowly at first, then lustily building to a furious, ferocious, final release.

Afterward, they lay in a heap with his head on her breasts. She felt the sobs that he tried to suppress, then the tears on her chest. She started to ask, then thought the better of it. Instead, she held him close and slowly stroked his hair.

*****

On Tuesday night, Jim asked Mrs. Gladden if he could talk to her after class. "Mrs. Gladden, when do you think I can take a progress test?"

"Well, Jim, I must say that you have advanced quickly over the last few weeks," she replied. "Let's get through Thanksgiving and Christmas and go from there."

"That'll be fine, ma'am. I'll be ready."

*****

During the next three months, Jim studied every weeknight and only allowed himself free time on weekends. Despite his busy schedule, the dreaded web of depression engulfed him frequently.

In November, Jim received a letter from his father.

Dear Son,

Well our man won. He will be a good president. My brother John won $25 on the election. I fired off 6 rounds in the air. Yore mother thought I was crazy. General Lee Sexton lost $100. 29 people in jail in Batesville. A man robbed and killed in Holston Landing. We broke up 2 stills last month.

Been rainy and cole. Rob Boatwright preaching now at church not as good as Dad but will do. Sherif says Benson out on parol. His son is missing in Kentucky. Mother ain't heard from him in months. Sawmill purty slow. Too much rain. Addie been sick. Hope you come for Xmas.

Yore father,

G.W. Taylor

Missing in Kentucky!

Jim read the letter again and then began to write a reply. His hands were shaking. He would take a long walk first. Later, he began the letter to his parents again.

Nov. 28, 1928

Dear Dad,

I won't be able to come home for Christmas. I can't get off work.

Business is good and Mr. Bivens is short a man or two. Will mail gifts for you and Mother. Tell everyone "Merry Christmas"—will come home in June.

Ray and family are well. Good winter wheat crop this year. Had Thanksgiving dinner with them.

Had to have transmission fixed on car—cost $28. I should have been a mechanic. They make good money. Weather is cold and windy. Bought a new coat so staying plenty warm.

The Benson boy that is missing probably went out West. Lots of men here are moving out there. The gangsters in Chicago are in the papers almost every day. Maybe they will kill each other off and rid us of the problems. Maybe the new President can have them all put in jail.

I'll close for now—give my love to Mother.

Your Son,

Jim

*****

Jim's first Christmas away from home, coupled with his instinct that something had changed about Lilly, was overwhelming. He settled into a melancholy that was hard to shake. He spent Christmas day at Toby's and was thankful for her company.

In January 1929, Mrs. Gladden tested his progress. "Eleven

point three, Jim," she reported as she handed him the progress report. "Your advancement has been just amazing."

"That's a junior, right?" he asked.

"Yes, one third of the way through your junior year."

"When do you think I'll finish?"

"At the rate you're going, my guess is about a year. Your progress will slow a bit, since the junior and senior years are the most difficult."

"Thanks, Mrs. Gladden. I'll see you Thursday night."

On his route the next day, he informed Toby of his progress. "That's great, Rascal. We'll have to celebrate when you get the time."

"How about tonight? Are you free."

"Sure. Same time?"

"I'll be here at 6:30, and I'll bring something to celebrate with."

After completing his route, he walked home, thinking of the celebration that night. After a hot bath, he dressed, then eased the bottle of bourbon from his drawer.

When he arrived at Toby's, she hugged him tightly and pressed her breasts firmly against his chest.

"What's for supper?" he asked as he squeezed her.

"Nothing fancy, but something you like—hot dogs. What's in the bag?"

"A little something to celebrate with," he replied as he pulled the bourbon from the bag.

She took the bottle and placed it on the table. After pouring them a drink, she asked if he had had a good day.

"It was freezing today. Maybe this will thaw me out," he said as he lifted the glass.

"Wait!" Connie replied as she clinked her glass to his and offered a toast. "To your success in night school."

After dinner and several drinks later, he asked her to take a bath with him.

"Sorry, Rascal, I can't. It's that time of the month."

He remembered her helping him to bed and taking him into her mouth, but little else. Waking to the smell of bacon, he jumped up and asked, "What time is it?" The pain in his head pushed him back down on the bed.

"It's 4:35. You got a little high last night."

"High? I was drunker than a bicycle!"

She laughed until tears appeared. She caught her breath and started to say something, but was cut short by giggles, then hearty laughter again.

"What's so funny?" he queried.

"I just never heard that expression before. The bath is ready. Get cleaned up. Then we'll have breakfast."

It was the first time he had spent the night with a woman, and he remembered very little of it.

CHAPTER 18

The letter from Lilly came in late April. She would graduate the following month and would be spending a great deal of time trying to secure a teaching job. She would be very busy, but hoped to see him while he was in on vacation in June.

He reread the letter, hanging on every word. What was she telling him? He had assumed they would be spending almost every day together.

Something has changed, he thought. She would be a college graduate, a teacher. He was just a delivery–truck driver. There was no future for them. Is that what she was saying?

What should I write back to her? he wondered.

He sat on his bed, hurt, numb. Finally, he decided to wait a couple of days before responding. He would like to ask Connie's advice on what the letter meant. Would she be upset that he was asking for advice concerning another girl?

A few days later, he sat at Toby's kitchen table with the letter.

She read it twice. "I don't know, Rascal. What were her other letters like?"

"Well, she would tell about things at college and at home. And she would tell me how she missed having my arms around her."

"What about letters just before you were coming home?"

"She would have suggestions on places we could go—you know, a picnic or to lunch in Dawson, things like that."

"Did you have sex when you went home?"

"No, just playing around. You know, everything but the real thing. Why, what's that got to do with it?"

"Maybe nothing. I'm just trying to figure out how close y'all were."

He paused to think, then said, "I told her I was saving up for a ring, but she always said we were too young, and that she needed to finish school and teach awhile."

"Do you know if she's been dating other boys?"

"Just for dances and stuff. She said they didn't mean anything to her."

Connie rubbed the back of his hand as tears came to his eyes.

"Rascal, it may be nothing. Maybe she was just in a hurry when she wrote the letter. You know it has to be hectic right now. She's studying for final exams and going through preparation for graduation. She has a lot on her mind right now. Or it could be—"

"Or it could be that she's met someone else," he finished the sentence for her.

"That's not what I was going to say, but truthfully, that's always a possibility. She may have met someone, or she may just be thinking of her future. She's graduating from college. Not many girls accomplish that. She's going to be a teacher—a professional. Just think! Ten years ago, women couldn't even vote in an election."

Jim took a deep, quivering breath and wiped the tears from his face. "Thanks for listening, Toby."

She hugged him, hiding her own tears. Was she crying for Jim or herself? She wasn't really sure. Maybe both, she thought.

*****

On Sunday morning, Jim answered Lilly's letter. He wrote that he looked forward to seeing her in June and congratulated her on her upcoming graduation. A few minutes later, he joined the others for breakfast downstairs.

Only four other men had opted to get up early for the full breakfast. John Simmons asked Jim if he was going to church with him this morning.

“Sure am,” replied Jim.

“Okay, Jim. Meet you down here at 10:45.”

Several months prior, John had invited Jim to attend the Baptist church down the street from the boarding house. Ever since, they had gone together almost every Sunday. Jim was struck by the difference between this Baptist church and the one back home. Piney Level was a one–room log structure. This church was a large brick structure with a basement and classrooms for Sunday school.

He enjoyed the services, especially the singing and silent time for meditation and prayer. It seemed to help combat the bouts of melancholy and depression that plagued him from time to time.

*****

Two months later, in June, Jim arrived at his Virginia home just after daylight. He was tired, but not sleepy. His mother had held off cooking breakfast until he arrived. He was looking forward to her sawmill gravy and cat head biscuits.

His father caught him up on all the local news but didn’t mention old man Benson or his son, Tom. Jim considered asking about the missing boy but decided not to stir that pot.

“Is Rob out of school for the summer?” Jim asked.

“Yep. Saw him last Sunday. Said for you to come see him.”

“Well, I think I’ll get a couple of hours sleep, then take a ride over to his place.”

“Be sure and visit your Aunt Addie. She’s not well.”

“I’ll go by her place when I get up.”

He hardly recognized his Aunt Addie. Drastic weight loss had sapped her strength and revealed deep wrinkles in her skin.

"Let me help you out to the porch, Aunt Addie. The sunshine'll do you good."

"No, honey, I don't have the strength," she replied. "Can't even make it to the outhouse. Have to use that blame chamber pot."

"How do you manage here by yourself?"

"Your mother comes several times a day. Stays some nights, too. Darlin', the truth is, I'm dyin'. But that's okay. I've had a good life, and I'm ready for the Lord to take me."

"Don't talk like that, Aunt Addie. You just need to gain a little weight. You'll be fine."

"Hand me that pipe, will you, son?'

Jim handed her the corn cob pipe and asked, "When'd you start smoking?"

"Snuff got to where it made me sick to my stomach," she lamented as she lit the pipe. She exhaled the blue smoke and tried to lean up in her chair. "Jim, I'm at peace except for one thang. I wanted to live to see the son of a bitch that killed Annie hang. Promise me that you won't let 'em give up lookin' fer him."

Jim was taken aback. He had never heard Aunt Addie cuss before. "We won't give up. He'll pay," Jim promised.

*****

Mrs. Boatwright came to the door wearing a big smile and wiping her hands on her apron. "Jim Taylor, it's so great to see you! How've you been?"

"Just fine, ma'am. How're you and all the folks?"

"Oh, we're tolerable. Rob's been looking forward to seeing you. He's out at the barn. Go on out there."

"Thanks, Mrs. Boatwright."

Jim eased to within six feet of Rob's back and yelled, "Hey, preacher man!"

Rob jumped, dropping the shovel. "You scared me half to death," he said as he pumped Jim's hand.

"Need some help?" asked Jim.

"No, no. Pull up a hay bale and tell me what you been up to."

They chatted easily, catching each other up on their lives for the past year. Finally, Jim turned serious. "Rob, I need to talk to you confidentially."

"As a friend or as a minister?" Rob asked.

"What's the difference?"

"Well, if you're talking to me as a minister, anything you tell me is completely confidential. No one will ever know. I've been officially ordained as of two months ago."

"Yeah, I heard. Congratulations. I guess I'd like to talk to you as a minister."

"Okay. What's it about?"

"I, uh, I've been having sex with a woman in Ohio."

Jim relayed the entire story of his relationship with Toby. "I've asked forgiveness several times, but I keep going back to her."

"Jim, God created us, and he created us with desires. He knows that those desires are strong and that we are weak. Jesus said that you could be forgiven not seven times but seven times seventy."

"So you mean that someone can keep on sinning and just repent after each time?" Jim asked.

"No, that's not what I mean. It means you can be forgiven if you repent and are truly sorry. If you keep committing the same sin over and over, you must question whether you're truly sorry."

Noticing the contortions of confusion on Jim's face, Rob added, "Just remember, God's love is an unconditional love, no matter how bad the sin."

After a long pause, Jim asked, "No matter how bad the sin?"

"No matter how bad the sin," Rob repeated. "Anything else?"

"No, that's it," replied Jim.

"Stay for lunch with us," Rob insisted as he stood up.

"Well, it's hard to pass up your mother's cookin'. Let's go."

While they were walking to the house, Rob mentioned that Jim should go see Lilly. "I saw her last Sunday at church. She said to be sure and tell you to come see her."

After lunch, Rob walked him to his car and once again mentioned that he should go see Lilly.

*****

Lilly, dressed in overalls, was on her knees weeding a flower bed with her mother when Jim approached.

"Hey, college graduate!" Jim called out.

Lilly gave him a hug.

"Hello, Mrs. Larkey."

"Hello, Jim. It's good to see you. How's your Aunt Addie?"

"She pretty feeble. Lost a lot of weight."

"How about a glass of lemonade?" Lilly offered.

"Sounds good. Can I help with the flowers?"

"You kids go on and visit. I'll finish up here," Lilly's mother interjected.

They sat on the porch making small talk.

"That's a pretty necklace. Whoever picked that out has good taste," Jim joked.

"It was a beautiful Christmas present from a fellow up in Ohio, and I appreciate it very much."

"Mrs. Lowery, my landlady, helped me pick it out."

Lilly thought of the more expensive necklace hidden away in her room upstairs and felt a pang of guilt. "Well, she did a good job. It's very pretty. Jim, let's take a walk down by the river."

"Let's go."

On the river path, he took her hand. "I've never seen you in overalls," he said. "You look mighty sexy."

She stopped abruptly and blurted, "Jim, we need to talk."

"Okay. Let's talk.

"I've been practicing different ways to say this, but I'm just going to be direct. I've been dating other boys at school."

"I see," he said in a subdued tone. "Several different boys or just one?"

"Several," she lied. "I want you to date other girls, too. I think we're too young to get so serious. I want to get married and have children eventually, but I want to teach a few years first."

Jim studied her face intently.

"Say something, Jim. Tell me how awful I am, how dishonest I've been." She began to cry.

He took her in his arms and held her close as she sobbed. Finally, he whispered, "It's okay. Everything will work out." He stroked her hair. "You're not awful. You're the best person I've ever known. Shhhh. Shhhh."

He was shaken, hurt. But he was determined not to show it. He knew that he was guilty of far worse.

She broke the embrace and kissed him on the cheek.

Before she could speak, he asked, "Can we have lunch tomorrow?"

"I'd like that," she said as she wiped tears from her face and eyes. She felt as if a great burden had been lifted. She had dreaded this moment for months. It had been difficult to concentrate at school. Even though she felt a sense of loss, she was glad she'd taken her roommates' advice.

*****

After lunch the next day in Batesville, they returned to her house and walked along the river. He pulled her to him and kissed her tenderly.

"I think you'll be a great teacher, Lilly. You're smart and you have a good heart. Even if you find someone else, I want you to know that I'll always love you." Before she could speak, he put a finger to her lips, signaling that she didn't need to answer.

As they walked back to the house, she asked him, "Will you write me?"

"Absolutely. Will you write me?"

"Of course. Will I see you before you go back?" she asked.

"Probably not. I know you're busy with the job hunting, and I need to spend some time with my folks, especially Aunt Addie."

She walked him to the car and kissed him goodbye.

He drove to the river and crossed the swinging bridge to their special spot.

He sat there for two hours, absent-mindedly tossing rocks into the river and thinking, thinking. Finally, he walked back to the car and drove to the cemetery.

His visit with Annie was interrupted when his cousin, Scott, rode up on a horse. "You're mother said you might be up here. You need to come home. Aunt Addie's took a turn for the worse."

"How bad, Scott?"

"They don't think she'll make it through the night."

Jim hurried home and drove up the wagon road to her house. His mother was wiping Addie's face with a cool rag. Jim looked at Addie and then his mother. His mother shook her head slightly to signal that there was no hope.

"I'm goin' to go cool this rag," said his mother. Then she whispered, "She's too weak to speak, but you can say your goodbyes."

Jim placed his hand on Addie's cheek and leaned in close. "Aunt Addie. Aunt Addie."

She slowly opened her eyes and blinked twice as if to say hello.

He placed his lips near her ear and said, "We got him. We got Annie's killer. He's dead!"

She looked at him. Her dim eyes opened a little wider. Then she closed her eyes as the beginning of a smile formed on her lips.

*****

Addie took her last breath just after 2:00 a.m. that night. Less than 36 hours later, she was buried four graves down from Annie.

Lilly walked with Jim from the cemetery to the car. His father was sitting in the front passenger seat, his mother and Aunt Lois in the back.

Lilly said goodbye as she squeezed his hand, then added, "Remember to write."

"You, too," he replied, studying her face as if trying to memorize every feature.

"Goodbye," she said again.

"Goodbye," he said, almost in a whisper.

CHAPTER 19

1929–1930

Lilly and Jim continued to exchange letters infrequently. She had secured a job teaching eight grades in a one-room school, Chinquapin Elementary. Lilly relayed that her 21 students were aged six to 16 and that it was difficult work, but she loved the job and the kids. She didn't mention dating others, and neither did he.

On October 29th, the stock market crashed.

Everyone in town was talking about it. Jim didn't own stocks and didn't know anyone who did except for Mr. Bivens. From what he heard around the warehouse, Mr. Bivens had lost a great deal of his life savings. Within a few weeks, he knew it was true. He could read it in Mr. Bivens's face.

The widespread effect of the downturn came into sharp focus when Toby told him her business was off by 30 percent.

"Why?" he asked.

"People are cutting back—just buying the essentials."

"Why?"

"Because they're afraid it's going to get worse."

Over the next few months, Jim noticed the reductions in orders from his customers. That means Mr. Bivens's business is really hurting, he worriedly concluded.

He wrote home and asked his parents how they were getting by. They answered that they were fine, but that the plant in Dawson had let some people go. His father relayed that the sawmill business had really dropped off, but that he was still a part-time deputy.

Jim received a devastating letter in late February 1930. Lilly was engaged to someone named Robert Leatherwood.

He sat on the bed, his head in his hands. Lifting the letter off the floor, he stared at it as he ran a hand back and forth through his hair. The words were now a watery blur.

Jim felt sick and took deep breaths to stave off the nausea. Finally, he stood up and removed the bottle from the writing table drawer. Lilly's smiling face looked back at him from the frame on the table. He turned away and took a long pull on the bottle.

Within minutes he was in the bathroom, vomiting into the commode.

Did she know this was coming when he was with her this summer? he wondered.

Clutching the cold porcelain, he threw up again.

Back in his room, he read the entire letter.

She was sorry if she had hurt him. She knew he would be okay. He had probably met another girl by now. She wished only the best for him. She would always remember him as her first love. She hoped they could still be friends....

He sleepwalked through the next few weeks, missing three classes at night school and two Sundays in a row at church. Recurring depression was a problem.

Connie asked him the same question as the people at work.

"Nothing," was his pat answer.

"Look, Rascal, I think I know what's bothering you. Come see me and talk it out," Toby offered.

"I'll think about it," he replied to shut her up.

That night he sat at Connie's table and spat out all the details.

"Rascal," she said, "I know it hurts really bad, but you've got to snap out of it. You're a few weeks from taking the final test for your diploma. Don't throw away two years of work. If this recession gets worse, you'll need all the education you can get." Toby caressed his face and held him close, but she sensed that he didn't want it to go beyond that.

Finally, Jim took her advice and plunged back into his work and studies. Mrs. Gladden informed him that he needed to make up the missed classes before taking the test for his degree.

"I thought I could take it at any time—that it was based on my progress."

"That's true, Jim, but you need the last two math classes and the workbook exercises, in my opinion."

"Okay, Mrs. Gladden," he said as he expelled an exasperated breath.

In the meantime, Mr. Bivens had cut the work day for everyone from 10 hours to eight hours. The recession, later to become known as the Great Depression, was worsening. Jim's brother Ray was making it okay on the farm, but his brother John was laid off in Detroit. Jim had learned from talk at Mrs. Lowery's that the two banks in Oxford were in trouble and would probably merge. He didn't understand how that would succeed. In his opinion, the result would simply mean that the town would have one bank in trouble instead of two.

*****

He finished the test in an hour and 15 minutes and nervously handed it to Mrs. Gladden.

"Can you grade it now?" he whispered.

"No. I'm sorry, Jim. I'm not allowed to grade it. The state will grade it and notify you by mail."

"What if I fail?"

"I'm sure you did just fine. Try not to worry."

"But what if I do fail?"

"In that case, you'll have to put up with me for few more

lessons," she said with a smile.

"Mrs. Gladden, I really appreciate all you've done."

"You're welcome, Jim. I've enjoyed watching you grow as a student. Good luck!"

Two weeks later, Mrs. Lowery handed him the oversized envelope. He looked at the upper left-hand corner: *The State Board of Education, State of Ohio.*

He raced up the steps, tearing open the envelope as he went. He stopped at the top of the stairs to read the letter: *It is a distinct pleasure to inform you...*

He sat on his bed and carefully removed the stiff cardboard and the accompanying certificate.

It was one of the proudest moments of his life. He thought about his family and the fact that no one else had ever finished high school. If Annie were alive, she would be very happy for him, and she would certainly have been the next graduate in the family.

He had wanted to surprise Lilly with the news. That had been his plan all along.

Well, it certainly doesn't matter now, he thought.

Mother would congratulate him with that special sparkle in her dark eyes. Father would say little, no doubt. But he knew deep down that his dad would be very proud of him. Connie would be happy for him and would want to have a celebration party.

He looked at the clock—6:50 p.m. Since her business had fallen off, she had started closing later, at about 7:00. On his way downstairs for supper, he decided he would go see her and give her the good news.

It was a quarter of eight when he knocked on her door for the first time in over a month. He heard movement inside. He shifted the bag with the bottle to his left hand and knocked again.

The door opened just wide enough to reveal Connie's face.

"Hi, Jim," she said.

"Hey, Toby, I've got some good news!"

"Now's not a good time," she said.

"What's wrong? Not feelin' good?"

"No, uh, it's just not a good time. How about tomorrow?"

"Do you need help?" Jim asked. "Can I help with somethin'?"

"No, Jim. I have a visitor."

"A visitor?" He paused in awkward silence, then asked, "You mean a date?"

"Yes. Jim, I'm sorry. I haven't seen you in quite a while. I thought you didn't want to see me anymore. I'm sorry."

"No, that's okay." He stumbled through the words, trying to think of something to say, his face reddening by the second. He thought he heard a man's voice call out.

"Jim, can we talk tomorrow?" Connie said quickly.

"Yeah, that'll be fine. I shouldn't have just showed up like this. I'm sorry. I'll see ya."

For the first time, she noticed the bag in his hand as he walked to the car. She had been nervously concentrating on his face—that stunned look. "Damn, Rascal, damn!" she whispered to herself.

Jim was stunned and angry, too. Not at Connie, but at himself.

What did I expect? he asked himself. I've been foolish and selfish, thinking only of myself—thinking I could see her anytime I want.

He realized now that he had taken her for granted, had used her when it was convenient. Nevertheless, it had hurt him to the core and shaken his confidence.

As he lay in bed staring at the ceiling, the thought kept creeping back into his consciousness: Does she make love to him the way she did to me?

*****

In early May, Mr. Bivens sent word for Jim to come by the office.

"Hi, Jim. Come in and have a seat."

Jim looked around the office apprehensively. Mr. Bivens's normally clean desk was in disarray. A ledger book was open atop a sea of coffee-stained papers. The leafless, lifeless plant in the corner held wads of paper around the base of the brittle stem. The route map on the wall facing him contained scores of small holes where tacks, representing stores, had once been.

"Jim, my business has dropped to the point that I have to consolidate some routes. I'm sorry, but I have to let you go. I want to keep as many of my older employees as possible. I hope you understand. They have families."

"I understand, Mr. Bivens. I appreciate everything you've done for me."

"What will you do now? Where will you go?'

"Well, I'm not sure. I've got a brother in Detroit. He's laid off right now, but he might help me find something."

"What about your other brother, the one with the farm?"

"I could live with him for a while, but I doubt that he has work for me."

"You've been an excellent employee, Jim. I'd love to have you back when things get back to normal," Mr. Bivens said as he stood up and offered his hand.

Jim shook his hand and said, "Thank you, Mr. Bivens. Thank you for everything."

Jim worked the remainder of the week and picked up his final paycheck on Friday.

There was no work available in Detroit, and he was back home in Virginia within three weeks.

CHAPTER 20

Eight Years Later

1937

Jim awoke with a start. In his dream, he and Rob were racing their horses in a clearing on the bluff back home. His mother and Annie were picking berries, and he and Rob stopped to help. Rob's hands were bloody from pricks of the blackberry briars. They tried to help him, but the bleeding wouldn't stop.

Lilly stirred beside him, changing positions without waking up.

Fully awake, now, he stood in front of the window, staring into the darkness toward the lake. He didn't particularly like Detroit, but the money was good. He had first worked at a service station here until he got on at the Ford plant.

So much had happened since he had left home over nine years before. He recounted the events in his mind.

Lilly and I were dating—just kids, he now realized. She went off to college, and I left for the job in Ohio. She met Leatherwood, and I met Connie. I often wondered whether Lilly had slept with Leatherwood. After all, they were engaged. I stopped short of asking her many times. I didn't ask because I didn't want her to ask the same question of me.

I tracked down Benson and made sure he would never kill again.

Jim shuddered as he saw the red eyes in his mind's eye.

Other than hearing that Benson was missing, his name had never come up again.

Lilly began teaching, then wrote me that she was engaged. I graduated from high school and then lost my job early in the Depression. Going back home was difficult. I felt like a failure. It was good to see all my folks, but it wasn't easy to readjust. It was hard seeing Lilly from time to time, knowing that she was with someone else. I maintained my savings in the bank at Batesville, hoping I could still buy her a ring.

Then there was the farm work and the odd jobs—the six months of driving for Foremost Dairies before being laid off again. I remember how I would sneak off occasionally to the new movie theater in Dawson just to get away from everything and everyone.

I wrote Connie, telling her where I was and apologizing for the way I had treated her. She wrote back, catching me up on life in Eaton, Ohio and assuring me that no apology was needed. In the next letter, I told her that I missed her and often thought of her. I never received a reply.

The Depression worsened to the point that even the odd jobs dried up. As a last resort, I applied for Roosevelt's CCC program and spent six months near Richmond.

"That was the loneliest time of my life," Jim whispered to himself. "But before it was over, it became one of the happiest."

I wrote the letter to Lilly from camp after a weekend of drinking—telling her how much I missed her in my life. To my surprise, she wrote me back a warm letter, relaying the local news from back home and ending with a few lines telling me that they would be moving to California after the wedding.

Later, I wrote her back, thanking her for the books she had sent and describing my two years of study for a high school diploma in Ohio. She replied that she had no idea that I had been going to school all along, and how impressed she was with my determination. I still remember the exact words: "Learning that you were in night classes the entire time I was in college has had a profound effect on me." And I remember thinking: If I'd known it was going to have that effect, I would've told you a hell of a lot sooner.

Finally, I wrote her congratulating her on the upcoming wedding and telling her how much I admired her accomplishments in life. I wrote about my feelings for her and said that I would always love her.

Not long after that, she wrote that she had broken off her engagement. She didn't want to marry Leatherwood, and she didn't want to go to California. The shocking end of the letter informed me that it wasn't California that bothered her. It was that she was still in love with me!

Out of the window, Jim noticed the faint light of the winter sunrise on the lake. It became a spreading glow, changing from slightly pink to a pale blue accentuated by star-like electric lights on the horizon across the lake. The trees to his left gradually changed from formless shadows to stark skeletons, with every branch now visible against the emerging winter dawn.

Lilly turned over again, this time calling his name.

"I'm watching the sunrise. Go back to sleep, baby. You need your rest," Jim said in a hushed tone.

Her rhythmic breathing told him that she had fallen back asleep. She was six months pregnant with their second child. Their first, Shelly, was asleep in the adjoining room. She was 18 months old and thankfully slept like a log—usually not up before 8:00.

Jim spotted a long-necked bird in the shallows of the lake. Fishing for breakfast, he thought, as he lapsed back into his earlier recollections.

I was back from the CCC camp and seeing Lilly on a regular basis, but I couldn't find work. John was back on at the plant in Detroit and encouraged me to come up here. Lilly agreed to marry me after I got settled in Detroit.

There were the love letters back and forth, and the aching desire to see her. I eventually got on at the plant, and Lilly was teaching back home. Then the plans came together early in 1934. Lilly would finish the school year. I would find a house in Detroit. I could only get off work for the weekend plus one extra day. It turned out to be a busy three days.

I made a whirlwind trip to Virginia. Got a few hours of sleep, then we hit the road. We stayed in Ohio at my sister's house and got married just across the state line in Boston, Indiana.

Several of my Ohio relatives attended the wedding reception at my sister's home. Not one of Lilly's relatives was present, and I'm sure they were none too pleased back in Virginia. Our honeymoon consisted of one night in a hotel in Richmond, Indiana. But what a night it was—fresh flowers, champagne, room service, and making love to the love of my life. That night is probably the closest I'll ever come to heaven, he thought.

Then there were the letters from home detailing my father's health problems. He was suffering the effects of an apparent heart attack. The doctors weren't sure.

Lilly sat up in bed. "Come and snuggle with me," she invited.

He eased into bed beside her. Snuggling always turned into lovemaking; it had become their code word. Lilly went to relieve the pressure of the baby on her bladder. She returned, removed her gown, and pressed her body against him. They made love slowly, but passionately. According to Lilly, Jim's concern that he might hurt the baby was unfounded, but nevertheless, he worried each time.

"You're really something, woman!" he joked.

"Why?" she asked. "You know how I am when I'm pregnant."

"Yeah, I think the word's horny."

They lay as spoons. Jim loved to hold her this way, with one hand on her belly, anticipating the baby's kick. It was Saturday. They could enjoy the day together.

"Did you hear Shelly?" Lilly asked.

"Yeah, I think she's awake."

At last they heard her playing with a rattle. As always, they lay embraced, listening to her baby sounds until she called out. Finally, they heard her little voice: "Ma, Ma, Ma, Ma."

"Stay put. I'll get her," Jim offered.

He came back with Shelly and placed her between them.

*****

In April, Jim raced Lilly to the hospital, where she delivered a baby boy. Lilly had named Shelly, so it was Jim's turn. He named him Robby, after his best friend. "Maybe he'll be a preacher, too, like Rob," Jim commented.

The following months were difficult for them. Jim's father died, and they raced home in time for the funeral. Shelly was just under two years old when Robby was born. Lilly hadn't had a chance to make many friends, and the only relatives in Detroit were Jim's brother John and his family, who lived on the other side of the city. Jim sensed that Lilly was not happy, although she bravely tried to hide her feelings. She was homesick but would never admit it.

The problem came to a head in August, when Jim announced that he was going to be laid off. Lilly suggested that they call home and inquire about the job market, and Jim agreed. Lilly was glad to be going home, but she hated the thought of giving up the lake house.

It was a furnished, two-story clapboard house in excellent condition. Downstairs consisted of a living room, dining room, kitchen, and two bedrooms. The living room had a marble fireplace, and, like their bedroom, faced directly onto the lake.

The bath had a shower on city water.

She loved the shower. It reminded her of dorm life in college. The warm water on her neck and shoulders had eased her through many hectic days while tending to two babies still in diapers.

She seldom used the tub except for an occasional bath with Jim. The rooms upstairs were never used and were closed off to conserve heat. The breeze off the lake in summer kept the house cool and pleasant. The kitchen had an electric refrigerator, which eliminated the bother of an icebox.

*****

Back home, they lived with her parents on the river, and Mrs. Larkey's help with the kids was a godsend. Robby was less than six months old when they moved; Shelly was 28 months.

Jim immediately began looking for work after the move. He visited old friends and acquaintances to catch up on the local job scene and began applying for various jobs. He was told repeatedly that no jobs were available, but they would keep his application on file.

Jim and Lilly exchanged visits with Rob and his wife, Cindy, almost every weekend, and they were looking forward to entertaining them today.

Arriving at the Larkeys' right on time, the Boatwright family was welcomed to the chairs in the shade of the large porch. Robby Boatwright had met Cindy in business college. Now they had a boy, Hamilton, and a little girl, Jenny. Rob kept busy managing his father-in-law's sizable hardware and feed operation consisting of three stores. In addition, he preached at Piney Level every other Sunday.

"Why just every other Sunday?" Jim asked.

"It's a throwback to the days when the church alternated Sundays with the Methodists."

"I understand that," Jim said, "but since the Methodists don't use the church anymore, why not use it every Sunday?"

"People got used to going to other Primitive Baptist churches on the off-weeks and just never changed," said Rob. "Since most everybody has a car these days, one church is about as convenient as the next. Speaking of church, are you coming to the September Meeting next Sunday?"

"Wouldn't miss it for the world," Lilly and Jim said in unison.

The September Meeting, as it was called, was the annual homecoming. People from all around, including many from out of state, came back to their roots for the "all-day dinner on the ground" service.

On Sunday morning, Jim yelled upstairs, "Are you ready?"

"Not quite," Lilly answered, "You go on and pick up your mother. I'll bring the kids with Mom and Dad."

Jim, his mother, and her sister, Aunt Lois, arrived at the church about the same time as Lilly and her parents and sat together inside.

It was a difficult time for Jim. His father had passed away only months before, and his childhood experiences in this old church flooded his mind. The elderly reverend, Ben Boatwright, spoke of the saints from this church that had gone on to glory to claim their reward. Jim thought of his father and grandparents who had grown up in this place.

Rob preached next and ended with an altar call as the congregation sang:

Where He leads me I will follow
Where He leads me I will follow
Where he leads me I will follow
I'll go with him, with him, all the way.

Jim bolted from his seat and Lilly followed. They knelt at

the altar and rededicated their life to Christ. With tears in their eyes, Rob and Jim hugged unashamedly in front of the packed house.

After the morning service, blankets, quilts, and tablecloths were spread on the ground. Food of every description was placed on a communal hay wagon that served as a buffet.

It was Jim's favorite part of the day. Rob blessed the food, then sat with Jim and Lilly and a number of their mutual friends.

Jim, Lilly, and the kids skipped the afternoon service to visit the cemetery. He would come back for his mother after the service.

Ray and his family, two of Jim and Ray's sisters and their families, and several other relatives were already there. Jim took the flowers from Lilly. Someone had already put flowers on Aunt Addie's grave, so he divided his between his father's grave and Annie's.

Lilly and Jim had been home less than a month, but they had easily readapted to rural life. The worst of the Depression was over, and things were slowly returning to normal. Jim eventually secured a job driving a truck for the Southern Oxygen Company. He drove daily between Dawson, Tennessee and Harlan, Kentucky. Maneuvering the large tanker truck along the mountain roads was dangerous work, but Jim enjoyed the challenge.

CHAPTER 21

Fall 1938

The diesel–fueled Cummings engine pulled the tanker slowly up Blair Mountain. When it threatened to bog down, Jim shifted to yet another lower gear.

During these long drives, he tried to concentrate on the road and drive the dark thoughts of Annie's murder and her killer from his mind. At other times, he reflected on his family and what the future might bring. Occasionally he reminisced about dance night with Toby. The bulge in his pants was evidence of the effect it had on him. As always when he thought of Toby, he relived the feeling of rejection. Who was the man in her bed? Was he a better lover? Why had she not answered his second letter?

Now, rolling along on top of the mountain, he readied for the downshifting to conserve his brakes. Overheating the brakes on the descent was always a possibility and the most dangerous part of the trip.

Slowly, Jim maneuvered the rig through the hairpin curves into the valley below. He was looking forward to bantering with Betty, the waitress at Helen's Restaurant near Harlan, Kentucky.

The truck rumbled to a stop behind the restaurant, where he parked in order to leave spaces out front for the other customers.

"Hey, trucker man," Betty greeted him as she approached the booth.

"Hey, good lookin'!" he replied.

"What're you having today?" she asked.

He looked around, making sure no one could hear. "Same as always. I'd like to have you."

"I'm not on the menu today. Try back tomorrow. What are you drinkin'?"

"Same as always. Sweet tea."

He watched her as she walked away. She had medium–long, vibrant red hair, a pretty, pouty face, and beautiful blue eyes. He loved Betty's sense of humor, but what turned him on most was watching her bottom and rounded hips sway in those tight–fitting jeans. Her blouse always had only the top button unfastened, never revealing even a hint of her small breasts.

She was back. "Have you decided, hon?"

"Yeah. I'll have the chicken and dumplings special."

On the trip back to Dawson, he was considering what to do about finding a rental house. One of the other drivers had told him that renting was just throwing money away. Jim needed to buy a house and build equity, the man had said.

Why not? he asked himself. We have over $3,000 in savings. I could make a down payment and get a 30–year loan.

The sign interrupted his thoughts.

DAWSON 20 MILES

Almost home, he said to himself. I can't wait to see Lilly and the kids!

Lilly met him at the door with Shelly beside her and Robby on her hip. She kissed him as he took Robby from her. Shelly hugged his leg and wouldn't let go. He walked her across the room with a stiff–legged limp as she hung on relentlessly.

That night in bed, he broached the subject of buying a house.

"Don't you like living here?" Lilly asked.

"Yeah, its fine. But we need a place of our own. We can't live with your parents forever, hon."

"I know," answered Lilly, "but it sure is nice to have Mama's help with the kids. And think of all the money we're saving in rent!"

He rolled on top of her and kissed her lightly. "Don't you know, with our own house, you wouldn't have to worry about your parents hearing us."

Lilly opened her legs, and Jim forgot all about houses.

*****

I love Saturdays, especially when it's warm like today, thought Lilly, as she helped her mother prepare the meatloaf.

"What time are they coming?" her mother asked.

"Supposed to be here about three o'clock," Lilly replied.

Rob and his family were coming for a visit. Lilly was looking forward to seeing them and their children. They played so well with Shelly and Robby.

"I'll go tell Daddy and Jim to get cleaned up," said Lilly.

She walked to the barn and yelled, "Y'all come on! It's time to get ready."

"Okay," Jim yelled from the loft.

The weather was warm enough to move the supper outside to the two picnic tables. The kids ate quickly and were playing on the tire swing under the century–old oak tree. Hamilton was the oldest at age five. Next were Jenny and Shelly at three years each. The baby, Robby, was snug on Lilly's lap, drinking from a bottle.

Rob was entertaining the group with stories, and Lilly had laughed until her sides hurt.

Jim whispered to Rob, "I've got a stash hidden in the barn. Wanna go?"

Rob answered by standing up and saying, "Jim and I are

going to talk a little politics. We'll be back in a little while."

They eased away as Mrs. Larkey was sharing her recipe for coleslaw. Mr. Larkey was more than a little offended. He had found Jim's "politics" in the barn over a month ago.

As they neared the barn, Rob said, "I ought to abstain. I don't want to offend anyone."

"It's okay, "Jim assured him. "It's vodka. They won't smell it on our breath."

They sat opposite each other on hay bales and passed the bottle.

"Tell me about Cindy," Jim said. "Sorry Lilly and I couldn't come to the wedding," he quickly added.

"We met at a party at the business college and married two years after I graduated. Her family owns a farm, where she grew up. It's about 60 miles north of here. Her parents are getting on in years. She's an only child and would like to move back to the home place someday."

"So that farm will be yours someday, along with the hardware stores." Jim made it a statement rather than a question.

"Well, I guess so," replied Rob, as he had another drink. He paused before he spoke again. "Jim, you remember the woman you told me about in Ohio?"

"Yeah," Jim replied cautiously.

"Well, I suspect that you've been with a number of women."

"A few," Jim answered, fearful of where this was going.

"Well, I, uh, Cindy and I aren't getting along all that well—you know, in the bedroom."

"What's the problem?" Jim asked with a silent sigh of relief.

"I don't know. The honeymoon was great, but after that, I really wasn't very excited about being with her again. It's almost like I want to be with a woman once, then move on. Any idea what causes me to feel that way?"

After a long pause, Jim said, "You know you was raised as a

preacher's son. Maybe you just have guilt feelings about doin' it."

"Maybe that's it. One of my college psychology classes touched on that very thing." He stood up. "Jim, we have to get back. About that woman in Ohio—I've never mentioned that to anyone, and I never will. I hope you'll treat me the same way."

"Don't worry. It's one of our many secrets that we'll take to our graves, ole buddy," Jim assured him.

They shook hands, Jim hid the bottle, and they headed back. The wives greeted them coolly as they cleared the table and carried the dishes inside.

"See y'all at church tomorrow," the Boatwrights yelled as they headed for the car.

*****

Monday morning, the fog rolled in on the mountains, and Jim maneuvered the truck down the steep grade with extra caution.

Wonder what Betty's been up to, he thought as he released the air pressure from the brake system. He dismounted, locked the truck, and walked around the building to the entrance.

He picked a booth and settled in. Betty emerged from the kitchen to deliver an order across the room. Same tight jeans, Jim observed.

"Hey, Jim," she said in a subdued voice.

"Hey, Betty. What's good today?"

"I don't know. It's all good, I guess."

"What's wrong with my girl?" he inquired.

"Nothing," she replied.

She took his order and returned to the kitchen. Jim had never seen her like this. She brought his food and turned to leave.

"Betty," he called and raised his finger as if he needed

something.

She returned to the table and stared at him.

"You need to talk it out. What time do you have lunch?"

"Around one o'clock. Why?'

"Come to my truck out back and bring your lunch."

"I can't do that," she said flatly and walked away.

When Jim finished lunch, she brought the check. "My truck is gonna be parked out back until somebody calls the law and makes me move it," he said.

"You're crazy," Betty said as she walked away.

Jim sat in the truck, catching up on paperwork. Ten minutes after 1:00, and no Betty. He was beginning to wonder if she would come when the door opened. Betty slid into the seat and said, "Satisfied?"

"No," he replied. "I'll be satisfied when you tell me what's bothering you."

"It's nothing that concerns you, Jim, but I appreciate the fact that you noticed. That's more than I can say for the people I work with."

"I know it's none of my business, but it still helps to talk to someone."

She sat silent for a couple of minutes, and he did nothing to fill the void.

"It's my crazy family," she finally said. "My father's a drunk, and day before yesterday, he beat up my mother. My two brothers won't do anything about it because they're Dad's drinking buddies. What kind of boys won't protect their own mother?" she asked rhetorically.

He didn't answer—didn't think she wanted an answer.

She began to cry. He pulled her to him and cradled her against his chest, rubbing her back with his free hand. He didn't say anything. He let her have a good cry. When the sobs finally subsided Betty said, "I'm sorry."

"No, it's your dad and brothers that are sorry—sorry

excuses for men! Couldn't you and your mom just leave, start a new life?"

"No. She would never leave home."

"Is there anything I can do?'

"No, but it's sweet of you to ask," she said as she raised her head to look at him.

He wanted to kiss her, but stopped himself. "How old are you, Betty?"

"Twenty," she replied. "How old are you?"

"Thirty. Where's your lunch?"

"I'm not hungry. If I get hungry, I can grab something," she said as she dried her eyes.

"Listen to me," he said, locking eyes with her. "Find a way to get away from this situation. If your mother is not willing to leave, you've got to go without her."

She dropped her eyes to avoid his gaze.

He gently shook her shoulders and repeated it.

Betty nodded that she understood, then kissed his cheek. "I've gotta get back. Thanks, Jim. Your wife is a lucky woman."

She was out and gone before he could reply.

*****

A week later, Betty greeted him with, "Hey, cowboy!"

"Hey, sweet thing. Are you on the menu today?"

"You're married, remember?"

He motioned for her to bend down closer. "I don't know about Kentucky, but in Tennessee, they don't castrate men when they get married."

She laughed. "You're crazy."

"Things improve at home?"

"Depends on which day you ask."

"At least you've got your laugh back."

"Hard not to, with you around," she answered. "What're you

having today?"

"Surprise me," Jim said.

"I might just really surprise you someday," she said matter-of-factly as she met his eyes.

He was caught off guard—couldn't think of a witty reply. She had already turned and was walking away when he muttered, "I'd like that."

She was back with beef stew, coleslaw, and corn bread. He kept his quivering hands under the table. "Got any lunch plans today?" he asked, trying to appear calm.

"I'm eating on the run. The girl that works the register is out today, and I'm pulling double duty."

"I'll be here Tuesday, out back at one o'clock. Bring us a couple of sandwiches."

"I can't, hon, but thanks."

As she turned to leave, he said, a bit too loudly, "I'll be there."

She quickly looked around to see if anyone had heard, met his eyes briefly, and then walked away.

He left the usual generous tip and met her at the register. She counted out his change and avoided eye contact.

"I'll be there," he stated emphatically.

She didn't answer.

*****

He and his conscience wrestled on the drive back to Tennessee.

How would it feel to undress her and see her body for the first time? he wondered. How would it feel to be inside her? What kind of lover would she be? So young!

Stop it! his conscience countered. You have a wife and kids. It's a sin to betray them.

I love Lilly more than anything in the world, he told himself.

I can't do this to her.

His thoughts eventually turned to Toby and the awful feeling of rejection.

Damn, he said to himself.

*****

Tuesday morning, long before daylight, he made love to a sleepy Lilly.

"I love you," he said as he stood up.

"Love you, too," Lilly yawned.

After getting dressed, Jim tiptoed into the kids' room and gave them a goodbye kiss. He paused at the bedroom door for a few moments to watch their peaceful faces.

CHAPTER 22

At the terminal in Dawson, Jim poured a cup of coffee as he looked over his route sheet. "Hello, old man," he greeted Bob, the young dispatcher. He had dubbed him "old man" because Bob was always so nervous and fretful.

"Hey, Jim," Bob replied. "Got a minute?"

"Sure. Whatta ya need?"

"I just wanted to give you a heads up. I heard the boss on the phone with headquarters. I think they're selling the company," Bob whispered.

"So, what's wrong with that?" Jim asked. He glanced around to make sure no one could hear.

Bob shrugged and said, "I don't know, but I guess I'm just worried about our jobs."

"That's exactly why I call you 'old man.' You're always worrying about everything. Relax. There's nothing to worry about. Especially you. They couldn't run this place without you."

"Be safe out there," Bob said in a caring tone.

Jim smiled at him, thinking, That's what I like about Bob. When he says, "Be safe out there," he really means it.

"See ya tomorrow, Bob."

Jim approached the idling rig and climbed aboard. As usual, the yardman had started the engine after pumping his dangerous cargo into the pressurized tank that was coupled to the cab. In one fluid motion, Jim shifted into first gear with his right hand and released the parking brake with the other.

He wrestled with the decision all morning before stopping

at a market. Jim quickly spotted the rubbers behind the counter and moved on through the store. He was embarrassed to ask the young female clerk for them. Finally, he picked up a pack of gum and lifted a bottle of Coca-Cola from the metal box of cold water.

Thank goodness the men playing checkers are at the back of the store, not near the counter, he thought.

He laid the two items on the counter. It was decision time.

"Will that be all?" the young woman asked.

Jim looked past the clerk to the rubbers in the glass case behind her.

"Is this gonna be it?" the clerk asked again.

"Yeah, that's it, I guess," he sighed.

Back in the truck, he threw the gum on the dash, retrieved the "church key" from the glove box, and opened the Coke bottle.

She probably won't show up anyway, he thought.

Jim eased the truck in behind Helen's Restaurant. He took the empty bottle from between his legs and put it in the glove box. He looked at the back door, then back at his watch for the sixth time.

Twelve minutes past one.

His hands were shaking so badly that he gave up trying to make entries to his log book. Then Jim saw movement to the right out of the corner of his eye.

Betty was easing the screen door shut to avoid having it slam in the wind. She jumped inside the cab and tossed the bag of sandwiches onto the dash.

"I thought he would never leave," she said.

"Who?" Jim asked.

"The owner. He went into town to buy supplies."

"How long do you—"

She kissed him in mid–sentence.

He pulled her onto his lap and teased her with his tongue. His right hand rubbed her leg, then her hip. Jim scooted their bodies to the right and squeezed her rigid bottom without breaking the kiss. He clumsily tried to unbutton her jeans. Now free of the steering wheel, she broke away, unbuttoned the tight jeans, and struggled to get one leg out. At the same time, he lowered his pants and underwear to his ankles. He was hard and ready. He closed his eyes to kiss her and reached between her legs to massage her through her panties. She had already removed them.

Betty straddled him and took his erection into her hand. "Do you have some protection?" she asked breathlessly.

"No, I, uh..."

She lowered herself onto him without commenting. She rocked back and forth until his final lunge signaled that they were through.

Betty kissed him tenderly until his erection had subsided. Then she moved to get her leg back into her panties and jeans.

Jim said, "I'm sorry I don't have a cloth or anything."

"No problem. I can clean up in the restroom. I've got to go," she said as she buttoned her jeans.

"Whoa! Let's talk awhile and eat our sandwiches," said a surprised Jim.

"Can't. Don't have time." She kissed him on the cheek and reached for the door handle.

He grabbed her arm and said, "What's the big hurry, Betty?"

"I've got to be there when he gets back. Bye–bye."

She was halfway to the back door when he said, "'Bye."

*****

After church on Sunday, Jim, Lilly, and the kids drove his mother back to her home. She had prepared dinner for them early that morning before church. Jim loved his mother's cooking, and Lilly enjoyed the leisure time while Esther warmed the food. Esther always insisted on doing the work while Lilly sat at the table to keep her company. Jim played with the children in the yard until dinner was called.

During the meal, Jim casually asked his mother, "Did anything ever turn up about that Benson boy—you know, the one that was missing in Kentucky?"

"Don't know. I never heerd any more about it, but I heerd that his daddy had got religion and was attending church with his wife in Holston Landing."

"That's good," Jim replied.

"I'm glad I don't have to worry 'bout them moonshiners comin' after yore daddy anymore. What I do worry 'bout," Esther added, "is that ole Roosevelt draggin' us into that war across the pond."

Jim locked eyes with Lilly as they broke into a mutual smile.

"Did Jim mention *our* big news?" Lilly asked Esther.

"No, honey, he didn't mention anything," Esther replied as she looked first at one, then the other.

"We've been looking at houses. It's time that we owned our own house," Jim said.

"Well, good. I'm glad to hear it!" his mother said enthusiastically.

*****

A few weeks later at work, worry was evident on the faces scattered around the room as the two men from the home office were introduced. Jim was not particularly worried. He had applied for a job with the Fain County Sheriff's Office, and the chief deputy was an old friend of his father's.

The older man was outlining the improvements the company had made in equipment and working conditions over the last several months. Then the younger man began to explain the need for route changes that would be made over the next several weeks. He finished by informing the drivers that they would meet individually with Bob, the dispatcher, for their new assignments.

Jim joined the line forming outside Bob's office. He passed the time thinking of the improvements he needed to make at the four-room house that he and Lilly had bought. It was a few miles out of Dawson in the growing community of Springdale.

"Hi, Jim, come in," Bob welcomed him.

"Hey, Bob. What's up?'

"Jim, I know you're a family man, so you're probably not going to like it. They're adding stops to your route. You'll be away from home two nights a week."

"I can live with that," Jim answered as he thought of the deputy's job.

"Of course, the company will pay the expenses. Here's a list of three motels that will bill the company directly, and this sheet explains the per diem for meals," he said as he handed them to Jim.

"The per what?" Jim asked.

"The per diem. It means the maximum amount the company will pay per day for meals."

"Oh, okay. And get that worried look off your face, Bob. Things will work out just fine."

Three days later, Jim was on his way to Kentucky to service his Monday route. The new route assignment will start exactly two weeks from today, he calculated.

Lilly was none too pleased with the prospect of his being away from home, and bringing up the deputy's job didn't help, either.

His thoughts turned to Betty. She was the strangest girl—woman, he corrected himself—that he'd ever known. Their occasional trysts in his truck were always over in minutes, and she was out and gone before half of her 30-minute lunch break was over. Other than her face, he had never seen Betty from the waist up. She never had time to remove her blouse and bra.

"Takes too much time to get the bra and top back on," she'd said.

He had worried about that first unprotected time with her. Thank God she had not gotten pregnant. Each time since then, he had used a rubber.

I need to break it off and not see her again, he thought. I'll use the route change as my excuse. I'll tell her today.

"Hi, Betty," he said as she removed the order pad from her pocket.

"Hi, Jim."

"Got some bad news, sweetheart," Jim began as he turned to check the booth behind him.

"What?"

"They've changed my route. I won't be able to come by and see you."

The disappointment was evident on her face.

"I'm sorry, Betty, but I can't imagine that you're very satisfied with, you know, so quick—and in a truck," he added as an afterthought.

Her penetrating blue eyes bored in on him as if searching his soul.

He leaned slightly toward her and lowered his voice. "What we're doing is having sex, not making love."

She hesitated as if trying to think of an answer. "Then let's spend the night together," she said.

Jim had not anticipated her answer. Finally, he said, "Okay. We'll work it out somehow."

Three weeks later, they met in his motel room, 22 miles west of Helen's restaurant. The room had a double bed with small oak tables on either side. A pitcher of water had been placed on a spindly side table, along with a radio. There was a worn armchair in one corner, and a straight-back chair in the opposite corner by the bathroom. Four clothes hooks had been screwed into the wall next to the door. The small bath contained a tub, a commode, and a sink with a mirrored medicine cabinet above it.

Betty had borrowed her cousin's car, and she also gave Jim the cousin's phone number. "You can always get a message to me through that number," she told him.

He offered her a glass of wine.

"No, thanks," she said coolly. "I've seen what that stuff can do to people."

"Sorry," Jim said as he set aside the unopened bottle. "Are things improving at home?" he asked.

"Right now, it's great. My dad and brothers are in jail."

"Jail?" Jim raised his eyebrows in surprise.

"Somebody called the law on 'em. They were drunk and brawlin' in the front yard yesterday."

"Let's hope they keep 'em there for a while," Jim said.

"Oh, they'll probably beat me home tonight," she said sarcastically.

He walked the two steps to her armchair, bent down, and kissed her. She barely responded. Jim sensed her nervousness as he pulled her up into his arms. Taking her place in the chair, he guided her onto his lap.

It was the first time he had seen her in a dress. "You do have two legs after all," he said, acting surprised.

"What on earth are you talking about?'

"Well, I'm used to seeing you with one leg in and one leg out of your clothes," he teased.

She pulled her dress to her thighs to expose beautiful legs. "Two, see," she said, playing along.

"Yeah, I see, all right!" he said, as he caressed her legs from calf to thigh.

She lifted her head from his chest and kissed him tenderly as his hand stroked her inner thigh. As the kiss became more passionate, she parted her legs slightly, signaling him to feel.

He expected cotton panties, but felt skin instead. "No panties," he mumbled through their kiss.

She tilted her head back and said, "I wanted to surprise you."

"You're full of surprises."

She unzipped his pants and pulled them off, along with his underwear. Then, as she mounted him, he reached around her, trying to find the zipper of her dress.

"No," she said and pulled his hand around to her breast.

"I want to go to bed and get all our clothes off," Jim pleaded.

"No, I want it now, honey," she said.

Jim shifted his weight slightly to sit more upright.

"Something's wrong. What is it, Betty?"

She said, "Nothing. I just, I just..." She began to cry.

"What's wrong? Tell me," he demanded in a calm voice.

She started slowly, and the story gushed out.

Her father had started molesting her when she was eight years old. He was sadistic and violent at times. He had burned her breasts with cigarettes when she tried to resist.

She collapsed into Jim's arms. He held her close and let her cry as he stroked her back.

Finally, she allowed him to pull the dress down to her waist. He gently removed her bra and examined the scar tissue on her small breasts. His hands were trembling with rage as he replaced her bra and zipped her dress. He dressed quickly, and they talked for two hours, exploring ways she could get away and start a new life.

Finally, Jim said, "Betty, I can make him stop."

"How?" she asked.

"I can kick his ass so bad that he will never touch you again."

"Oh, no, I couldn't do that. He's still my father, no matter what. Besides, he doesn't bother me that way anymore. He can't get it up anymore—because of the liquor, I guess."

Jim's anger subsided somewhat. The flashback of his defenseless sister and that monster Benson, along with the mental image of Betty being tortured, had drained him.

"I don't know what to do, then," he finally admitted.

"There is a way. You could leave your wife and we could run off," she offered.

"I'm sorry, Betty, I truly am, but I could never leave my wife. Besides, I have two kids," he added.

With her eyes glued to the floor, she mumbled, "I know. I understand."

He took her into his arms and held her. He felt completely helpless and at the same time realized that Betty had probably felt helpless and powerless all her life.

She began to sob again. "Jim, I've misled you. I had sex with you hoping you would run away with me. I'm sorry."

"No, it's my fault. I'm old enough to know better," he said as he thought of Connie. He walked her to the car and opened the door for her.

She turned to face him. "Don't worry about me," she said. "I've got another plan. I'll be fine."

"What's the plan?"

"Can't tell you." She kissed his cheek and got in.

Jim watched her taillights until they disappeared down the dark two–lane highway.

"Good luck," he whispered.

CHAPTER 23

1940

The contractor was scheduled to be there at 6:30 a.m. Consequently, Jim and Lilly were having an early Saturday morning breakfast. They were converting from cistern water to city water, which would require rearranging the plumbing in the house and digging a line to the street to tap the Springdale Water Company's line. At about the same time, another workman would permanently close the cistern with a concrete slab.

The four-room house was situated on four small lots—enough space to keep a milk cow, chickens, and a couple of hogs. The hillside lot closest to the house was to be used as a garden area for fresh vegetables. The cellar's hard clay floor and walls could be expanded later beyond the coal bin and stoker-fed furnace. The outhouse sat on the back lot line, a short walk from the back door.

The two front rooms served as a bedroom and a living room. The bedroom was furnished with two single beds for the kids and a chest of drawers that had belonged to Aunt Addie. The living room was partly furnished with a sofa and two armchairs. Later, a gift of a coffee table from Lilly's parents would be added.

One of the two remaining rooms in back served as a combination kitchen/dining room. The other was Jim and Lilly's bedroom. The small kitchen was partially lit by two windows, one along the north wall and the other on the west. The sink beneath the west window was bracketed on the left by a counter with cabinets above and pantry below and an electric stove on the right. The oven door of the stove barely cleared the refrigerator, which was adjacent to the back door along the north wall. The table and four chairs were crowded along the southern wall, opposite the door to Jim and Lilly's bedroom.

The only luxury afforded the couple in their private chamber was a closet containing a bar for hanging clothes with a shelf above. The room contained a double bed, dresser, and chest of drawers, all from Lilly's bedroom at the Larkey home.

Jim's job for the day was two-fold: supervise the contractor and erect a clothesline for Lilly. The week before, he had painted the iron posts for the clothesline using the white paint left over from the kitchen cabinet job. The posts had been welded after work in the truck terminal shop by a friend.

As Jim dug the two holes on either side of the back yard, he thought of his father. He would have liked to show him the house, especially the stoker and furnace. At least he could show it to his mother this afternoon.

He was to pick her up at 4:00 and bring her to spend the night. She would sleep with Lilly, and he would bed down on the sofa in the living room.

His thoughts turned to Betty.

Wonder what her plan is? he said to himself. Was she going to run off with someone, maybe her cousin? He suddenly stopped digging and stood erect. Surely not. Or did she mean that she would kill herself? The thought chilled him to the bone.

"What?" Jim stammered.

"I said, here's you a glass of cold water. Do you feel all right?" inquired Lilly.

"Yeah, I'm fine. I was just thinking about Mama comin' this afternoon."

"Okay. I'll check back in a little while."

He watched Lilly walk back to the house as he rubbed the cool glass across his brow.

Jim backed out of the driveway and headed to the old home place, just eight miles away across the Virginia state line. After Jim's father had died, his mother had decided to stay there alone, which had been a constant worry for Jim and his brothers and sisters. Then last fall, Esther's sister Lois had volunteered to move in with her. Such a relief, Jim said to himself.

"You sure you won't come with us, Aunt Lois?" Jim asked for the second time.

"No, honey. I've got work to do. Y'all have a good time. I'll see you tomorrow."

Esther's excited, Lilly thought. She's got that "dark-eyed sparkle" that Jim talks about. I guess she's happy to be in our new home.

Over dessert, it became apparent what was on Esther's mind. "Jim," she said, "I want you to do me a big favor. I want you to get aholt of your brothers and sisters and tell 'em to come to the September Meetin'. We'll make apple butter on Saturday and all go to church together on Sunday."

"I'll start work on it after church tomorrow," Jim replied. "It'll be good to see everybody."

"We ain't all been together since your father's funeral," Esther observed. "I's so tore up I don't remember much about it—seems like a dream."

Jim reached over and patted her back. "I know exactly what you mean, Mama."

Later, he commented to Lilly that he could feel the bones in his mother's back. "She's lost some weight," he commented.

"Well, having all her kids at home in September will perk her up," Lilly said.

Over the next several months, Jim received commitments from everyone except John in Detroit. John indicated that he would do everything short of losing his job to be there.

*****

Some of Jim's siblings had taken an entire week off in September. Others would be in on Thursday, and John would arrive with his family on Friday.

Jim had secured his mother's copper boiling pot from her brother, who had borrowed it several years before. He spent half a day cleaning it with vinegar and salt. The inside shone like a new penny, and he was confident that it would pass the inspection of his mother's critical eye.

Ray arrived at the home place about daylight to begin the fire. Jim arrived next and retrieved the long L-shaped homemade paddle from the barn. The unusually long handle allowed the apple butter to be stirred out of range of the considerable heat generated by the fire. John chopped extra wood. The women peeled apples as they chatted and traded the latest family news.

Tradition held that each one of George and Esther's children was obligated to tell a story from his or her childhood on that person's first turn at the paddle. Also, it was customary for the oldest child to take the first turn, with each succeeding child stirring in order of their birth from first to last. Opal went first, then John, Mamie, Ray, Ida, May, and finally Jim.

Jim told about a time that he and their dad were searching for a still. "We walked around about two hours, but no still. Then we came to a small clearing and saw a cow. The cow looked funny. Something wasn't right about her. She stood with her legs wide apart. Dad always called her the 'spay-legged' cow. Finally, Dad said, 'That cow is either sick or drunk.'"

They all laughed, even though most of them had heard the story several times before.

"We watched her for about 30 minutes, and then she staggered off into the woods. We followed her all the way to a large still—biggest I'd ever seen. The cow drank some of the sour mash and wobbled off. We stayed till almost sunset, but nobody came to tend the still. It was after dark when we got home."

"What happened to the still?" Ray asked. He knew the answer but asked for the benefit of any of the kids that hadn't heard the story.

"Well, I left home for Ohio, but Dad and some deputies sneaked back there several times. People started complaining so much about funny tasting milk, the lawmen finally gave up on catching the 'shiners and just busted it up."

Opal and Mamie headed off to help Esther and the other women with food preparation. They were cooking enough to feed everyone today as well for the "dinner on the ground" tomorrow.

May and Lilly stayed to help stir.

Jim asked, "Can you girls handle it for a while?"

"Sure," they answered in unison.

He and his two brothers eased out to the barn to have a nip of moonshine. Ray didn't drink anymore, but he made an exception for homecoming. They passed the jar and laughed at the stories they dared not tell in front of the women and children.

John, as the eldest brother, returned thanks before dinner. Ray counted everyone present and came up with 15 adults and 17 children. After dinner, they gathered on the front porch and in groups scattered throughout the front yard to catch up on each other's lives. One of the adults manned the paddle at all times.

The sound of children at play filled the house and yard. Shelly hovered over Robby. Although only two years older, she had practically become his second mother.

Esther was the center of attention. She sat on the front porch in her favorite cane-bottomed chair like a queen on her throne. Parents and children alike rotated in and out of the preferred seats at her feet on the porch.

By late afternoon, Mamie yelled above the din, "The apple butter's ready to take off!"

Everyone looked at Esther, knowing that it would have to be inspected first. She eased off the porch and approached the boiling pot.

She pursed her lips and blew on the apple butter in her wooden spoon. Then she tasted it, moving it around in her mouth. Esther was making sure there was enough sugar to overcome the tartness of the sour apples without making the mixture too sweet. In addition, she was checking for a hint of cloves and for the taste of cinnamon. She wanted it balanced with the other flavors to the point that folks would argue as to whether it actually contained cinnamon or not.

"Mamie's right. It's ready," she pronounced. The Mason jars and lids had been sterilized in boiling water, and the wax was ready for sealing.

After the glowing embers of the fire had turned to ash, Esther and her children posed for a picture behind the apple butter pot. Esther held the paddle and concentrated on stirring the empty pot. She was somewhat embarrassed by the playacting, but her nephew, the photographer, insisted.

As daylight ebbed to dusk, some of Esther's children and their families began to drift off. John and his family were staying at the home place. Others from out of state were staying with siblings or other relatives. Everyone was looking forward to seeing old friends and other relatives at the church homecoming tomorrow.

Rob was the lead preacher, now. His father, relegated to the front row as a proud spectator, thumped his cane and hurled Amens toward his son at the appropriate times.

After the service, the younger folks hiked and their elders rode to the Taylor cemetery. The children scampered around the graveyard, calling out to each other. Some of the older children read epitaphs to the younger kids. Teenagers huddled among the cars parked outside the fence, exchanging frustrations and wondering if the day would ever end.

Most of the adults gathered around the adjacent graves of their father and their sister Annie. As the group dispersed to visit other graves, Jim remained.

"Dad and Annie," he said quietly, "I hope you're pleased with what I did. I know it was a sin, but I believe it would have been a bigger sin to let him kill again. Rest in peace. I love you."

*****

Early Monday morning, Jim drew a cup of coffee from the communal urn in the terminal as Bob approached him.

"The boss wants to see you in his office," Bob informed him.

"What about?"

"Don't know, but there's some other men in there with him."

"What on earth?" Jim mumbled as he headed for Mr. Flanagan's office. Jim knocked and Flanagan greeted him at the door.

"Come in, Jim. These men want to talk to you. This is Detective McCrary. I'll let him introduce the others," Flanagan said as he left the room and closed the door behind him.

"Mr. Taylor, this is Detective Hubbard and Detective Murray with the Kentucky State Police, and I'm with the Dawson City Police Department. They want to ask you a few questions. Have a seat."

Fear saturated Jim's body. Benson's red eyes quickly materialized in his mind.

The coffee cup was trembling in Jim's hand, and he welcomed the opportunity to place it on the table where he sat. The fact that he never picked it up again did not go unnoticed by the detectives.

"What's this about?" asked Jim, trying to hide the quaver in his voice.

"Will you state your full name for the record?" asked Detective Hubbard.

"James Taft Taylor, but I go by Jim." Jim concentrated on breathing slowly and deeply to calm his nerves. His mouth was dry. Did he dare take a sip of coffee and expose his trembling hands?

"Taft. Unusual name. Can you spell it for me?"

"T–a–f–t," Jim answered.

"Mr. Taylor, you've been through the state of Kentucky a lot over the years, haven't you?" Hubbard asked.

"I guess so. Why?"

"Look, Taylor, you know why we're here. Don't pull that dumb act on me!" Hubbard said in a raised voice.

"Would y'all mind telling me what's going on?" Jim finally replied.

Detective Murray spoke for the first time. He sat directly in front of Jim across the table. He had a friendly, mellow voice. "Jim, we know that you're a good man. We've checked you out. You're a family man—go to church. I'm betting y'all had a fight—you didn't mean for it to happen, but it did happen, Jim."

He placed both arms on the table, leaned forward, clasped his hands and continued. "Jim, I know it's been hard living with this, like a great weight on your shoulders—on your mind. Jim, this is your chance to get rid of that guilt and be free of it." He leaned even closer. "We found the body in Kentucky."

A chill swept through Jim's body as his heart lurched in his chest. He wondered if the officers noticed his arms moving as he wiped his damp palms back and forth on his trousers under the table. Then a calming warmth spread over him like a drink of moonshine. The detective was right; the guilt seemed to have lifted from his mind and soul. He replied in a calm and steady voice, "I have no idea what y'all are talkin' about."

Hubbard took over again as McCrary, the Dawson City detective, stood up and eased out of the room.

"You're goin' to make us do this the hard way, aren't you, Taylor?" he said. "We know you did it. What we want to know is *why* you killed her!"

Jim's breath quickened as he thought, Did he say *"her"*?

"I have no idea what you're talking about," Jim replied. Now he really didn't.

"We're talking about a dead girl, Betty Winters. A girl that you were screwing. A girl that used to meet you in your truck."

"You mean Betty, the waitress?" Jim asked, surprised.

"You know exactly who we're talking about. Detective McCray is searching your truck as we speak."

They continued questioning Jim for over an hour. He denied any relationship with Betty other than trying to give her fatherly advice on how to handle things at home. They asked why Jim stopped eating at Helen's Restaurant about the same time that Betty disappeared. Jim answered honestly that his route had changed.

As the detectives departed, they indicated to Jim that he would probably see them again.

Jim went straight to Mr. Flanagan's office after the interview.

"What on earth is this all about, Jim?"

"The best I can figure, Mr. Flanagan, a waitress at a restaurant in Kentucky has been murdered. I used to stop there before my route changed. I always joked around with her. I guess she disappeared about the same time that I stopped going there. I just can't believe they think I had anything to do with it."

"Thank goodness they're gone. You better shove off. You're already way behind on your route."

Jim walked to his truck with the mixed emotions of relief and great sadness.

CHAPTER 24

1939–1943

Almost a year later, Jim sat in the drivers' meeting wondering which rumor to believe. Was the company being sold yet again, was it closing down, or were they just rearranging routes for the third time?

This time, Jim was worried. Every time he had checked with Chief Deputy John Smoot, it was the same answer: "We're not hiring due to budget problems." He had applied at the Dawson Police Department, as well, but Detective McCrary might hurt his chances there.

The managers from company headquarters were there. They announced that the Dawson terminal was closing and moving to Nashville. They explained all the reasons, but Jim only caught bits and pieces: changing customer base, drivers welcome to transfer, fuel costs, etc.

His mind was on finding work; he was not moving his family to Nashville. Other than the Grand Ole Opry, he had no interest whatsoever in Nashville.

That night in bed, he broke the news to Lilly. "Don't worry, Lilly. I'll find another job. I always do."

"I know, but I still worry. I could go back to teaching to help out."

"That won't be necessary."

"Mama could keep the kids."

"Lilly, the school year's already started. Besides, I'd rather you stayed home with the kids. Lord knows, I've been away half the time; they don't need you gone, too!"

She snuggled close and put her arms around him. Their standard remedy for relieving tension and worry was lovemaking, and they did it freely and passionately.

Less than a week later, Jim secured employment with the Sunburst Coffee Company. He would drive a panel truck and deliver coffee door to door. Some customers paid him directly, while others paid monthly by mail. Part of his job was to convince cash-paying customers to switch to the monthly pay-by-mail program. Jim didn't particularly like his new job, and it paid considerably less than his previous position.

Shifting the two-pound can of coffee to his left hand, he knocked on the door. The door opened with a flourish to reveal a pretty, wet-haired woman dressed in a white silk robe. Her straight blond hair hung past her shoulders in damp, golden strands. Jim was stunned by her icy blue eyes. Even without makeup, her pinkish-pearl complexion was without blemish except for the beauty mark to the right of her mouth. Her thin lips were drawn tight to match her furrowed brow.

She started to say something, then changed her mind. "You're new," she finally said in a lilting voice.

"Yes, ma'am. I'm the new delivery man," Jim replied as he tried not to stare.

"Well, thank God!" she said emphatically.

Jim was at a loss for words.

"The other man was rude, unfriendly," she added.

"Uh, he's not, uh, with the company anymore. I'm his replacement."

"I'm glad to meet you. I'm Judy Sawyer." She offered her hand and a smile, revealing perfect white teeth.

Jim shook her hand and said, "I'm Jim Taylor. Glad to meet you, Mrs. Sawyer."

As she paid Jim, he asked her if he could talk to her about

their pay-by-the-month program.

"Could we do that next time, Mr. Taylor? My hair is wet. I just got out of the shower."

"Yes, ma'am," he answered as his eyes met hers. She held the gaze a bit longer than necessary, then quickly pulled her robe together at her throat and said, "Goodbye."

That night in bed, he told Lilly about Mrs. Sawyer's house. "I've never seen anything like it. It's a two-story brick. You could fit eight or nine of our house in it. Some of the hedges are higher than my head. I bet they have full-time servants and yardmen," Jim gushed. "Two weeks from now, I'm supposed to explain the monthly pay plan. I'll tell you what it looks like inside."

"You mean you go inside these houses?" Lilly asked, trying to mask the worry in her voice.

"Some of 'em, yeah. I sit down with them and try to talk them into signing up for the plan."

Judy Sawyer answered the door and welcomed Jim in to explain the new program. She was wearing a different robe and her hair was pulled back into a ponytail. She led him to the kitchen.

"Have a seat. Would you like a cup of coffee?" she asked.

"Sure," he replied. "Thank you, Mrs. Sawyer."

"Call me Judy," she said as she secured two cups from the cupboard.

As she bent to pour his coffee, her robe opened enough to reveal the cleavage of her breasts. He wanted to look away to avoid being caught, but he couldn't resist, and she didn't seem to mind.

He had an overwhelming urge to kiss her, to see her naked, and to make love to her. After explaining the new pay plan, Jim insisted on serving the second cup of coffee. When he leaned over to pour, she lifted her head to thank him. Their eyes met, and he kissed her. He placed the coffee pot on the table and pulled her out of the chair.

Her robe was open now. One of her erect nipples brushed his company–issued wool jacket. Jim slipped his arms inside the robe and felt the warm skin of her back as they kissed. He removed his jacket and shirt as he bent to kiss her breasts.

"We can't do this," she said.

He answered by lowering her panties to her ankles and lifting her onto the table. Her panties fell to the floor as he kissed her again while lowering his pants.

"We can't do this!" Judy exclaimed as he entered her. He lunged repeatedly until she started to climax. As she did—"Oh, yes, yes, yes, *oh, please!"*—she spread her arms wide, knocking the metal coffee pot and one of the cups to the floor. Her hands gripped the edges of the table as she raised her legs higher.

Afterwards, he kissed her slowly and passionately until he was no longer inside her. Judy lay on the table with legs dangling as he watched her breasts move up and down with every breath.

Jim pulled up his underwear and pants and bent to pick up the coffee pot and broken cup.

"Leave it," she said. "Come here and kiss me."

Avoiding the mess, he gingerly moved to the side of the table and kissed her softly, warmly.

"Judy, I'd like to stay, but I'm going to get in trouble if I don't get going." He picked up the single cup left on the table and held it above her face. "Our cup from now on," he said.

*****

Lilly held his jacket to her nose and sniffed a second time. She immediately called him into the bedroom and angrily confronted him. He vehemently denied her accusations and gave two plausible explanations. His explanations seemed to be credible, and she desperately wanted to believe them.

Jim was determined to break off the relationship, but two

weeks later, he made love to Judy on her back porch in broad daylight. It was a cold November day, and they raced inside to warm up. He told her about his wife's suspicions and asked her to stop wearing perfume.

"Let's take a shower to make sure," was her reply.

In the following weeks, they made love on almost every visit. They were quickies, but torrid and lusty. Today, they made love in the back seat of her car inside the garage. As always, they showered together in her upstairs bedroom. As he soaped her back, he confessed that he was scared.

"What of, Jim?" she asked.

"I'm afraid that I'm falling in love with you," he lied. "I love my wife, and I don't want to lose her and my kids."

"I know, honey. I'm beginning to feel the same way," she replied.

They rinsed in silence.

Finally, Jim said, "We've got to stop."

"I know," she agreed.

Downstairs in the foyer, he kissed her and said, "Goodbye. I'm goin' to miss you."

"Goodbye, Jim. It was beautiful while it lasted."

Two weeks later, she answered his knock dressed only in a garter belt, black nylons, and high heels. He took her savagely on the carpet of the foyer. Just before climaxing, he picked her up and bent her over the hallway side chair. As he entered her, he noticed the carpet burns on her back and bottom. This merely added fuel to the fire of his rabid desire.

Later, in her bed upstairs, she stretched out on her tummy as Jim applied the soothing salve.

"Are you happy in your marriage, Judy?" he asked.

"Yes, I'm very happy."

"Then why are we doing this?"

"I don't know. I really don't. I just know that within a few days of your leaving, I start looking forward to the next time."

"Does your husband satisfy you? In bed, I mean."

"Yes, he does, and I love him very much."

That was not the answer he had expected, but he could relate to the feeling.

She turned over and lay with her back on the towel. He looked into her face, as if trying to understand what was going on in her mind. His eyes took in her incredible beauty: the rounded breasts, the reddish-tinted curls between her thighs, and the long, slender legs.

She could read it in his face, his eyes. He was looking at her for the last time—trying to memorize her features.

"Is this really goodbye, Jim?" she asked in a voice barely above a whisper.

He paused, and then looking into her gorgeous blue eyes, he kissed her tenderly and replied, "Yes."

Two weeks later, there was no knock on the door. By mid-morning, she gave up and found the can of coffee on her doorstep.

*****

Two years later, on December 7, 1941, Pearl Harbor was bombed by the Japanese.

The Taylor household was fearful and tense. Jim had registered for the mandatory draft the year before, but now he wanted to go downtown and volunteer.

"Everybody's signing up to do their part, Lilly," he insisted.

"Those are the younger guys. You have two children to provide for," retorted Lilly.

"I'm 32 years old and in my prime. I can't sit by while other men go fight for the country!"

Exactly seven days after the bombing of Pearl Harbor, their third child, Lois, was conceived. It was almost as if Lilly had willed herself to get pregnant to keep her man out of the war.

*****

Lois, named for her great–aunt, was born on September 15, 1941 in Detroit, Michigan. The family had moved there the previous April. Before that, Jim had gone to the draft board in Dawson to join the Army. However, the recruiting sergeant checked his status and told him to go back home and take care of his wife and kids.

Then, in late March, Jim approached Lilly with a different idea. "If I can't fight for the country, I can at least go to work at one of the defense plants in Detroit. They pay triple what I make now. We could replenish our savings to build onto this house. Now that we're going to have another child, we have to have at least one more bedroom. We could build a bathroom, too. And—"

"Whoa, whoa, slow down, Jim," she interrupted him.

"And John says to hurry. They're hiring hundreds of people a day," he finished with a deep breath.

"What about this house?"

"I've already thought about that. My cousin Gerald says he will rent the house if we give him a two–year lease."

He was shocked when she said, "That sounds like a pretty good plan, but we have to find a good school there for the kids." He hadn't expected it to be so easy.

He left for Michigan a few days later. He planned to stay with John and his family until he could get on at one of the plants.

Four days after arriving in Detroit, he had passed the company physical, was processed through personnel's bureaucracy, and was building military jeeps for the Ford Motor Company. He raced home after his first day of work to talk to John.

"John, you're not going to believe this! They've got me working with a nigger!"

"Jim, you better get used to it. Your kids will be going to school with them, too."

"Oh, no, they won't," Jim said emphatically.

"We'll see," said John.

Jim lucked into a furnished rental house belonging to one of John's friends. It was a three–bedroom house with a living room, a small dining area, and a bath. The owner assured Jim that the local school was one of the best in Detroit. Robby would start kindergarten, and Shelly would be in first grade.

Two weeks later, Lilly and the kids were in Detroit, settling into the new house. Jim was shocked when Lilly mentioned that a cute Negro boy was making friends with little Robby.

"My kids are not goin' to school with niggers," Jim said in a raised voice.

"Jim, don't use that word."

"What word?"

"It's not nigger, it's Negro," Lilly retorted loudly.

Jim was taken aback. Lilly had used that tone only two or three times with him since they'd been married. "I have to work with one all day, Lilly," he said in exasperation.

"How could you possibly have anything against Negroes?" she asked, and then continued before he could answer. "You didn't know any Negroes when you were growing up. You probably never even saw one before you were 12 years old."

"I don't have anything against them. They're just different. They need to stay with their own, and I'll stay with my own."

"So what you're saying is, they need to stay where they are: in poor housing, low–paying jobs, on their side of town, and in rundown schools."

Jim stood up and walked out to the front porch to be alone.

A few minutes later, Lilly opened the screen door and touched his shoulder. "I don't want to fight, Jim."

He touched her hand and looked up. She kissed him and squeezed his hand.

"I didn't know you felt that way about nig— uh, Negroes. It took me by surprise," he said.

"We'll talk about it another time. I want to tell you about a class I had in college, but only when we have plenty of time," she said as she left to check on the kids in the back yard.

She quickly came back to the door behind him and asked, "By the way, what's his name?"

"Who?"

"The Negro that you work with," she replied.

"Joby," he answered.

"Try to make friends with him, Jim."

Before he could answer, she was gone.

Over the next several months, Jim got to know Joby, and he liked him. Joby was always nudging him to tell about life growing up in the hills of southwest Virginia. Jim slowly opened up and described his life helping his father to break up stills, going to church and church socials, and how he courted Lilly when they were kids.

Jim, in turn, asked Joby about growing up in Birmingham and was surprised to learn that Joby had two years of college. His father was a college professor, and his mother played the piano at church.

"Why did you quit college?' Jim asked.

"All the men left for the war, and the college was near bankruptcy. My father's job was eliminated. I came here to make money—same as you."

"How come you weren't drafted?" Jim asked.

"I was, but they turned me down—failed the physical." He didn't offer the reason, so Jim didn't ask.

*****

Over the ensuing months, their friendship grew. In addition to taking breaks together, they began to have lunch together as well. One day Joby asked Jim to tell him every racial joke that he knew. Jim could think of only two. "Why do you want me to do that?" Jim asked.

"I want to know if there're any I haven't heard."

Jim told the two jokes, and Joby beat him to the punchline both times.

Jim then asked Joby, "Why do you not like to be called nigger?"

Joby paused then asked, "Why do you want to know?"

"I guess the same reason you wanted to know the jokes," Jim retorted.

"Well, let me see." He paused. "Would you want me to call you a dumb-assed, egg-sucking, rednecked, dullwitted hillbilly?"

Jim's face turned red. He took a deep breath, then said, "I reckon not."

"Well, multiply how that felt by a thousand times, and you might be in the ball park of how it makes my folks feel."

Jim said, "I'm not sure I understand it all, but I'll never call you that. And by the way," he added, "I ain't never sucked an egg."

They laughed until tears were flowing.

A few weeks later, Joby was peppering Jim with questions about his family, their beliefs, and their upbringing.

"Do you ever run out of questions?' Jim inquired

"Let me explain," Joby said. "I'm interested in different cultures. Sociology was my major in college. I'd really just gotten started on my major when I had to quit. I'm not just being nosey. I really find it interesting."

Jim turned the tables on him and asked point blank, "How does it feel to be black?"

Joby thought for a few moments, and then replied, "You've sort of hit me between the eyes with that one. Of course I know how it *feels*, but I believe you're asking me if I can make you understand that feeling."

"Exactly."

"Give me a few days. I'll figure it out," said Joby. "Now let's get back to work."

The following Wednesday morning, Joby asked Jim if he had plans for Friday night.

"Nothing I can't change. Why?"

"I may have an answer to your question. I want you to go to the club with me on Friday night."

"What do they do at the club?"

"Oh, it's mostly couples dancing, socializing, and a little drinkin'."

"Where is it?"

"In Paradise Valley, where else?"

"I... I don't know, Joby."

"You'll be my guest. Come on!"

"Okay, but are you sure you know what you're doing?" Jim asked.

"Trust me. It'll be fine."

*****

Joby arrived at Jim's house at 6:45 p.m. and quickly became the center of attention. Jim and Joby walked to the car under the intense stares of neighbors who were sitting on their porches fighting the heat.

"Don't worry, Jim. They probably think I'm the yard man," Joby joked.

When they arrived at the club, the band was swinging and the place was rocking.

Jim's breath caught in his throat as they entered the large ballroom. There must be 500 people here, all black, he thought. I wonder if they employ off-duty policemen as security.

Joby led him through the tables of partiers all the way to

the back bar. Each group grew silent as they approached. All eyes were on Jim as they passed each table. Some muttered snide comments.

"What the—"

"Hey Joby, what's you doin'?"

"Man, look *at this.*"

"You lost, boy?"

Jim stuck close to Joby and looked straight ahead.

"Hey, Mooky," Joby greeted the bartender.

He nodded. "Joby."

"Give us two whiskey sours."

"What you tryin' to prove?" Mooky asked.

"Just give me the drinks, Mooky," Joby demanded.

Jim whispered, "Joby, let's go on home."

"We'll go in a few minutes. I just want you to get the *feel* of the place, so to speak."

When Joby mercifully led Jim toward the door, catcalls from around the club could be heard.

"What's your hurry, boy?"

"Not soon 'nuff fo' me."

And from one buxom lady, "I think he's kinda' cute!"

Jim could hear laughter from the building as they made their way to Joby's car.

On the ride home, Joby spoke first. "How'd you feel back there?"

"Well, if you wanted to embarrass me, you did a good job," Jim said dejectedly.

"I didn't want to embarrass you, and I apologize for putting you through that. But I wanted you to feel what it's like to be black. Those feelings you felt tonight, I've felt all my life. I feel like that when I go to the Post Office or a movie theater. I feel like that when I walk through a department store to spend my hard-earned money or walk by the lunch counter where I'm not allowed to eat. I feel that way when I go to the hospital or for a job interview."

"That's enough, Joby. I get your point."

They rode in silence to Jim's home. Joby stopped the car and offered his hand. "Still friends, you egg–sucking hillbilly?"

Jim shook his hand and replied, "I ain't never sucked an egg."

CHAPTER 25

Summer 1943

In June 1943, Detroit erupted into racial violence. It started on a muggy Saturday evening at the popular Belle Isle Amusement Park. Fights between black and white teenagers spread throughout the park.

When over a hundred white sailors from the nearby Naval Armory joined the fray, it evolved into an all–out brawl. It spread to the bridge between the island and the mainland and then into the city as rumors spread. Both whites and blacks fanned the flames with untrue stories of atrocities.

Elements of the white mob claimed that a black man had raped and murdered a white woman on the bridge, and the story quickly spread in the downtown area. Likewise, stories spread throughout Paradise Valley, the huge black ghetto where over 200,000 blacks were squeezed into substandard, unsanitary housing. The most prominent rumor asserted that a black woman and her baby had been thrown over the Belle Isle Bridge. Enraged blacks swarmed in and around Paradise Valley, burning white–owned businesses, attacking white people, and burning their cars. At the same time, white mobs forced streetcars to stop and savagely beat the black passengers who were on their way to work.

Black leaders encouraged Mayor Jefferies to request federal troops to quell the violence. The mayor refused and only relented once white mobs attacked sections of Paradise Valley on Sunday evening. Later that night, U.S. Army troops cleared the streets and calmed the situation. Over the next few days, there were flareups, but for the most part, the uneasy truce held.

At Lilly's insistence, Jim stayed home from work until Wednesday. Lilly feigned fear for herself and the children, but her real concern was that Jim would somehow become involved.

"Where's Joby?" Jim asked on Thursday as he started his shift with a new partner on the line.

"Don't know," said the man. "They just told me to work here today," he added.

Later, Tom Foster, the foreman, walked by and Jim asked him about Joby.

"Joby's in the hospital," answered Tom.

"Hospital? What's wrong with him?"

"Injured in the riots, is what I'm told."

"How bad is he? Where'd it happen?"

"I don't know, Jim, but it must be pretty bad, 'cause they said it could be a while 'fore he gets back."

On his lunch break, Jim called three hospitals before locating Joby. I'll go see him on the way home this afternoon, he thought.

"Room 415," the hospital volunteer answered.

Jim thanked her and took the elevator to the fourth floor. After wandering down two corridors with no results, he asked directions at the central nurses' station. On the right track, now, he walked into 415 and quickly determined that the man in the hospital bed was not Joby. He had turned to leave again when a woman's voice called to him.

"Are you Jim?" she asked.

Jim turned to see a petite black woman who apparently had been in the bathroom.

"Uh, yes, I am," he answered.

She approached him, offering her hand. "I'm Olivia Talbot, Joby's wife. He said you'd come."

"Yes, ma'am, but where's Joby?'

"Why, he's right there." She pointed to the man in the hospital bed.

Jim was speechless as he tried to make sense of the situation. Joby's face was swollen beyond recognition, his left arm was in a cast, and his head was bandaged so heavily that he appeared to be wearing a white toboggan.

"I didn't recognize him," Jim said sheepishly.

"I know. Don't feel bad; even I didn't recognize him at first. Have a seat, Mr. Taylor," she said as she motioned toward a chair in the corner of the room near the bed.

"How is he?" Jim asked as he sat down with her.

"He's hurt very badly, as you can see, but the real worry is that he may have internal injuries. The doctors say that the injuries you can see aren't life threatening, but they worry about swelling of the brain and possible damage to his organs."

"Has he been awake at all?"

Oh, yes. We've talked a little, but they're keeping him doped up so he doesn't move too much. He's had a terrible headache, as you can imagine."

"Yes, ma'am. Is there anything Lilly and me can do for you? Do you need anything here or at home?"

"No, but thanks for offering. Once he's fully awake, he'll want to see you, though."

"Oh, yes, ma'am. I'll be here, Johnny on the spot."

True to his word, Jim visited Joby and Olivia every day after work. On Friday night, Lilly baked a rhubarb pie to take to the hospital on Saturday morning. Also, she made arrangements with Mrs. Johnson next door to keep the kids. After breakfast Saturday morning, she and Jim drove to the hospital.

"Are you sure Mrs. Johnson doesn't mind keeping the kids?" Jim asked.

"Oh, no, she loves them, and you know how lonely she gets."

As they approached the hospital room, Lilly's stomach

began to churn. She was anxious to meet Olivia but was concerned as to how she would be received. Olivia stood to greet them.

"How nice to finally meet you, Mrs. Taylor," Olivia said as she took her hand.

"Please, call me Lilly. I'm so sorry to meet you under these circumstances. How is he this morning?"

"He seems to be a little better. He's sleeping right now, but he's had a good night, even been talking some," she said as she looked at Joby.

"I brought this for you. I hope you like rhubarb pie."

"Oh, I love it! Mama used to bake rhubarb pies when we were growing up in Alabama."

Jim stood by the bed looking at Joby while the women fell into easy conversation.

"So you grew up in Alabama, too," said Lilly. "Were y'all childhood sweethearts?"

"Not exactly. We met in college. I grew up in a small town, and Joby grew up in Birmingham. Joby tells me that y'all were childhood sweethearts in Virginia."

"Yes. We've known each other almost all of our lives."

"Joby, do you know me?" Jim asked.

Joby opened his eyes and looked straight at Jim. He stared as if he was trying to focus. "Jim," he whispered.

Jim grinned and touched his hand.

"Sucking eggs," mumbled Joby.

"Did he say he was craving eggs?" asked Olivia.

Jim laughed and said, "No, I'll tell y'all about it later."

Joby went back to sleep and Jim entertained the ladies with Joby's "egg-sucking hillbilly" story.

On the ride home, Jim noticed that Lilly's mood had changed. "What's wrong?" he asked.

"Nothing. Just thinking."

"About what?"

She hesitated, then said, "I was thinking about how unfair life is, about how awful it is that Joby was almost killed for nothing—just because of who he is, just because he was born a different color than us. Why? *Why?*" she asked as her voice grew louder and tears began to flow.

Jim reached over to hold her hand, but he didn't have an answer. Finally, he said, "I don't know. It's just the way the world is."

"Just the way the world is," she said with heavy sarcasm. "Do you know that Olivia has been at the hospital for a week without going home even once—afraid that she'll be attacked?" she continued.

Jim gripped the steering wheel and pretended to be concentrating on the road.

"She and Joby came to Detroit for the same reason we did, to better themselves—to make a decent living and save up some money. They're doing their best to get along, then he's beaten senseless by complete strangers. Why? Why?"

"Only God knows why, Lilly."

"No, that's not true. *I* know why! It's because of hatred and ignorance! Blind hatred and ignorance beyond comprehension. Only a softening of hearts and education—lots of education—will overcome this mess. Look around. The stores are closed, the kids haven't been to school all week, and I doubt that anyone will be at church tomorrow. Disgusting, just disgusting!"

Jim started to say something, then thought the better of it. They stopped for an early lunch at a deli a few blocks from their house. Halfway through his hot dog, Jim commented on the rumors that had been circulating all week.

"Jim, those are just rumors, not facts. According to the newspaper, virtually none of those rumors turned out to be true."

"How do you know that? We don't even take the newspaper!"

"I read Mrs. Johnson's paper almost every day," Lilly replied.

Jim looked perplexed. What else don't I know about her? he wondered.

"It's important to understand the big picture—what really causes problems like this. Thousand of poor blacks and whites have moved to Detroit to work in the defense plants. The blacks are forced into Paradise Valley under terrible conditions. They live two, three, even five families to a house. The southern whites bring prejudices ingrained in them since childhood. The local people resent the invasion of both. It makes for an explosive situation."

"Lower your voice. People are going to hear you," he whispered.

"I don't care. Maybe they need to hear it."

They finished their meal and ordered hot dogs to go for Mrs. Johnson and the kids.

In the car, Lilly apologized. "Jim, I'm sorry. I didn't mean to be so preachy. Let's enjoy the weekend with the kids."

Jim nodded and forced a smile as he tried to make sense of the feelings bouncing around inside. Later Saturday night, Jim suggested to Lilly that she approach Mrs. Johnson about sharing the cost of the newspapers.

"After she reads the paper, she could pass it along to us," he offered.

"That's a great idea!" Lilly responded.

*****

Monday was a beautiful summer day. The kids were back in school for their final week before summer break, and on his way to work, Jim noticed that there were fewer Army troops on the streets. After work, Jim stopped by the hospital and was pleasantly surprised at how much better Joby looked.

"Hey, Joby. Hi, Olivia," Jim said as he entered the room.

Joby was sitting up in bed, drinking water through a straw.

"Hi, Jim," Olivia said as she noticed the sparkle in Joby's eyes.

"Hey, hillbilly," Joby said through cracked lips.

"How ya feelin', Joby?"

"Better, better."

"I'm amazed at how much better you look. You're gettin' your ugly back!"

"Well, the doctors say that I'm comin' along. Swellin' of my brain has gone down, and I've quit passin' blood. So I reckon I'll be going home soon."

"The doctors haven't said anything about him going home," Olivia interjected. "That may be wishful thinking," she added. "I'm going downstairs to grab a bite to eat and let you menfolk visit awhile."

"Would you like for me to drop you off at your house, maybe to pick up a few things?" Jim asked her.

"No, no, that's not necessary, but thanks for offering," she replied. "I'll see y'all a little later."

Jim turned to Joby. "You've had a rough time of it, ain't ya, buddy?"

"Pretty rough, I guess," replied Joby.

"Joby, what happened? I know a mob beat you up, but how did it happen?"

Joby took a deep breath and thought for a minute. "Well, Jim, I'm not sure you would understand. The fact that you offered to drive Olivia home tells me you probably wouldn't understand. A white man couldn't drive to my place in Paradise Valley right now—too dangerous."

"Well, I'm sure I don't understand it all. But I believe the problems go back many, many years and that black folks are forced to live in real bad conditions. And I believe that most of it is caused by racial hatred and ignorance and that love for each other and education is the way out of it."

Joby stared at him. "Damn, hillbilly, sometimes you amaze me."

Jim smiled as he raised the straw to Joby's lips.

Joby told Jim how a white mob had stopped the trolley car on Woodward Avenue and had dragged him and several others out onto the street.

"They beat me with their fists, and a couple of 'em had sticks or ball bats, I'm not sure exactly. I fought 'em till they knocked me to the ground. Then came the worst part, kicking me and striking me with all manner of things. I made it up on one knee and saw a policeman and yelled for help. He looked straight at me then turned his back—no ears for a black man!"

Joby paused for a breath. "They beat me back down, and I gave up. I asked God to help me, and they laughed and kicked me some more. I'm not sure what happened after that. The next thing I knew, I was in this bed."

Jim took Joby's hand but didn't speak.

Joby broke the long silence. "When I get on my feet, we're moving back to Alabama. We want to have kids, and this is no place for that."

"Is it any better there?" asked Jim.

"I don't know, maybe not, but at least there, God has ears."

"Well, we're going home, too," Jim informed Joby.

"Because of the riots?"

"That, and other things."

*****

Three weeks later, in early August of 1943, Jim and Lilly had Joby and Olivia over for a goodbye dinner. They promised to keep in touch—promises that both couples knew wouldn't be kept.

CHAPTER 26

Beginning several months before the riots, Jim had sensed that something was not quite right with Lilly. She was the strongest person he had ever known. Her outward appearance was the same—lovely brown eyes to match her hair, beautiful soft-featured face, and a figure that was still the envy of other women. But he could tell that something was different inside.

Maybe she's just homesick, he thought, or maybe worn out from caring for two kids and a baby. At other times he was convinced that she was tired of the hustle and bustle of the city.

It came to a head on a Friday night. She turned down his offer to go to a movie.

"Lilly, something's going on. Something has changed. I'm going to keep asking till you tell me."

She said, "Nothing's wrong. Please stop asking me."

He sat across from her at the kitchen table, trying to read her face. Suddenly, Lilly began to cry. Jim went to her and pulled her up into his arms.

"Lilly, I love you. I want you to be happy."

"I know, I'm sorry," she sobbed and hugged him tightly. "Jim, I want to teach. I've always wanted to teach. That was my dream, and I don't want to give it up. I know I'm being selfish. I've got a family to take care of. I've got to think of you and the kids," she said between short, jerky breaths.

He held her until she was quiet and breathing normally. It gave him time to think. "We're going home to Virginia and you're going to teach," he said emphatically. "Besides, this is no place to raise kids."

"No, no, Jim, we can't do that. The house in Springdale is leased for another six or seven months. You're making good money, and our savings account is growing. I appreciate your concern, but I'll be fine. Why, it's probably just getting close to my time of the month. Let's go to bed and snuggle."

The decision to go home to Virginia had first started developing in Jim's mind a few weeks before the outbreak of violence. The riots had merely sped up the process.

He turned in his notice at work on Monday, July 19th. Two weeks later, they were headed to Virginia with three kids and no job or house. Lilly had resisted the notion, saying it was crazy, but Jim had won her over.

The rental payment on the Springdale house essentially took care of the house payment, so they didn't have to worry about that. The Larkeys insisted that they live with them until they could get into their own home.

The former chief deputy of Fain County, John Smoot, was now the sheriff. The department had three openings, and Sheriff Smoot hired Jim on the spot. A new payroll cycle would begin on the following Monday, and that was when Jim would start.

Lilly applied at the Fain County, Tennessee Board of Education, as well as the Shelby County, Virginia school district. She was offered a job by Shelby County and was to report on September 13th to Greenwood Elementary School near Holston Landing to begin the new school year. Jim and Lilly dipped into their savings and purchased a used car for her to drive to school and back. Lilly hired a responsible 20–year–old girl to help her elderly mother look after Lois. Shelly and Robby would enroll at Greenwood and ride to school and back with their mother.

After washing the dishes from Lois's first birthday party, Lilly hugged Jim and said, "Can you believe it, Jim? We've been home for less than two weeks, but we both have jobs, and I even have my own car! The Lord has really blessed us."

"He sure has, sure has."

"I don't worry as much about your law–enforcement job as I did before. The way everything just fell into place tells me that it's God will. He'll protect you."

*****

Jim rode with an experienced deputy for two months before he was allowed to patrol alone. Sheriff Smoot called him into the office on his last day of training.

"Jim, I wish your daddy was alive to see this. According to your trainer, you're a natural at law enforcement," he said as he perused the training report. "You scored a 98 on your live fire training, and your high–speed driving skills he rated as excellent. It's the last comment in the report that worries me a bit."

"What's that, Sheriff?"

"He says that you're fearless, and that concerns me."

"I don't understand, Sheriff."

"Well, this is a dangerous business. A good dose of fear can help keep you from getting hurt or killed. We deal with some pretty bad folks out there. I want you to be careful. Me and your daddy were good friends. He'd tell you the same thing if he was alive."

"Yes, sir. That's true. I'll do my best for you, and I appreciate the job."

Time passed quickly for Jim. He enjoyed the people he met on the job. Even some of the drunks he arrested could be interesting and comical.

Lilly cherished her time in the classroom. During the first three months of school, she interviewed every child to learn more about their strengths and weaknesses and to ascertain as much about their family life as possible. She thrived on watching their progress and gaining their respect through doses of discipline and lots of love.

Jim concentrated on learning the back roads of the county and the streets of Dawson, where he occasionally served civil papers. That was the only part of the job he didn't enjoy. Within three months, he was earning extra money moonlighting at the local race track on Saturday nights and the wrestling matches on Wednesday nights at the Dawson Civic Center.

In mid–April, the Taylors would be able to move back into the house in Springdale. In the meantime, they hired a contractor friend of Jim's to build a new addition onto the back of the house—a kitchen, a bedroom, a bathroom, and a small back porch.

*****

On Tuesday, May 16, 1944, Jim answered a "dead man in the river" call.

He was less than two miles away, so he was the first deputy on the scene. A jon boat was tied to a small sycamore tree, and its apparent owner paced back and forth along the shoreline. Jim lit a cigar—a habit he had picked up over the last few months—as he picked his way down the rocky bank.

He recognized the young man as Jimmy Manis, whom he had picked up for public drunkenness a couple of weeks before. On the way to jail, Jim had a change of heart and, over Jimmy's protests, took him home to his father.

As Deputy Taylor approached, Jimmy lit a fresh Lucky Strike from the dying embers of the stub between his yellow–stained fingers.

"Hey, Jimmy, what's going on?"

"There's a body over there against the bridge," replied Jimmy.

The body had snagged on a large tree limb, which in turn had caught on the bridge pier in the north fork of the Bedford

River.

"You sure it's a body?"

"Well, hell, yeah, it's a body! I saw it up close. Scared the shit outta me!"

"What were you doing out here, Jimmy?"

"I was scoutin' out a place to set a trot line when I spied it. It didn't look right, didn't look natural. So I paddled over to it, and—"

"You sure it's a human body?' Jim interrupted him.

"Yeah, I'm sure," Jimmy said as he began shaking again. "You can take my boat over there and look for yourself."

A siren whined in the distance. "No, that's okay. The rescue squad will be here any minute now."

The volunteer-manned rescue squad pulled the body onto the bank and waited for Doc Williams, the county coroner.

"Probably fishing and fell in somewhere upriver," said one of the squadsmen.

"I'll go see if I can find his gear," Jim replied.

Picking his way upstream, Deputy Taylor checked every obvious spot worn bare by fishermen for half a mile. Finding nothing, he returned to the scene to find a man on his knees examining the body.

"You must be Doc Williams," Jim said.

"Yes. And who are you?" the corner asked without looking up.

"Jim Taylor, with the Sheriff's Department."

"Well, glad to meet you," he said as he stood up without offering his hand.

"You figure he fell in and drowned?" asked Jim.

"Don't know. Probably. He's got a skull fracture at the left temple. Coulda fallen on a rock, I guess. I'll take a closer look when we get him to the morgue."

Jim climbed the bank to his cruiser and drove farther upstream, looking for the man's fishing spot. The road ran parallel to the river for over two miles. The deputy was in and out of the car and up and down the bank six or seven times before he spotted it: a Chevrolet parked in a pull-off with no one around it.

Jim looked it over, then walked down the path. There by the river lay a fishing rod with the tip end in the water and a small, well-worn tackle box opened near the reel end of the rod. Jim took a quick look around, then sat down to study the scene. Around the fishing gear, the half moon-shaped ground was bare, with no overhanging tree limbs. Deputy Taylor took a fresh cigar from his shirt pocket and lit it.

The department had issued short-sleeved shirts on May 1st, and the day was unusually cool for mid-May. Beyond the half circle were trees and scrub brush, broken only by the narrow path back up to the pull-off at the road. It appeared to be a good fishing spot—open enough for casting, but room for only one fisherman.

It's the kind of spot I would pick, Jim thought. Don't like being crowded when I fish.

He lifted the rod and reel and noticed that there was no hook, fly, or lure on the line. Holding the rod with the limp line swaying in the breeze, Jim tried to picture in his mind how the man had fallen.

Had a fish hooked, and it was so big it broke his line. The man was excited, jumped up to wrestle the fish, then slipped and fell, hitting his head.

Jim began to shiver from the cold breeze off the water. After gathering up the tackle box and rod, he carried it to the cruiser and locked it in the trunk.

Deputy Taylor depressed the mike button. "109 to headquarters."

"Station. Go ahead," the dispatcher answered.

"Need to run a tag, Tenn 7042."

"10-4."

Five minutes later, Jim was startled by the pop of the cruiser radio. "Station to 109."

"109. Go ahead."

"Tag is on a Chevrolet registered to John Gibson, 609 Well Street, Dawson."

"10–4," Jim said as he jotted it in his book.

That night in bed, he relayed the story to Lilly. "Something bothers me about it, but I can't figure out what it is," he told her.

Three days later, Jim called Doc Williams.

"Hi, Doctor Williams, I'm Deputy Taylor. I met you the other day down at the river."

"Yes, I remember you. How are you doing?"

"Fine. I just read your report on—let me see. Yeah, John Gibson. Noticed that you ruled the cause of death as undetermined."

"That's right."

"So you're not sure that he drowned, right?"

"Well, he probably did, but I can't say that, since the skull fracture could be the actual cause of death."

"Is there no way to tell for sure?" asked Jim.

"Well, there was water in his lungs, but not as much as I expected to find. Technically, he could've died from either one. That's why I logged it as undetermined. Either way, I suspect that it was an accident; otherwise, I would have called it homicide."

"So the head injury was bad enough to cause death?"

"Definitely. His head injury was severe enough to be fatal."

"Is there any way to find out for sure which one he died of?"

"Look, Taylor, I'm up to my ass with work here. The body was released yesterday. It may be in the ground by now. But to answer your question, I ran all the standard tests. Good day."

Jim made a mental note to apologize to the coroner at his earliest opportunity. Back on patrol, he was on the lookout for reckless drivers and drunks while keeping an ear on the radio chatter.

Suddenly it came to him. The coroner had said, "Coulda fallen on a rock."

Rocks! I don't remember rocks at the fishing spot.

He turned the cruiser and headed for the river. Once there, he searched for anything that could cause a skull fracture. There were two rocks on the bank within a few feet of where the fishing tackle had lain. Both were flat and level with the ground. Also, there were three rocks underwater near the shore, but after using a stick to measure the depth, he estimated all to be within four to six inches beneath the surface.

Jim drove to the Public Safety Building in downtown Dawson. The three-story building was a joint project of the city and county. Both city police and county deputies had offices and squad rooms there, along with the court system and a shared jail.

After retrieving his lunch bag from the locker, Jim walked toward the squad room.

"Hey, Jim." It was the desk sergeant, Bill Summins.

"Hey, Bill."

"I've got a callback for you. It's Doc Williams. Here's his number."

"Thanks," Jim said unenthusiastically. I dread this call, he thought.

After lunch, Jim returned the call.

"Hi, Doctor Williams. I wanted to apologize for the other day. I'm pretty new at this, and I—"

"Don't worry about it, Deputy Taylor," the doctor interrupted. "I'd like for you to drop by here, if you have the time."

"Yes, sir. How about right now?"

"That would be fine."

"I'll be there in five minutes."

Jim was a little nervous when he knocked on the open door

to Doc Williams's office.

The doctor looked up from the paperwork in front of him. "Come in. Close that door, if you don't mind."

Dang! This is goin' to be a real butt chewing if he wants the door closed, thought Jim.

The office walls were bare except for the Hippocratic Oath and the doctor's diplomas that hung on the cinderblock wall behind the desk. The room was painted a pukey light green. Along the wall on the left, a shelf contained a set of what appeared to be medicine-related volumes. To the right, there was a table with papers and folders of various descriptions stacked a foot or more high. Williams's desk was relatively clean and orderly compared to the rest of his office.

"Deputy Taylor, I've been thinking about this John Gibson case. Your call spurred me to look at it again. I'm bothered by the head wound. It's perfectly round, two and one-eighth inches in diameter. I can't picture a rock like that. Maybe a root, but not a rock," Doctor Williams said as he handed over the grainy pictures of John Gibson's head.

Jim studied the pictures, then excitedly shared with Williams his findings at the site. Doctor Williams agreed that rocks a few inches below the surface couldn't be a factor and that flat rocks were not likely to produce the unusual head wound.

"I've seen lots of blunt force trauma wounds, but this one is unusual. A bat or heavy stick produces an oblong fracture. A hammer wound is the right shape, but they're considerably smaller in diameter."

"Maybe a sledgehammer," Jim offered.

"Could be, but I think the wound would be deeper, considering the heft and weight of a sledgehammer. The only wound I've ever seen that matches it was made by a slapjack. I saw it back in the early Twenties when I was a resident at Cook County Hospital in Chicago. Do you have a slapjack, by any chance?" the coroner asked.

"Sure, right here," Jim said as he retrieved it from the slot on the pants leg of his uniform.

Doc Williams examined it closely, turning it over and over in his hands. It was about a foot long and, unlike a blackjack, it was flat rather than round. Heavy leather covered the lead pieces in either end. One end—the striking end—was larger than the smaller gripping end. The imprint of the circular piece of lead embedded in the cover was plainly visible.

"Let's measure it," suggested the doctor as he secured a ruler from his desk drawer.

He measured the circle of lead bulging from the leather cover. "Two and one-eighth inches," he said as he handed it back to Jim.

"Whatta ya think, Doc?" Jim asked.

"I don't know what to think. We certainly don't have enough information to prove that he was murdered by a blow from a slapjack, but it does make one wonder. Why don't you see what you can dig up, and I'll keep an open mind on it?"

After interviewing Gibson's widow, Helen, Jim was no closer to a solution. She answered his questions freely as she dabbed the corners of her eyes with a handkerchief. Deputy Taylor returned to patrol. He could only devote about an hour a day to the case in order to keep up with his regular duties.

*****

"Jim, wait up." It was the chief deputy, Jim Scott.

"We heard that you were asking around about the Gibson drowning."

"Uh, whatta ya mean?"

"I mean that it's a city case, and we got no business messin' with it."

"How's it a city case?"

"The body was found in the city. The fishing spot upstream is in the county, but the sheriff and the chief of police have agreed that the city will handle it."

"But we don't know where he was murdered."

"Murdered? *Murdered?* What're you talking about? The city is getting ready to close the case as a drowning. You keep your nose out of it and let the city detectives handle it. The sheriff will have your ass if you embarrass him. Do you understand me?"

"Yes, sir, Chief."

CHAPTER 27

Jim thought about it over the next few days and came up with a compromise. He would work on the case on his time off. After work, he drove to Mrs. Gibson's house.

"Hello, Mrs. Gibson. Could I have a few minutes of your time?"

"Well, I thought, er,... The police said... Why, sure. I guess it wouldn't hurt. Come in."

"I was wondering if you could show me Mr. Gibson's fishing gear."

"Sure. It's in the garage. Come this way."

She led him through the small garage to the back wall. There, neatly arranged, were six rods and reels held by nails that would accommodate seven rods.

"One's missing. I guess that's the one—" Jim stopped in mid-sentence. "Sorry, ma'am. Do you know where he kept his tackle box?"

"It was always here next to this workbench. It's gone, too, of course."

"Yes, ma'am. Well, thanks a lot. I'm sorry to bother you."

Back at the car, Jim wrote in his book: *Wednesday May 24, 609 Well St., rod, reel, and tackle box missing.*

Thursday evening after work, Deputy Taylor interviewed the homeowner at 605 Well St. and wrote in his book: *Nothing helpful*. He repeated this process up and down the street every evening except Sunday. By the next Tuesday afternoon, he was at 619 Well Street.

"Hello, sir. I'm Deputy Taylor. Could I ask you a few questions regarding Mr. Gibson from up the street?"

"Of course. John was a friend of mine. I sure hated to hear about him. I don't know what poor Helen will do."

"Would you say you were good friends?"

"Sure was. We fished together quite a bit."

"Really? Where'd y'all fish?"

"Mostly out on the lake."

"Did you ever know of him river fishing?"

"Well, no. Like I say, we generally went to the lake. But I wasn't that surprised to hear that he had been fishin' at the river. He just loved to fish, you know. I was a little surprised that he was night fishing."

"Oh? Why is that?"

"Well, he just never mentioned night fishin', and I hadn't ever seen a lantern in his garage."

"A lantern?"

"Yeah, you know, for night fishin'. I guess maybe he'd bought one, although I'd a been glad to loan him ours."

"Sure. One more thing, Mr., uh—. Sorry. I didn't get your name."

"Ralph Taylor."

"Taylor. My name's Taylor, too."

"Yeah, I noticed that right off."

"Would you mind looking at a rod and reel and tell me if you recognize it?"

"Sure."

Deputy Taylor opened the trunk lid and retrieved the fishing gear.

Mr. Taylor looked at the rod and reel carefully. "This rod looks familiar, and that reel is definitely John's. But John wouldn't have used this reel."

"Why?"

"He hated that reel. Helen gave it to him as a Christmas

present a couple of years ago. It's a cheap Shakespeare. He took it along a few times so Helen would think that he used it. He swore me to secrecy—you know, that I wouldn't let on to Helen. John wouldn't have been caught dead using this reel."

Mr. Taylor's face turned red as soon as the words were out of his mouth. "I'm sorry, I didn't mean—"

"It's okay, Mr. Taylor, I know what you meant," Jim interrupted, then asked, "What about the tackle box? Do you recognize it?"

"Nope. Never seen it before."

"Are you sure you've never seen it in Mr. Gibson's garage?"

"No. Besides, it's a cheap box. John's box is bigger. That little box wouldn't hold a third of John's stuff."

"Thanks, Mr. Taylor. I appreciate your time. If you think of anything else, you can reach me at the Safety Building. You shouldn't have any trouble remembering my name."

"Nope. Taylor. I should be able to remember that." He laughed.

Jim entered notes of the interview in his book, with *No lantern* underlined.

It was dark by the time Deputy Taylor exchanged the cruiser for his civilian car. Sitting in the car with the windows down, he tried to figure out the discrepancy of the fishing tackle. Having made up his mind, he started the car and pulled away from the Safety Building.

On the second knock at 609 Well Street, Helen Gibson opened the door. Jim had forgotten how pretty she was, or maybe this was the first time he had seen her with makeup. She was dressed as if going out for the evening, and the high heels added several inches to her stature.

"Your hair is different," Jim greeted her.

"What? Uh, well, I had it done today. You know, trying to get my mind off things."

"Can I come in? It won't take but a minute or two."

"Look, Mr., uh—"

"Taylor, ma'am. Deputy Taylor."

"Deputy Taylor, the city police told me no one would bother me again. I'm getting tired of being bothered. A widow oughtn't to have to go through this."

Jim disappeared for a second, then reappeared with the fishing tackle. "I just need for you to look carefully at this rod and reel and the tackle box and tell me if they belong to your husband."

"Yes, they're his."

"Look carefully. Make sure, ma'am."

"Yes, I told you. That was his favorite reel. I got it for him Christmas before last."

"What about the tackle box?"

"Yes, that's his."

"You positive? 'Cause we found this down at the river, and we want to get it back to the rightful owner."

"Deputy, please. That's his fishing box. I've seen it a thousand times."

"Okay, ma'am. You've done a good job. Sorry to bother you. I'll get a release on these things and get 'em back to you."

"Thank you, Deputy. Good night."

Driving back to the Safety Building, Jim gripped the steering wheel to calm his shaking hands.

I'm knee deep in a murder case and not authorized to pursue it, he thought. What do I do now?

Back at the office, he tried unsuccessfully to concentrate on paperwork generated by the automobile accident he had investigated earlier in the day. Outside, darkness was approaching as he pushed the starter of his 1939 ford. It was the third car he had owned since the 1927 Model A back in Ohio.

Lucky I traded for it before the war, he thought. Cars are hard to come by now.

He switched off the headlights before easing up the one–

way alley behind the houses on Well Street. He parked two doors down from the Gibsons'. With two cars between him and Helen Gibson's back yard, he felt sufficiently hidden from view. Ten minutes later, Jim pulled the cotton trench coat around himself and leaned back in the seat.

I wish I was home with Lilly and the kids, he thought. Picturing them having supper with Mr. and Mrs. Larkey reminded him that he was hungry.

An hour later, just when Jim was ready to give up, a car slipped by him and parked behind the Gibson house.

No headlights, he observed. They obviously don't want to be seen.

After five or six minutes, someone emerged from the car and approached the back door of Helen's house. The door opened immediately and light spilled out onto the porch. Jim caught a glimpse of a man wearing a jacket and hat. The door quickly closed behind him.

Jim walked to the car and knelt behind it to copy the license number: Tenn 6–3910. He returned quickly to his car and resumed watching the back door of the house.

Less than 20 minutes later, the porch light flicked on, then almost immediately back off. Someone had turned it on by habit, then, realizing their mistake, had quickly extinguished it, Jim surmised.

The man returned to his car a minute later and eased down the alley without lights.

Should I follow him? Jim wondered. Don't need to. Got his tag number.

Later, in bed, he told Lilly what he had learned. A part of her was intrigued by the story, and she hung on every word. Another part of her was very fearful for her husband. She made him promise that he would report everything to the sheriff and get plenty of help from other deputies.

Once satisfied that Lilly was asleep, he spent the next hour planning his next move.

Early the next morning, after the shift change meeting in the squad room, Jim walked down the hall to the registrar's office and looked up the owner of Tennessee plate 6-3910. The name jumped out of the book at him. Jim read it again, even took a straight edge to make sure he was reading on the correct line.

Johnny W. McCrary.

Maybe it's a different Johnny McCrary, he thought, not Detective Johnny McCrary.

Deputy Taylor copied the address: 419 Wadsworth Street, Dawson, Tennessee.

Cruising past 419 Wadsworth in his civilian car, Jim observed that there were no cars in the driveway.

Good, he said to himself as he pulled up in front of 415, two houses down from McCrary's. A young high school-aged boy answered the door.

"Hello, I'm Don Baker. I'm looking for Johnny McCrary."

"He lives two houses down that way," the boy said, pointing toward 415.

"He's a carpenter, right?" asked Deputy Taylor.

"No, no. He's a policeman. A detective, actually."

"Oh. Must be the wrong person. Thanks anyway. By the way, how come you're not in school?"

"Memorial Day," the boy said, his inflection implying that Taylor was an idiot.

Back at the station, Jim quickly exchanged his car for the cruiser and headed for home, just across the state line. Rummaging through the box in their bedroom closet, he finally found the book *Crime and Detective*, by John Tickerling. He hurriedly explained to Mrs. Larkey that he couldn't stay for lunch.

On the eight-mile trip back to Dawson, he wondered how many department rules he had violated. Two quickly came to mind: crossing the state line in a county car when not in hot pursuit, and working on a case that he had been ordered off.

Just outside Dawson, he found a pull–off and pretended to be monitoring traffic. Normally, it was amusing to watch cars come tearing down the road and then slowing quickly when they spotted the cruiser. Not today; he had bigger fish to fry.

He reread pertinent parts of the book. *Murders are committed for passion or greed or both.*

Detective McCrary and Helen Gibson are obviously having an affair, Jim thought. That could account for passion. What about greed? Wonder if she had a life insurance policy on John?

Back at the station, Jim found a dark office, picked an insurance agent at random from the phone book, and dialed the number.

"Hello. Milton Roberts. Can I help you?"

"Yes, this is Deputy Sheriff Jim Taylor. How are you today?"

"Fine, Deputy Taylor. What can I do for you?"

"I need some information. How would I go about finding out if there was a life insurance policy on a deceased subject?"

"Well, in the old days, we would have to call every company and inquire about it. But now we can call an insurance dick and find out pretty quickly."

"An insurance dick?"

"Yeah, you know, an insurance detective."

"Oh, yeah. Well, how exactly does that work?"

"All the insurance companies pay a fee which funds three detectives, one for each grand division of the state. I could call the one here in east Tennessee and find out for you."

"I'd appreciate it. The name is John Gibson here in Dawson, on Well Street. I need to know if there's a policy, and how much it's for."

"You want to know the beneficiary, too, I bet."

"Yes, sir."

"Well, give me a couple of hours, and I'll find out and give you a call back. What's your number?"

"Let's see," Jim hesitated. "I'll be on patrol. Could I just drop by your office instead?"

"That'll be fine. I look forward to meeting you, Deputy."

Later, Deputy Taylor began to feel like he was in over his head. Mr. Roberts had just told him that the Trans-State Insurance Company had approved payment of $10,000 to Mrs. Helen Gibson. Now he had motive and some circumstantial evidence, but no witnesses. Apparently, the only witnesses were Helen Gibson and Detective McCrary. It was decision time, and Jim's stomach was churning. The best course of action, he determined, was to get a confession from Helen. He would put all of his eggs in that basket and go for broke just before daylight tomorrow morning.

At the crack of dawn, Deputy Taylor drove up the alley to make sure that McCrary was not there. He circled the block and pulled into the driveway. After five knocks, the door opened to a surprised Helen Gibson.

"Oh, no, not again!" she exclaimed. "What could you possibly want now?"

"We need to talk, Helen," he said, as if addressing an old friend.

"What about?" she asked.

"Do you have coffee made?" he asked as he stepped by her and into the living room.

She hesitated, then said, "Yes."

After pouring two cups, she sat across from him at the kitchen table. "What do you want to talk about?"

"The murder of your husband."

"What?" she asked, seemingly in total amazement.

"Look, Helen, we have Johnny in jail. He's told us everything."

"I don't have a clue what you're talking about."

"I'm talking about the murder of your husband and dumping his body in the river. Johnny's told the whole story and the city police are buying it. How you killed your husband and then called Johnny in a panic. How he reluctantly, against his better judgment, helped you dispose of the body. I'm talking about how he has pled guilty to two relatively minor charges: abuse of a corpse and failure to report a crime. I'm talking about how I don't buy it, how I think it's just the reverse. I'm talking about how he'll lose his job and get a slap on the wrist—probably probation. I'm talking about how my boss, Sheriff Smoot, thinks I may be right and whole city police department may be wrong. I'm talking about how I think I'm a pretty good judge of character, and how I think you played the minor role and Johnny the major. I'm talking about how you're going to the electric chair and it ought to be the opposite. I'm talking about the fact that Johnny has two other girlfriends besides you, and how you're being played for a fool," he lied. He purposely did not mention the insurance money.

Jim took a sip of coffee as Helen cried with both hands covering her face. He waited patiently until she stopped crying and took a deep breath. "How did I let him talk me into this?" she asked, shaking her head from side to side.

Jim didn't answer. He waited for her to begin instead. She started slowly.

"Johnny told me everything would work out and we could be together forever. He killed John in the garage and told me to follow him in John's car down to the river. I would ride back with him. He let me out in the alley and I slipped in the back door. He told me that if someone asked, I should say that John went night fishing. He practiced with me, questioning me, trying to trip me up so I could answer any questions if the police came around. He said to act like a mourning widow for the next month or so, and that we should have no contact."

"Why was he here the other night, then?" Deputy Taylor asked.

"I called him because I was worried—you know, about to

panic, because you kept coming around asking questions. He came over for a few minutes to calm me down and reassure me. He was upset with me—afraid I would do something stupid, and he seemed really worried about the tackle box you asked me about. But then he calmed down and hugged me."

"One other question. Why didn't he take John's tackle box to the river?"

"When he hit John, John's head fell onto the tackle box and got blood on it. Johnny said it could be evidence. He told me to bring one of John's rod and reels and that he had a backup box he could use."

"What happened to John's big tackle box?"

"I don't know. Johnny took it."

"Anything else you want to tell me?" Jim asked.

"No." She lowered her head to the table and began to cry again.

Jim sipped the coffee; it was cold. "Can I get you a glass of water?" he asked.

"Yes, please," she sobbed.

Jim poured water from the refrigerator jug. "Helen, you're under arrest. Let me explain to you what we're going to do. We're going to talk to the sheriff. You're going to tell him the whole story. Then we're going to try to help you. Let's get you a jacket. I'm supposed to cuff you, but I don't want the neighbors to see it. I'll wait till we get to the sheriff's office, okay?"

"Okay," she sniffed.

Jim used Helen's phone to call the office.

"Sheriff's office, can I help you?" said Mrs. Laura Simmons.

"This is Deputy Taylor. I need to meet with the sheriff in 25 minutes and—"

"Wait a minute, Deputy. The sheriff is tied up. You don't make appointments for him, I do. And—"

"Hush and listen a minute! This is urgent. I'll be there with a prisoner in 25 minutes. See if you can reach Detective Roberts to be there, too," he said as he hung up.

Once there, Deputy Taylor cuffed Helen and escorted her to the second-floor office. As they entered, Mrs. Simmons, the sheriff's secretary, gave Jim an angry stare. After showing Helen to a seat, Jim approached Mrs. Simmons and whispered, "I'm sorry. It's been a long night. I owe you lunch."

She replied with a nod of her head toward the sheriff's door. Jim knocked, and the sheriff barked, "Enter."

Jim relayed the entire story, from arriving on scene at the river to Helen's confession. He added that he had worked on his own time for the most part. Detective Roberts was strangely silent.

Before the sheriff could say anything, Deputy Taylor said, "She's outside. I want you to hear it from her."

Sheriff Smoot frowned and finally said, "Bring her in."

After Helen finished her story, she answered questions from both the sheriff and Detective Roberts. Then she was escorted by another detective to his office, where she wrote out a formal confession. She was taken downstairs to be booked.

Back in the sheriff's office, the atmosphere was tense. Detective Roberts chewed on Jim until the sheriff finally intervened.

"Deputy Taylor, you failed to follow orders. This was a city case, and you went around our detective division. Detective Roberts is upset because he was cut out of a case that should have been his. In the future, if something like this comes up, you are to hand it off to the detective's division. Is that understood?"

"Yes, sir. I'm sorry for the screw up."

"Now, let's get down to business and plan how to make the arrest on Johnny McCrary. He'll be armed, desperate, and dangerous."

In the meantime, Helen was transported to the jail of an adjoining county to hide her from Johnny McCrary or anyone else who might tip him off.

The plan was essentially the sheriff's idea. Detective Roberts would call McCrary and ask him to a meeting with the sheriff and the detective division. He was to be told that it was a big case and couldn't be discussed over the phone. The sheriff would brief Chief Jamison in Dawson.

The sheriff assured them that he would personally disarm McCrary, which made everyone a little nervous. "I need a minute with Deputy Taylor, if y'all will excuse us," announced the sheriff.

Alone with him now, Sheriff Smoot told Jim to have a seat. "I don't know whether to fire you or to hug ya," he began. "This is probably the biggest case we've ever handled. You're a rookie—been here only six or seven months. Your methods are a little unorthodox, but you produced results. If it hadn't been for your work on this, a murder woulda been chalked up as an accident. I appreciate your initiative, but from now on, you need to follow our rules. Understand?"

"Yes, sir," Jim replied.

The sheriff stood up, offered his hand, and said, "Good job. Your daddy would be proud of you."

"Thanks, Sheriff. One more thing. McCrary may be onto me. I better hide in another office till he's under arrest."

"Fine, Jim, fine," answered the sheriff.

Detective McCrary walked into the sheriff's office at 3:00 p.m. sharp for the meeting.

"Close the door, Johnny, will you?" asked Sheriff Smoot.

Johnny closed the door and took a seat.

"Hey, before we get started, I want to show Johnny the gun trick," the sheriff beamed. "Johnny, a prisoner trustee showed me this last night. You're goin' to laugh your ass off. Who's got a gun? What're you carrying, Johnny?"

"A .38 snubnosed," replied Detective McCrary.

"Yeah, that'll work. But unload it first, of course."

McCrary smiled, unloaded his gun, and handed it to Sheriff

Smoot. Detective Roberts rose from his chair and stood in front of Johnny as two deputies moved into place behind him. "You're under arrest for the murder of John Gibson. Stand up."

McCrary was speechless, docile, and white as a sheet. The two deputies pinned McCrary's arms behind his back and placed handcuffs on his wrists.

Jim entered the room, lifted the back of Johnny's jacket, and removed a slapjack from his pocket. "Evidence," Jim stated.

It took the June 6, 1944 Allied invasion of France to finally knock the story out of newspapers all over the region.

Three months later, on September 14, 1944, Johnny Werner McCrary was on his way to death row in Nashville, and Jim was headed home to celebrate Lois's second birthday with Lilly, the kids, the Larkeys, and his mother, Esther.

He and Lilly had asked Esther several times to come and live with them. They were back in their Springdale home and enjoying the added space. Esther refused, but she agreed to stay with them temporarily so May and her family could move into the home place. Jim's thoughts turned to his mother and the family events of the recent past. Aunt Lois had passed away a couple of months ago, and the family had been shocked when Esther accepted the offer of her son, John, to come live with them in Detroit.

Even though Jim and his family, along with his sister May, had visited Esther often, she opted to move to Michigan—new territory, she called it. Madge and her husband had agreed to buy the house and small farm. At least it will stay in the family, Jim thought.

Finally, he allowed himself to think of Helen Gibson and the lies with which he had tricked her. She was sentenced to 20 years in prison for conspiracy to commit murder and five years for insurance fraud.

"This can be a dirty business," he whispered.

CHAPTER 28

1944–1945

Lois was the center of attention at her birthday party, and Shelly and Robby were jealous. Their grandmother, Esther Taylor, was spending as much time with them as possible. She would be riding back with John and his family to Detroit after the September Meeting on Sunday.

Having learned over the last few months how it worked, Jim realized that he would be back in the headlines in the following day's newspaper.

First were the headlines when the case was solved. Jim had tried to deflect credit to Doc Williams, but the coroner had told reporters that the case was solved by "Taylor's natural curiosity and tenacity."

Another round of publicity started with the trial and continued every day until the jury came in with a verdict. Jim had been an excellent witness, according to the District Attorney. After the trial, the DA was quoted as saying, "Taylor was calm and stuck to the facts on cross–examination. Mighty professional for a rookie cop," he added.

Tomorrow's lead story would detail the death sentence handed to the former city detective, but it would also rehash his love affair with the victim's wife, the arrest, and the subsequent trial.

At first, Jim had enjoyed the attention of the public spotlight, but it was becoming a bit of a burden. Some of his fellow officers had made comments to the effect that he had merely been in the right place at the right time.

Jim sought advice from his two best friends in the department, Jimmy Ray Johnson and Cam Barker. Cam was well known for his exploits as a lawman. His broad red nose and gravelly voice were a testament to his life-long affection for moonshine and Pall Malls. His growing waistline revealed another addiction, his love affair with fried foods. Jimmy Ray's bigger-than-life personality, booming voice, and constant swagger belied the fact that he was a benevolent man with a big heart. His red face and rotund build portended a deadly combination—high blood pressure and diabetes.

Jimmy Ray and Cam were a little older, and both had experienced high-profile cases with intense publicity. Jimmy Ray's advice: "Forget it. This too shall pass." Cam assured him that some of the men might be jealous but that he certainly had their respect.

All of Jim's siblings were at the annual church homecoming except Ray. Esther would see him on Monday, since they planned to spend the night at his house in Ohio before going on to Michigan.

Rob preached an ole timey, gut-wrenching sermon on Sunday morning, and shouts of several elderly women echoed throughout the old building on the hill. Jim was quite the celebrity at church. Everyone had either read the Sunday paper or at least heard about the murder case. Even Rob had cornered him and asked for details. Lilly came to Jim's rescue by taking Rob by the arm and whispering, "It's time to return thanks. People are starving."

After the dinner on the ground, the Taylors gathered at the cemetery. The grassless mound in front of Aunt Lois's grave marker was a stark reminder of her recent death. The family gathered around it and reminisced about her colorful life.

Jim slipped from the circle and walked over to Annie's

grave. After placing a daisy at the base of her stone, he began to talk to her. Lilly watched him, saw his lips moving, and wondered what he was saying to her.

"Well, Annie, it's a beautiful fall day. I wish you could be here to see it. You always knew which leaves turned first and last and everything in between. I hope to get back up here and sit with you a while next month, when the colors will be at their peak. It hit me as were driving up here that you would be 30 years old this year. Don't seem possible. I love you," he mouthed, then eased back over to the group.

By late afternoon, they had all gathered at the old home place, where they had a party as a sendoff for Esther, John, and his family. John now had a phone at his Detroit house, and Jim and Lilly were having one installed the following week. They would be able to talk long distance, but the conversations would have to be very brief to hold down costs.

That night, long after Jim had fallen asleep, Lilly lay in bed thinking.

I wonder what he was saying to Annie. He's the sweetest man I have ever known. He makes everyone laugh with his mischief, and people are naturally drawn to him. He's great with the kids, always teasing and hugging.

It feels good to be in our own house, and Shelly and Robby enjoy playing with their new friends in the neighborhood. I'm glad we moved back from Detroit. School starts next week, and I love working with the kids. I'm glad to be out of Detroit. I would have resisted going back there the second time if it weren't for my uneasy feelings and the rumors. I was afraid women were chasing Jim, or maybe he was chasing them. My sister told me the rumors she had heard, but I didn't believe her, or maybe I just didn't want to believe her. He said that in his line of work there would always be rumors, but there've been no hints of infidelity in Detroit or since we've been back in Tennessee. He's a good man. We've been through a lot together.

Lilly nuzzled him and pressed against his body, and for the first time in their marriage, she awakened him from a deep sleep to snuggle. He sleepily made love to her, and they fell asleep in each other's arms.

Less than two months later, President Roosevelt won an unprecedented fourth term and the nation sensed that the end of the war was in sight.

Jim and Lilly entertained relatives from both sides of the family at a Christmas open house at their house in Springdale. Lilly's old kitchen, now referred to as the middle room, served as a small den, with the living room still on the front side of the house and the new kitchen on the back. A newly added bedroom and bath completed the addition. Lilly served punch and cookies from the kitchen, which allowed her to speak individually with each guest. A white apron covered her new red Christmas dress, an early present from Jim. He was floating among groups in the living room, middle room, and kitchen. Shelly insisted on helping her mother serve, while Robby played with three of his cousins in the front bedroom.

Just after nine o'clock, when the last guest departed, the Taylors gathered around the Christmas tree to exchange presents. Shelly and Robby took turns giving out the gifts, and Lois helped Mama and Daddy unwrap their presents.

Lilly allowed the children a few minutes to play with their new toys, then shooed them off to bed. "Santa Claus won't come until everyone is asleep," she told them. Lilly rocked Lois while Jim read a Christmas story to Shelly and Robby. After the kids were asleep, Jim and Lilly sat at the kitchen table sipping eggnog.

"I think everyone enjoyed themselves," commented Lilly.

"Yeah, it was a good party," Jim replied.

"We better get to bed. Santa Claus has to get up early to put out more presents."

"No, I think I'll put 'em out now so I don't have to get up

again."

"Okay. Get them out of the car and I'll clean up this mess."

"Okay," Jim said, as he headed out the back door.

Later, in bed, Jim was dreaming that the school bell was ringing, but the school day was only half over.

Robby was playing a trick, or maybe his friend Barry...

Suddenly he was awake, or almost.

"It's the telephone, Jim. Wake up," Lilly said as she nudged his shoulder.

"Hello," Jim answered.

"This is Dispatch. The sheriff has ordered everybody in. Go to the civic center. Big fight."

Jim grabbed his clothes and hopped around the foot of the bed on one leg, trying to get into his uniform pants.

"What is it?" Lilly asked, trying to mask the fear in her voice.

"Nothing to worry about. Just a fight at the civic center. I'll be back soon."

"Why do they need you?"

"Must be a pretty big fight," he said as he hurried out with his shirt unbuttoned.

When Jim arrived on scene, the worst was over. He helped subdue and cuff one particularly large man, then transported three to jail.

"What happened?" he asked a city officer at the jail.

"Big Christmas shindig got outta hand. Several officers injured. Too many for us to handle. I guess Chief Jamison called the sheriff for help."

As Deputy Taylor headed for home, he noticed that his shirt pocket had been ripped during the scuffle. Have to ask Lilly to sew it back on, he thought.

Lilly was awake when he crawled back into bed.

"What happened?" she inquired.

"Just a ruckus. Had to transport some people to jail. Lilly, you can't lie awake every time I get called out. Let's get some sleep."

"I know, I know," she replied.

A few minutes later, he turned over and kissed her cheek.

"Good night. Merry Christmas," he whispered.

"Merry Christmas," she replied.

Jim was off duty for Christmas Day, and the kids were in high gear. Shelly and Robby had been fussing off and on all day, while Lois observed them with somewhat detached interest. The excitement over Santa's toys and the sugar from Christmas candy had resulted in Robby getting a spanking and Shelly a warning or two.

Lilly was in the middle of one of those warnings when the phone rang.

Jim said, "I'll get it."

"No, it's right here beside me," answered Lilly.

"Hello."

"Hello. Is Deputy Taylor there?" blared the gruff voice on the other end.

"Yes, just a moment."

It was Dispatch, asking Jim if he could answer a domestic call.

"It's a domestic there in Springdale. We're running a mite thin. Can you help us out?"

"Yeah, what's the address? Okay, I'll handle it," Jim said as he jotted down the address. "Gotta go, Lilly. I'll be back shortly."

The disturbance was located less than a mile away. When Deputy Taylor arrived, he could hear the loud voices inside as he got out of the car. A child of about seven was sitting on the porch, crying.

"What's goin' on, son?" Jim asked.

"Daddy hurt Mama," he sobbed.

Jim knocked on the door and the loud voices quieted. He knocked harder a second time, then a third. He started to step off the porch and try the back door when he heard a loud voice.

"Don't answer that!" Then louder still, "I said, don't answer that!"

The door opened, and Jim saw an unkempt woman dressed in jeans and a bloodstained blouse. Her light-brown hair hung limp and stringy, and she was nursing a cut over her eye with a dirty dish rag.

"What's goin' on, ma'am?' Deputy Taylor asked.

"Nothing. Everything will be all right. We're fine."

"You don't look fine."

"Yeah, I'm okay."

"Tell your husband to step outside a minute."

"I'm not coming out. I'm not stupid," came a loud voice from somewhere behind her. "I'm drunk, but you can't touch me in my own house!"

Jim pushed by the woman and stepped into the house. The man ran to the kitchen, stumbling and staggering as he went.

Jim followed him into the kitchen. About Jim's age but slightly taller, the man was rummaging through a cabinet drawer.

"You've done it now! You're in my house without a warrant!" he yelled as he turned around.

"What're you holding behind you?' Jim asked as he approached the man.

"Wouldn't you like to know?" he mocked.

Jim hit him hard in the jaw with his fist. The man fell backwards near the sink, and a butcher knife skidded across the dirty linoleum floor. Deputy Taylor twisted his arm, bent him across the sink, and cuffed him.

Hearing the commotion from the kitchen, the wife screamed, "Don't hurt him! Don't hurt him, please!"

Jim led the man to the car and placed him in the back seat. After turning him over to the jailer and signing the necessary papers, Deputy Taylor headed back to Springdale. On the drive back, he wondered if the wife would bail her husband out.

Of course she will, and then the process can start all over again, he thought. "Merry Christmas," he mumbled to himself.

In early January, Lilly returned to work and resumed the routine of dropping off Lois and then chatting with Shelly and Robby on the drive to school.

Jim had the weekend off, and Lilly was planning a special meal for Saturday night. A call from Dispatch during dinner resulted in Jim being gone for almost three hours. Lilly finally got the children to sleep and waited up for her husband. Jim returned tired, and they fussed for half an hour.

Monday afternoon after school, a new electric clothes washer was delivered to Lilly. It was Jim's way of apologizing.

The delivery men set it up in the small basement and showed her how it worked. Later, Jim cautioned her to be careful with the wringer as he showed her the cut–off switch for the third time.

That night, they were passionate in bed. As Jim reached for the night stand drawer for a rubber, Lilly stopped him. "No. I want to feel *you* tonight, not that."

"We shouldn't take a chance," cautioned Jim.

"It'll be all right," Lilly assured him as she snuggled underneath him.

In late March, Lilly broke the news to Jim. "I'm pregnant."

Jim was strangely silent. Finally, he said, "Are you sure?"

"Yes."

"I should have known. You've been awfully frisky lately. You'll have to quit teaching, you know," he said sympathetically.

"Maybe not. I've given it a lot of thought. I can wear loose clothing. No one will suspect until the last month of school," she added.

The month of April started with a burst of color. The retiring ruby–tinted redbud trees signaled that the vibrant dogwoods would soon bound into bloom. However, bright hopes of spring rebirth were quickly dashed with the news of

President Roosevelt's death on April 12, 1945. Three days later came news that Lilly's father, Henry Larkey, had died.

While the nation gathered around their radios mourning the death of the president, the Larkeys and their in-laws huddled around Mrs. Larkey, the matron of the family. Lilly's sister Mary would move her family into the big house on the river to care for their mother.

Much-needed good news arrived a few weeks later on May 7, 1945. Germany surrendered, and a relieved nation turned its attention to the Pacific. Jim, Lilly, and the kids drove into Dawson to join the celebration. The honking of horns, the ringing of church bells, and the pops of firecrackers filled the air. Lilly tried her best to explain the commotion to the kids as Jim joined in the revelry.

The last Thursday of May was one of spectacular beauty as Deputy Taylor drove into the foothills of the southeast section of the county. The dazzling sun, already high in the pale blue sky, enhanced the spring-green hue of grassy knolls and trees alike.

Jim turned onto Simpson Road and headed up Gentry Mountain. It was good to be in the mountains, but serving civil papers was a part of the job he didn't particularly enjoy. He was reminded of the woman whom he had served with eviction papers the previous month. She was at the end of her rope; it showed in her face. She was about 35, but looked 50. She was alone, raising two kids. He stood in her kitchen explaining that if she wasn't out in 10 days, deputies would come and set her furniture on the side of the road.

When she went out back to check on the kids, he opened the refrigerator door to make sure they had food. The refrigerator was empty except for a jug of water and half a stick of butter. He placed a $20 bill under the jug and shut the door quickly when he heard her footsteps on the porch.

After he had negotiated a switchback curve, two men who were working on a rickety fence came into view on the left side of the road. They wore overalls with no shirts underneath, and due to the steepness of the hillside, they could hardly stand erect.

Jim rolled to a stop and greeted them. "How y'all doin' today?

"Pretty good, I reckon," answered the older of the two.

"I'm lookin for the Boucher place. Can ye help me?"

"Henry Boucher?" the same man asked.

"Yes, sir. That's the one."

The man's lower foot began to slide in the crumbly shale. He grabbed the fence and straightened up.

"Go to the top of the hill and turn left down the lane. There's a rusty old sign; says somethin' 'bout apples for sale."

"Thank ye. Appreciate it," Jim said as he started to pull away.

"Hey!" the man shouted.

Jim stopped the car and backed up a few feet. "Yeah?"

"You might ort to be careful. The Bouchers is strange people."

"Whatta ye mean?"

"Well, they've got a quar turn to 'em."

"How's that?"

"They don't like people comin' round their place, 'specially strangers."

"Okay, thanks. Much obliged," answered Jim as he pulled away.

"He lives there with his two old maid sisters," the man yelled as an afterthought.

Jim waved his thanks without looking back.

Deputy Taylor turned left and slowly proceeded down the narrow passage that tunneled through the forest, following the ridgeline. Jonquils with blooms long gone dotted both sides of the lane in a haphazard sort of way. The daylight ahead revealed a rundown shack. Clucking chickens scattered as he pulled into the yard. An old man and two women were working in a small garden to the left front of the house.

Jim got out of the car and threw up his hand. "How y'all doin' today?" he asked.

They stared at him without comment. The two women were dressed in long dresses with sunbonnets. One of them—the one dipping snuff—reminded him of his Aunt Addie.

The old man finally spoke as the women retreated to the front porch. "What you want? This is private property." He was dressed in grimy, gray pants and a tattered, long-sleeved, checkered shirt.

Probably a logger in his younger days, Jim thought. "Just need to talk to ye a minute," Jim replied. "Could a man get a drink of spring water?"

Boucher stepped up to the remnant of an aging picket fence. "You got no business here. Git offen my land."

The women were talking at the same time—cackling words that Deputy Taylor couldn't make out.

Jim said, "I've got some papers for you. Then I'll be gone."

Boucher stared at him without reply.

At first, Jim couldn't make out what the women were saying.

"Git the axe, Henry. Git the axe! *Git the axe, Henry!*" they repeated, louder each time.

Boucher moved from behind the fence toward the corner of the porch where a double-bladed axe was partially buried in a chopping stump.

The two women were chanting now in unison, "Kill him Henry, kill him!"

Never taking his eyes off the deputy, the old man worked the axe handle back and forth to release it from the stump.

"Wait! I'm not here to arrest you. I've just got papers to serve!" yelled Deputy Taylor.

Boucher freed the axe, raised it over his head, and began methodically trudging toward Jim.

"Stop! Put the axe down!" Deputy Taylor ordered as he unsnapped his holster.

Boucher kept coming as Jim retreated to the rear of the cruiser.

"Put the axe down! *Now!*"

The old man kept coming, egged on by his sisters. Jim backed up as the man advanced. With "Kill him, kill him!" ringing in his ears, Deputy Taylor drew his pistol as Boucher backed him around the car for the second time.

Finally, the old man stopped. Thank God, Jim said to himself. The old man looked at the deputy, then the car, then back at the deputy. Suddenly he buried the axe in the hood of the car.

"Stop!" Jim yelled as he charged toward the old man.

Boucher quickly raised the axe, which stopped Deputy Taylor in his tracks. The old man stared at the deputy, then smashed the axe into the windshield of the cruiser.

Boucher held the axe at port arms across his chest, staring at Jim through bright, intensely blue eyes. Then he slowly raised the weapon over his head with both hands and took a step toward Jim.

Jim took careful aim and shot him in the leg. The bullet shattered Boucher's kneecap. The axe fell behind the old man, and he tried to step toward Jim, but the leg gave way. The old ladies screamed and ran into the shack.

Lord, please don't let them come back out with a gun, the deputy silently prayed.

Old man Boucher began to moan—the first sound he had made since picking up the axe. Jim depressed the mike key and radioed for an ambulance and backup, then tried to comfort Boucher while keeping an eye on the house.

A few days later, the District Attorney ruled the shooting self–defense, and other deputies served the papers on Boucher at the hospital. The newspaper ran a picture of Deputy Taylor and his "chopped–up cruiser."

CHAPTER 29

1945–1947

Lilly was beginning her eighth month of pregnancy in early August when the good news came. The United States had developed a super bomb that completely devastated a Japanese city 25 times larger than Dawson. Lilly thought of the thousands of deaths it must have caused. But sadness turned to joy when she realized that it could shorten the war.

Three days later, a second Japanese city was completely destroyed, and shortly thereafter, the war in the Pacific ended almost as quickly as it had begun. Lilly was surprised at the sudden news of total victory. The radio and movie newsreel broadcasters had repeatedly said that the Asian island nation would fight to the last man, woman, and child.

After assurances from Lilly that she would be fine, Jim left to celebrate with Cam and Jimmy Ray at Jimmy Ray's old home place on the river. The two-story house with a large wraparound porch faced the river. Johnson's parents had willed the place to him, and he used it on weekends and holidays. News of the party spread quickly, and off-duty deputies, policemen, and their friends filled the house and spilled out into the yard.

Two months later, Jim and Lilly's fourth child, a boy, was born at Dawson Memorial Hospital. Lilly had decided to take a break from teaching for a couple of years to be with the baby, and Jim had happily agreed. They would live off Jim's salary and dip into savings only if absolutely necessary.

Lilly had named the third child, so it was Jim's turn. Several months earlier, he had picked Sally if a girl and Henry, in honor of Lilly's father, if a boy.

Two days after the birth of their son, the new father paced around the hospital room. Lilly said, "Jim, you've tinkered and fiddled with everything in this room. What's on your mind?"

"Well, I've got something to ask you, but I'm afraid you'll be disappointed." He hesitated as he searched for the right words.

"C'mon, out with it. You won't hurt my feelings."

"Uh, it's about the baby's name."

"Yes? Go ahead."

"The nurses keep asking—you know—for a name to put on the birth certificate."

"*Yeeees.*" She strung out the word as if to say, "Out with it."

"Well, every time I think of the name Henry, I think of that old man I shot, Henry Boucher," he said quickly, out of breath.

"Honey, it'll be fine to change the name. My dad would understand," she said with a giggle.

"But we could have his middle name be Henry," he suggested.

"Yeah, that'll work just fine," she agreed, then asked, "What's his first name gonna be?"

"I was thinking Barry, after my friend that drowned. You remember Barry, that drowned in the river when we were 12?"

"Sure, I remember. You, Barry, and Robby were thick as thieves. I haven't thought of Barry in years. I like the name—Barry Henry Taylor."

"I'll go tell the nurses right now!" Jim said as he hurried from the room.

Rob and Cindy Boatwright visited the Taylors at their Springdale home in early November to see the new baby. Rob said a special prayer thanking the Lord that mother and child were both healthy.

*****

Fifteen months later, the entire first week of January 1947 was blustery and cold. Every day since the New Year had dawned had seen precipitation of one form or another, but today was an exception. Jim stared out the squad room window to watch the sun as it cleared the rooftop of the newsstand across the street. He shifted the wool overcoat on his lap. He wondered if the Christmas present from Lilly would be needed again today.

The shift leader called out for everyone to listen up and copy down a BOLO (Be On Lookout). Jim jotted down the tag number and description of the stolen car in his log book. He waited impatiently for the pass–along meeting to end. He needed to see Dawson police Officer Brady Ketron about a case they were prosecuting in General Sessions Court later in the week.

As the meeting broke up, Jim scurried down the hall and slipped into the city PD squad room. Brady Ketron was not there. The city shift sergeant, Tom Corker, was just finishing the pass–along on the same stolen car information to the city's day shift.

"Listen up. This last item is important. We have a tip from one of our informants that Harley Pesterfield got a load of liquor in late last night from Hot Springs, North Carolina. It's stashed in the weeds by a telephone pole just outside his store building. As all of you know, Pesterfield is a dangerous character. He's a convicted felon—spent time in prison for murder. Anybody know him well enough to reason with him? We don't want anyone to get hurt over this."

The uneasy silence was finally broken by a voice from the back of the room. "I know him. I'll bring him in."

"Well, Deputy Taylor, welcome to our meeting," the shift sergeant said. "This is inside the city, so we'll get a city officer to go with you."

A rookie officer, Carson Baxter, spoke up. "I'll drive him out there."

"Fine. I need a word with you two. Everyone else is dismissed. Have a good day. Keep your eyes open and your head down," cautioned Sergeant Corker. "Okay, Deputy Taylor, you're more experienced. You're taking the lead on this, right?"

"Yeah, no problem. I served some civil papers on Pesterfield last month."

"Good," replied Sergeant Corker. "Remember, if he resists, back off and call for backup. According to our informant, the liquor will be in gallon jars and hidden in weeds by a telephone pole beside the store. He leaves it there all day and pays an old man to watch it—you know, so no kids stumble onto it, and so forth. After dark, he moves it inside and pours it into pint and quart jars for resale. Any questions?"

"Nope," both replied.

"Okay, you two, be careful." He turned to Baxter. "One more thing. You are still in training. Stay in the car and summon help if Jim runs into trouble. Understand?"

"Yes, sir."

Harley Pesterfield was the second-largest bootlegger in the Dawson area. He operated a combination store and cab stand at Greasy Corner. The neighborhood supposedly derived its name from grease tracked over the area by workers at the meat packing plant that had once operated there.

On the ride to Greasy Corner, Deputy Taylor cautioned the rookie to stay in the car once they arrived on scene.

Officer Baxter pulled a few feet past the store building as instructed, so that Deputy Taylor's door was opposite the telephone pole. Jim rolled down his window to get a better look. Outside and toward the rear of the store, an old man sat in a wooden chair canted back at an angle, with the top of the chair resting against the side of the building.

The deputy was within a few feet of the pole when the old man woke up. He jerked his feet to the ground to bring the chair upright and quickly disappeared around the back corner of the store.

Thirty–one gallon jars and four quart jars, according to Jim's quick count. "Must've run out of gallon jars in North Carolina," Jim said with a laugh. He unscrewed the lid of a quart jar and noted the pungent odor of moonshine.

Heading for the front door, the deputy shifted the jar to his left hand and unsnapped his holster with the other. He paused a few seconds inside the door to let his eyes adjust to the dim light.

Harley was leaning forward with his outstretched hands on the counter in front of him. Meagerly stocked shelves lined the left side of the room. A well–worn horsehair sofa sat against the wall to the right. Two lights hung from the ceiling, one near the front of the store and one over the counter.

Jim hesitated. Something looked different from the month before, when he had last been here. What was it? The Christmas tree! That was it. The Christmas tree was gone.

The old man who had warned Pesterfield was standing at the back door, back lit by bright sunshine. Jim recognized the silhouette.

Harley's black mustache accentuated his dark eyes and high cheekbones, which hinted of his Cherokee ancestry. His oily, coal–black hair was combed straight back.

"Good morning, Harley," Jim greeted.

Harley smiled, but said nothing.

Deputy Taylor slowly approached the counter, talking as he walked. "Got some bad news, Harley," Jim said as he raised the jar of moonshine from behind his left leg. "We found your stash. You're gonna' have to go downtown and make bond."

The old man shifted in the doorway and rested his head against the door facing. Sunlight streamed through when the man moved.

It was a bright, blinding light, the whitest white imaginable—then beautiful purples, reds, and blues—then the pain.

The moonshine crashed to the floor. Jim's hands went to his head as he instinctively staggered toward the front door.

His thoughts came in abrupt, incoherent flashes. Get away, shot, moonshine hands, wet, can't see.

Outside, Officer Baxter heard the shot, hesitated, and then keyed the mike to call for assistance. The radio blared with static; it was malfunctioning again. Meanwhile, Pesterfield and the old man jumped into a cab out back and fled.

Deputy Taylor stumbled blindly to the front door and collapsed. The blood that he had thought was moonshine streamed from his head wound, down his face, onto his shoulder and chest. Officer Baxter saw the blood, frantically tried to get the radio to work, and then raced away, looking for a telephone.

The funeral home hearse/ambulance rushed Deputy Taylor through city traffic to the hospital where his son had been delivered just three months earlier. Emergency room doctors asked the attendants what they knew about the situation.

One of the attendants answered, "He was semiconscious on the way in. He's a deputy sheriff shot in the head by someone at Greasy Corner. The only words I could make out were something about red eyes."

"We applied pressure to the wound," the other attendant volunteered.

The doctors asked that a neurosurgeon be summoned and then sent the patient for X-rays. As the doctors and nurses worked feverishly to save the lawman's life, officers from police agencies throughout East Tennessee and Southwest Virginia fanned out to search for the shooter.

Lilly was called by the sheriff's department, given sketchy details, and told to head to the hospital. She quickly took the baby to a neighbor's house and then drove herself to Dawson. She pulled up in front of the emergency room and hurried in, leaving the car door open with the keys in the ignition. Personnel inside told her that her husband had been sent to surgery. A hospital volunteer walked her to the waiting area.

Rookie cop Carson Baxter, who had followed orders exactly, was devastated as he answered his supervisor's questions. "Why didn't you assist Deputy Taylor? Why did you leave him there?"

Over 200 lawmen joined the manhunt for the man who had shot one of their own. Three days later, acting on a tip, state troopers in Virginia surrounded the house of Harley Pesterfield's cousin and demanded that Pesterfield give up. Harley surrendered without resistance. At that same moment, Jim was en route by ambulance to the University of Virginia Hospital in Charlottesville, some 278 miles away. He was there for brain surgery and several weeks of recovery.

Lilly would later claim that it was one of the happiest times of their marriage. During his recovery, she pushed him around campus in a wheelchair. They enjoyed movies at the college theater and relished the stress-free environment of the university. The children had been split up among relatives and were in good hands.

In June 1947, after Deputy Taylor was well enough to testify in court, Pesterfield was convicted and received 30 years in prison. Meanwhile, Jim was spending time in a different type of prison.

*****

Lilly handed Jim his cane and helped him out to the front porch. He eased into the chair as a rooster crowed in the distance, signaling the start of another warm June day. Lilly kissed him on the forehead and retreated into the house to wash the breakfast dishes.

What had the brain doctor said about his recovery? "You may feel anxious or even angry at times, but you have to work through that. Every brain injury is different, and it takes time for the brain to heal or adjust."

The dull ache of sadness settled over him as he watched his neighbor, David, fiddling with his car before leaving for work. Watching him drive off sparked the recurring sense of being left behind. It reminded him of how he had felt the day after Annie's death. Day-to-day life continued. People went to work, church, and even a Fourth of July celebration. It didn't seem right.

At least the bills were being paid, thanks to Lilly. She had bravely appeared before the county commission to plead their case. The newspaper had quoted her: "The men of the Sheriff's Department put their lives on the line every day to enforce the laws and protect our citizens. The least we can do is pay their medical bills when they are killed or injured in the line of duty."

The county commission voted 20 to 1 to pay all medical bills, including those of the hospital at the University of Virginia. The newspaper ran an editorial backing her position and also established an account at the First National Bank for donations to help the family with day-to-day expenses.

Jim balked at the thought of taking handouts, especially from people he didn't know, but Lilly convinced him otherwise. "People want to help, and it wouldn't be right to deny them the opportunity," she said. "We have a new baby, three other children, and house payments to make. Be thankful that people want to pitch in to show their gratitude. Concentrate on getting well so you can go back to work."

I've got a lot to be thankful for, he thought as he watched bees flitting from one marigold to the next by the front steps. Lilly's been with me every step of the way, and the sheriff assured me that a job will be waiting for me when I get on my feet. There's been a steady stream of family members and friends coming to see me. Rob comes every weekend, and folks bring food almost every day.

The sound of movement inside the house behind him interrupted his thoughts. Lilly opened the screen door with her hip and eased into the adjacent chair with Barry and his bottle. He studied her serene face, mindful of the baby's intermittent suckling sounds.

"We have a lot to be thankful for, Lilly."

She glanced at him for a quick read of his face and nodded her agreement. Barry's tiny hand gripped and released his blanket in rhythm with the pursing sound of his mouth.

As the baby shifted in the crook of Lilly's arm, Jim thought, I haven't been true to you Lilly. I'll do better, I promise. You're a good woman. I don't deserve you.

Touching her arm, he said, "I love you."

She turned to reply and noticed the tears in his eyes as he looked away. Her first impulse was to ask what was wrong, but instead, she placed the baby and bottle in his arms and kissed him. Then, with their faces just inches apart, she replied, "I love you, too."

*****

Over the next few months, they settled into a comfortable routine. By September, Jim had been cleared for light duty. Lilly would get the kids off to school, then, along with Barry, drive Jim to work. Since he hadn't been cleared to drive a cruiser, he worked in the office, helping the department's two detectives clear cases.

Even though Jim worked only half days, Sheriff Smoot insisted on paying him for full time. Deputy Taylor gradually began spending afternoons reestablishing his street contacts, and in late October, the doctors cleared him to drive. The bank account at First National contained just over $2,000, and Jim used a small portion of it to pay his street contacts in return for information on crimes. He was able to assist the detectives in solving an armed robbery and several burglaries.

On Tuesday, December 2, 1947, Sheriff Smoot called Deputy Taylor into his office.

"Jim, Detective Cox is resigning to accept a security job at the plant. Effective immediately, I'm promoting you to detective. It means a little more money and your own car. The downside is that you'll be on call 24 hours a day. Whatta ya say?"

Jim stared at the sheriff in disbelief. Six months earlier, he had worried that he would never work again, and now he was being promoted. He fought back tears, which seemed to come without warning since his injury. His mind was a jumble of thoughts. Working major crimes, no more civil papers to serve, my own car, working unsupervised, a pay raise—I gotta get home and tell Lilly!

The sheriff nudged, "Jim, aren't you gonna say something? A simple 'yes' will do."

"Yes! Yes, sir. Thank you, Sheriff. I won't let you down."

"I know you won't. Get with Mrs. Anderson and complete the paperwork," the sheriff said as he stood and shook hands.

At home, Jim shared the good news with Lilly. She enjoyed the sparkle in his eyes as he relayed the conversation with the sheriff.

"You're not cooking tonight," he added. "We're all going to Wanda's Restaurant to celebrate!"

Later, back home, once the kids were asleep, they cuddled passionately.

"Lilly?"

"Uh-huh."

"I'm gonna take a few days off for Christmas. We didn't really have a Christmas last year. I don't recollect it at all."

"That's good," she replied sleepily.

Then, suddenly awake and alert, she said, "I want to talk

about something."

"What's that?"

"I want to go back to work next year. Lois will be starting school, and I can pay Mrs. Chambers to keep Barry."

Jim thought of Annie and her dream of going to college and then working as a nurse, a doctor, or a teacher. "That's fine. I just want you to be happy," he said as he pulled her tighter against him.

Lilly was surprised. She had expected him to object. She had practiced the argument in her mind many times and had been waiting for the right moment to broach the subject.

They lay spooned, with his hand on her belly. Long after his rhythmic breathing signaled sleep, she whispered, "I love you, Jim."

CHAPTER 30

A few nights later, Jim was supervising Robby's bath when Deputy Johnson called.

"Jim, we've got Johnny Clayton here on a burglary charge. He says he's got information to trade, but he won't talk to anybody but you. Wanna talk to him now or wait till morning?'

"I'll be in to talk to him. Give me an hour or so, okay?"

"Sure. See ya later."

Jim finished Robby's bath, kissed Lilly, and headed for the office. Pulling behind the jail to park, he noticed a commotion at a sheriff's cruiser near the jail intake. Thinking an officer might need assistance, he turned the car to shine the headlights in that direction.

The bright light revealed a black, bloody, sullen face with eyes staring straight ahead. The man's hands were cuffed behind his back. His shirt was torn open, and sweat glistened on his chest.

Jim recognized Deputy Simpson and heard him yell a question, but he only caught a few words. The black man didn't answer and took another fist to the mouth.

"Hey, stop!" Jim yelled as Joby and Detroit flashed in his mind. "What's goin' on here?" he asked as he approached the two.

"Teaching this nigger some manners, that's all."

"The man's cuffed. Don't hit him again," Jim said with authority.

"Keep outta this, Taylor. None of your business." The

deputy turned back to the prisoner. "Had enough, nigger?"

The prisoner stared at Simpson.

"I guess not," Deputy Simpson said as he drew back to deliver another blow.

Detective Taylor grabbed Simpson's wrist. "There'll be no more of that."

Simpson jerked his wrist away and pushed Jim hard in the chest, propelling him backward. "This is my prisoner, and you're interfering with an arrest. Now get the hell away from me, or you'll get some of the same!"

Jim regained his footing, his heart racing, adrenaline flowing. He stared at the deputy for an instant and then took a deep breath as he closed the three steps between them. "You're forgetting one thing. I'm not cuffed," he said as he smashed Simpson's face with a right haymaker.

Deputy Simpson bounced up and they exchanged several licks before two deputies and a jailer pulled them apart.

Chief Deputy Grey Stallings was called in from home. After talking with all involved, he informed Jim that he was in trouble and that he was to be in the sheriff's office at 8:00 sharp the next morning.

Later at home, Lilly nursed his wounds and assured him that he had done the right thing.

"You don't understand, Lilly. I'm probably goin' to be fired."

"I don't care if they do fire you. The important thing is that you stopped further abuse of that poor prisoner. You can get another job."

"I don't want another job!"

"Jim, be sensible. What if that fight had dislodged the steel plate in your head? You could have died instantly. Do you want these kids to grow up without a father?"

Jim didn't answer. They went to bed, but neither slept much. The next morning, they talked over coffee.

"Jim, my advice is to resign. Don't let them fire you. It'll go on your record and hurt you when you apply for another job."

"I don't know, Lilly. We'll see," he replied as he kissed her goodbye.

Jim arrived at the sheriff's office at 7:55 a.m. Mrs. Anderson informed him that the sheriff was conferring with others, and he was to wait in the chief deputy's office. Forty minutes later, Detective Taylor was summoned to the sheriff's office.

"Good morning, Sheriff. I'm sorry about all this," Jim said as he approached the desk.

"Good morning, Jim. Close the door and have a seat," Smoot said in a reserved tone.

"Jim, you know how you said a while back how lucky you've been?"

"Yes, sir," Jim replied anxiously.

"Well, your luck may have run out."

Jim nodded as he noticed the bowling trophies on the shelf behind the sheriff. In addition to the trophies, there were various pictures of his family, along with a knick–knack or two. Absent were the many law–enforcement awards Sheriff Smoot had received in his long and storied career. Jim recalled that just the year before, he had been named Sheriff of the Year by the association in Nashville. The other walls were decorated with pictures and paintings: one of a water–wheel mill, another of the Smoky Mountains, and other scenes from the region. How strange, Jim thought, that he has nothing to signify his successful career.

"Jim, are you listening?"

"Yes, sir."

"As I was saying, this is serious. Deputy Simpson is going to the DA and insists that you be prosecuted for interfering with an arrest. I'm afraid you're in for big trouble."

"Yes, sir, I understand. I don't want to cause you any trouble or embarrassment, so I'm going to resign."

"It's not that simple, Jim. Don't worry about me. You need to worry about yourself and your family. Simpson claims that Fain resisted arrest, then you interfered, and—"

"Who's Fain?" Jim interrupted.

"Hawthorne Fain. He's the Negro that Simpson arrested, and he's not saying much. I talked with him at the jail about 6:30 this morning. I'm afraid he's not goin' to be much help in clearing this up."

Jim nodded.

"This next part I'm goin' to say never happened. I didn't say it. You understand?"

"Yes."

"Do you know the DA, Fred Winstead?"

"I know of him, but I don't really know him," Jim replied.

"Well, I do. I've been around him quite a bit, socially and otherwise. He hates—or I should say he really dislikes—Negroes. I've personally heard him refer to FDR's wife, Mrs. Roosevelt, as a 'nigger lover.' Look, I don't know what went on last night. You've told Chief Deputy Stallings that Simpson was beating a prisoner who was cuffed. Simpson claims that he was trying to cuff Fain and Fain was resisting—that you interfered and picked a fight."

Jim straightened in his chair to reply forcefully when Sheriff Smoot raised his hand, signaling him to wait.

"What I'm telling you is that the DA may delight in prosecuting you. I think I know what happened, and you probably did the right thing, although two of my officers getting into a fistfight doesn't reflect well on any of us. Nevertheless, you don't want to resign. It would look like an admission of guilt.

"I believe the DA will take this to the grand jury for indictment. So, Jim, here's what I'm gonna do. I'm ordering you and Simpson to stay away from each other until the courts decide what's what. You two will not approach or talk to each other. If either of you breaks this order, he will be fired. The county attorney advised me to suspend both of you, but I'm short of manpower and money, so this is my decision. Any questions?"

"No, sir. I understand."

"One more thing," the sheriff said as he stood to signal that the meeting was over. "You'll need a good lawyer. Take this."

Jim looked at the card. It read Harlan Hughes, Attorney at Law. "Thanks, Sheriff," Jim said and extended his hand.

Detective Taylor quickly found an empty office, called Lilly, and relayed the gist of the meeting with the sheriff.

"I'll tell you more tonight. I'm goin' to find Jimmy Ray and Cam and ask for advice. Okay, love you, too. 'Bye."

Next, he called the Dawson office, hoping to catch Cam Barker and Jimmy Ray Johnson. Barker was there and agreed to round up Jimmy Ray for lunch after Sessions Court adjourned.

They settled into a back booth at Shirley's Restaurant in downtown Dawson and ordered lunch. Jim laid out the entire story for them.

"Why'd you get in the middle of this nigger mess to start with?" asked Cam.

"First, it's Negro, not nigger."

"Whatever," Cam drawled.

"Second, it's not right to beat a man with his hands cuffed behind his back."

"Well, you're right there," Jimmy Ray asserted. "That's downright chickenshit. If I'm gonna' beat a man, I give him a fightin' chance. I cuff him in front."

Cam and Jimmy Ray horse laughed as Jim tried again.

"Look, I need some advice. They're gonna try to put me in jail over this, and I don't even know if Hughes'll take the case, not to mention the cost," Jim said with some trepidation.

"Hey, listen, dumbass, the sheriff's already talked to Hughes, or he wouldn't have given you the card. By the way, Hughes is the best lawyer in three counties. Probably owes the sheriff a shitload of favors," reflected Cam.

"Speaking of the sheriff, where does he stand on all this?" Jimmy Ray asked.

Jim thought of the sheriff's off-the-record comments but decided not to mention that part of their conversation. "He's ordered both of us to stay away from each other. Gonna let the courts decide what really happened."

The waitress brought their orders, and Jimmy Ray flirted with her in his distinctive, loud voice. Once she was out of hearing range, Cam asked, "You say this prisoner wouldn't talk to the sheriff?"

"The sheriff said he wouldn't say much about it," Jim replied.

"Well, first off, we need for him to talk, even if he is a nig—uh, Negro. The judge might give some weight to his testimony. Of course, it depends on which judge draws the case."

"What're the two deputies and the jailer saying about it?" asked Jimmy Ray.

"Don't know. Haven't talked to 'em."

Cam advised, "You probably ort not talk to 'em. Maybe Jimmy Ray and I can find out somethin'."

Jim informed Lilly that the grand jury would begin meeting in late January. After discussing various options, they decided that Jim should contact the attorney.

Located just two blocks from the Safety Building on the second story of Goldman's clothing store, the Hughes and Beeson law firm housed four attorneys, three secretaries, an investigator, and one runner. Jim thumbed through yesterday's newspaper as he waited, feigning interest in the old news.

Harlan Hughes burst into the room wearing a broad grin. As Jim's father would have put it, he was "grinnin' like a mule eatin' yaller jackets." He was a big man, maybe 6' 3", 230 pounds or so, with an athletic build. A photo of a younger, slenderer version of the same man, dressed in a yellow jersey with the number 26, hung on the wall next to the door of his office.

His big smile drew attention away from the hint of jowls on his wide, ruddy face; his graying, wavy hair was combed straight back, like that of a gospel quartet singer. A squarely built body revealed that he was about 25 pounds over his Georgia Tech playing weight. Hughes was known to be street smart and quick on his feet. Many friends of the UVA Law School graduate had suggested that he dive into the murky waters of Tennessee state politics. But Harlan loved trying cases, and his easy manner and disarming charm had won over jurors for 20 years.

"I'm Harlan Hughes. You must be Detective Taylor," he said as he extended a huge right hand.

"Yes, sir. Glad to meet you."

Hughes ushered him into the office and listened intently as Jim relayed the entire story without interruption. The attorney studied his notes, then asked, "What was in your mind that night when you intervened?"

"Whatta ye mean?" asked Jim, a bit perplexed.

"You saw this happening as you got out of your car. What was your first thought?"

"That it wasn't right."

"Why?"

Jim hesitated, thinking before answering. "It just ain't right to beat a man with his hands tied behind his back."

"Did you know this, uh, Mr. Fain?" Hughes asked after glancing at his notes.

"No."

"Ever have any dealings with him?"

"No."

"What about Deputy Simpson? Ever have any dealings with him? Any run–ins or disagreements?"

"No. I'd seen him a few times, but never worked any cases with him."

"Well, Detective Taylor, that about wraps it up. I'll be in touch," Hughes said as he stood up.

"What happens next?" asked Jim.

"I want to give it some thought and have our investigator check a couple of things, and then I'll get back to you."

"Well, uh, how much is this gonna cost?"

"Oh, I don't know, but we won't collect until you have a rich uncle die," Hughes laughed as he ushered Jim out.

The following Wednesday, Harlan Hughes arrived at the courthouse to check the criminal court docket before climbing the creaking stairs to keep his 9:00 a.m. appointment with District Attorney General Fred Winstead.

"Good morning, General," Harlan greeted his old rival.

"Good morning, Counselor. To what do I owe this rare privilege?"

"I just need to have a short chat about a private matter, General."

"Well, I've asked Assistant General Mathews to join us. Can I get you a cup of coffee?"

"Yes. Black, please. And if you don't mind, I'd like to meet with you alone."

While Winstead instructed his secretary to get coffee and cancel Mathews, Harlan edged along a wall of the corner office, reading citations, plaques, and awards. The opposite wall was lined with mahogany bookshelves filled with legal journals, textbooks, and a complete leather-bound set of the *Tennessee Code Annotated.*

"Here we go, Counselor." Winstead handed him the embossed cup, then closed the door.

"Thank you, Fred."

"What can I do for you, Harlan?"

Hughes retrieved a pack of Camels from his suit jacket and offered one to Winstead.

"No, thanks. I'm a pipe man. But you go ahead."

Harlan carefully sipped the hot coffee, then took a deep drag on his cigarette. "I represent Detective Jim Taylor, who I believe you are targeting for indictment for interfering with an arrest," Hughes drawled as short bursts of smoke accentuated each word.

"Wait just a minute, here! You can't interfere with deliberations of a grand jury. You're treading on dangerous ground."

Hughes raised his hand, the palm facing Winstead, as he interrupted. "Hold on! Let me finish. Rumor has it that you're considering a run for the state senate next time. I'm here to help you. I'm worried that you're fixin' to screw up. This thing is gonna get messy—lots of publicity, lots of bad publicity—which is not good for a campaign. This isn't a case about a Negro resisting arrest. It's about simple right and wrong. It's about a prisoner being beaten without any way to defend himself."

"So, you're suggesting that I not take this to the grand jury—just let your client walk away? Have you thought of *your* career, Harlan? Have you considered the ramifications of a charge of extorting a public official—the attorney general, no less?"

Harlan was mesmerized by the attorney general's bow tie, which twitched with each word spoken by the state's prosecutor.

"No, no, that's not it at all. I'm torn by this case. Canon of Ethics and all. On the one hand, I'm duty bound to pull out all the stops in defending my client. On the other, this community could be torn apart, and the publicity could go nationwide. This thing could get out of hand very quickly. Even if you get a conviction from a white jury—and I don't for one minute think you will—we would win on appeal as well as on the editorial page. Then there are the civil suits that would be tried around election time, and people goin' on and on 'bout a deputy beating a handcuffed man, and all the bad publicity brought on the area."

"Civil suits? Winstead interrupted. "Have you lost your mind, Harlan?"

"Well, I don't think so. We'd be forced to sue you, the county, the state, and of course Deputy Simpson."

"So you don't think it would be wise to take this to the grand jury," mumbled the attorney general as he nervously tamped tobacco into a briarwood pipe.

"I think it would be very ill advised," offered Hughes. We should settle out of court," he added.

"Settle? Settle what? There isn't even a case yet!" Winstead said incredulously.

"Well, I mean settle before it gets that far. I think $500 for Mr. Fain and $200 for my client would be a pittance, considering what all's on the line here," Harlan answered. "Of course, we expect the charges against Mr. Fain to be dropped," he added.

"You represent him, too, do you?" the attorney general sarcastically inquired.

"Yeah, you could say that."

Winstead's face reddened, his jaw muscles twitched, and Harlan could count the elevated heartbeat from the protruding, pulsating vein in the attorney general's left temple. Winstead called on all his experience and training to restrain himself, to keep his cool and mask his rage.

Harlan rose from the leather-lined chair. "General, after you've had time to think about this, I'm satisfied that you will thank me. Send a check to our office, and I'll have our investigator distribute the money—anonymously, of course."

A week later, as Jim maneuvered his 1946 Chevrolet Fleetline into a parking spot behind the Safety Building, a man approached him.

"Detective Taylor?" the man inquired.

"Yes?"

"I'm Jimmy Tindall, special investigator for the Hughes and Beeson law firm. Mr. Hughes wanted me to give you this." He handed Jim an envelope.

Jim opened it to reveal $200 in cash. "I don't understand,"

he said.

"It comes with very specific instructions. Mr. Hughes wanted you to know that there will be no indictment. Everything is settled. He asks that you give your word that you will never reveal the source. I'm also instructed to tell you that the settlement includes $500 for Mr. Fain, and his charges have been dropped. He's out of jail."

Stunned, Jim stared at the envelope in his hand. "There's nothing to sign? What's the money for?"

"Detective Taylor, I have no idea. It's apparently on a need-to-know basis. Mr. Hughes mentioned that it was for doing the right thing. Have a good day," Tindall said as he turned to leave.

"Doing the right thing" echoed in Jim's mind. His thoughts quickly turned to Benson and the killing. Doing the right thing?

"Wait!" Jim blurted.

The investigator stopped and faced Jim.

"Do you have Fain's address?" Taylor inquired.

"Yeah, I'm headed there now."

Jim handed him the envelope. "Put this with Mr. Fain's money and tell Mr. Hughes that he has my word. Tell him to send me a bill for his services," Jim added as an afterthought.

"I'll tell him," Tindall said over his shoulder.

As Jim had promised Lilly, he took three days off for Christmas.

CHAPTER 31

Ten Years Later

1957

On Tuesday, May 14, 1957, Jim took a comp time day off for extra hours spent working a murder case. With three roses in hand, he lifted the trunk lid to retrieve the folded lawn chair. As he approached the cemetery gate, he noticed the old saw blade, covered with rust and hanging at a skewed angle. I'll fix it on the way out, he thought to himself as he unfolded the chair and placed it at the foot of the three graves—his mother's, father's, and Annie's. After leaning a fresh rose against each tombstone, he sat down to think and talk. He had come here to be alone with his family almost a week before Decoration Day.

Mother's been dead over a year, he thought as he read the tombstone: Esther R. Taylor, Beloved Mother and Wife, Born April 13, 1871—Died April 17, 1956. Dad's been gone 20 years, and Annie—it doesn't seem possible—has been dead almost 30 years. You would be 43 years old this year, Annie.

As always when he thought of Annie, he was reminded of their childhood days. He had grown to dread the Fourth of July holiday because of the painful memory of her tragic, violent death.

If only I could have gone berry picking with her on that July 2nd, he lamented to himself.

He recalled tracking down her killer, and he could vividly remember the sickening thuds of the blackjack on Benson's head.

"I wonder if Toby's still alive," he asked in the silence. It was broken only by the singing birds and the drone of a barely audible chainsaw in the distance. She would be about—he did the math in his head—63, he thought with amazement. I wonder if she ever married, and who was the man in her bed? And Betty, what happened to poor Betty? Shortly after I was promoted to detective, I checked the Kentucky State Police report. Death by gunshot to the head by unknown person or persons, it had said. Did her no-good father shut her up by shooting her? Had it been by her own hand or someone else's?

A black-capped chickadee alighted on George Taylor's tombstone, cocked its head to one side to observe Jim, then flitted away.

"Dad, General Eisenhower is in the middle of his last term. I remember that in '52, when he was elected, Mama jumped for joy. I went out in the yard and emptied my revolver into the air. Lilly thought I had gone plum crazy. I wish you could have lived to see it."

Patches of the past pushed the present out of his head. Memories and feelings flooded through him: the feeling of being shot and the long recovery; Lilly's courage and commitment; the births of their children; murder cases and major crimes, solved and unsolved; Shelly's college graduation; and Robby's leaving for the Army.

Jim turned his attention back to the graves in front of him.

"Lilly and the kids are fine. Two of them are grown, and the other two are headed that way. Lois is in high school, and Barry's in the sixth grade. My headaches are down to two or three a month. Aspirin is one of my best friends."

A drop of water on his shoulder pulled his eyes skyward. The morning's pale blue sky had become partially masked by various shades of gray.

"I need to meet Lilly for lunch. See you next time."

On his way out, Jim lifted the dangling end of the old saw blade, reattached it to the S–hook, and headed home.

*****

Three weeks later, on June 5th, he was on the day shift, working contacts with the rookie officer, Benny Hawkins, whom he had been assigned to train. Earlier in the day, an APB had been broadcast to all officers regarding Billy Wampler, a convicted murderer from this county. He was being transported by a state trooper from prison back to Dawson to face a second charge. The details were sketchy, but somehow he had gotten a gun. He shot and killed the highway patrolman when they stopped for a traffic light on the edge of town.

All officers except for a small patrol crew had been assigned to the manhunt task force. Turning up the volume of the Motorola XLE police radio, Jim haltingly answered the questions from Officer Hawkins between transmissions.

"All task force officers stand by to copy," boomed the dispatcher's voice as the two fell silent in anticipation. "All task force members report to the Dawson office for a 9:45 a.m. briefing, this date. Repeat, all task force officers report this date at 9:45 a.m. to the Dawson office."

Detective Taylor and his trainee claimed two seats in the rear of the courtroom near the door. Sheriff Jackson Flynn waited patiently in front of the judge's bench, chatting with Dawson police chief Darrell Webb.

Sheriff Flynn had won the 1952 election when the former sheriff, John Smoot, was elected to the state senate. Smoot eked out a victory over Attorney General Fred Winstead in the primary race and went on to handily win the August general election.

Two years later, Jim's old nemesis, Fred Winstead, won his old office back in a close election for attorney general.

Sheriff Flynn opened the meeting by announcing that the Tennessee Bureau of Investigation would be taking overall charge of the manhunt for Billy Wampler. He and Chief Webb explained that search sectors had been established, and that after the meeting, the two departments would meet in their respective squad rooms for sector assignments.

Chief Webb reviewed a detailed description of Wampler and passed a picture around the packed room.

"This man has murdered at least two people, including a highway patrolman. He is obviously armed and very dangerous. There have been no stolen cars reported this morning, so he may be on foot. Any stolen car report will be broadcast immediately county wide. The two bus stations, both here and in Brighton, are under surveillance. Any questions?"

After several questions and answers, the city and county officers reassembled in their respective department squad rooms for assignments. Sheriff Flynn caught Jim on the way into the room. "Detective Taylor, you will not have a sector. You'll be our rover. I need for you to work contacts and leads. You and Hawkins can go ahead and hit the road."

"Okay, Sheriff. We'll keep in touch."

Jim worked informants for two hours before breaking for lunch at Sandy's Diner. Each contact was told to ask around and give a call if they heard anything. During the meal, the trainee peppered the experienced detective with questions. As they waited for the check, Jim asked, "Where do you think he is, Benny?"

Surprised but pleased that the veteran officer wanted his opinion, Hawkins replied, "I think he's here in Dawson, holed up till the heat dies down."

"I agree," Jim said. As he turned to look for the waitress, he spied Cam and Jimmy Ray headed their way.

Jim waved and scooted over next to the wall. Jimmy Ray plopped down beside him as Cam said, "Move over, rookie."

Jimmy Ray opened the conversation. "Well, where is he, boys?"

"Benny here thinks he's holed up here in Dawson, and I agree," Jim offered.

"Bullshit! You two couldn't find your ass with both hands. Wampler had a plan. Me and Jimmy Ray just came from Dawson PD—found out the trooper's gun was still in his holster, hadn't been fired. If he went to enough pains to get a gun slipped to him in Nashville or somewhere between there and here, he certainly would've had a ride lined up. Nope, he's long gone—probably in Kentucky or Georgia by now."

The waitress, Toni McConnell, placed the check by Jim's Coke and asked, "What're you two vagrants having?"

"Two hot dogs with chili, sweet tea, and a big, sloppy kiss," Jimmy Ray exclaimed.

"How about you, Cam?" she asked without acknowledging Jimmy Ray's comment.

"A bowl of beans with a slice of onion, cornbread, and buttermilk."

Toni finished writing and stared at Jimmy Ray.

"What?" Jimmy Ray asked.

She ginned. "You gonna' give Cam that big sloppy kiss now, or are y'all gonna' wait till you're in the car?"

Toni walked away, leaving one of them red faced and the other three in stitches.

As they got into Jim's 1955 Ford cruiser, Benny asked, "What's next?"

"Let's run by the office. I've got a couple of phone calls to make, and we can check in with the sheriff," Jim replied.

Desk Sergeant Bobby Raines, cradling a phone between his ear and shoulder, waved to get Detective Taylor's attention and looked for the note on his cluttered desk. "Hang on just a second," he said into the phone as he retrieved the note and handed it to Jim. Covering the mouthpiece with his right palm, he said, "This guy's called three or four times. Won't leave a message. Please call him and tell him not to tie up this line," Raines said in an elevated voice.

Detective Taylor directed Hawkins to check with the task force leaders for an update while he placed the call.

"Hello."

Jim recognized the voice of Jerry Compton. He had been one of the detective's paid informants since the early '50s and was on Jim's afternoon call list.

"Hello, Jerry."

"I need to meet ya. It's important!"

"Where?"

"In the alley behind the pool hall. Come alone."

"I can be there in 10 minutes. Is that okay?"

"I'll be there," Compton said nervously.

Detective Taylor called Hawkins out of the squad room and headed to the car. "I'm goin' to let you out at Granny's Market. I'll be back to pick you up in a few minutes," he informed Hawkins.

Jim spotted Jerry among the 55-gallon garbage barrels behind the pool hall. His slender profile and blond flat top were easily recognizable even in the shadows of the alley. Jerry was street smart and cunning enough to make a living stealing hubcaps and shooting pool.

Compton cupped the Lucky Strike in his left hand as if hiding it would somehow make him invisible. As Jim was rolling to a stop, the informant brushed the lit end of the cigarette against the brick wall, put the stub in his shirt pocket, and slid in the passenger side of the cruiser.

"What's up?" Taylor asked.

"It's 'bout Billy Wampler. A cousin of his told me the family's scared. Billy's 'bout half nuts, you know."

"Why are they scared?" Jim asked as he lit his second cigar of the day.

"Afraid he'll show up at one of their houses," replied Jerry.

"His mama's and brother's houses have already been checked," Jim assured him.

"Yeah, but he has an aunt that lives in Highland Acres. Johnny—I mean my friend—says that the aunt don't get along with Billy's mom; they don't talk. Anyways, he's called the aunt several times, but nobody answers. He's afraid Billy might be there. I figure this information is worth double the usual."

Jim pulled a $10 bill from his billfold and handed it to Compton. "If it's good information, I'll be back with another 10," promised Detective Taylor as he popped open the glove box in front of Jerry.

While Jim rummaged through the glove box, Compton nervously looked up and down the alley. "Same deal as always—this meeting never happened, right?" Jerry asked.

"Right," Taylor said as he handed two packs of Lucky Strikes to the informant. "Do you have a name and address on the aunt?"

"Yeah." Jerry opened the folded paper and handed it to the detective.

"219 Rose Avenue," Jim read aloud. "Do you have her name?"

"Nope. Never asked. My friend don't wanna be involved. Same deal—nothing came from him either, right?"

"Right," Jim reassured him.

Compton scanned the alley, then got out.

Jim drove to the market. Hawkins sat on a bench in front of the store, sweating from the June sun reflecting off the Clabber Girl Baking Soda sign next to him. The trainee got in, killed the last third of a six-ounce bottle of Coke, and dropped the empty onto the floorboard in back.

"No, no. Don't ever leave a bottle in the car. A prisoner can take the back of your head off with that," Jim instructed.

Hawkins retrieved the bottle and set it on the store bench.

"Sorry 'bout that," he said sheepishly as he reclaimed the passenger's seat. "Where to now?"

"Highland Acres, on a tip," Jim replied. "Probably another wild goose chase."

At 219 Rose Avenue, Mrs. Wiggins strained to hear with her ear to the bedroom door. This was the third time she had approached the door in the last half hour. Each time, she lost her nerve and slipped back into the living room. She wiped her sweaty hands on the calico apron and gripped the doorknob, slowly and quietly turning it until it stopped. She hesitated, afraid to ease open the door, but afraid to let go. Finally, she pushed inward ever so slowly. She peered into the two-inch gap. Billy's motionless body lay on the bunk that he had pushed against the window.

Asleep at last, she thought. Now's my chance.

She made her way to the small living room in the front of the house and bolted out the door.

Detective Taylor and Deputy Hawkins stopped in front of 219. As they exited the car, a woman rushed down the front steps toward them.

"Just a minute, ma'am. We need to talk to you," Jim said, rushing his words to match her haste.

"Don't have time. Gotta see a neighbor. I don't wanna buy anything today," she said as she scurried off.

Benny's first impulse was to yell, "We're not salesmen!" Instead, he turned to Detective Taylor with a questioning look.

"Something's wrong, Benny," the detective said as he turned to look at the house.

Before Hawkins could ask, Jim commanded, "Radio for backup. Get the shotgun outta the trunk, and then go around and cover the back. Be careful. He's got nothing to lose, and he's a crack shot."

"What's going on?" Benny asked as he lifted the Remington 12-gauge shotgun out of the trunk.

"She's scared, no pocketbook, still got her apron on," Jim said as he unsnapped the holster and drew his .38 S & W police special.

Jim headed for the front porch as Deputy Hawkins radioed for assistance. With his back against the wall next to the door, he tried the knob with his left hand. Unlocked!

Benny rushed past the porch, heading toward the rear of the house.

Jim's mind was awash with fearful thoughts—the gunshot to his head at Greasy Corner; Lilly and the kids; my trainee! Wampler will make a break for it out the back. It's a natural instinct. Damn! Why didn't I take the back?

Taylor gripped the knob and eased the door open. He peeked around the door and surveyed the living room. The only exit from the room other than the front door was an opening to a hallway leading to the back of the house.

Jim slipped inside and sidestepped to the left. Keeping his eyes glued to the hallway opening, he quietly edged along the walls until he reached it. The detective sneaked a quick look down the hall. All clear. He looked again. One door on the left and one on the right, in the middle of the passage. Since he could see the doorknob fully protruding into the hallway, he deduced that the door on the left was completely closed. He believed the door on the right to be slightly open, since most of the handle was hidden by the door facing. Two bedrooms, no doubt, he said in his mind. The room at the end of the hall appeared to be the kitchen. Sunlight from a window over the sink flooded the kitchen with light that spilled into the hall.

Jim realized he had been holding his breath. After slowly exhaling and taking a deep breath, he began inching down the hall toward the kitchen. He could hear his heart pounding in his chest and feel the beat next to the steel plate in his left temple.

Should I check the kitchen first to make sure Wampler's not there, drawing a bead on Benny? he asked himself.

He heard Cam's gruff voice in his mind. "Don't ever leave a room behind you unchecked."

He inched along ever so slowly, his back against the wall. Strangely, the closer he got to the bedroom door, the calmer he felt.

Which door first? he asked himself.

The door in front of him to his right was slightly ajar.

That one, he thought. If the closed door to his immediate left opened while he peeked, he would hear it and turn quickly.

The detective took a slow, silent step forward and peeked through the crack.

He's there! Jim's mind screamed.

Wampler was asleep, his back to Taylor.

Jim crouched as he nudged the door open a few more inches and glanced at the reflection in the window. The detective eased back the hammer and fired into Wampler's back. A second shot rang out, and Jim flinched. He stood up slowly as Deputy Hawkins burst from the kitchen with the shotgun at the ready.

The detective stared at the white T–shirt turning red from the middle of Billy's back to where his body met the bed.

"Red eyes," Jim mumbled as he leaned against the door jamb for support. Splatters of red, as if cast off a painter's brush, filled the wall and window beyond the body.

He and Hawkins turned Billy onto his back to reveal a large chest wound and a revolver in his right hand. His glassy eyes were open wide. His slack jaw drooped to expose part of his tongue.

"Shot in the chest," observed Hawkins.

"That's an exit wound, son," corrected Jim.

"You shot him in the back?" asked Benny in a shocked tone.

"Had to," the detective quietly answered. "Damn! We

haven't cleared the other bedroom. Go check it, will ya, Benny?"

Officer Hawkins cleared the room across the hall and returned with a question. "You said something about red eyes when I first ran in. What was that about?"

"I didn't say anything about red eyes. You must've misunderstood." Jim eased into a chair across from the bed to gather his thoughts and emotions. "Go call this in, Benny," he instructed.

"Already radioed for backup."

Jim slowly became aware of the background noise, sirens getting louder by the second.

"Go outside and tell the officers everything is secure here. Go slow. Leave the shotgun here, and show 'em your hands as you go out. Don't want to get you shot." His voice trailed off.

"What happened, Jim?" Jimmy Ray asked him later as he stepped onto the porch.

"I've gotta get a cigar from the car," Jim replied as he headed in that direction. "We'll talk later."

Cam flipped the hinged lid of his Zippo lighter and held the flame under Jim's cigar. "It'll take a couple of hours for your nerves to calm down," Cam said, as if reading Jim's thoughts.

"Thanks, Cam. I've gotta go. The TBI wants to interview me—debriefing."

"Okay. Me and Jimmy Ray'll catch ye later."

*****

Jim was getting impatient. The questioning was deep into the second hour, and he knew that Lilly was waiting down the hall. Jimmy Ray had called her out of the classroom to give her the news. She quickly made provisions for child care and drove straight to Jim's office.

Detective Sergeant Kyle Bivens said to Jim, "Tell us one last time what happened. Then you can see your wife."

Jim looked from Bivens to the TBI agent as if to say, "Can't you put an end to this?"

Agent Bailey did not respond.

"Okay. We arrived on the scene to find a lady rushing from the house. I instructed my trainee, Benny Hawkins, to radio for backup and cover the rear of the house. Then I became worried that Wampler would bolt out the back and shoot Benny.

"I entered the house and made my way to a bedroom in the middle of the house. The door was open a couple of inches, and I saw a man in bed with his back to me. I pushed the door open a few more inches and saw Wampler's reflection in the window. He was on his right side facing the window. He was holding a pistol against his chest. I observed that his eyes were open. I could see them blinking. He cocked the revolver, and I shot him."

"Did it occur to you to yell 'Police!' or 'Drop the weapon,' 'Let's see your hands'—anything like that?" asked Agent Bailey.

"No. I knew he would roll over and fire. I was afraid he would run out the back and shoot Officer Hawkins, then flee to kill God knows how many others."

"Will you change your mind about giving us your informant's name?" Bailey queried.

"No. I told you, I can't do that. I gave my word."

"That's all for now, Jim. Go see your wife; we'll yell at ya later if we think of anything else," said Detective Bivens.

Lilly hugged him and asked, "Are you all right? I was so worried!"

"Yeah, I'm fine. Just tired."

"Go home and catch your breath. I'll pick up the kids and see you there," Lilly said with a smile to mask her concern.

*****

Three months later, in mid–September, Jim sat studying the picture on the wall across the law office waiting room.

Number 26, Jim observed. He must've been a fullback. Looks like a new jersey.

This was the third time he had been to meet with Harlan Hughes since he had been charged with second-degree murder. Everyone seemed to be surprised when they learned that Attorney General Winstead had gotten a grand jury indictment against Taylor—everyone, that is, except Harlan Hughes.

I guess he's seen it all over the years, Jim thought. Maybe nothing surprises him anymore.

Hughes ushered Jim in and pointed to the two chairs in front of his desk. A junior partner, Thomas Riley, and special investigator Jimmy Tindall occupied the leather sofa to Jim's left.

"I believe you met Mr. Riley last week, and you know investigator Tindall from way back," said Hughes as he negotiated his way around the desk.

"Hey, good to see you," Jim greeted them as they stood to shake hands.

"Have a seat, Detective Taylor, and let's get started," directed Hughes. "As you know, this case hinges on the reflection you saw in the window. Mr. Tindall has been to Mrs. Wiggins's house several times trying to duplicate the conditions. I know that this is mid-September, and the shooting occurred in mid-June, and the angle of the sun would be somewhat different. But we haven't been able to see a reflection in the window. Tell us again exactly what you saw."

"I saw him from about the waist up. The sun was bright. I saw the pistol against his white T-shirt. His eyes were open. I could see them blinkin'. He cocked the gun and I fired."

"Investigator Tindall, here, has another theory we wanted to bounce off you. Wampler is awake, his nerves obviously on edge, given the circumstances. He has the gun cocked and ready. His hands are shaking. He accidentally fires the revolver, and you shoot as a natural reaction. Isn't it possible that his weapon discharged first?"

"No. I fired, and then his gun fired a split-second later, although at the time I didn't know who fired the second shot. I wheeled around to look at the other door behind me. I was concerned that a second shooter might be behind me, but the door was still closed. Officer Hawkins ran in about that time. He cleared the other bedroom, then went outside to tell the other officers that the house was secure."

"Jim," Hughes began, "we go to trial about a month from now. If you have anything you're holding back, we need to know. We need to know it now. I'm gonna excuse Mr. Tindall. He's not protected by attorney-client privilege."

Investigator Tindall left the room, and Harlan Hughes turned to Jim. "Mr. Riley here also represents you. He'll be assisting me at trial. The one thing that really bothers us is surprises. We need to know everything. Any skeletons in your closet?"

"No, other than I went out on my wife a couple of times many years ago," Jim answered.

"How many years ago?"

"Twenty, maybe more."

"Anything else?"

"No, sir."

"Well, we've finished depositions, witness lists, and so forth. Any questions?

"Just one. Why is the attorney general pushing this?"

"Well, Detective Taylor, I've wondered the same thing. It could be payback for the little misunderstanding we had about 10 years back involving you and a sheriff's deputy. I feel partially responsible, and that's why we intend to represent you pro bono. Or he may simply believe that you shot Wampler in the back. You know, to get the glory and attention for bringing down the man who murdered a fellow peace officer."

"What do you believe?"

"Doesn't matter what I believe."

"It matters to me," Jim said with conviction.

"For what it's worth, I believe you saw his reflection in the window and saw him cock the pistol. I believe Wampler would have tried to kill you, Officer Hawkins, and anybody else in his path. I believe you did the right thing."

"The right thing." Words Jim tried to brush aside, words that evoked memories of Benson's demise, which invariably led to his questioning his own actions and whether he should answer to the law.

CHAPTER 32

October, 1957

Strangely, courtrooms felt much like church to Jim. The congregation was behind him. The choir was in the jury box at his left front. The judge's bench was in the front center where God himself presided. The door at the front right where prisoners were escorted in and out represented the gates of Hell, ready to receive the condemned.

It was almost 11:00 a.m., and only three jurors had been seated. Jim leaned over and whispered in Harlan Hughes's ear, "How long will this take?'

"Probably be over by close of court today. Usually speeds up some in the afternoon," the attorney responded in a hushed tone.

At 4:15 in the afternoon, Judge John Merriweather declared that the 12 jurors and two alternates had been empanelled. He turned to the jurors and informed them that since they were not sequestered, they were free to go.

"Let me caution you once again. You are not to discuss the case with each other or anyone else. That includes your families. You are to be here tomorrow at 8:45 a.m. sharp. We should be ready to proceed around 9:00 a.m., and at that time, I will give you detailed instructions. That should take 30 to 40 minutes. The trial will then begin with opening statements from the attorneys. We thank you for your service, and we'll see you tomorrow."

Jim stood and leaned over the rail behind him to hug Lilly. "Pretty boring, huh?" he said.

"No, I thought it was interesting," Lilly retorted sincerely.

"Good afternoon, Miss Lilly," Harlan Hughes greeted her. "Jim, we need to meet either now or after supper," he continued.

"Let's do it now," Jim suggested.

Jim kissed Lilly's check. "I'll see you at home."

At the law offices, Harlan announced that they had decisions to make. "Jim, we still haven't decided whether or not to put you on the stand. Mr. Riley is against it, and I haven't made up my mind yet."

"I need to testify—tell 'em how it happened," Jim insisted.

"That's all fine and good, but it gives the state a chance to cross–examine. It could open up all sorts of possibilities. Would you be willing to go along with our decision, whatever it is?"

Jim looked at the two lawyers, then out the window to his right. Darkness had begun to creep over the city outside.

"Yes," he finally answered. "I trust y'all, and I'll do whatever you say."

"Mr. Riley and I have a lot of work to do tonight. It'll be two or three days before you take the stand, if that's what we decide. You go home to your wife and kids. We'll see you at court tomorrow."

The court opened at 9:00 a.m. sharp with the bailiff's familiar refrain that ended with "the Honorable John Merriweather presiding." Everyone took a seat, ready for opening statements.

"Mr. Mathews, is the State ready?" asked the judge.

"The State is ready, Your Honor," answered Assistant District Attorney Jim Mathews.

Jim whispered in Harlan's ear, "Where's Winstead?"

"Probably doesn't want to get his hands dirty," whispered his attorney.

"Ladies and gentleman of the jury," Mathews began as he

approached the jury box, "this is a complicated case. A state trooper is shot and killed in his cruiser sitting at a traffic light here in Dawson. A convicted felon, Billy Wampler, flees from the car. Detective Taylor here"—he pointed to the defendant—"killed the escapee. End of story, one might surmise. But the story doesn't end there. You see, we may never know who shot the trooper. As yet, no witness has surfaced. We may never know because Fain County Detective Jim Taylor shot and killed Billy Wampler. Shot him in the back while he slept in a bed at his aunt's house.

"Did Billy Wampler somehow wrestle the gun from State Trooper James Thaxton? We know that didn't happen because Thaxton's gun had not been fired recently, and it was still snapped securely in the trooper's holster at the murder scene. Did Billy Wampler by some miracle produce a gun from his prison-issued clothing and shoot Trooper Thaxton? It seems very unlikely, since the prisoner was thoroughly searched before leaving the prison. Did an accomplice follow them into town, get out of his car, and shoot the trooper? We may never know, because Mr. Taylor killed the one witness we are sure of, Billy Wampler. Shot him in the back, Jesse James style."

Jim flinched and turned to Harlan Hughes. His attorney put his forefinger to his lips, signaling Taylor to remain quiet.

"Was someone simply settling an old score with Trooper Thaxton? If so, Billy wasn't going to stick around and take the blame," the assistant attorney general continued. "If Billy had an accomplice in a car behind him, wouldn't he have jumped in the car for a quick getaway? Of course he would have. Instead, he made his way on foot just eight blocks from the scene to his aunt's house, where he could catch his breath and think. Would he have turned himself in? We'll never know, because the defendant murdered him, shot him in the back. Why did he do it? Was it for fame? The man who shot Billy Wampler! Was it for the admiration and respect that would come from fellow officers? We don't know what was in his mind.

"The one thing we do know is that the gun that killed Trooper Thaxton was not the gun Billy had when he was murdered. The state will offer incontrovertible evidence of that.

"This is a nation of laws, laws that apply to you and to me. Without the rule of law, society would be in a constant state of chaos. The law not only applies to you and me. It applies to law-enforcement officers, and it applies to Detective Jim Taylor," he said, his sarcastic voice rising slightly as he pointed to the defendant.

Later, Mathews closed with, "Thank you, ladies and gentleman. I have confidence that you will render the right decision, using your common sense and the rule of law."

Judge Merriweather signed a paper, handed it to the bailiff, and turned his attention to Harlan Hughes. "Is the defense ready, Counselor?"

"The defense is ready, Your Honor," Harlan said as he stood. Harlan gathered his notes, then put them aside and walked empty-handed to the jury box.

"Good morning. I'm Harlan Hughes, and I represent Fain County Detective Jim Taylor. The state prosecutor, Mr. Mathews, told you this is a complicated case. The state may try to complicate it, but it's really pretty simple.

"Officer Taylor, my client, is a respected and highly decorated veteran of the Sheriff's Department. Many years ago, as he was attempting to serve civil papers, an old mountain man came at him with a double-bladed axe over his head, ready to strike. Officer Taylor, just a second or two from a sure death, shot the man—not in the upper torso, as he had been trained to do, but in the leg, so the man could live and provide for his family.

"Just 10 years ago, Officer Taylor was shot in the line of duty while protecting the people of this county. He's not new to this business of keeping the peace. He's a family man—got four kids and a wife. He attends church virtually every Sunday that he's off duty.

"Yes, ladies and gentlemen, this is a simple case. Billy Wampler, a vicious convicted killer, was on his way from the state penitentiary to Dawson to stand trial for armed robbery. Somehow, he obtained a gun—from where, we'll probably never know. He killed a second time—this time, State Trooper James Thaxton, who was also a family man. He left behind a young widow to raise two kids alone.

"Wampler fled to his aunt's house, throwing the gun in a creek along the way. He terrorized her and forced her to give up her deceased husband's gun. He was very tired—exhausted from being up the night before, planning his escape upon arriving in Dawson. He was loaded into the trooper's cruiser at 4:10 a.m. Central time near Nashville. They stopped near Cookeville, Tennessee at the state garage for gas at a little after 6:00 a.m. They arrived in Dawson about 9:00 a.m. Eastern time. After Billy Wampler murdered Trooper Thaxton, he arrived at his aunt's house about 9:20 a.m. to hole up and wait for dark.

"We will show that he was nodding off to sleep at Mrs. Wiggins's kitchen table. She convinced him to go to bed. Once he was asleep, still clutching the gun, his aunt hurried from the house. Detective Taylor, along with Deputy Hawkins, arrived on scene just as she rushed out the door. Detective Taylor instructed his trainee to cover the rear of the house. Then he began to worry that the rookie officer could be hurt or killed if Wampler bailed out the back door.

"Detective Taylor had a strong suspicion that Wampler was inside, so he decided to enter the house—not for fortune and fame, but to stop a cold-blooded killer from escaping and killing again. The bedroom door was slightly ajar. Taylor observed Wampler in the bed. Then, from the reflection in the window, he saw the gun in Wampler's right hand. He saw his eyes blinking. He saw the killer's right thumb cock the pistol, so he fired.

"He could have waited until Wampler rolled over. He could have waited for Wampler to fire. He could have waited for another officer to be killed. He could have waited for a neighbor to be killed. And he could have waited for a child playing in the backyard next door to take a stray bullet. But he didn't. He acted. He did what you and I pay him to do.

"Yes, this is a simple case, a case of simple right and wrong. What Officer Taylor did to protect us was the right thing. Once you hear the proof in this case, I believe you will do the right thing, the decent thing, and let this brave man go home to Miss Lilly and their four children. Thank you."

Judge Merriweather turned to the jury. "Ladies and gentlemen, we're going to take a 15-minute recess. You are reminded of my admonition to not discuss the case among yourselves. We will reconvene at 10:35."

The remainder of the morning was taken up with mundane testimony. The state established that the shooting occurred within the city limits of Dawson on June 8, 1957, and they called the officer from the prison who patted down Wampler. The attendant from the state garage in Cookeville testified that the prisoner was handcuffed when escorted to the restroom and then locked in the car when Officer Thaxton went inside briefly to use the restroom and get a cup of coffee.

Much of the afternoon was spent on the testimony of Wampler's aunt, Mrs. Wiggins. She testified that she was not "scared of Billy," but when confronted with her pre-trial statement saying otherwise, she would admit only to being "concerned."

The next morning, the prosecution's expert witness, an engineer from Virginia Tech, testified that he had tried to duplicate the condition in the bedroom window but could not produce a reflection. On cross-examination, Harlan pressed him hard, establishing that it would be difficult to reproduce the exact conditions since his tests were conducted in September, almost two and one half months after the shooting in June. The engineer used charts to show the angle of the sun in June and the calculations he had used to compensate for the difference in September. The defense attorney questioned him on the thousands of variations possible from sun filtered by clouds, no clouds, the effects of variations in temperature and humidity, etc.

Jim found the testimony extremely tedious, but over lunch, he discovered that Lilly found it fascinating.

He changed the subject to their son's upcoming birthday. "Barry will be 11 years old. I think I'll get him a gun to hunt with," Jim announced.

Lilly quickly and firmly vetoed the idea and returned to their conversation regarding the trial.

The afternoon session included a ballistics expert who began to explain that the bullet that passed through Wampler's body and lodged in the wall matched the—

"If Your Honor please," Harlan interrupted as he rose from his chair. "We can save the court some time. We stipulate that the bullet in question was fired by my client's gun and that he is the subject that fired it."

"Well, this court is all for saving time," the judge stated as he turned to Mathews. "Anything further from the State for this witness?" he asked.

"No, Your Honor," the prosecutor answered.

"Next witness, Mr. Mathews," the judge ordered.

"The state calls Billy's mother, Mrs. Mae Wampler."

The petite woman raised her hand and swore to tell the truth. After taking a seat, she placed her pocketbook on the floor by the witness chair.

Jim became increasingly more uncomfortable as Mrs. Wampler fulfilled her mission, which was to humanize her son. The State wanted the jury to realize that Billy was a living, breathing soul who had it tough growing up with an abusive father, and that he was an accomplished musician, someone who had dreams and ambitions.

Harlan could have shot holes in part of her testimony but decided to accomplish that later with witnesses of his own. When the prosecutor finished, he turned to Hughes. "Your witness, Counselor."

Harlan rose and nodded politely at Mrs. Wampler. "No questions, Your Honor."

"The State rests, Your Honor," announced the Assistant Attorney General.

Judge John Merriweather sent the jury home, then heard the defense's motion to dismiss, which he promptly rejected.

The defense called its first witness Wednesday morning: Robert R. Smith, a cab driver who saw a man fitting Billy Wampler's description throw something into Hetti Creek where it crossed Boone Street.

Harlan asked him to state his name for the record.

"Hack Smith," he replied.

"Is Hack a nickname, Mr. Smith?" Harlan inquired.

"Some people call me Hack, and some call me Smitty."

"I see. But your name is Robert R. Smith, is that correct?"

"That's right, but nobody calls me that." Prompted by Hughes, Smith went on to give his full address and the number of years he had lived in Dawson.

"And what is your occupation, Mr. Smith?"

"Cabby," he replied.

"I believe you own your own cab. Is that correct?"

"Sure do."

Harlan led Smith through questions, at times over the objections of the prosecutor. Smith testified that a man fitting Billy's description threw a dark object into the creek and that the time was between 9:00 and 9:30 a.m. on the morning of Trooper Thaxton's murder.

The defense attorney turned to Mathews and announced,

"Your witness."

"May we approach the bench, Your Honor?" asked the prosecutor.

"You may," answered Judge Merriweather.

The Assistant Attorney General informed the judge that he intended to challenge the credibility of the witness. "I can prove through independent witnesses that he has a drinking problem, is known for the tall tales he spins, and is generally unreliable."

Hack Smith sat just six feet away, all ears. He caught bits and pieces of the discussion of his credibility.

"These so-called witnesses are not on the witness list, Your Honor," retorted Hughes.

Judge Merriweather ruled that witnesses not on the list would not be heard, and he directed Mathews to proceed with his cross-examination.

"Mr. Smith, tell the court in your own words what you were doing the morning of June 8th of this year," demanded Mathews.

"First, I wanna know what all this has to do with my credit. I heard y'all talkin' about it!"

"That's something we lawyers talk about that you cab drivers wouldn't know anything about. Just answer the questions, Mr. Smith," Matthews admonished.

The Judge frowned at Smith and directed him to answer and to limit his comments specifically to the attorney's questions.

"Now, Mr. Smith, I will ask you again. Tell the court in your own words what you were doing on the morning of June 8th."

"Well, me and some of the boys was just hobnobbing around."

"Hobnobbing? *Hobnobbing*? What is hobnobbing, Mr. Smith?"

"That's somethin' us cab drivers talk about that you lawyers wouldn't know nothin' about," replied Hack.

The courtroom erupted in laughter. The judge turned his

head to hide his own reaction as he banged the gavel.

Once order was restored, the prosecution team huddled as if they were planning their next move.

The prosecutor approached the witness stand and smiled at Hack. "Mr. Smith, I noticed a pair of glasses in your shirt pocket. Were you wearing glasses the morning of June 8th when you observed this man at Hetti Creek?"

"I don't know. Prob'ly not."

"So you just wear them to read?"

"Mostly."

"Mr. Smith, do you see the court bailiff, Mr. Lankford, back there by the door?"

"Yep."

"Can you describe him for us?"

"He's got dark brown hair, and from the looks of his belly, he dranks more beer than I do."

The cabby gloated as they rolled in the aisles.

Judge Merriweather quickly curbed the laughter, and Matthews tried again. "Mr. Smith, about how far can you see clearly without your glasses?"

"I can see the moon on a clear night, but I don't know how fer it is."

The judge let them laugh this time while glaring at Mathews as if to say, "When are you going to end this farce?"

Finally, the judge called the court to order and cautioned the audience that he would clear the courtroom if there were further disruptions. "You may proceed, Mr. Mathews."

"No further questions, Your Honor."

"Its 10:05, still early, but we're going to take a short break. Be ready to go at 10:25," Judge Merriweather instructed.

Jim turned to Lilly. "My favorite witness so far," he joked.

The assistant attorney general approached Harlan and asked, "What asylum did you drag him from?"

"Just one of our many local characters, Counselor," Hughes

answered with a big smile.

The remainder of the morning and part of the afternoon were filled with testimony from the defense's expert witness, Dr. Timothy Sigmund, an East Tennessee State College professor of atmospheric science. His testimony was much like that of the State's witness from the day before. He referred to angles of the sun, atmospheric conditions, and angles of the viewer to the window glass.

Finally, Harlan Hughes guided the witness to what Harlan called the rainbow example.

"The reflection in question here can be compared to a rainbow," Dr. Sigmund asserted. "We've all seen a rainbow appear when the sun shines through misty or rainy conditions. But we've also seen the same apparent conditions that did not produce a rainbow."

On cross-examination, Dr. Sigmund admitted that a reflection in a window and the appearance of a rainbow were two entirely different phenomena. "They are, however, similar in that they both depend on very precise variations of atmospheric conditions," Dr. Sigmund maintained.

Over lunch, Hughes informed Jim that he would not be taking the stand. He explained that after hearing the State's case, he felt it was in Jim's best interest to not be cross-examined.

Thursday afternoon closed with testimony of three character witnesses on Jim's behalf.

Judge Merriweather inquired as to how many witnesses there were for the following day.

"Only one, Your Honor. Shouldn't take more than 20 to 30 minutes," answered Harlan.

"Okay, ladies and gentlemen," the judge said as he swiveled his chair to face the jury. "We will hear the last witness tomorrow morning. Then the State and the defense will make their closing statements. Depending on how long that takes, I will charge the jury. That means I will cite the law and give you detailed instructions—either before lunch, or sometime shortly thereafter.

"You're excused for the evening with the reminder that you are not to listen to or read the news, and you're not to discuss this case among yourselves, with family, or anyone else. You may go get a good night's rest. We will see you at the regular time tomorrow."

*****

Friday morning, Sheriff Flynn took the stand and testified to Jim's good work record. Cross–examination was brief. The prosecutor made sure that the jury understood that the sheriff could testify to Jim's record only during the five years the sheriff had been in office.

The closing statements were designed to make a lasting impression on the jury, but they were remarkably similar to the opening statements.

The little ditty, "Mr. Jim, the dirty little coward that shot poor Jesse in the back," played in Jim's mind throughout the trial. Now he wondered if it had been the same for the 12 people who would decide his future.

Judge Merriweather patiently explained to the jury that they had several options: guilty or not guilty of second degree murder, and guilty or not guilty of either voluntary or involuntary manslaughter. The next hour was consumed with the judge's charge to the jury, explaining the fine points of the law. After completing the formal instructions, he ordered the bailiff to escort the jurors to their conference room for deliberations.

Attorney Hughes suggested that Lilly and Jim go to lunch with him so he could answer any questions they might have. Lilly nervously queried Hughes as they walked across the street to Shirley's Diner. He explained that they must stay in the area that afternoon in case the jury came in with a verdict.

"Don't venture too far, and leave a phone number with my office where you can be reached. When they come in, I'll need you to be here within 10 minutes or so," Hughes instructed them.

Three hours later, the phone at Lilly's sister's house rang. The jury had reached a verdict.

The jury filed into the room and took their assigned seats. The judge confirmed that all parties were present and then asked the jury foreman if they had reached a unanimous verdict.

"We have, Your Honor," the foreman answered.

Judge Merriweather ordered the defendant to rise. Harlan Hughes stood at his side.

"What is your verdict?"

Jim took a slow, deep breath, knowing that his life and that of his family could be changed forever by the answer about to be given. His casual demeanor regarding the trial over the last few months had been a front. He had wanted to keep a lid on his feelings and not worry Lilly and the kids.

He had relived the shooting over and over—thinking, wondering, questioning...

Should he have yelled at Wampler? Should he have waited for backup? Should he have waited for the killer to turn over? At times he was very confident that he had acted properly, and at times doubt filled him with uncertainty.

"Not guilty on all counts."

Jim exhaled with a sigh of relief, and Lilly sobbed behind him. He hugged her and at the same time shook hands with Harlan Hughes, as Lilly refused to release him.

"I don't know how I can ever repay you," Jim said to Hughes over Lilly's shoulder.

"The service you have given to the people of this county is thanks enough."

Once outside the courtroom, Jim hugged Lilly tightly and

fought back tears.

"Let's go home," he said, then added, "How about a date tonight to celebrate?"

"I'd love that. I'll get a sitter."

Upon their arrival at the house, Jim was bombarded with questions about the trial by Lois and Barry.

"Well, we won," said Jim. "I'm tired, and I need a nap. Your mom can tell you more about it. Okay?"

"Okay," they said in unison.

Shortly thereafter, Lilly was on the phone making long-distance calls to Shelly and Robbie to give them the good news.

She hung up the phone and informed Jim that Shelly was thrilled, but she had not been able to reach Robbie.

"I left a message for him to call us. Now get some rest, and I'll pick a place for our date," she said as they embraced.

Jim could hear the muffled voices of Lilly and their kids discussing the trial as he drifted off to sleep.

Two hours later, Jim awoke to the sound of running water. Lilly is taking a bath—getting ready for our date, he thought.

He tapped lightly on the bathroom door, then eased it open. Lilly was reclined in the water, surrounded by bubble bath suds. Jim sat on the edge of the tub and asked, "Want me to wash your back?"

"That would be great."

After sponging her back, he bent to kiss her shoulder. "Thank you for everything," he said. "I know it's hard to be an officer's wife. You teach school, raise a family, plus have to worry about your husband getting killed or hurt. I don't see how you do it all."

"Well, it's trying at times, but it's also rewarding. We have great kids, we have our health, and we have each other. The Lord's blessed us, but I want you to promise me you'll be careful. We need you. We love you."

"I will," he replied.

"She fixed her eyes on his and said, "You promise?"

"I promise," he said as his lips met hers.

"Your turn. I'll draw you some fresh water," she said as she stood to take the towel he offered.

He commented on her well–proportioned body as he drew back the towel each time she reached for it. Finally, she snatched it from him and said, "You'll have to wait until later tonight, mister."

"Where are we going. You picked yet?" he asked.

"Yes. We're going to Raymone's, near the train station. Do you remember our dates at the depot?"

"How could I forget? Remember in the car in the depot parking lot?"

"Yes, I remember that a slick–talking boy took advantage of a little country girl. At least we didn't go all the way."

"Maybe you didn't, but I did," he said with a twinkle in his eyes.

"Your bath is ready now. Get in and stop being naughty," she said without conviction.

Later, they parked at the depot and walked to Raymone's Italian Restaurant. They were fortunate to get a window table, where they could watch couples strolling by.

Jim ordered red wine for himself and iced tea for Lilly. To Jim's surprise, Lilly changed her order to wine also.

"Well, we're celebrating. I'll have a sip or two, and you can finish it for me."

Jim ordered lasagna and Lilly chose ravioli. Suddenly, Lilly blurted, "Oh, I forgot to tell you that Robbie called while you were in the bath. He was excited with the good news and asked a hundred questions about the trial!"

Jim marveled at Lilly's beauty in the flickering candlelight as she relayed everything Robbie had said. Reaching across the table, he took her hand in his and squeezed gently as he listened.

After dinner, they strolled hand in hand down Main Street past the depot and turned the corner onto Cherry Street. At Elm Street, they decided to stop at Kenny's Bakery Shop for pie and coffee.

Later, they made their way to the library, and Jim guided her to a park bench. They chatted about the day's events, the kids, and the loan for Shelly's college expenses. Finally, he told Lilly a joke that Jimmy Ray had told him earlier in the day during a court recess.

Lilly laughed until tears rolled down her cheeks. He handed her his handkerchief, and she dabbed her eyes. Then, as they walked toward the depot, she got tickled again and laughed uncontrollably.

As they approached the car in the depot parking lot, Jim dropped her hand, put his arms around her, and drew her lips to his. As his hands caressed her back, she squeezed him tightly. Stroking her bottom revealed that she had worn a garter belt in place of a girdle.

Once in the car, they embraced and kissed again. Jim cupped her breasts and kissed her more passionately.

Lilly caught her breath and whispered, "Let's go home and straight to bed."

Jim kissed her neck and whispered, "I want to finish what we started here 30 years ago."

"No, we can't. We might get caught!"

"We won't get caught. It's dark. No one can see us."

"No, Jim. It's too dangerou—"

He interrupted her with his lips on hers. His hands now moved all over her body, stroking her breasts, then hips, then thighs, and finally between her legs. Lilly's resistance yielded to passion as she unzipped his pants and massaged him. He slipped his pants down to his ankles, while she unsnapped her garters. Then she raised her bottom to allow him to remove her panties.

Jim eased Lilly onto her back and settled between her legs.

As their rhythmic lovemaking plunged toward mutual reward, Lilly suddenly pulled herself upright.

"What's wrong, Lilly?"

"I thought I heard something!"

They both looked all around. Nothing.

"We're fine, Lilly."

"Are you sure?"

"Yes," he said as he pulled her to him.

Lilly moved onto his lap. "Let's finish this way, and I'll keep a lookout." She clung to him, rocking in rhythm until they both reached the pinnacle together. Afterward, Jim's hands moved effortlessly up and down her back as they talked.

"Wow, what a night. I love you," Jim said as he handed her his handkerchief.

"I love you, too."

CHAPTER 33

Ten Years Later

1967–1968

"Mr.Taylor? Mr. Taylor?" the doctor prodded.

"Red eyes," Jim murmured.

"Mr. Taylor, can you hear me?" Doctor Turner tried again.

The patient finally focused on the doctor's white jacket and wondered if he were in heaven.

"Do you know where you are?"

"No, I…" Jim mumbled.

"You're in Dawson Memorial Hospital, recovering from a heart attack." Dr. Turner turned to Lilly, "He's coming around. The drugs are working their way out of his system. His vitals are much improved. I'll be back later today when he's fully awake."

"Thank you, Doctor," Lilly said appreciatively.

The remainder of the day, Jim alternated between long periods of sleep and short stints of small talk with Lilly. By day's end, he had convinced her to go home and get a good night's rest. She reluctantly agreed and kissed him goodbye.

Over the next few days, as Jim became more lucid, he became impatient with the hospital routine—especially the ever–present IV and the regimen of being awakened to take the prescribed pills.

He tried to peer through the fog of the last few days. He

recalled the short visit from the kids.

It was good to see Rob Boatwright and his son, Hamilton, yesterday, he thought. Or was it the day before? Lilly says lots of friends have been by, but the doctor and nurses won't let them up here. Wonder how Rob and Hamilton got in?

As he stared at the walls of his room, he began to laugh. If Cam were here, he thought, he would call the paint color baby-shit green. So much has happened, he observed as his thoughts took him on a tour of the last decade.

A few days after the trial in 1957, Jimmy Ray threw a party at his river house to celebrate the Not Guilty verdict. Jim parked in the side yard and entered through the back door.

Years before, Cam had donated an old jukebox for use at the party house. Three couples danced to Elvis Presley's "Love Me Tender" and others lined the walls or sat on one of the three couches in front of the large fireplace.

Jimmy Ray and Cam were bartending in the kitchen. Clyde Hankins, an off-duty officer, yelled, "Hey, the guest of honor has arrived!"

Jim blushed as he walked the gauntlet of well-wishers bestowing handshakes and pats on the back. Cam rescued him with a glass of Jack Daniels and Coke as he drew him into the kitchen to Jimmy Ray. As they talked, Jim noticed a beautiful woman in a black dress standing by the fireplace, talking to Deputy Franklin and his wife, Judy.

She glanced repeatedly at Jim as he talked to his friends. Finally, Jim asked Jimmy Ray, "Who's the woman in the black dress?"

"Oh," said Jimmy Ray, "she's been wantin' to meet you. I promised her I would introduce you."

"Why?" asked Jim.

"Hey, you've been in the news for weeks, dumbass."

"Bull," Jim replied.

"Come on. I'll introduce you."

Jim followed him into the living room, admiring her as they approached. Her simple black dress revealed a shapely body. She was close to Jim's height, but high heels added another two or three inches. Her blond hair was cropped short to conform to her angular face. Red lipstick contrasted with her lively blue eyes. He guessed her age at about 40.

"Mary, this is Jim Taylor. Jim, this is Mary Martin. I gotta get back to help Jimmy Ray," he stated as he retreated to the kitchen.

"Glad to meet you, Deputy Taylor. I've been reading about you. Saw you on TV, too," she quickly added before Jim could speak.

"I'm glad to meet you, Miss Martin. Are you a friend of Jimmy Ray's?"

"No, I'm a friend of Wallace Franklin and his wife, Judy. She invited me to come and meet you."

"Just to meet *me*?" he asked with raised eyebrows.

"Well, you're famous. I might want your autograph."

"Oh, no. Just another deputy, like the others here. Can I get you a drink?" he offered.

"Yes. Rum and Coke. How nice of you."

"Be right back with it."

Jim worked his way through the partiers to the kitchen and secured the drink. When he returned, Mary was chatting with a couple he didn't recognize. Mary introduced them, then Jim excused himself and moved around the room to thank everyone for coming.

Later, with a waltz playing on the jukebox, Mary approached Jim. "Any space left on your dance card?" she coyly asked.

"Sure," he replied as he took her hand and struggled to find an opening on the crowded floor.

The press of the crowd limited dancing to standing in place and swaying with the music. Once Mary ran out of questions, she rested her head on his shoulder and slipped both arms around his neck. Jim breathed in her perfume and felt himself growing hard as she pressed her warm body into his. She raised her face to his ear and whispered, "I can feel you against my tummy. Let's go outside to the car."

He faced her and looked into her glittering blue eyes. "I'd love to. You're a beautiful woman. But I have a wife waiting for me at home."

As the flow of drinks and the volume of the party increased, Jim slipped out the back door and headed home to Lilly.

Later in the year, Shelly married in Dawson, then moved to Ohio, where her husband had secured a good job. She eventually found a teaching position and they made a down payment on a house.

Robby was in the Army, stationed near Washington, DC. His unit provided honor guard services for burials at Arlington, Jim remembered. I received a letter from his commanding officer stating that Robby was a good soldier and a credit to his unit. I was thankful the country was at peace and that he didn't have to go overseas. He met a girl there and later, after being discharged, went back to marry her. They live just outside of Washington.

In 1958, Rob's father, Reverend Boatwright, died. His was the largest funeral I had ever seen. The church was packed, and the church yard was full of mourners.

A couple of weeks later, Rob came to see me and cried like a baby. Apparently he was closer to his father than I had realized. Rob asked me if I was sure I'd been saved. "Yes," I replied, "I'm sure."

"Jim, we all have our crosses to bear, but it is very important that we receive forgiveness for our sins," Rob stressed.

"I know, Rob. Lord knows I've committed my share of sins, and then some. But I feel like I'm over the hump—on the right path." I relayed to him the story of the beautiful woman at the party, and how I was able to resist the temptation.

"I'm glad to hear it, Jim. Girls have been the downfall of many a boy, but the Lord is forgiving if we are truly repentant," Rob assured me.

In 1960, Lois graduated from high school and started college. At the same time, Barry started high school.

Then, in 1961, I was injured trying to break up a brawl at the race track. I took a blow to the head causing a concussion—still don't know what they hit me with. The doctors were concerned that the steel plate in my skull might have been dislodged. X-rays confirmed that it was still in place; however, the recurring headaches are still a problem.

In 1963, President Kennedy was shot and killed in Dallas. The only thing we had in common was that we were both shot in the head. LBJ is from the South, but I don't care much for his politics, either.

The following year, 1964, Jimmy Ray died from complications of diabetes and heart disease. He left a detailed note requesting that in lieu of a funeral, a party be held in his memory. Oddly, he demanded that only fried frog legs, biscuits, and Cam's moonshine be served. We followed his instructions and had the party at his river house.

Lois graduated from college and moved to Ohio near her sister, Shelly. Barry entered college and told me he wanted to be a lawyer. Shortly thereafter, I noticed a shortness of breath when walking upstairs. The doctor diagnosed my problem as enlargement of the heart due to cholesterol buildup in my arteries. He prescribed a blood thinner, a diet, and rest. No more country ham or biscuits and gravy, he said. I followed his instructions for a few months, then gradually dropped back into my normal routine. Maybe if I had followed his advice, I wouldn't be here in this hospital bed, Jim thought.

Still not daylight outside. I thought the sun was coming up

an hour ago. Musta been streetlights instead, he concluded, as he fell into an uneasy sleep.

The nurse nudged him to take his pills. As he shifted positions in the hospital bed and listened to the nurse's retreating footsteps down the hall, Jim resumed his thoughts from earlier.

In 1965, Lois married a boy she met at the Health Department where she worked in Ohio. She and Shelly live just across town from each other.

Cam Barker died in 1966 after a lengthy bout with lung cancer—too many Pall Malls, I guess. I should quit smoking cigars, or I'll end up the same way. Cam's funeral was quite an affair, and an article in the newspaper detailed his colorful life. Chief Jamison of Dawson PD was quoted as saying, "Cam Barker was the bravest and most fearless man I have ever known."

I miss Jimmy Ray and Cam. Jimmy Ray made me laugh every day without fail, and I could always depend on sound advice from Cam.

His thoughts were interrupted upon hearing Lilly's voice outside his door. She was talking with someone, but Jim couldn't make out what they were saying.

She entered the room with a big smile on her face. "Good morning, sweetie," she chirped as she grabbed his toes with both hands.

"Good morning, Mrs. Taylor," he replied.

"Your toes are cold, as usual," she observed.

"Your hands feel good and warm."

"I've got good news. The doctor says you can go home today if you promise to follow his orders."

"Great! Get my clothes."

"Not so fast. It'll take a couple of hours to process everything. Just relax."

*****

Within a few weeks, Jim was released to go back to work on light duty. The sheriff informed him that he would be assigned to the process server detail. Jim protested, but the sheriff made it abundantly clear that the decision was final.

Deputy Taylor settled into a daily routine of serving civil papers until around 3:00 p.m., then going home for a short rest. As weeks turned into months, he began to make minor crime arrests such as DUIs, PDs, and misdemeanors. The sheriff either hadn't noticed or didn't mind.

On April 25, 1968, Jim was separating civil warrants from garnishee papers when his office phone rang.

"Hello. Deputy Taylor speaking."

"Jim, it's Lilly. I have some bad news."

"What?"

"Rob Boatwright died earlier today."

"What! Are you sure?"

"Yes. I'm sorry. I know how much he meant to you. Can you come on home?"

"How did it happen?" Jim asked in a robotic voice.

"According to his sister, he fell off his house. She said he was adjusting the TV antenna for better reception."

"I'll be on home," he replied, as he slowly placed the phone in its cradle.

Jim's brother Ray, who was also close to Rob when they were growing up, came in from Ohio. Two of Jim's sisters also made it in for the funeral.

Bewildered and grief stricken, with Lilly by his side, Jim trod wearily through the next two days of family visitation, the funeral, and the burial. After the burial service, Jim asked Lilly if she minded if he stayed at the cemetery for a while. "You can ride home with Ray," he said.

"Of course. Take all the time you want. I'll see you back at the house."

After everyone departed, Jim stood over Rob's grave and

talked about their childhood. Talking with Rob somehow seemed to ease the pain and anguish. Next, he stepped over to the graves of his dad, mom, and Annie.

"Well, we lost another loved one. I guess he's with you guys now. I'll probably be joining you before too long." He turned to Annie and said, "Annie, I feel better about what I did. God has forgiven me. Instead of payback for you, I think of it as stopping him from doing it again—to another little girl like you. By the way, on July 2nd, I'm going to pick some blackberries and bring them to you. My old heart won't let me climb the bluff, but I'll find some around here."

Approaching the gate, he straightened the rusty old saw blade, then turned to look at the graves. "I love y'all."

Early the next morning, Lilly and Jim were up to insure that Ray and his family had a good breakfast before heading back to Ohio.

"No biscuits for you, Jim," Lilly told him as she passed them to Ray.

They said goodbyes all around. Then Lilly convinced Jim that he should go on to work to keep his mind busy.

At the Safety Building, Jim secured the civil papers from the court clerk's wire basket and thumbed through them as he walked down the hall to his office. Waiting for him there—to Jim's surprise—was Hamilton Boatwright.

"Well, what a surprise!" exclaimed Jim as Hamilton rose to shake hands.

"Mr. Taylor, I'm headed back to the University of Richmond. My students have exams tomorrow, but I wanted to bring you this first," he said as he handed Jim a small book.

"Oh, well, thank you, Hamilton. What is it?"

"It's a diary I found while going through some of Dad's things. Since y'all were so close, I thought you should have it. It starts when he was about 17 or 18 years old."

"You sure you don't want to keep it, Hamilton?"

"No, sir. We've got lots of his papers. I think he would want you to have it—you know, to remember your boyhood together."

"Well, I really appreciate it. I'm proud to have it. Thank you."

"You're welcome, Mr. Taylor. I've got to run."

"Drive safely. I thought the world of your dad," Jim said as they shook hands.

"Yes, sir, I know. Goodbye."

"Goodbye."

Jim sat at his desk flipping pages of the diary, which were blurred by his watery eyes.

"This will bring back some good memories," he said under his breath. "Might as well start on page one."

June 1, 1927: Hot day, worked tobacco.

June 2, 1927: Went swimming with Jim and Ray.

No entry for June 3 or 4.

June 5, 1927: Saw her at church. Dad's text: "Woman at the well."

June 6, 1927: Smiled at me yesterday. I think she likes me.

June 7, 1927: Rained today.

June 8, 1927: Went to Batesville with Daddy. Stopped by her place.

June 9, 1927: Dreamed about her last night. Got to "know her."

June 10, 1927: Hard work today hoeing corn. Cow died calving.

June 11, 1927: Bought gold pocket watch from Tom Benson for a Beagle pup and $10 to boot.

The words struck Jim like a sledgehammer. He quickly reread it and was staggered as the words unraveled the last 50 years of his life.

Oh, God, please, no, no, no!

His guts churned inside; he was going to be sick.

Take a deep breath, take a deep breath, he commanded himself.

"Jim."

No answer.

"Jim!"

"Wha—what?" Jim finally got out.

It was Jack Bowie, the court bailiff. "The judge is ready for your prisoner. Are you all right, Jim? You're white as a sheet!"

"Yeah, yeah, I'm okay. I'll go get him."

Deputy Taylor stood—dizzy—then sat back down with another deep breath. The knot in his stomach grew tighter as he made his way to the stairs of the second-story jail.

Halfway up the steps, the pain punched him in the chest. It was sharp, but not unbearable. The light of the stairwell began to dim.

Must be working on the power lines, he thought.

As he eased to the floor of the stairs, his words were but a whisper. "Red eyes."

CHAPTER 34

Dawson Memorial Hospital

After completing the story—confessing to Lilly the lie he had been living for so many years—he was mentally and physically exhausted.

Fighting back tears, Lilly stammered that she couldn't talk right then. She feared that the ordeal had been too much for him and immediately summoned a nurse. Finally convinced that he was okay, Lilly told him she would return the next day and then slipped out of the room.

The nurses woke him every three hours for medicine. Other than those brief periods, he slept for 11 hours.

"No, no, please," he hissed. His eyes opened slowly and blinked repeatedly to focus on the all too familiar hospital room.

"Shhh, shhh," Lilly soothed him. Her caring voice belied the anguish he read in her face.

"Lilly, over the last few days, I've given this situation a lot of thought. I've made some decisions, and I need for you to hear them."

"Jim, wait until you're fully awake—maybe after breakfast."

Later, Jim began. "Lilly, yesterday I asked if you could forgive me. It would mean a lot to me—it would mean the world to me. I'm not asking that you forget, just that you forgive me. I've asked the Lord to forgive me a thousand times through the years, and I'm confident he has.

"Next, I love you more than you can ever know, but I'm

willing to give you a divorce so you can go on with your life. And once again, I want you to understand how sorry I am for hurting you—for betraying you."

"Jim, I—"

"No, please, don't talk," he interrupted. "Just listen until I finish. I intend to turn myself in to the police in Richmond, Kentucky. I want to stand trial and pay for the murder. There, I said it. Murder. It's the first time I've allowed myself to say or even think that word. I always referred to it in my mind as the killing, but it *was* murder. And even worse, as you know, I murdered the wrong man.

"I want to apologize to our kids as soon as possible. And last, I want to ask a big favor. Will you call my brothers and sisters and tell them I'm going to turn myself in? I don't want them to hear it on the street. Tell them that when I'm able, I'll talk to them."

"Yes, Jim, I'll let them know," Lilly said in a low, trembling voice. "Jim, I was up most of the night thinking and praying. Like you, I've also made some decisions, and I want to share them, so don't interrupt," she said, looking down at her notes.

"First, I don't want a divorce. I'm upset with you, but I love you. It will be difficult to forget, but I do forgive you. Only time will tell if you can build back the trust I've always had in you.

"We will have to live with this the rest of our lives, but it occurred to me last night that we also have many good memories. Those should not be forgotten as we go forward. Mistakes have been made, but we both have accomplishments to be proud of.

"I'm deeply hurt by the things you told me yesterday. I feel like a fool—married to a man I really didn't know through all those years. I opened my Bible last night and read the story of Job. I prayed for us, and in my mind I kept hearing the words, 'This too shall pass.' So I want to go on together and work our way through this.

"Lastly, as to turning yourself in to the authorities in Kentucky, you need to make sure you know what you're doing. My advice is to talk with an attorney before you do anything. I'll call Harlan Hughes and ask him to come see you when you can have visitors.

"There's one more thing. I promised myself that I wouldn't ask, but I've got to know. Why did you betray our love? Why did you go out on me? Was I not a good enough lover?"

"Lilly, I've asked myself that same question hundreds of times over the years. You are a great lover. It had nothing to do with that. The only answer I've ever come up with is that it was just lust, and I know now how selfish that was. My mother would have said that I got too big for my britches. I've never loved any woman but you, and I never will. If you'll give me the chance, I'll spend the rest of my life trying to make it up to you. Lilly, I love you, and I'll never lie to you again. As long as I know that you love me, I can get through this."

"We can talk later, but first, you've got to get well," she replied.

Next, Lilly broached the subject of who would be hurt over these revelations besides their own family. "Tom Benson's parents have passed away, so they won't have to deal with this, but I really feel for Hamilton and Jenny Boatwright. Learning that their father raped and murdered Annie will be a crushing blow."

"They will never know about it. You and I are the only ones that know, and I don't intend to ever tell anyone."

Lilly sat in silence, absorbing the meaning and consequences of what Jim had just said. "Jim, if you face a judge or jury without giving a reason for your actions, they will show no mercy. When you told me you were going to turn yourself in, I immediately thought you might get a light sentence because you thought you had a good reason to kill him. But if you take away that motive, they will view you as a coldblooded killer!"

"I know, Lilly, but I've ruined enough lives already. Also, I've prayed about this, and I've forgiven Rob. I don't want to wipe out the memories that people have of him. I'll never know why or how he could have done such a horrible thing, but I'm not going to destroy the Boatwright family. No one will ever know."

"I understand, Jim, but please wait until you've talked to Mr. Hughes before you make a decision. I've got to make those calls to your brothers and sisters, and I'll let the lawyer know when you can have visitors."

Jim handed her the key to his locker at the Safety Building. "Lilly, I need your help with a couple of things," he said.

*****

Lilly returned at 10:30 the next day and handed Jim the requested items. He signed the letter of resignation and handed it back to her for mailing. Then he opened the envelope marked *Annie* that Lilly had retrieved from his locker at work. He removed the broken watch fob and showed it to Lilly. She examined it and gave it back to him without comment.

Later that night, Jim took the watch fob from the envelope and gazed at it through misty eyes. Next, he slowly made his way to the bathroom and dropped the fob into the commode. As he watched it circle out of sight, he noticed the wall sign above the commode. *Toilet Paper Only, Please.*

*****

Harlan Hughes stopped Jim in mid-sentence and asked for a dollar.

"What?" Jim asked.

"Give me a dollar and hire me before you say anything else. You know the routine—attorney-client privilege."

"My wallet is in the drawer," Jim pointed. "Help yourself."

Jim gave Hughes the short version of the murder, leaving out the part about Rob Boatwright. He merely stated that he had found that he had killed the wrong man.

"How d'ya know it was the wrong man?"

"Sorry, can't tell you that," Jim said with enough authority that Hughes knew not to ask again.

"So what do you want to do?" the lawyer asked.

"I want to plead guilty, and I don't want to fight extradition."

"Let's slow down and think this through. My advice is to think long and hard about what you're fixin' to get into. What's your reason for doing this?"

"I want to pay the price for my mistake—my crime. I've already made the decision, and it's final."

"Okaaay," Harlan said, stringing out the word as if he thought Jim had lost his marbles. "If your mind is made up, I recommend we hire an old friend of mine. He practices criminal law in Lexington, Kentucky, and he's an excellent attorney. I'll set up a meeting with him when you're able to travel."

They shook hands as Harlan told Jim to follow the doctor's orders and get well. Hughes paused at the door. "One last thing, Jim. Resign from the sheriff's department. Don't wait for them to fire you. It may save your pension. Good luck, partner."

"Thanks, Harlan, I appreciate everything you've done for me over the years."

"Don't mention it, Jim. By the way, can I ask a favor?"

"Sure."

"Confidentially, and just out of personal curiosity, what did you see in the window just before you shot that escapee?"

"Just what I told you. I saw that he was awake, and I saw him cock the pistol."

"I thought so. You just won me a $20 bet. See ya, buddy."

*****

Jim, with Lilly at his side, answered questions posed by Johnny Jackson, Harlan's old teammate at Georgia Tech. "So you won't tell me who really raped and killed your little sister?" Jackson asked.

"No," Jim answered emphatically.

"That doesn't leave me much to take to the Commonwealth's district attorney," said Jackson.

"I know, but my decision is final."

"Okay, it's your decision. My advice, then, is to negotiate a plea deal. We'll stress your long and meritorious service with the sheriff's department, your advanced age and poor health, and the fact that you are freely admitting your guilt. Also, I'm going to point out that this Tom Benson shot at your father, threatened to 'get him,' and that you feared he would ambush your dad."

"That's fine," Jim agreed. "We appreciate your help."

*****

Jim was sentenced to four years in the Bell County Forestry Camp Prison near Pineville, Kentucky. The newly reformed Kentucky state prison system afforded him excellent medical care, along with a healthy diet and regular exercise.

Lilly made the trek to Pineville twice a month—sometimes alone, and at times with one of their children or other relatives. Jim completed two college courses while there, and he taught a popular inmate seminar entitled "Life Decisions."

Inmate number 1692 was paroled on February 5, 1970, after serving 18 months. Lilly drove him to their Springdale home to begin a new life together. Two days later, on Sunday, the congregation of Piney Level Primitive Baptist Church welcomed him back to the fold.

Over the next six years, Jim managed a small grocery store and assisted Lilly in spoiling their five grandchildren. He died in 1976. The newspaper article chronicling the life and death of the popular lawman was entitled "Last of the Big Three Dies." It detailed the lives of Jimmy Ray Johnson and Cam Barker, and it noted that with the death of Jim Taylor, an era had ended.

Lilly lived another 13 years, keeping busy with volunteer work and helping the less fortunate. The day before she died—sensing that her time was near—she slowly unfolded the fragile, heavily creased letter and read it for the last time.

May 5, 1934
CCC Camp
Richmond, VA

My Dearest Lilly,

The sun came up this morning, shining brightly on the tree tops. As always, I thought of you—so warm and bright. I hope you have a happy marriage and enjoy California. They tell me it is always sunny there.

You won't have any trouble finding a good job. You are a great teacher. I respect and admire what you have done with your life.

I feel blessed when I think of our time together, and I will always cherish those memories. If Annie had lived, I believe she would have been a lot like you. You were her heroine.

I want you to know that I am very proud of you, and I love you. I will always love you. Sometimes my soul aches, and I think my heart will surely burst. I say that not to complicate your life, but so you will know how I feel and carry it with you always.

I am very lucky to have known you, and I'll always fondly remember my first and only love.

Yours forever,
Jim

About the Author

Gary H. Hensley grew up in the Bloomingdale community near Kingsport, Tennessee. He served as a drill sergeant in the United States Army and attended East Tennessee State University, where he received a Masters of City Management degree in 1971.

He served as city manager of Loudon, Tennessee for seven years before moving to Maryville, Tennessee, where he retired after 28 years as city manager. He resides in Maryville with his wife, Sherry. They have three children and two grandchildren.

Mr. Hensley's parents—Iva Nell Addington Hensley and Howard Hensley—grew up in the hills of Southwest Virginia. Iva Nell was a teacher in the Sullivan County system for many years. For most of his adult life, Howard was a lawman in Sullivan County, Tennessee. His life is the inspirational starting place for this work of fiction.

Editing and Publishing Assistance

This book was proofread and edited by David and Leonore Dvorkin, of Denver, Colorado. David Dvorkin did the cover layout, the formatting and layout of the manuscript, and the publication of the book in e-book and print formats.

David and Leonore are both much-published authors, with a total of 31 books (both fiction and nonfiction) and many articles and essays to their credit. Almost all of their books are available for purchase on Amazon, Apple, Barnes & Noble, and other online buying sites in e-book and print formats. A few are in audio format and available from Audible.com.

David's most recent nonfiction book is *DUST NET: The Future of Surveillance, Privacy, and Communication: Why Drones are Just the Beginning* (© 2013).

Leonore's memoir, *Another Chance at Life: A Breast Cancer Survivor's Journey,* is available in both English and Spanish. Both are © 2012. The English edition is also in audio format.

For details, please see their websites:
David Dvorkin: www.dvorkin.com
Leonore H. Dvorkin: www.leonoredvorkin.com

Made in the USA
Lexington, KY
05 October 2015